A native of St. Louis, Missouri, **Tiffany Snow** earned degrees in education and history from the University of Missouri-Columbia, before launching a career in information technology. After nearly fifteen years in IT, she switched careers to what she always dreamed of doing – writing. Tiffany is the author of romantic suspense novels such as the Kathleen Turner series, which includes *No Turning Back*, *Turn to Me*, and *Turning Point*. Since she's drawn to character-driven books herself, that's what she loves to write, and the guy always gets his girl.

She feeds her love of books with avid reading, yet she manages to spare time and considerable affection for trivia, eighties hair bands, the St. Louis Cardinals, and Elvis. She and her husband have two daughters and one dog, whose untimely demise Tiffany contemplates on a daily basis.

Visit Tiffany Snow online:

www.tiffanyasnow.com
www.facebook.com/TiffanyASnow
www.twitter.com/TiffanyASnow

TIFFANY SNOW

PLAY TO WIN

piatkus

PIATKUS

First published in the US in 2016 by Forever Romance, an imprint of
Grand Central Publishing, a division of Hachette Book Group, Inc.
First published in Great Britain in 2016 by Piatkus

1 3 5 7 9 10 8 6 4 2

Copyright © 2016 by Tiffany Allshouse
Excerpt from *Power Play* copyright © 2015 by Tiffany Allshouse

The moral right of the author has been asserted.

A CIP catalogue record for this book
is available from the British Library.

ISBN 978-0-349-41157-6

Printed and bound in Great Britain by
Clays Ltd, St Ives plc

Papers used by Piatkus are from well-managed forests
and other responsible sources.

MIX
Paper from
responsible sources
FSC® C104740

*For Leah. Thank you for taking a chance on me.
(And I'm determined to make you an expert on
how to take a Muppet-free selfie.)*

ACKNOWLEDGMENTS

This book was particularly difficult to write, as some can be, and I have several people to thank for their relentless encouragement and endless patience:

To my editor, Leah Hultenschmidt, for whom this book is dedicated. I've been very lucky as a new author in this business to be surrounded by some of the kindest, hardworking, most knowledgeable people who've been as determined as I am to take my career to higher levels. You are one of these people. It has been an absolute pleasure working with you on this series. Thank you for the brainstorming sessions, the critiques that made this book better, the patience with deadlines and life in general. You're an amazing editor and a lovely person, through and through.

To my agent, Kevan Lyon, for making this deal happen. I don't know how you remember all that you do, but I'm in constant amazement. You're an amazing agent and I feel incredibly fortunate to have you. I still recall sitting in a hotel

Acknowledgments

room in Seattle, dumbstruck at your absolute confidence in the sale of this series. Thank you.

To my author friends who encouraged me and kept me going when even five hundred more words felt insurmountable: Tracy Brogan, Catherine Bybee, Jill Shalvis, Marina Adair, Melinda Leigh, Paige Weaver, and Kele Moon. It's such a huge relief to realize I'm not alone.

To Janeen Solberg and the wonderful ladies who staff Turn the Page Bookstore in Boonsboro. Your enthusiasm and support for my work is truly awe-inspiring and humbling to me. Thank you so very much not only for that, but for all the recommending and hand-selling you do of my books to your patrons.

To my family—my wonderful daughters and patient husband—who dealt with a very stressed-out mom and still managed to love me when at times I was quite unlovable. I treasure you.

And lastly, to the people who've made this series so great with their many talents and skills in marketing, graphics, PR, and branding: Jodi Rosoff, Fareeda Bullert, Dana Hamilton, Danielle Egnozzi, and the entire Forever team. Thank you!

PLAY TO WIN

PLAY TO WIN

PROLOGUE

"Parker and I slept together."

The words fell with the force of a bomb. Ryker stared at the woman he loved in disbelief. With his best friend? Really? Shock froze him in place and he couldn't move, could barely breathe.

This couldn't be happening. He couldn't possibly have understood her correctly. She was lying, or this was a really bad joke—

"I'm in love with him," she continued, as though completely unaware of the pain each word was driving into him. "And he loves me, too. We were going to tell you before, but..." Her words trailed away and she shrugged.

"But what?" he asked, his voice like a rake on gravel.

"But it's hard to hurt someone you love."

She moved closer until she stood within a hairbreadth of her abdomen touching his. Lifting her hands, she placed her palms on the bare skin of his chest. Ryker squeezed his eyes shut, his senses assaulted with her—the heat of her touch, the smell of her skin, the brush of her hair against him as it stirred in the breeze. The ceiling fan in the bedroom was a bare whir of sound.

"Parker put you up to this, didn't he?" Ryker said. That was the only explanation. Natalie was too sweet and trusting. She'd believe anything Parker told her. God only knew what he'd said to seduce her and make her think he loved her.

Grasping her upper arms so tightly she gasped, he pushed her back so he could see her eyes.

"Tell me the truth," he growled, trying to keep his temper in check. "He said whatever he had to in order to get you into bed. You love *me*. You want to be with *me*. Right?" He shook her slightly before he stopped himself. "Tell me!"

"N-no," Natalie stammered, her eyes wide. "I just can't keep up pretending with you, pretending that I don't have feelings for Parker—"

"He wants you for himself," Ryker interrupted, abruptly releasing her. Turning away, he shoved a hand through his hair. "I can't believe it."

It was unreal. Incomprehensible. Parker and he went back—way back—and had looked out for each other through street gangs, schoolyard bullies, drill sergeants, and enemy fire. Parker knew how much Ryker loved Natalie. He'd even talked to Parker about maybe proposing to her.

And he'd thought she was there, too—or at least, almost. She'd told him she loved him. They'd made love. She was like him—they came from the wrong side of the tracks, had a rough upbringing, and done what they could to help the ones they loved. Natalie had been the first woman to work her way past his wall of defenses to the man he was inside. He'd opened up to her, trusted her, fallen in love with her...

Then Parker had seduced her. That had to have been what had happened. He'd made her believe he loved her so she'd have sex with him. For Parker to have done something like that to someone as trusting and vulnerable as Natalie made Ryker's blood boil. Parker had finally shown his true colors. It had just taken a woman to bring out what Ryker had always suspected was there—a narcissistic asshole blinded by his own wealth and privilege. It must've amused him, all these years, playing the savior for the charity case kid from the shitty side of town.

A little voice in the back of his head said, *You know Parker's not like that. He's saved your life. He wouldn't steal your girlfriend.*

But the alternative to believing in Parker's loyalty...was believing in Natalie's *dis*loyalty, and he couldn't handle that.

He felt Natalie's hands on his back, lightly stroking his skin, gentling him.

"I'm sorry," she said. "You must hate me. I understand if you never want to see me again—"

"Don't be ridiculous," he interrupted her. The searing pain inside needed an outlet, but it couldn't be Natalie. It was Parker. He was the one to blame. He'd betrayed their friendship. The thought of Parker with Natalie—

No. He couldn't think about it, *wouldn't* think about it. It didn't matter what she'd done or been coerced into doing; Ryker couldn't live without her. His every breath was for her. If she left him...he'd have nothing and no one. He needed her more than he cared about his broken pride or wounded psyche.

"I forgive you," he rasped. "It's you and me. Together. Nothing will come between us. Especially not Parker."

Taking a deep breath, he turned around and took her in his arms, his lips finding hers in a searing kiss that melted his anger and turned his guts into a molten river of want.

She let him make love to her, their joining more desperate on his side than it had been before. As though his soul knew he was losing her, inch by inch.

* * *

Only a week later, his worst fears were realized.

Ryker didn't announce his presence when he walked into Parker's place. He hadn't been able to reach Natalie for the past hour, though they were supposed to meet for dinner after he got off work. On a suspicion he didn't want to dwell on, Ryker had come here.

He hadn't spoken to Parker since Natalie had confessed. Unable to know for certain what he'd do if he saw Parker, Ryker had avoided him all week.

Now he stood, frozen in Parker's bedroom doorway, aghast at the tableau in front of him.

Natalie, naked, her limbs entwined around Parker's hips. The sounds of her gasps and moans filled the air, pouring into his ears like acid. The sheets were tangled around their legs and the sight of Parker pumping between her thighs sent fury raging through him.

With a roar, he attacked, grabbing Parker and hauling him off Natalie. Parker hit the wall with a thud and a grunt before falling to the floor.

Parker's gaze met Ryker's, and shock and confusion were followed quickly by horror.

"What the fuck are you doing here?" Parker asked.

"Besides watching you fuck my girlfriend," Ryker spat, "I'm here to kill you, asshole."

He went for him, but Parker fought back, blocking Ryker's right hook and retreating.

"She said it's over between you two," Parker said. "You've got to accept that."

"Fuck you," Ryker growled, going after him again. This time he landed a good hit to Parker's jaw and gut before Parker was able to retaliate with several blows to Ryker's solar plexus, forcing him to pause to regain his breath.

"You've gotta stop," Parker said, breathing hard. "It's not worth this."

Nothing Parker said could have enraged Ryker more, and he yelled as he attacked again, this time his fury such that Parker's blows didn't stop him. Blood flowed and his knuckles ached, but all he saw through the haze of red in his vision was Natalie's body being desecrated by Parker's.

"Stop! You're going to kill him! Stop!"

Natalie's words broke through the rage at last and Ryker went still, his chest heaving from exertion. Parker lay on the floor, blood staining the skin around his mouth and nose. His eyes were closed and he didn't move.

"Oh God oh God oh God..." Natalie was murmuring over and over. She'd dropped to her knees and tenderly brushed back the hair from Parker's face. "I think he's just unconscious," she said at last.

She lifted her gaze to Ryker's, and he was stunned to see tears streaking her face.

"I can't do this. I can't watch you two tear each other apart," she said.

"You have to choose," Ryker said, his voice flat. "Him or me. You can't have both." Because now he knew. He knew by the look in her eyes that she hadn't told him the truth.

"Why do you even want me?" she asked. "I slept with your best friend. You should hate me." Her gaze was unflinching.

"I can't hate you. I love you."

Slowly, she got to her feet. "You shouldn't," she said. "For your own sake. I don't understand how you could possibly still love me."

"It doesn't matter what you've done. I love you no matter what."

"How can you expect me to believe that, Ryker?" she asked, incredulous. "I'm just supposed to trust you?"

She shoved her hands through her hair in exasperation, then crossed her arms over her breasts, making her petite frame look even smaller.

"Nothing you say or do is going to make me not love you," he said. "You just have to accept that."

She didn't answer, just silently gathered her clothes and dressed. When she was done, she stood in front of him.

"Kiss me," she said, and the look of despair in her eyes was heartbreaking.

He couldn't resist her. Hope was too strong of a pull and he leaned down, sealing her lips with his.

At last, he lifted his head, his eyes lazy to open. When they did, he stumbled back in shock.

For it wasn't Natalie in his arms, staring at him with a look of utter satisfaction on her face. It was Sage.

* * *

Ryker woke up with a start, sitting straight up in bed. He was covered in a sheen of cold sweat but he didn't notice. All he could see inside his head was Natalie and Sage, the thin, sharp blade of betrayal cutting him deep.

He got up and went into the kitchen, forgoing any lights. He knew his way in the dark.

Ryker absently filled a glass with water and took a deep swallow, letting the night air cool his sweat-slicked skin. Even now, years later, he remembered the horror of that night and the morning that had followed. The police had called with news that Natalie's car had been found in the river and they had sent in a recovery team to find the body.

The hole in his soul that Natalie had temporarily filled had been empty from that night on. Guilt, loss, regret...all of it overlaid with things he would've done differently if he'd had the chance. Natalie had been just like him—afraid to trust anyone, afraid to let anyone too close. He'd been so sure that fate had led them to each other...that he'd found the ethereal *true love* that he'd never before believed in.

Then she was gone.

He hadn't spoken to Parker since that night until four months ago, when he'd walked into Parker's office...and laid eyes on Sage.

Now he was on the brink of losing the woman he loved, again, to the same man who'd betrayed him all those years ago.

Ryker wasn't going to let that happen. He wouldn't lose Sage to Parker, and he'd do anything to keep history from repeating itself.

CHAPTER ONE

One Month Later

Parker's dead."

Ryker stared at me, seemingly uncomprehending. Not that I could blame him. I'd just arrived on his doorstep in the middle of the night, though it didn't look like he'd been asleep.

"They came to my apartment," I continued, my voice flat. "They took me and they killed him. They just...killed him." I couldn't continue. Tears poured from my eyes as I began to sob. I'd been numb before, the ordeal of being kidnapped necessitating a distance from the horror of what had happened in my apartment. Was Parker's body there even now?

I couldn't breathe. Ryker was talking to me but I couldn't hear him and I still couldn't breathe. My knees buckled and if he hadn't had a hold of me, I would've crumpled to the floor.

"Sage! Listen to me..." Ryker implored, but I barely heard him.

Suddenly, I was torn from his grasp. A hand forced my chin up and I blinked open my eyes—

Parker.

I gasped, stumbling backward, but he caught me.

"I'm okay," he said, his blue eyes boring into mine. "They didn't kill me. I'm all right."

My jaw was hanging open, my sobs abruptly cut off, and then I threw myself at him.

"Oh my God oh my God on my God," I kept repeating, my arms circling his neck so tightly I had to be choking him. Not that he seemed to mind. "You're here! You're okay." More tears, but this time of relief rather than heartbreak.

Parker held me just as close, his arms around my waist just this side of painfully tight. His face was buried in my neck and I savored the feel of him in a way I never had before...because I'd never been so close to losing him as I had come tonight.

The sound of Ryker clearing his throat brought me back to the here and now, and I pulled back, releasing Parker. He let me go, albeit reluctantly it seemed. An uncomfortable awareness settled over me as I stepped away to put some space between Parker and me. Ryker stood a few feet away, shirtless with a bandage covering the burn on his chest, watching us.

"So, um, how, uh, how did you get here?" I asked Parker, hurriedly swiping my wet cheeks. My voice was hoarse and I avoided both their gazes, instead sinking onto the couch. I glanced around hopefully for McClane, but remembered he was still recuperating at the vet's.

"Ryker showed up just in time, before Leo and his men decided to finish me off," Parker said.

Leo Shea. Crime boss, ruthless "businessman," and the guy who'd not only tried to kill me but had decided to kill

Parker, too. Lives meant nothing to him. Parker's had been for expediency; mine was for revenge. Only luck in the former and the timely intervention of my father in the latter had thwarted Leo.

"And your apartment needs another cleanup job, by the way. I'll call to get it done."

Good to know. I wondered if whoever the CIA used for that sort of thing offered a discount for frequent customers.

"I knew they'd taken you," Parker continued. "Ryker has weapons and ammunition, so we came here."

He didn't continue, but I could fill in the rest. They'd been on their way to rescue me. Well, at least they could agree on something at last.

And Ryker had ended up keeping Parker alive. I remembered now. Ryker had dropped me off at my place, then left to go to the police station, but had said he'd be back. Looked like his timing couldn't have been better. He'd saved Parker, a man he supposedly hated.

Now the two men stood a few feet apart, both looking at me. The enormity of all that had happened during the past few days washed over me and I lifted a hand to rub my forehead. Ryker had said he wasn't giving up on me, and Parker had told me he loved me. My headache seemed to grow exponentially, especially when images of Parker and me in my bed flashed through my mind.

"Let me get you an ice pack for your eye," Ryker said, heading into the kitchen. He was back in moments, crouching down next to me and gently pressing an ice cold bundle to my eye.

"Thanks," I murmured. The cold brought relief to my throbbing head. Leo had a mean right hook, but he'd paid for that and paid dearly.

A mobster and a bully—though that was probably

redundant—Leo Shea had kidnapped me and nearly killed Parker. Leo would've killed me if not for the precipitous arrival of a most unlikely savior: my dad. Well, not just him, but lots of large, gun-toting men who'd taken care of Leo and his goons in a very permanent way. It seemed my dad had secrets I'd known nothing about.

But I would wait until later to think about that because I had more pressing problems at the moment—in the form of two large, alpha men staring at me as though waiting for something.

"So, um, what now?" I asked the room at large, because I honestly had no clue.

I was with two men. I'd slept with both of them, I loved both of them, but everyone knew two was company and three was a crowd. I just wasn't sure at this point if *I* wouldn't be the one tossed from the group.

"You're exhausted," Ryker said. "You need rest."

Sleep. Yes, sleep sounded really, really good. My whole body hurt and my heart still ached from the beating it had taken over the past twenty-four hours. Before Leo had gotten involved and nearly killed Parker, I'd almost lost both him and Ryker to Viktor, a crazy Russian mafia guy who'd made me watch while he tortured them. I shuddered even now as images of them both—bleeding and bruised—flitted through my mind.

Taking my hand, Ryker pulled me to my feet to lead me from the room, but I put on the brakes.

"What about you?" I asked Parker. "Are you leaving?" The anxiety that thought produced had my stomach turning itself into knots.

He must've read my mind because he said, "Not if you don't want me to." He glanced at Ryker. "I'm sure Ryker won't mind me camping out on his couch tonight."

"That's fine."

Something passed between the two of them, but I was too tired to examine the tension in the air. Relieved that Parker wasn't leaving had me nodding. "Good. Okay, then."

I let Ryker lead me to his bedroom. He sat me down and removed my shoes. I shucked my jeans and climbed underneath the covers. Ryker had on a pair of sweat pants and joined me, turning off the bedside lamp before pulling me into his arms. I settled against his chest with a sigh that felt soul-deep, and was asleep in moments.

* * *

Screaming woke me, then I realized it was my own.

"Sage...hey, it's okay; you're okay..."

I was sitting straight up in bed and Ryker was next to me, his hand on my arm, his voice anxious as he tried to get through to me. He'd turned the light on, but apparently even that hadn't been enough to break through to me.

"Viktor..." I gasped. Images from my nightmare were still vivid inside my head: images of him torturing and tormenting Parker and Ryker.

The door flew open.

"Sage..." Parker said, standing in the doorway. His face was drawn in lines of worry as he looked at me. Instinctively, I reached for him. His hand was instantly in mine as he sat beside me.

"Oh God," I breathed, my eyes slipping shut. Ryker's hand slipped from my arm, but I grasped it, holding him tight.

No one said a word as I tried to gain control. Tremors shook me. Lord only knew how much therapy I was going to need in the future to move past what had happened, but tonight the only therapy I needed was holding each of my hands.

I lay back down on the bed, scooting until I was in the middle. Both Parker and Ryker were looking at me with their best poker faces.

"I'm tired," I said, looking at them both expectantly. I had a hold of each of them so unless one of them tried to pull away, no one was going anywhere. An odd request? Absolutely. But I'd had a really rough few days and I figured if I wanted to get any rest tonight, my subconscious was going to be appeased only one way.

Neither man looked happy with the situation once they realized what I wanted, but they both complied, lying down on either side of me in identical, stiff positions. Ryker turned off the light and I closed my eyes. I could feel both of them pressed against my sides, the warmth of their skin heating the chill of mine. If I listened, I could hear them breathe, and that sound comforted me. A smile flitted across my face, and I relaxed.

CHAPTER TWO

There might be better ways to wake up than sandwiched between two half-naked men, but if there was, I couldn't imagine what it would be.

Early morning light filtered through the window blinds as I blinked a few times and debated whether I wanted to move.

We were sleeping spoon-style, all three of us, my front pressed against Ryker's back with Parker cradling me from behind, his arm slung over my waist. It was warm and cozy and I felt like I never wanted to move.

They were both here, whole and safe. Ryker's chest rose and fell steadily and I could feel Parker's breath stir my hair. The terror from my nightmare seemed a world away. I felt safe with both of them looming over me in the bed, and I memorized the feeling. I'd felt *un*safe too often lately.

God, what day was it? I'd lost track with all that had happened. It wasn't like I had to get up for work. Last I'd checked, I was unemployed, thanks to telling my boss—the man currently spooning me—that I'd quit.

Not that I'd had much of a choice. Once you sleep with your boss and tell him you love him, that's pretty much a Point of No Return right there. Or maybe that point had been when I'd dated (and yes, slept with) his arch frenemy—the man *I* was currently spooning.

Being hunted by Russian mafia bosses and hit men would turn any girl's life into a soap opera, right?

Right.

I frowned, not wanting to think about the current disastrous state of my life. At this moment in time, everything was perfect, and I didn't want to face reality. Not yet.

Unfortunately, reality didn't feel the same way about me, because no sooner had I thought that than Parker's arm tightened around me. He snuggled closer, close enough for me to feel that his body was most assuredly not undergoing any lasting side effects from Viktor's torture, but was most wholeheartedly embracing the morning.

Okay, so I was a red-blooded woman who'd maybe read one too many romance novels, but the thoughts that flashed through my head weren't of a high standard at that moment. I cursed ethics and morals and all those things that kept me from pressing my lips to Ryker's naked back and pushing my hips back into Parker's.

Oh, for a bottle of tequila and an inadequate respect for propriety...

As though he'd heard my thoughts, Ryker stirred, turning onto his back. My hand fluttered for a moment, then settled softly on his chest. His dog tags were tangled about his neck and my gaze wandered over his chest and ab muscles to the white bandage covering the burn.

I thought I should probably get up before I did something

colossally stupid. It seemed my hormones wanted to celebrate the fact that we were all alive and well, an urge I heartily seconded but one which I doubted the men would appreciate very much.

Squirming a little, I tried to ease out of the smidge of space I was wedged into without waking either of them.

"If you leave me in bed alone with another man, I'll have to fire you."

Parker's murmured words in my ear made me smile in spite of myself.

"You can't fire me. I already quit, remember?"

"Yes, but I was hoping you didn't."

"So much for wishing this didn't really happen," Ryker interrupted, cracking his eyes open and slanting a look at me.

"Pretend it's the zombie apocalypse," I suggested. "We're huddling for warmth and survival."

His lips twitched. Then his gaze fell to where Parker's arm was around me, and even that tiny smile faded entirely.

Yep. Time to cut this short, since it looked like I was the only one already composing a letter to *Penthouse Forum* in my head.

I scooted down the mattress and got up before either of them could say anything else. Both sets of blue eyes followed me. Acutely aware that I wore only a T-shirt and panties, I scooted into the bathroom.

Squinting into the mirror, I grimaced. My eye was no longer swollen, but I looked like I'd been in a bar fight... and lost. Badly.

A long, hot shower later, I felt better. Of course, I had no clothes, so I wrapped myself in a towel and went in search of a T-shirt to borrow and my jeans. The bedroom was now deserted and I quickly grabbed what I needed, then went to find the men currently occupying my every thought.

I heard voices coming from the kitchen and paused where I stood in the hallway.

"...not the same type of person Natalie was," Parker was saying. "I know you don't want to hear about her, but I never lied to you."

"Natalie was never the problem. *You* were," Ryker retorted. "You think I didn't know how you were manipulating her?"

"What are you talking about?" Parker asked. "I didn't manipulate her. It was her idea. She said she had feelings for me, that she didn't love you anymore."

"She thought I would hate her for sleeping with you," Ryker argued. "But I loved her. I wasn't going to let her go just because she made a dumb mistake with you."

"It wasn't a mistake, and I wasn't going to be a part of her games any longer. I thought our friendship was worth more than a woman. She tore us apart, Ryker."

I winced at the leashed anger in Parker's voice.

"Bullshit. You betrayed me and our friendship. Don't blame Natalie."

"I wanted you to see that she wasn't who you thought she was," Parker argued.

"So is that what you're doing with Sage?" Ryker asked, also angry. "Using her to teach me a lesson?"

I sucked in a breath, shocked. That wasn't true, was it? Parker wouldn't do that. He cared about me. Maybe he didn't love me, but he cared on some level.

"Of course not—"

I breathed out a sigh of relief.

"—but we need to decide what's going to happen from here," Parker finished.

"It's not up to us," Ryker said. "Sage is calling the shots."

"And what are you going to do if she picks me?" Parker said. "You going to go apeshit?"

"Who says she's going to pick you?" Ryker shot back. "That's just like you, thinking you must be the one she wants. You've had the opportunity to be with Sage for over a year. I find it a little too coincidental that you wait until now to decide she's someone worth having."

"That's not true," Parker denied. "As usual, you're jumping to the absolutely wrong conclusion."

I decided I'd had enough of them arguing, and my eavesdropping. I stepped into the kitchen.

Both men fell silent. I looked from one to the other.

"I was really glad last night that you two seemed to have patched things up," I said. "But I'm not like Natalie. I'm not going to break something that's finally been repaired."

"What is that supposed to mean?" Ryker asked.

Parker remained silent, his gaze shrewd as he studied me, and I wondered if he knew what I was going to say before I said it.

"It means I'm breaking up... with both of you."

Hard words to say, and the frightened woman inside who'd needed both of them to sleep last night looked at me as if I'd lost my mind. I ignored her.

"Ryker," I began, walking toward him and resting my palm on his chest. "This has been an amazing few months with you. I've had a lot of fun and you... you've come to mean a lot to me. I wish you nothing but the best." Stretching up on tiptoe, I pressed a chaste kiss to his mouth, then turned to Parker.

"I've worked for you for quite a while, and I loved it. I respect and admire you, and will always cherish the time that we had." Tears were starting to clog my throat, but I swallowed them down. Repeating the same kiss with Parker that I'd given Ryker, I moved away from them both.

"Sage, don't do this—" Parker began, but I held up my hand to stop him.

"You two were best friends, in a way that should never have been broken. You were idiots to let a woman come between you then, and I'll be damned if I let history repeat itself."

A car honked outside.

"That's my ride," I said. I'd called my dad after my shower and asked him to send a car for me. He'd asked no questions. "So, I guess . . . I'll see you around."

Their faces were unreadable, and I memorized the way they looked, standing there together. Two formidable men with testosterone nearly seeping from their pores, their jaws shadowed with stubble, bruises and scars from the recent ordeals we'd been through marking their bare arms and knuckles. Even Parker seemed to have lost his veneer of sophistication; his edges were more raw than I was accustomed to.

The doorway seemed a long way away and it blurred as I hurried toward it. I swiped my cheeks, wondering how I'd managed to fall in love with two men . . . then lose them both.

I went out the door to the waiting car and climbed in the back.

"Where to, Miss Sage?" Shultz, my family's driver, asked.

"Take me home, please," I managed. "Real home. Not my apartment." I felt a sudden need to see my mother and hear her reassure me that everything would be okay.

And maybe it would be. Someday.

* * *

"Any plans today?" my mother asked as I poured myself a cup of coffee. It had been two weeks since I'd come home, and most of that time had been spent padding morosely around the house from one room to another. I couldn't seem to find peace of mind. Every place I went, I couldn't escape the images of Parker and Ryker inside my head. My bedroom was the worst. It was where Parker and I had first made love. I'd torn off the sheets and thrown them away the first night I'd been home, unable to face sleeping in them, imagining I could still smell him—smell us—on the fabric.

"Um, I dunno," I muttered. "I hadn't really thought about it."

"Well, I just thought it would be nice if you got dressed today," she said mildly. "Maybe do your hair? I could make an appointment at the spa for you."

Okay, so I'd been too depressed to worry much about my appearance. I was without a job and without a boyfriend, two states of being that I thought were worth a bit of self-pity.

"It's not like I smell," I said defensively. At least, I didn't *think* I smelled. I sniffed cautiously.

"Of course not, dear," she said. "But you can't go on like this. You have to pick yourself up and move on."

I sat in a heap at the kitchen table, head in my hands. My robe hung open over my pajamas, even though it was after noon.

"I know; you're right," I said with a sigh. "It's just… hard." I missed them. Both of them. I'd come clean with my mom the day I'd arrived, a sobbing mess with a nasty black eye. She'd held me and soothed my tears and listened.

"I know it is," she said now, sitting in the chair next to me at the table. "But the Sage I know is a fighter. You've mourned; now it's time to pick up and move on."

I knew my mom was just trying to help. She'd never kick me out if I wanted to stay, and lord only knew there was plenty of room for three people in their six thousand-plus square-foot home in the exclusive Chicago suburb of Lake Forest for three people. Well, five I guess, though Schultz—my dad's driver—and Rita—the cook—didn't actually sleep here.

"I guess I could go to the spa," I said. No sense jumping right on into a job search. Easing back into life sounded way better anyway. Even if I'd been the one doing the breaking up, I deserved a spa day, right?

"Good idea." Mom beamed as though I'd been the one to suggest it in the first place.

Six hours, one manicure, one pedicure, a massage, a haircut, and a facial later and I was feeling more like my old self. I decided it was time to confront my father.

I went to his study, knocking on the door before pushing it open. As I'd expected, he was behind his desk going through a stack of papers. My dad was a workaholic, but since he was at home rather than being at the office for twelve hours a day, Mom didn't complain. He glanced up.

"Sweetheart! Good to see you up and around. How was the spa?"

"It was fine," I said, settling into a chair opposite his desk.

"So what can I do for you today?" he asked.

I gave him a look. "Really? You really don't know why I'm in here?"

Giving me a small smile, he said, "I assumed we'd have this conversation at some point, yes. You're telling me that time is now."

"Who were those guys, Dad?" I asked, referring to the men with guns who'd accompanied him to free me from Leo Shea's clutches.

"They work for me."

"You employ men for the sole purpose of killing people?" I asked, incredulous.

Dad snorted. "Don't be ridiculous. They're security for my business. Most of them are former military. Men who have incredible skills that can sometimes go unappreciated in a civilian occupation. They're not just guns-for-hire."

"And why do you need that kind of security?" I asked.

My father sighed. "Sage, I realize you don't know a lot about how I run my business, but it's not easy being the largest liquor distributor in Chicago. I worked hard to get where I am, and people don't always play by the rules in business."

"Do you?"

He gave a slight shrug. "I do my best. I don't ship anything illegal, but that doesn't stop some people from wanting to infringe on my territory, or try to put me out of business entirely."

"Has it always been this way?" I asked. "Was I just oblivious growing up?"

"You don't remember—you were too little—but it started when someone threatened you and your mom," he said. "Your mother was driving you home from the pediatrician one day when she had car trouble. This was before cell phones. A man stopped, supposedly to help her. Instead he threatened her, told her what would happen if I didn't do what this rival...company...wanted me to do. It scared her. And me.

"I decided then that I had two choices," he continued. "I could capitulate, do what they wanted and forever be at the mercy of a man who wouldn't hesitate to hurt me or my family. Or I could fight back. I chose the latter."

"What happened to the man?" I asked.

"I made him understand that messing with me was a bad idea," he replied evenly.

I decided I didn't want to know the details.

"I never thanked you for coming for me," I said, changing the subject. "I don't know what I would have done if you hadn't shown up." Somehow I doubted I'd have survived the night with Leo.

"I'm glad I was in a position and had the resources to get you out of there," he said. "And no thanks is required. You're my daughter."

A moment of understanding passed between us. Although my dad was not much of a demonstrative man, I could appreciate what he wasn't saying.

"So now that you've quit your job, what are you going to do?" he asked.

It was my turn to shrug. "I don't know. Thought I'd try the museum again." Though without any kind of an "in" there, I didn't think my chances of landing a job were that good.

"You can come work for me," he offered.

I raised an eyebrow. "Work for you? Doing what?"

"Learning the business," he said. "You're our only child. I'd like to leave you my business and keep it in the family rather than eventually sell it."

I thought about this. I'd learned a lot at KLP over the past couple of years, especially by working for Parker. I liked business, and knowing I'd be working on a company that my father had started and grown from the ground up made it personal. A little flame of interest and eagerness lit in my belly.

"Is this a temporary thing or permanent?" I didn't want to get all excited about a new career if Dad just wanted to give me something to do to distract me from my heartbreak.

"It's whatever you want it to be."

Fair enough. "Okay," I said. "What do I do?"

My father was beaming. "You'll work downtown at the main office," he said. "I'll have Charlie start training you and you can shadow him."

Charlie was my dad's second-in-command and had been working for him forever.

"I'm usually in the office a couple days a week," he continued. "I can teach you more then. So when do you want to start?"

"Monday, I guess," I said. That would give me the weekend to get back to my apartment and back to real life. The thought of going back home wasn't as depressing as it had been before, and the thought of a new job in a new career perked me up.

"Wonderful. I'll make it happen."

I stood, rounding the desk to give my dad a hug and kiss on the cheek.

"Thanks, Dad," I said. And I didn't just mean the job. He'd worked hard to provide for me and my mother, and it seemed he'd had to do some dangerous things along the way. I was grateful for it, and for him.

"None of that now," he said, shooing me off as his ears turned pink. "Go love on your mother. Lord knows she's been worried enough for you these past few weeks."

My mom helped me pack up my things and rode with me back to my apartment, taking along some food and stowing it in my refrigerator, chattering to me as she did so.

"...love those throw pillows on your sofa," she was saying as I glanced around the apartment. Parker had said they'd do another cleanup job, and they had. Nothing was out of place, and those were definitely new throw pillows. I didn't want to think of what had happened to the old ones.

I let my mom putter around for a bit, then she kissed and hugged me good-bye and went on her way. It felt good to be home, and I felt more like myself.

But Monday morning, someone else will be getting Parker's coffee.

The thought sent a pang of jealousy and regret through me. I'd done the right thing. I had.

I'd opened my cabinet to reach for my cookie jar when I remembered. I'd thrown it at Parker and broken it.

Shit.

I was crying again and didn't even have my cookie jar full of M&Ms to make me feel better. What I did have was a bottle of wine and a television.

Two hours, a bottle of wine, a box of tissues, and *The Notebook* later and I was ready to give up on life and love. It was about this time that my cell rang. It was Megan.

"Yeah," I answered, still sniffling.

"I know what you're doing," she said.

"What am doing?" I asked, morose.

"You're moping. You quit your job—something you might have mentioned to me, by the way—and broke up with Ryker. How many bottles of wine have you gone through?"

"One," I mumbled, tipping up my glass to swallow the last bit. I figured hey, at least I'd used a glass.

"I suppose it could be worse," she sighed. "You could be passed out on your bathroom floor, hugging the toilet."

Yeah, I'd already done that at my parents' house. Thank God they hadn't heard me heaving and bawling at the same time. The house was too big for that.

"You're at your apartment, right?" she asked.

"Yeah."

"Then I'm coming over and I'm bringing food," she said. "Pizza and ice cream. Any requests?"

"More wine."

"You don't need more wine." Megan dismissed my suggestion. "I meant, vanilla or chocolate?"

"Why is that even a question?"

"True. Chocolate it is. I'll be there in an hour."

I didn't move from where I lay on my stomach on the couch, watching whatever had come on after the depressing movie from hell. Eventually, there was a knock on my door.

"A Friday night after a breakup should not be spent alone," Megan said, breezing past me. The scent of pizza wafted behind her and I followed her into my kitchen.

"It's been a couple of weeks," I said. "I'm fine."

She stowed the ice cream in the freezer and gave me a look. "Yeah, you look fine."

Okay, I couldn't argue with that sarcasm. I probably looked like hell after my crying jag.

"I got extra cheese," she said, opening the box. "Let's eat."

Three dripping slices later I felt moderately better. Megan had changed the channel to some comedy show ("Why are you watching Lifetime?" she'd complained. "That's television to slit your wrists to."), and we were sprawled on my couch. I eyed the pizza, considering another slice.

"So what happened?" she asked. "Quitting your job is a pretty big deal. And I thought you and Ryker were doing good."

"We were. Right up until I slept with Parker."

Megan's mouth dropped open in a little O of surprise and her eyes widened. I had the brief satisfaction of knowing I'd rendered her speechless. Of course, that didn't last for long.

"You slept with Parker?" she asked, her voice high and squeaky. "When...how...?"

"It was after that guy that Viktor hired came after me," I explained. "Parker showed up at my parents' house and I'd been worried for him, and he'd thought something terrible had happened to me and well..." I shrugged. "I thought it was a huge deal and would change everything—*he* said it changed everything—but then he must've had second thoughts because of Ryker, because when he showed up the next day—"

"Ryker showed up at your parents' house, the morning after you slept with his ex-best friend," she interrupted. I nodded. "Did you tell him?"

"No, but he knows I have feelings for Parker," I said. "He told me he wasn't going to give up like he did last time. Then Parker told me he loved me, and then it all went to hell."

Megan shook her head. "Damn. You were right. We really do need wine."

That got a laugh out of me, and she grinned.

"So let me get this straight," she said. "You have two men, each of whom say they're in love with you, and you broke up with them both, even going so far as to quit your job."

I nodded. "They're friends again, I think, and if I'd chosen one, I'd have just made them hate each other again. I didn't want to do that."

"It's not your fault they both fell in love with you," Megan argued. "I happen to think you're pretty awesome."

I smiled weakly.

"But I do think you're being ridiculous, tossing them both aside," she continued. "You're going to throw away your chance at love because they can't put aside their egos enough to still be friends no matter who you choose?"

I shook my head. "I already feel as though I'm living in a soap opera. I don't want to be a part of their drama."

"So you can just turn off your feelings?" Megan persisted. "And you're never going to see either of them again?"

My face crumpled and she muttered a curse as she hugged me. "I'm sorry. I didn't mean to make you cry again," she said anxiously.

I sniffed. "It's okay. I just can't think of it like that or

I...I..." My throat closed up and I couldn't say anything else, but I think she knew what I meant.

It took a minute, but I swallowed everything down and swiped at my eyes. Clearing my throat, I sat back on the couch. "Sorry about that," I said.

"Don't apologize. I'm the shitty friend who made you cry."

I laughed a little. "No, you're just saying what's true. I miss them. A lot. But what was I supposed to do? Make them compete over me?" I shook my head.

"Tell me the truth," she said. "If you had to pick one of them, could you?"

I thought about her question, his face floating behind my eyes, and nodded. "Yeah. Yeah, I could. But I can't, so I won't. It'd be wrong and make them fight again. It's over."

Megan seemed to accept this, though she looked sad for me. I appreciated the sympathy though I felt I hardly deserved it.

"So where are you going to work now?" she asked, and I was grateful for the change of subject.

"I'm going to try working for my dad," I said, "in the business. I start Monday."

"I didn't know you were interested in business," she said. "I thought you wanted to work at a museum."

I shrugged. "I minored in business in college, just as a kind of backup plan. Dad offered and it seemed like a good idea. I guess I'll see how I like it." I hesitated. "What about my old job? Has Parker...hired anyone yet to replace me?" I tried to pretend I didn't care what the answer was, but I don't think I fooled Megan, who shook her head.

"No. I think he's trying to pretend you're going to come back," she said. "They've had temps in there and he's been going through them like mad. The last one left in tears in the middle of the day. I heard HR was going to lay into him because the agency is refusing to send over more people."

"You're not serious," I said. Parker wasn't *that* bad. I mean, he'd never made me cry or anything. At least, not about work stuff.

"I think he's being a total ass," she said with a shrug. "And he'll probably keep being an ass until he realizes you're not coming back."

Well, that was food for thought, and I couldn't help the small niggle of satisfaction that he hadn't replaced me already. Not real big of me, but it was what it was.

We chatted for a little while longer, with Megan obviously trying hard to keep things light and cheer me up, before she left a little after eleven. I gave her a long hug when she left, glad I had a friend like her to talk to.

Too many memories of Parker and Ryker assailed me when I stepped into my bedroom: the horror of believing Parker would be murdered as he lay next to me, to echoes of Ryker and me making love under the sheets.

Would Ryker and I have worked out if I hadn't already had feelings for Parker? I didn't know. What I *did* know was that I couldn't be involved with him while I was still in love with Parker. And I couldn't be in a relationship with Parker, knowing it would cause another rift between the two men.

* * *

I was nervous Monday as I dressed for work. My dad didn't have a lot of employees in the main office, maybe a couple of dozen, and I couldn't help wondering if they'd resent the boss's daughter coming into the business in a blatant display of nepotism.

Wanting to look professional, I wore a black pencil skirt that hit just below my knees with a white button down shirt and a gray cardigan. I fastened a thin red belt around my waist and added matching red heels.

I didn't have to wear my hair up for a change, so I pulled it back in a low, loose ponytail. A chunky statement necklace and my purse and I was ready to go.

The bus took me on the same route, but I didn't get off at my usual stop. A pang hit me as I saw the Starbucks where I'd always bought Parker's breakfast, but I shoved the feeling aside.

Two stops later and I exited. My father's office was one block down. Another Starbucks was located on this corner, so I ducked inside for a quick grande gingerbread latte, nonfat and no foam.

"Hold the whip?" the barista asked as he wrote on the side of the cup.

"No. Extra whip." Time to break in a new Starbucks, I thought with a sigh. My old Starbucks barista would laugh outright at someone asking me that.

He gave me a wry look, the judgy little thing, but I ignored it, handing him some money to cover the bill.

I'd visited my dad's office a hundred times over the years, but today was different, as evidenced by how the receptionist, Carrie, greeted me.

"Good morning, Miss Muccino," she said with a smile.

I stopped in my tracks. "Carrie, you've known me for five years. Call me Sage."

She laughed. "Okay, if you insist. I just didn't want to start your first day on the wrong foot."

"I appreciate that, but I'm not pretentious and certainly not going to have people calling me *Miss Muccino*," I said, grinning at her. "Sage will do just fine."

"Charlie's waiting for you," she said, getting up from her desk. "But first let me show you your office."

"I get an office?"

She laughed. "Of course you do! I thought your father was going to burst with pride when he was in here Friday, tell us you were going to start working with him. Had the decorator in over the weekend to put in just the right furniture and drapes."

I was touched and had to clear my throat a couple of times. I'd had no idea it would mean so much to my father if I came to work for him. He'd never pressured me to join the family business, not batting an eye when I'd wanted to study art and art history, merely suggesting a minor in business "never hurt anybody."

"Here it is!" Carrie said, proudly opening the door to an office larger than I'd thought it would be.

The walls were a warm mocha, the desk and credenza wooden with graceful lines and a deep walnut finish. A couple of chairs upholstered in chocolate and burgundy-striped fabric added color to the room and stood in front of the desk. A settee in the corner had throw pillows that matched the chairs.

"This looks amazing!" I headed behind the desk and stowed my purse in a drawer.

"I'll tell Charlie you're here," she said with a smile.

I hardly noticed her leaving, so absorbed was I in taking everything in. A huge computer monitor was on the desk, tied to a laptop docked below. I sat down and toggled the keyboard. A login screen appeared. Glancing on my desk, I saw a thin folder with my name on the tab. Flipping it open, I saw it was a typical new-hire form for a new employee with logins and passwords for various systems along with my office number, fax line, e-mail, yadda yadda yadda.

"Sage! So glad you're here!"

I looked up to see Charlie had walked in. Tall and broad, the only hair on his head being his graying moustache, Charlie could exude warm grandfather one moment, then disapproving tyrant the next. He obeyed my dad without question and ruled the business with a strong hand.

He'd been born and grown up in Sicily, emigrating to the States when he was seventeen and hiring on with my dad soon after that. No-nonsense but fair, he'd been by my dad's side for years. Suddenly, I could see Charlie hiring those men who'd accompanied my father, his pragmatism no doubt unsurprised by the things that had been done over the years. After all, Sicily in the 1950s hadn't exactly been rainbows and unicorns, I was sure.

We spent the next few hours going over the business and the books, with Charlie explaining to me the process of what they did and how they did it. I found it more interesting than I thought it would be, and the time flew by. Before I knew it, Carrie was rapping on my open door.

"Thought you might be hungry," she said, coming in to set a package on my desk. "I picked you up a salad and sandwich while I was out."

"That's great, thank you," I said. Someone else getting *me* lunch; now that was new. And on a Monday. With a pang, I wondered who had gotten Parker's standard lunch special from Tony's today. Ruthlessly, I shoved the emotion aside. "I appreciate it. Here, let me give you some money." I reached for my purse but she shook her head.

"I put it on the company card," she said, heading back out. "Don't worry about it."

I ate my lunch as I went over the thick book Charlie had left me, detailing more about our suppliers. At about half past three, he popped in again.

"Just thought I'd check on you," he said.

"It's going well," I replied. "I've jotted down some questions I have for when you have time."

"Sure, no problem. We can look at those in the morning," he said. "Tonight we have our weekly financial meeting. I've got a problem with Albertson's over their latest delivery and need to go by and have a meeting with the owner first. Your dad wanted you to start dipping into how the financials work, so I was hoping you could come along."

"Yeah, sure," I said. "When and where?"

"It's over at that place on Polk and Clark. Blackie's. About six. The owner knows us so just tell him who you are. I'll meet you there."

I jotted it down. "Got it."

"Okay. See you then."

I waved good-bye and dived back into work. I got up for a cup of coffee a little while later, saying hello to a few people I knew as I walked to the kitchen. Everyone seemed friendly and if they thought it was tacky that the boss had hired his daughter, I couldn't tell.

At about five forty-five, I got a call from Charlie.

"What's up?"

"This meeting is running long and with traffic, there's no way I'm going to be able to make it," he said. "Go ahead and go, I'll just let him know I won't be there."

"Okay. Will do."

I was a little nervous as I touched up my makeup and caught a cab to Blackie's. This was my first official meeting in my new job so there were butterflies in my stomach. I really wanted to do well, not only for my father, but for myself as well.

Blackie's was a neighborhood bar and had been around since the thirties. It had lots of walnut wood and a historic feeling, and I liked it right away.

"Sage Muccino," I told the host. "We have a standing reservation?" I was a few minutes late, having misjudged the traffic.

"Ah yes," he said. "This way."

He led me toward the back, past tables that were mostly full, though I spotted a couple of empty ones. Several people sat at the bar in groups of two, enjoying drinks and appetizers by the look of it. I could smell the food and my stomach growled.

I wondered what exactly would be expected of me at this meeting, since Charlie wasn't there. If it was a weekly event, then it probably wouldn't last long, though hopefully I could learn more about the company's holdings and investments.

"Here you go, miss," the host said, pausing for me to sit at a table.

"Thank y—" I stopped, staring in surprise.

It was Parker.

CHAPTER THREE

Good to see you, Sage," Parker said, getting to his feet as the host guy melted away. He pressed his lips to my cheek.

My eyes slipped closed, a shaft of bittersweet pain lancing through me. I could smell him, the scent I'd always loved—his cologne mixed with his skin—and my throat closed up.

Then he stepped back and the moment was gone.

My eyes popped open and I cleared my throat, struggling for composure.

"What are you doing here?" I asked.

Parker didn't answer at once, pulling my chair out for me instead and waiting. Manners made me sit, though part of me longed to rush out of the restaurant like a hysterical teenager.

Retaking his seat, Parker said, "Your father contacted me. He said he wanted me to take care of the company accounts personally, rather than one of my account reps. Of course I said I would."

Dear lord. Could this get any more embarrassing? My father was setting me up, most likely at the behest of my mother. I'd known she was getting ideas the night we'd all had that disastrous dinner together.

"And did he tell you I'd be here tonight?" I asked, wondering how obvious Dad had been. Subtlety wasn't one of his best traits. Actually, I doubted he knew the meaning of the word.

"He told me you were working for him now," Parker said evenly. "You could say I hoped you'd be here tonight."

Our gazes met and held, too many memories flashing through my mind. Memories of our bodies pressed together, him moving inside me, his lips on mine, the muscles of his back underneath my fingers...

I tore my eyes from his, lifting my hand for the waiter hovering nearby, who immediately stepped up to our table.

"Grey Goose martini," I ordered.

"And for you, sir?"

Parker's eyes were still on me as he said, "Bourbon, on the rocks."

"So what do we need to discuss?" I asked, trying to get down to business. "I'm supposed to be brought up to speed on the company's financials."

"Why did you leave?"

I stared at him, nonplussed. Was he talking about my job? Or something else? I went with Option A, mostly because there was no way I could deal with discussing our relationship, or Ryker.

"I decided I needed a different career," I said with a shrug.

"That's not what I mean."

Well, shit.

"I don't want to discuss it," I said, my voice firm. I prayed he'd take the hint. This was the unavoidable and cliché accidental meeting with an ex, with all its awkwardness and heartbreak—though my relationship with Parker hadn't exactly been the usual boyfriend/girlfriend type of thing.

The waiter returned with our drinks and I took a hefty gulp of mine. The cold vodka burned a path down my throat to warm in my stomach.

"Are you ready to order?" he asked. "Or do you need more time?"

I hadn't even glanced at the menu.

"Give us a few minutes," Parker said. The waiter disappeared again. No doubt even he could feel the tension between the two of us, it was so thick.

I was nervous, my hands were shaking, and I didn't want to look at Parker again. I was afraid he'd see too much in my eyes. Instead, I studied the menu.

"What's good here?" I asked, forcing my tone to be light. They had burgers. Lots of gourmet burgers. Grease and fat and a side of fries smothered in ketchup sounded like just what I needed.

"We need to talk—"

"I said I don't want to discuss it," I interrupted, putting the menu down and giving him a look. Maybe he could tell by the near panic in my voice that I was inches away from getting up and leaving. His lips thinned and he sat back in his chair, studying me while I resumed studying the menu, holding it up so it partially concealed my face.

"Everything's good here," he said at last. "So get what you want."

"Great." A burger it was. Extra fries.

After we'd ordered, Parker pulled some files and papers

from his briefcase and began going over them. I had enough of a business background and my experience as his assistant at the firm to understand most of it. What I didn't, he took time to explain, making sure I understood before moving on. I was worried I'd look dumb, but he didn't talk down to me or make me feel like an idiot. He was a good teacher and I could see why he was popular with his clients.

Dinner came and we worked as we ate. He'd ordered the salmon, but snagged some fries off my plate in an oddly intimate gesture that I decided not to comment on. I had another martini, which may not have been the wisest decision, but I figured the beef I was consuming would help soak up the alcohol.

Time flew by as we talked, and I was a whole heckuva lot more at ease discussing money and investments than anything personal with Parker. He was funny and easy to talk to, and it made my heart hurt when I thought of how much I missed him.

Parker paid the bill over my objections when we were finished, citing the fact that I was his customer now and he picked up the tab for customers. I couldn't argue with that, not when I knew it was the truth. After all, I used to be the one to do his expense reports.

We walked outside and I was about to lift my arm for a cab when Parker stepped in front of me. He was close, closer than I was prepared for, and I took a step back.

He followed me, his hand closing around my elbow, and I couldn't back away again.

"Let me take you home," he said. "My car's just around the corner."

That was such a bad idea, I didn't even bother putting my refusal into words.

"I'll grab a taxi," I said, looking over his shoulder at the

street and the light traffic going by. I could feel his eyes on
me, and the touch of his hand on my skin felt like a brand.

"Look at me," he said.

I didn't, knowing I'd cave if I gazed into his eyes.

"Look at me, Sage," he said again, more insistent. He
moved closer, and our bodies nearly touched. Reluctantly, I
lifted my chin until our eyes met.

The intensity of his gaze made me suck in a breath. My
pulse was racing and every inch of me wanted to press
against him.

"Don't try to pretend you don't still have feelings for
me," he said, his voice a low rasp that made a shiver dance
across my skin. "Or that you don't want me, because I know
it's not true."

He bent until his lips were near my ear. My eyes slid shut
at the barest touch of his skin against mine. The warmth of
his breath caressed my cheek as he spoke.

"I remember your taste, the feel of you beneath me, the
sounds you make when I'm inside you," he whispered.

I couldn't breathe. The urge to turn toward him until our
lips met was nearly overwhelming. I clenched my hands into
fists, the images his words provoked running through my
head.

"You and I belong together, and no matter how long it
takes for you to realize that, I'm not giving up."

His mouth grazed my jaw in a touch that made me swallow down a moan, then he took a step back, releasing me.

My eyes flew open to find him watching me, his brows
drawn together in a frown.

I couldn't speak, and even if I could, I had no idea what
I'd say. He'd thrown me utterly.

Taking a shaky step, I glanced at the street and saw a taxi
driving past. Parker did, too. He let out a piercing whistle

and lifted his arm. The cab pulled over and idled at the curb.

"I've gotta go," I said, my face flushing with heat as I moved quickly past him. But he was already there, opening the car door for me.

"See you soon, Sage," he said, his lips twisting in a half-smile, as if he knew how hard it was for me to walk away from him when every cell in my body was screaming to do just the opposite.

The door shut and the driver stepped on the gas. I couldn't help twisting in my seat to look out the back window for one last glimpse of Parker standing on the sidewalk.

* * *

I was completely thrown by the dinner with Parker and what he'd said. I felt as though all the progress I'd made in the past two weeks had evaporated into smoke. And thoughts of Parker made me think of Ryker.

Regret stabbed at me. Did Ryker hate me for how things had turned out? Did he think I'd done what Natalie had? Played them against each other just for the fun of being wanted by two men and driving a wedge between them?

Stripping off my work clothes, I pulled on a pair of pajama pants and a tank top. As I glanced in my closet, my eye caught on a small stack of T-shirts. They weren't mine. They were Ryker's, left over here from the many times he'd stayed over. I also had a couple of pairs of his jeans and a gray tank.

I'd have to get his stuff back to him. Not to mention, he had a key to my apartment. Probably should get that back. A tingle of anticipation as well as a heavy sense of dread settled over me at the thought of seeing Ryker again. Then nerves set in. Was there anything more awkward than returning your ex's belongings?

Looked like I'd have to find out—as soon as I screwed up my courage.

* * *

The courage didn't present itself until Saturday. I procrastinated all week, learning my new job and the ropes around the office. Then the weekend rolled around and I knew I couldn't put it off any longer.

I elected not to call first. A mistake? Maybe. But talking over the phone would be just as awkward and I was hoping he might be working and I wouldn't have to face him at all.

Okay, who was I kidding? I was dying to see him again, but too chicken to try and arrange it.

I dressed carefully, changing clothes a half dozen times. That was too dressy. That too casual. That looked like I was trying too hard.

Finally, I decided on shorts and a retro Van Halen T-shirt I'd picked up at a vintage shop. It was black and cut for a woman, and so was flattering in a subtle way. I left my hair down and packed up Ryker's belongings into a Nordstrom shopping bag.

I'd delayed long enough and it was early afternoon by the time the cab pulled up to Ryker's house. It was at times like these that I regretted turning down my dad's offer to buy me a car. Having my own mode of transportation—without calling Schultz or a taxi—would be really nice.

There was a sinking sensation in my stomach when I saw that the front door was open, with only the screen door blocking the entry.

He was home.

Getting out of the car, I hefted the bag. "Can you wait, please?" I asked the driver, who shrugged. I took that as a yes.

I'd made it halfway up the walk before the door burst open and McClane came barreling toward me.

I stopped in my tracks at the sight of the huge German shepherd and his twin rows of sharp, white teeth. A police academy dropout, McClane had a huge doggie crush on me, despite my unreciprocated affection. He smelled. He shed. And he drooled.

He'd also saved my life, getting injured in the process.

With a sigh, I set down my bag just as he jumped up, his paws settling nearly to my shoulders. His tongue lolled in a grin and I carefully avoided the wet slobber, patting him on the head.

"Hiya, McClane," I said. "Glad you're all better now." I noticed the hair was just starting to grow back from where they'd had to shave his belly.

"I knew it had to be you. There's only one person he'd knock down my door to get to."

I glanced up, my heart skipping a beat at the sight of Ryker. He must've been working on his truck, because the white tank he wore was torn and stained, and he was wiping black grease from his fingers onto a rag.

His shoulders and arms were covered in a fine sheen of sweat and I found my gaze wandering over all the exposed muscles and skin. Ryker had a raw edge to him that was as potent as catnip and as intoxicating as the strongest Hurricane Mardi Gras had to offer.

"Um, yeah," I said, pushing McClane down. It was like trying to move a gorilla and I had to give him a mean look before he dropped back to the ground. Even then, he sat close, gazing up at me in doggie adoration as his tail swished the grass.

I couldn't avoid Ryker's gaze any longer, though it hurt to look into his eyes. I felt guilt and a strong sense of loss, as though things would've been very different if all that had come between us had never happened.

"I brought your things," I blurted, not knowing what else to say. "Thought you might want them back." Nervously, I glanced away from him.

"There are a lot of things I want back. My clothes aren't one of them."

My startled gaze met his, but he was moving toward me, and before I could even think of stepping back, he was kissing me.

Hot and sweet, his lips on mine. His arms were around my waist, lifting me up on my toes, and it was instinct to clutch his shoulders, hard underneath my fingers.

Ryker didn't just kiss; he put all he had into it, his tongue sliding against mine and making my head swim as though I'd downed a shot of tequila. I breathed in deep the scent of heat and sweat tinged with motor oil. It may not sound sexy, but it was all man and it made my knees weak.

"God, I've missed you," he muttered, finally breaking the kiss. I was breathless. "Tell me you've missed me, too." He let me slide down until my feet were on the ground, and I wanted to whimper at the press of his hard cock against my abdomen. His hands drifted down to cup my ass and his mouth moved to my neck.

"What are you doing?" I managed to ask, my eyes slipping closed. "We-we broke up."

"You broke up. Not me."

He was sucking on my neck, turning me boneless, and I struggled to think.

"Ryker," I said. He didn't reply, just brushed his lips up to the tender skin under my jaw. "Ryker," I said again, stronger this time. "Stop." I pushed at him and he finally relented, easing his hold on me until I could take a shaky step back. Then I was at a loss for words.

"I was hoping that after you had some time, you'd reconsider," he said after a beat. "A lot's happened the past couple of weeks. You needed space, so I gave it to you."

"I haven't changed my mind," I said. "You and Parker have started putting the pieces of your friendship back together. I'm not going to be the one who screws that up."

The taxi driver honked, then stuck his head out of the window. "Hey, lady! You 'bout done?"

Before I could yell back for him to chill out, Ryker was striding toward the car. Leaning through the window, I saw him hand the driver some money, then the cab was backing out of the driveway.

"Hey!" I said, jogging over to where Ryker stood. "That was my ride."

"I'm your ride."

That statement sent way too many images through my head, most of them X-rated, which was so *not* helping.

He turned and headed for the house, pausing to examine the state of the screen door. After a moment, I had no choice but to follow. Grabbing the bag with his clothes, I walked up the porch steps, McClane trailing me.

"Did he break it?" I asked.

"Nah. It's all right. Just banged it up a little."

McClane looked completely unrepentant, his attention focused on wherever I was going. Which, at the moment, appeared to be inside Ryker's house.

Don't look toward the bedroom. Don't look toward the bedroom. Don't—

"You want something to drink?" Ryker asked. "I've got beer, pop, and some wine that appeared while I was gone." His lips lifted in a half-smile.

Ah. The bottles of wine I'd bought with Parker when I thought I'd be staying here. The thought of Parker and last night, and knowing I was now in Ryker's house had me nodding.

"A glass of wine would be great."

I followed him into the kitchen, feeling a little like he was the Pied Piper and I was the one unable to resist trailing wherever he led. He washed his hands and uncorked a bottle of chardonnay I'd left in the fridge. After he poured me a glass, he popped the top on a bottle of beer.

"Come on out back," he said. "It's a beautiful day."

One thing I missed from home that I didn't have in my apartment was a place to sit outside. Ryker had a really nice deck in the back that he'd said he'd built himself after tearing off the old one. Since it was an older neighborhood, he had a few big trees as well and had hung a hammock between two of them.

I eyed the hammock as he sat on the wicker couch and patted the seat next to him. I knew I probably shouldn't—I should sit in that chair over there where I couldn't touch him or smell him—but I obediently sat on the couch anyway.

"So where'd you go the past couple of weeks?" he asked. "Home? Or further away?"

"I stayed with my parents for a while," I said.

A beat passed.

"Your dad talk to you about that night?"

I hesitated. We were heading into risky territory now. Ryker had accused my dad of being a mobster and as it turned out, he'd been partially correct. "Yes. I guess I hadn't realized all these years how dangerous it was to be in his business."

"You know Leo Shea has disappeared, don't you?"

A sick feeling churned in my stomach. I'd deliberately not asked my dad about what had happened to Leo.

"I didn't, but I'm not surprised," I said. "He was going to kill me."

Ryker's hand clenched into a fist and I felt his body tighten. "That was my fault," he said.

"I don't want to play the blame game. I just want to... forget about it." I'd woken up a few times over the past weeks, my skin in a cold sweat, and Leo Shea's grinning visage in my mind. Between what Viktor had done to Ryker and Parker, then reliving Leo's order to kill Parker and what he'd done to me, the flashbacks were killing me.

I took a healthy swallow of my wine, the cold, fruity liquid a nice bite on my tongue. Birds chirped on the breeze and I took a deep breath, letting the sunshine dispel the darkness inside my head.

"Are you back at work yet?" he asked.

"I told you I quit. I have a new job now." Might as well get this part over with.

I felt his gaze on me through his mirrored shades, though I didn't look at him.

"What's that?"

I swallowed before answering. "I've gone to work for my father." I winced a little at the hint of defensiveness in my voice.

"So keeping it in the family then?" he asked.

"Keeping what in the family?" And now there was no mistaking my defensiveness. "My father hasn't done anything he wasn't forced to do because of other criminals threatening him and his family."

"It doesn't matter the reason. The point is he's a force in this town and now you're a part of that."

"Does it matter?" I asked bitterly. "You and I are through anyway. What do you care?"

His hand closed over mine, slotting our fingers together.

The roughness of his palm against the smoothness of mine sent a flicker of sadness through me. I hated good-byes.

"I don't want us to be through."

This time I did look at him. "I don't understand," I said, shaking my head in confusion. "You know I have feelings for Parker. I slept with him, for crying out loud. Why in the world would you want to get back together?" I honestly was befuddled. By all rights, he should hate me. I'd betrayed him the same way Natalie had, though for different reasons, I supposed.

"I love you. That hasn't changed. And I think you love me, too. What we have is worth fighting for."

"And it'll drive you and Parker apart again." I shook my head.

"It's...different," he admitted. "At first, I felt it was Natalie all over again. But I don't think Parker's using you. I've seen the way he looks at you, what he did in that warehouse to get to you." His expression was stark. "We're both in love with you, Sage, as crazy as that sounds. And neither of us wants to give you up."

I jumped to my feet, his words scaring me more than I wanted to admit.

"That's crazy," I said. "You make me sound like some weird...femme fatale or something. I don't want two men in love with me! I don't want to be the person who'd do that to someone."

I paced the deck, my agitation making my fists tighten until my nails cut into my palms.

"It's not up to you," he said grimly, getting to his feet. He stepped in front of me, halting me in my tracks. "There's three of us in this, and we all get a say."

Reaching out, he brushed the hair back from my face, tucking it behind my ear.

I didn't know what to say. The leap of hope inside sickened me with guilt. How could I choose one man over the other? Why was I so happy at the thought that I wouldn't have to give them up?

I opened my mouth to speak, but suddenly McClane leapt to his feet, a growl emanating from his throat. Startled, I turned to look, but he took off, back inside the house toward the front door.

"Shit," Ryker muttered. "If that's the mailman, he's not going to deliver my mail for a month."

We hurried after McClane to the front, where the screen door let in the breeze and sunlight. McClane was standing in front of it, growling at a woman waiting outside.

"McClane! Heel!"

Ryker's command had no effect on McClane's growling, and as I got closer, I got a better look at the woman just as Ryker froze.

"Natalie?" he asked, his voice a mix of awe and horror.

CHAPTER FOUR

D ean," the woman said with a tentative smile. "It's good to see you."

Ryker moved forward as though in slow motion. McClane shuffled aside. I stuck close because a) this was unreal and b) I thought Ryker was about to pass out.

"But... you're dead," Ryker said.

She gave a little shrug, looking slightly abashed. "False alarm. Can I come in, Dean? I have a lot to tell you and explain."

Ya think? My spidey senses were firing off all kinds of warnings. Why was she here? How was she even alive? And why did she keep calling him "Dean" in that familiar way that made me want to rip out her long, shiny hair?

"Um, yeah, of course." Ryker stepped aside and held open the screen door. He still looked dazed, as though he were responding automatically. McClane growled again as she walked in the door and that seemed to break Ryker from his trance. "McClane," he snapped, and for once the dog obeyed, quieting.

Natalie paused when she saw me, her eyebrows lifting in surprise. "Oh," she said. "I didn't realize you had company. Am I interrupting?"

Um, yeah, you're interrupting his life.

I couldn't explain why I instinctively didn't like her, didn't trust her, and felt a knot in my gut that said this was bad bad bad—it just was.

"Oh, yeah—um, Natalie, this is Sage, my girlfriend. Sage, this is..." He seemed at a loss for words so I stepped up and shook her hand.

"Hi, Natalie," I said with as friendly a smile as I could muster. "I must admit, I'm surprised to see you. Ryker had told me you passed away some years ago." She looked just like the photo I'd seen of her, Ryker, and Parker. Like she hadn't aged a day. Which, unless she was a freaking vampire, was impossible.

And no, I didn't bother correcting Ryker on referring to me as his girlfriend.

Natalie's smile had grown more brittle when Ryker introduced me, but was still firmly in place.

"I was hoping I might have a private moment with Dean to explain," she hinted. I just smiled and said nothing. "But...ah...I suppose if you're his girlfriend, then you'd want to hear the story, too."

You got that right, I thought but didn't say. Instead I replied, "That would probably be best."

"Have a seat," Ryker said, gesturing to the sofa. He sat heavily in a chair opposite, and I thought he was still struggling with his shock. I chose to remain standing and felt a small bit of satisfaction when McClane came and plopped his butt on top of my feet.

At least the dog liked me better.

Natalie walked by me and that's when I realized how little she was...and how huge I felt in comparison. She couldn't have been more than five feet, four inches tall, which was a good four inches shorter than me. Talk about feeling like an Amazon...

She sat primly on the sofa and brushed her hair back from her face. She was even prettier and more delicate in person than she had seemed in the photo. Her hands twisted in her lap as though she was nervous. Wearing a summer dress a soft shade of pink, she looked beautiful and innocent.

"When I left Parker's that night," she began, "I went home. It was there that I got the message."

"What message?" Ryker asked.

"The message that my...husband...was out of jail."

"You told me your husband was dead."

"There were times I wished he were dead," Natalie said. "He was violent. Possessive." She shuddered. "When he went to jail, I was relieved. I was free. Or so I thought. But his dad...he pulled some strings and got him out early. I had to run."

Natalie's story conveniently would elicit sympathy, especially from Ryker...which made me immediately suspicious as to its veracity.

Don't be judgy, I chastised myself. *At least wait and hear the whole story,* then *be judgy.*

"Where is he now?" Ryker asked.

Natalie's brow furrowed and she chewed her lip. "Dead," she said. "Killed in a drug deal gone bad."

Ryker just looked at her. "So you...what? Faked your suicide? Why?"

"I hoped he'd believe I was dead," Natalie said, tears welling in her eyes. "I'm sorry that I had to let you and

Parker believe it, too. I was afraid if I told you the truth, you wouldn't believe me. Or worse, try to confront him and get hurt."

"So your solution was to break his heart by making him think you'd committed suicide?" I asked. "And that it was his and Parker's fault?" I couldn't hide the derision in my tone and her eyes flashed when she looked at me.

"I was young and confused, and I didn't know what to do," she said. "You have no idea what my husband was capable of. For all I knew, he'd go after my friends. I couldn't risk it."

Damn. I couldn't argue with that and I felt a twinge of doubt about how I'd thought of her as conniving and manipulative. What if she was telling the truth?

She looked back at Ryker. "Just like now. I hope you can forgive me, Dean, because I need your help."

"What could you possibly need my help for?" he asked.

Um, yeah. I wanted to hear that, too.

"It's my sister," Natalie said.

"Jessie?"

"Yes. She's disappeared."

"What do you mean?" Ryker's brow creased in a frown. "What happened?"

"A few weeks ago. She never came home from work. I filed a missing person's report, but the cops have done nothing."

"How long has she been gone?"

"Nearly two weeks." Her eyes welled with tears again. "I'm so scared, Dean." She moved forward and wrapped her arms around his waist, resting her head on his chest.

I waited to see if Ryker would push her away—in a nice way—but he didn't. Instead, he hugged her back, holding her.

Hmmm.

I waited a beat—this was so awkward—then cleared my throat, which seemed to make Ryker realize I was still there. His gaze flew to mine over her head and I raised an eyebrow.

"So I'm going to get going," I said, because really, what else was I supposed to do?

"Yeah, I said I'd take you home," Ryker said, *finally* extricating himself from her clutches. Nice of him to remember that little bit. He'd been the one to send the taxi away, after all.

I was trying to be sympathetic—the woman said her sister was missing—but the whole thing was leaving a bad taste in my mouth. I tried to convince myself I wasn't jealous. I shouldn't be jealous—Ryker and I were done—but the hypocritical little green monster poked his head over my shoulder anyway.

"Will you help me?" Natalie interrupted, turning pleading eyes on Dean. I mean, Ryker.

"Where are you staying?" he asked. "I'll come by after I drop off Sage."

Oh really?

Natalie rattled off the name of a hotel that wasn't cheap, which made me wonder what she did for a living to be able to afford a place like that.

"Room 815."

Ryker didn't write it down, but I didn't think he probably needed to. The way he was looking at Natalie, as though he was seeing a ghost he'd desperately longed for, had me questioning the wisdom of letting him go alone.

She gave me the briefest of nods on her way out and I watched her get into a Toyota sedan and drive away. I could feel Ryker's presence behind me, also staring after her.

"That was…interesting," I said at last, turning around. "What do you think?"

He looked down at me and his eyes grew shuttered. "I think I should get you home." He grabbed his keys from the table by the door.

"You're kidding, right?" I asked, grabbing his elbow as he passed by me. "Natalie, your presumably dead-by-suicide ex-girlfriend shows up, and that's all you're going to say?"

"I'm a little in shock at the moment," he said, pulling away from me.

"I know you are, which is why you should probably talk about it."

"I will. Just not right now."

"Not right now? Or not with me?"

"Both."

Well, okay then.

I shut my trap and followed him out the door. Whereas usually we'd take his bike on a day as pretty as today, instead he headed for his truck. And there was plenty of space between us on the seat as he drove me home.

The silence wasn't a bit awkward.

Right.

Finally, I couldn't stand it anymore. "Ryker, I think we should talk about this. I don't trust her. I don't know how *you* could trust her. She's only showing up now to tell you she *isn't dead* when she should've told you years ago. And just because she needs your help. It's just so strange. She could've called you when her husband died or like a thousand other times..."

"What would you have me do then, Sage?" he asked. I winced at the irritation in his voice. "Tell her to go? She blindsided me."

"I don't know. I just thought it was really weird," I said. "And cruel. To let you and Parker think—"

"Don't even think about telling Parker," he interrupted.

I shot him a look. "You're joking, right? You're not seriously considering keeping Parker in the dark about this?"

"She should tell him herself. Or I should. Not you."

"I know, but—"

"End of story."

I wanted to whack him upside his thick skull. How he
would still hold a grudge to the point of not telling Parker
about Natalie's un-death was incomprehensible to me. But
I pressed my lips closed against the protest that wanted to
emerge and let it lie. Ryker could no more tell me what to do
than apparently I could tell him.

He'd barely parked the truck before I was out of the cab
and slamming it shut. "Thanks for the ride," I tossed through
the open window. "Give Natalie my best."

"Sage, wait—"

But I was already inside the building, and I'd no more let
my apartment door close behind me than I was on my phone.

"Parker, it's me."

* * *

I wouldn't tell him over the phone what was going on, so he
made it to my apartment pretty darn quick.

"Thanks for coming," I said, stepping aside to let him
enter.

"You sounded like this was urgent," he replied. Since it
was the weekend, Casual Dress Parker was in evidence and
I took a moment to admire the way his designer jeans fit him
very well indeed...

"Sage."

I jerked my guilty gaze up to his face and swallowed. The
ghost of a smile flitted across his face at catching my obvious stare.

"Um, yeah, well, you'd better sit down," I said. "And have a drink."

I poured a shot of bourbon from my cabinet into two glasses, handing him one.

"What's going on?" he asked. "Are you pregnant? Is that what you want to tell me?"

Holy shit.

I stared at him, openmouthed, then downed my drink in one swallow.

Pregnant.

I shook my head, coughing. "Not pregnant," I managed to squeak out. "Wow. I can't even..." I shook my head again, words failing me.

"Then what is it?" He'd set his glass on the table and still hadn't sat down. "You can tell me anything. You've got to know that. What's wrong? Is it your father? Ryker?"

"It's Natalie," I blurted. "She's not dead. She never was. And she's back."

I waited, but he showed no outward reaction to this news. His face was blank and he went very still.

"She showed up at Ryker's while I was there," I added, just to make sure he knew I wasn't making this stuff up. Who could??

Parker picked up his glass again and downed the liquor as I had, only without the coughing and sputtering afterward.

"Tell me."

So I did, starting with her appearing at the door and ending with Ryker supposedly going to her hotel after he'd dropped me off.

When I finished, I studied him and chewed my lip. How would he react to the news? Ryker had been blindsided, then immediately sucked back in. There was a lead weight in the pit of my stomach that Parker would be the same way.

"That's...unexpected."

I waited, but he said nothing more. I plowed on.

"Did you know Jessie?"

He shook his head. "No. She was younger than Natalie by a few years. Ryker knew her, though. He mentioned her a few times, that she was a sweet kid."

"Do you believe her story?" I asked. "That her husband got out of jail and that's why she left?"

"I'm not sure, but nothing she did would shock me. She's a manipulative liar."

"But you don't think she's lying about Jessie."

"I don't see why she would, no. She did always seem to genuinely care about her sister, even if the rest of her feelings were more difficult to read."

I mulled this over for a second, absently pouring each of us another shot of bourbon, but this one I drank more slowly.

"How did you feel about Ryker's reaction?" he asked.

I glanced up at him to find his shrewd gaze studying me. I shrugged.

"It's impossible to compete with an obsession," I said. "And whatever his feelings for me, I don't think he's ever gotten over her."

Parker gave a slow nod. "I'd agree with that."

I hesitated. "I guess the more pressing question on my mind is...have you?"

Parker's brows flew up in surprise. "Me? Have I gotten over her?"

Nerves twisted my gut, but I kept going. In for a penny... "I know how you felt about her. You can't just discount those feelings. And now she's back." *And still gorgeous*, I thought with a little sinking sensation. "Ryker looked like he'd seen a ghost. And not necessarily in a bad way."

Parker frowned. "I was young and stupid. And I'm not

ecstatic about her return, believe me. I mean, I'm glad that she's not dead, yes; that's a revelation. But she messed with Ryker's head so bad, I'd hate to see him lose his shit again over her."

That was hard to hear. Yes, I thought Ryker and I were pretty much over, but Natalie being back put the nail in that particular coffin. And I felt a twinge of disappointment. But even harder to take was that Parker had noticeably not said anything about his feelings for her—if he was over her. Or not.

Parker's gaze was still on me, reading every expression that crossed my face. Embarrassed, I turned away just as my cell phone rang. I glanced at the caller ID and sighed.

"Hey, Dad," I said. "What's up?"

"I'm in town," he said. "Let's go to dinner. I want to hear what you thought of your first week on the job. I'll pick you up in ten."

"Dad, I can't," I said, scrambling for an excuse. I wasn't up to dinner with my father. Not tonight. "Um, Parker's here."

"Excellent! Bring him! See you in a few." The line went dead.

"Dammit!" I tossed my phone onto the counter in frustration.

Parker raised an eyebrow. "Care to share?"

"My dad is on his way here to take me to dinner," I groused. "You too."

"Well, with that kind of invitation, how can I refuse?" His dry humor made me crack a smile. Not a big one, but a smile nonetheless. He could do that. Parker could change my mood from one spectrum to another with just a few words.

"Sorry," I said. "I'm just not in the mood tonight, but my father never takes no for an answer."

"And it's served him well."

I shrugged.

"I don't have to come along, if you'd rather I not?"

Parker asking? This was new. My manners kicked in and, let's face it, my desire to be with him. Now that he was here, he assaulted my senses. From how incredible he looked—his arms and chest filling out the long-sleeved polo he wore—to the smell of his cologne, to the tousle of his hair that said he'd been running his fingers through it.

No no no. I couldn't think like that. Especially now that Natalie was back. If I started to consider Parker and me being a couple, would I get kicked in the teeth? He may have been talking big about being over Natalie, but what would happen when he actually *saw* her? It might end up a completely different story.

"It's fine. My dad wants you to come, so come." I shrugged like I didn't care either way. *Right.*

I went in my bedroom and changed into a clingy cotton dress with elbow-length sleeves to protect against the chill of an air-conditioned restaurant and the nippy autumn night air. It also showed off my cleavage in a really great way. I told myself I just wanted to look my best as I rearranged the girls inside Victoria's best push-up. A squirt of perfume later and a brush through my hair and I was ready to go just as Dad buzzed from downstairs.

Parker gave me a once-over with a look that burned, our eyes meeting in a clash of want that had my breath coming faster. I knew that look...

"Ready?" I asked, only a little breathless. Thoughts of Natalie were far away when Parker looked at me like that.

"Ready for what?" he replied in a voice that begged me to rip his clothes off.

Hoo-boy.

"Okay then," I stammered, pulling open the door.

"Don't forget your purse," Parker said, handing it to me.

"Oh yeah, thanks." Okay, now I felt like a smitten teenager.

It was weird—almost as though Parker and I had started over since I'd quit my job as his secretary. *Executive Assistant*, I automatically corrected myself. A new start, a new relationship.

I wanted that. More than I even could admit to myself.

Dad was already having a cocktail in the back of the limo when Parker and I showed up. He handed me one without my even asking, glanced at Parker and did the same.

"My girl is a natural businesswoman, isn't she, Parker?" he asked. The note of unabashed pride in his voice made my cheeks warm.

"Yes, sir, she is," Parker replied. "Not that I had any doubt. Sage has always been an exceptionally quick learner. A very smart, intelligent woman."

I shouldn't let a man's praise go to my head, especially when, hello—what else would he say to my father?—but I couldn't help the preening of pride at Parker's words.

"Exactly." My father was nearly beaming.

Shultz drove us to a restaurant that made me glad I'd taken the time to put on a dress. The maître d' recognized my father immediately and led us to a private corner table.

"So what are the plans for the two of you?" my father asked once the waiter had taken our orders. I choked on the glass of wine the sommelier had poured.

"Pardon me, sir?" Parker asked, which I thought was a more cogent response than my coughing and sputtering. He handed me a glass of water.

"You two are together, right? My wife assures me she knows about such things and that's what she said."

I was so going to strangle my mother.

"I'd certainly like to be," Parker said. "But that's up to Sage."

Dad's gaze whipped around to me like a spotlight.

Cancel that. I was going to strangle Parker first, *then* my mother.

"Sage? What's wrong with Parker? He's good-looking, got a good job, decent family, military history. I approve and so does your mother."

"Dad," I struggled for words. "I-it's not that simple."

He snorted. "Bullshit. Of course it is. Unless there's not much there in the bedroom?"

Oh God. Could this conversation get any worse?

Parker snorted a laugh, covering it quickly with a cough.

"I cannot believe you just asked that," I chastised my dad. "Seriously?"

He finished his wine. "I don't sugarcoat, sweetie. It's better to know the truth. I don't lie to myself or my family. Neither should you."

That's what passed for fatherly wisdom and I gave an internal sigh.

Parker changed the subject to business, for which I was grateful, and dinner continued. I could follow the conversation this time and the three of us were talking long after dessert had come and gone. It was nice, really nice, to have something new that I could contribute to and have a stake in myself. I'd been part of Parker's life and career for so long, it was a new feeling to have things reversed. Now he was part of my career.

What a concept.

We'd finished off the second bottle of wine when dinner was through and I was feeling relaxed. *Natalie? Natalie who? Pfft.*

We were standing outside the restaurant on the sidewalk, waiting for Schultz to bring the car around. Parker's arm was around me, his palm resting lightly on my back, and I didn't mind at all. I may have even edged a bit closer to him; the wine was doing things to my hormones that made it seem like the best idea ever.

A car drove by, but I hardly paid attention. The only reason I even noticed was because it was going kinda slow. I glanced over as an automatic curious reaction just as a sharp sound split the night.

I had no time to react because Parker wrapped his arms around me and took me down to the ground so fast, I barely knew I was no longer vertical before the sound came again and this time I recognized it for what it was.

Gunshots.

Several of them, in rapid succession. Muffled, because Parker was covering me, his entire body shielding mine.

Fear for my father gripped me as tires squealed, and I heard an engine fire as the car sped away. I hadn't counted the gunshots, but it had seemed like a lot. A dozen, maybe? Had Dad reacted as quickly as Parker had? Or was he hurt? Possibly dead?

I struggled, trying to get out from underneath Parker. He was heavy and I couldn't catch my breath as the thought came that he could be hit, too. Sirens screamed in the distance, coming closer, and I could hear people yelling.

Something lifted Parker off me and I sucked in a breath, then scrambled to get to my knees, looking around frantically. The skin of my knees scraped against the asphalt, but I barely noticed.

"There's blood on her!"

Someone yelled it, but I knew I wasn't hurt. I crawled to Parker's prone body.

"Somebody get her some help! She's bleeding!" The guy who'd lifted Parker was still yelling and pointing at me.

"It's not mine!" I tore open Parker's navy sport coat, the vivid stain on the shirt beneath like a punch to my gut.

"This guy's hurt, too! Get the paramedics!"

I whipped my head around to see three people standing over my dad, who was lying on the ground. He wasn't moving either. Schultz appeared, parking the car haphazardly in the middle of the street and running to my father.

"Oh god oh god oh god . . ."

I couldn't think, didn't know what to do. My hands clutched at Parker's shirt. I knew nothing that could help him. His eyes were closed and I watched his chest, relieved to see it rise and fall with his breathing.

"Parker—" I choked out. This couldn't be happening. It had to be a nightmare and I'd wake up any second.

Parker's eyes opened to mere slits and my heart leapt as he focused on me.

"You . . . 'kay?" he murmured.

Tears spilled over and ran down my cheeks. I nodded frantically. "I'm fine."

His eyes drifted closed, but he was still conscious because he spoke again. "Good."

Sirens were closer, screaming inside my ears, but I didn't take my eyes off Parker. He seemed to drift into unconsciousness now.

"Ma'am, we need to get to him," someone said, moving me aside in a gentle but firm way. Someone else immediately took hold of me, turning me to face them. It was a paramedic.

"Are you hurt? Do you have pain anywhere?" he asked.

I shook my head, craning my neck to see Parker, then swiveling to try and spot my dad past the paramedics swarming him. Two ambulances had come as well as fire trucks and police. The whole sidewalk was practically swarming with emergency personnel.

"My dad," I choked out. "He's hurt..."

"We're doing our best to help him," the guy said. "We need to focus on you, though. Can you tell me what happened?" He took my vitals as I stammered my way through what little I knew. We were standing there, then there was the car, then gunshots. Then Parker was bleeding and my dad wasn't moving...

I couldn't breathe and tremors shook me. There was blood on my hands and clothes. Parker's blood...

"It's okay. Take a deep breath. You're hyperventilating. Look at me. Focus on breathing..."

The paramedic's words penetrated, but I still couldn't breathe, and now I was sobbing.

"Parker...Dad..."

"It's okay—"

But it really wasn't, and I had to watch as they loaded both Parker and my dad into separate ambulances, still trying desperately to regain control. Schultz climbed in with my dad, looking more shaken than I'd ever seen him. The paramedic with me helped me into the ambulance carrying Parker, and with the sirens screaming, we roared away into the night.

CHAPTER FIVE

The bullet that had struck Parker had gone clean through, so he needed stitches, blood, and antibiotics. He'd be fine with only a scar. My dad, though...my dad was a different story.

I stood there, dried blood on my clothes, listening with as much control as I could muster as the surgeon described to me my dad's condition. He'd been hit three times. He needed surgery. One bullet had fragmented off a rib and they were prepping him now to go in and remove the metal shards. He was stabilized, but at his age surgery would be hard on him. Depending on the extent of his internal injuries (which wouldn't be known "until we open him up"), he might need to be put into a medically induced coma for an indeterminate period of time.

I nodded like I was taking it all in, but my hands were still trembling and Parker's blood was on me. Schultz stood by my side, his solid presence comforting to me. He'd worked for our family for as long as I could remember, all the way back to driving me to school in the back of our Rolls.

"Surgery may take several hours," the doctor was saying. "You're welcome to wait in the surgical waiting room rather than in the ER. It'll be more comfortable for you." He gave us a last little nod, then turned and headed back through a set of swinging doors.

Schultz wrapped me in a hug, but I didn't allow myself the luxury of tears. I squeezed him hard, then took a step back. There were things that needed to be done, and I had to be the one to do them.

"I'll call Mom," I said. "Do you think you can go get her, bring her here?"

"Of course."

I already had my cell out. "I also need to call Charlie. He'll know the implications and what we need to do for the business if Dad's going to be—" I had to stop and clear my throat. "If Dad's going to be laid up."

There was also Parker.

I had his parents' phone number in my phone. I'd put it there a while ago just for emergencies. I needed to call them, as well as his office, and tell them what had happened.

I phoned Charlie first and to his credit, he didn't seem shocked at the news. Upset, yes, but nothing fazed him apparently, not even the fact that my dad had been hit in a drive-by shooting. It was as I was talking to Charlie that it occurred to me perhaps it hadn't been a random thing. I remembered what Dad had said about the problems he'd had over the years and the tough-looking ex-military men he'd hired to secure his business.

"Charlie, do you think Dad could have been targeted?"

There was a hesitation on the other end. "Maybe," he said

at last. "It's hard to know just yet. If he was, it shouldn't take long to find out."

"Can you find out?"

"Absolutely. I'm on it."

I hung up, my mind working. I didn't want to know exactly how Charlie would go about investigating this, but I did want to know the answer. Because if this hadn't been random and my dad *had* been a target from a rival...well, then there'd be hell to pay, courtesy of his daughter. I could feel the anger in my veins at the thought and I took a deep breath before dialing again.

"Hi, Mom. It's me," I said when she answered.

"Goodness, Sage, what are you doing calling at this hour? Is everything all right? Are you okay?"

"I'm fine," I reassured her. "It...it's Dad." Best to make this quick, like ripping off a Band-Aid. "He's been shot and they have him in surgery. They think he'll be fine, but they won't know more until later."

I could feel the shock in my mom's silence and tears stung my eyes again. I blinked them back.

"Thank God you're okay," she said at last. "What hospital?"

I told her, then added, "Shultz is on his way to pick you up. He should be there soon."

"Good. Do you need anything?"

Just my mom. But I didn't say that. "No. I'm okay. I'll see you when you get here."

I had to take a couple of minutes to regroup after that phone call before I made the next one.

"Hi, Mrs. Anderson? This is Sage Reese—"

"Parker's secretary?" she interrupted.

I bit back the automatic "Executive Administrative Assistant" that wanted to pop out. "Yes, ma'am."

"How can I help you?"

As gently as I could, I explained that Parker had been wounded in a drive-by shooting downtown. "But he's doing all right," I hastened to tell her. "He's stable and they're keeping him comfortable. He should recover fully without any problems."

There was silence on the other end, long enough that I checked to make sure the call hadn't dropped on my phone. Finally, she spoke.

"I see. I will let his father know. Thank you for calling, Sage."

The line went dead.

I stared at my phone, nonplussed. I knew Parker wasn't particularly close to his parents—hence the fact that I, not them, was his in-case-of-emergency person—but he'd been *shot*, for crying out loud. Surely that merited a bit more concern than what his mother had just shown?

I didn't have time to dwell on it; I had more calls to make, but it bothered me. I couldn't imagine having a child and then seeming to care so little about what happened to them. It wasn't any of my business, of course, but I felt angry and slighted on Parker's behalf.

Next I phoned Parker's office—my old one—leaving a voice mail for his new assistant and giving her detailed instructions on what had to be done for Parker since he would be out for several days. No doubt Rosemary would wonder how I knew all that, but I didn't take time to explain, just leaving my cell number in case she had questions.

I felt more in control when I got off the phone, having hit the big lines on the To Do list. I glanced at the clock, wondering how long my dad would be in surgery. I wanted to see Parker, but had one last call to make.

"Ryker, it's me. Sage."

"I'm surprised to hear from you," he said. "You seemed pretty pissed earlier."

Gee, I wonder why? "I didn't call to talk about that," I said, biting back the retort hovering on the end of my tongue. "I called to tell you that there's been a shooting. Parker was shot and so was my dad. We're at Cook County."

"A shooting? What kind of shooting?"

I told him about the car and the slow drive-by.

"Were you hurt?"

"No. Parker covered me, which is why he was the one hurt." The lump in my throat grew at that, but I swallowed it down. No time to fall apart right now. I'd lose my shit later in the privacy of my apartment.

"I thought you might want to know—"

I stopped talking then because I could hear another voice on Ryker's end. A woman's. Natalie. He covered the mouthpiece and it muffled his words, but I imagined him relaying to her what I had told him.

"We'll be right down." He hung up.

We? Oh shit...

They let me in to see Parker and I thought I'd been keeping it together pretty damn well...until I saw him.

He was shirtless, with bandages stained slightly with blood that had seeped from the wound, machines quietly monitoring his vitals, an IV drip in his arm, and his hair in a spiky disarray that at any other time would look sexy but now just made me that much more aware of his injured state...It was enough to break anyone, and it broke me.

I put my hand over my mouth to muffle my sob. Guilt didn't even begin to describe the emotion I felt at seeing him this way. Because of *me*. And likely because of my father as well. I still held out a small hope that it had been a freak of circumstance, but I also wasn't an idiot.

Parker's hand lay on top of the covers and I gently covered it with mine. I couldn't believe this had happened. It was surreal, like a nightmare from which I couldn't wake.

As if to punctuate the whole *nightmare* theme, the door swung open and Natalie walked in, followed by Ryker.

"You're kidding me, right?" I hissed at Ryker, heading him off at the pass and getting all up in his business. "Parker's been shot and you bring *her* here? You think *now* is the best time for a reunion?"

"She wanted to come," he said. "It wasn't like I could tell her no."

"So it would seem," I spat. He heard the scorn in my voice—it was hard to miss—and his gaze turned cold.

"Does it matter? Tell me the first thing you did when you got home wasn't to call Parker and tell him everything."

I didn't dignify that with an answer. Turning on my heel, I nearly gagged at the sight of Natalie, her hand cradling Parker's, running her fingers through his hair. Twin tears trailed down her cheeks in perfect crystal rivulets.

"You're going to wake him," I gritted out, trying to keep my voice down. I knew they'd given Parker pain medication, but the way she was messing with him was sure to pull him out of any drug-induced haze.

Sure enough, no sooner had I thought it than his eyelids fluttered open.

I hurried back to his side—the *other* side, as Natalie had taken my previous position—and saw his eyes open and focus. Unfortunately, they focused on Natalie, and his brows drew together in a frown.

"You've got to be fucking kidding me."

The rasp of his voice was low but even so, the words were unmistakable. I hid a triumphant grin, disguising it with a slight cough.

"Parker, it's me. It's Natalie." The tears had stopped and she smiled the perfect blend of sad and hopeful.

"Yeah. I know." He winced as he turned his head, pulling his hand away from hers as he did so, until his gaze landed on me. His hand fiddled with the controls to the bed. "There you are," he said to me. "Glad to see you're all right. What did the doctor say?" He completely ignored Natalie as he pressed the button to adjust the bed to sit more upright.

I gave him the rundown of his diagnosis and prognosis, ending with "And I called Rosemary and told her what to do about your meetings this week and the month-end reports. Your parents have been notified as well." That last one I kind of glossed over because I didn't want to go into detail about how *un*concerned his mother had seemed to be.

"Good. Thank you." He blinked kind of slow-like, resting his head back on the pillow, then saw Ryker standing behind me. "Man, what are you doing?"

Ryker stiffened. Parker hadn't said it meanly, more like the way I'd ask a girlfriend why in the world she'd start texting the ex who'd taken forever to go away.

"We'll talk when you're not drugged up," he said, approaching Natalie and taking her elbow. "Let's go."

Natalie let him lead her out of the room, but her gaze remained on Parker and what I saw chilled me: desperate longing and determination.

They went through the door and a noise from the bed had me swiveling, my attention now caught on Parker.

His eyes had shut but opened to slits when the door snicked closed.

"Are they gone?"

"Yeah, I'm sorry," I said. "I thought Ryker should know, but I didn't realize he'd bring her."

Parker sighed. "'S'okay. Best to get it over with sooner rather than later."

"Is there anything you need? Anything I can get for you?"

He shook his head. "No, I'm fine. Thank you."

Parker was clearly *not* fine—he was shot and in a hospital—but I got the message well enough. I'd been dismissed and I turned to go.

"Wait…"

I was afraid to hope when I turned back.

"Stay for a while?" he asked.

My smile nearly broke my cheeks, it was so wide. I nodded, perhaps a bit too enthusiastically. "Yeah, I can do that. I'll just go check on how my dad is doing, then I'll be back, okay?"

He nodded and I hurried out to the waiting room, finding a nurse who was able to tell me my dad was still in surgery but things were going well so far. I told her where I'd be and asked if she'd come to Parker's room to update me. She smiled in a nice way and said she would. Shultz hadn't yet returned with my mom and I knew it would still be a while before they got here.

By the time I got back to Parker's room, he'd fallen asleep, but that was okay. After Natalie had woken him, I was sure he needed the rest. And I didn't care what he said about not having any reaction to Natalie's return other than his exasperation at Ryker's behavior—it would be a shock for anyone, especially considering their history. Maybe he just didn't want to tell me for the same reasons I didn't want to know.

I moved one of the chairs in the room closer to the bed, which took some doing as I was trying to be quiet and it was a heavy chair, made for people to sit in for long vigils and have some measure of comfort.

It was late and I stifled a groan when I sank into the cushions. Worry for my dad gnawed at me and I tried to keep my eyes open, but exhaustion—emotional and physical—proved too much and before I knew it, I'd nodded off.

A gentle hand on my shoulder woke me. I jerked upright from where I'd been slumped, then immediately winced at the crick in my neck. It would appear I was too old to be sleeping in chairs.

"I'm sorry to wake you, but I thought you'd want to know that your father came out of surgery okay," the nurse said quietly. "He's in the ICU now and your mother is with him. You can visit him in the morning. You can talk to the doctor then about his condition, but for now the surgery went well and he's stable."

I glanced at the generic clock on the wall. It was after three in the morning.

"Yeah, okay, thank you."

She disappeared out of Parker's room as quietly as she'd apparently entered. The lighting had been turned down so only the faint glow from the panel of windows on the door lit the room. I tried to find a new position in my chair that would provide any semblance of comfort. Impossible.

"Sage."

Parker's voice startled me. I thought he'd been asleep.

"Yes?"

"Come here."

Thinking he was in pain and needed something, I jumped to obey. "What is it? Do you hurt?"

"No. I'm fine. But you look like the proverbial princess and the pea, trying to sleep in that chair. Here. There's plenty of room. Climb in."

I eyed the space next to him in the bed that he indicated.

Even small, it looked decidedly more appealing than the chair, and not just because it was next to Parker.

I shucked my shoes and climbed in, being careful of his cords and monitors, though they were all on his other side.

He slid an arm around my shoulders and tucked me into his side. A deep sigh eased from me and I didn't resist the temptation to rest my arm across his abdomen and snuggle closer.

In that quiet moment, it hit me, and tears began leaking from my eyes. I didn't sob, thank God, but neither could I halt the flow dripping down my cheeks and onto Parker's chest.

"What's the matter?" he asked, his fingers brushing my wet cheek.

I had to swallow—twice—before I could speak.

"I nearly lost my dad today," I choked out, my voice barely above a whisper. "Nearly lost you. A few seconds' slower reaction time from you and you'd be—" I couldn't finish.

His arm squeezed me tighter.

"Shh. It's all right. I'm fine and your dad will be fine. I promise. No one died and no one's going to die."

His word choice made me wonder for a moment, then I shrugged it off. I was too relieved that we were all okay to worry about it. He was on painkillers and likely didn't know what the heck he was saying.

I felt him press his lips to the top of my head and my eyes slipped closed. I savored the feel of his skin, the sound of his heart beating strong under my ear, and the rise and fall of his chest as he breathed.

Before I knew it, I was once again out like a light.

* * *

Voices woke me and I cracked my eyes open against much brighter light than I would have wished for. My head was hurting from too little sleep and it took a fraction of a second longer than normal for me to remember where I was and what had happened.

I was in bed with Parker, who'd been shot.

My eyes flew open and I tried to sit up, but Parker's hand tightened on me, keeping me in place.

"The doctor will be in to discharge me this morning, correct?" he asked the nurse who was busy removing his IV, and looking none too happy about it.

"He'll be in to see you, yes," she said. "Though whether or not he'll discharge you is up to him—"

"I'm sure we'll work something out," Parker interrupted, giving her a smile I'd seen work on weaker women, and it didn't fail now. She mustered a small smile in return, her displeasure at his demanding to be discharged softening.

After she left, I twisted to look up a Parker. "Discharge?" I didn't think I had to say any more and also didn't want to because, *hello*—morning breath.

"No way I'm staying in here any longer than I have to," he said, his fingers trailing through my hair. "And your mom stopped in earlier. I told her I'd send you her way once you woke."

Alarm shot through me. "My dad—"

"Is fine," he interrupted. "He's doing well and is stable. Your mom went to the cafeteria for some breakfast. Why don't you go join her while I deal with the doctor?"

Coffee sounded better than air at the moment, so I just nodded. This time he let me slide out of bed and I padded on bare feet to the bathroom, where the image in the mirror made me wince. My makeup was long gone, save for the morning-after raccoon-eye thing I had going on, thanks to too many tears mixing with my non-waterproof mascara.

After washing my face and doing all the necessary things one did in the bathroom, I combed my fingers through my hair the best I could and came back out. Parker looked better than any man should, especially after what he'd gone through. But other than the bandages and him looking more tired than usual, he could've been recovering from a late night out with the guys rather than a bullet wound.

"Do you want anything?" I asked.

"Coffee."

I didn't know if he was supposed to have coffee, but I nodded anyway. I could ask the nurse or something.

My mom was sitting by herself in the cafeteria, a plate of barely touched food in front of her, and sipping from a Styrofoam cup. She was staring off into space, but focused on me as I sat in one of the three empty chairs at the table.

"You look exhausted," she said. "Are you all right?"

"I could say the same to you."

"I wasn't shot at last night." Her hand reached to grasp mine, holding on tightly. "But my baby girl was."

"I'm fine, Mom." I squeezed back. The bones in her hand felt fragile and delicate. "How's Dad?"

Her face clouded. "He did well and the surgeon was very thorough. But it was quite serious and they have him in an induced coma at the moment."

My stomach sank. I knew that had been a possibility, but to hear that I wouldn't be able to talk to my dad for who knew how long was a blow.

We sat in silence, both of us absorbing our new reality. Dad was our rock. He'd always seemed such a force of nature, unstoppable. Now someone had hurt him, nearly killed

him, and I felt the anger rising inside again. The feeling became more familiar each time I felt it, like greeting an old
friend.

"Can we see him?"

She nodded. "But you should eat something. You look
dead on your feet." She winced at her word choice, but our
gazes caught and I cracked a smile.

"Mom being less than tactful? What's the world coming
to?" I teased lightly.

Mom grimaced. "Yes, I know. Obviously, I need more
coffee."

We both rose and headed for the coffee machine. I got a
cup for myself and one for Parker, adding a banana and a
granola bar. He might be hungry, too.

The hospital was bustling with early morning activity and
the changing of shifts as we headed back upstairs to the ICU.
The sight of my dad in the bed had tears leaking from my
eyes again.

"So many machines..." I murmured, looking with dismay at how my dad was surrounded.

My mom and I held tightly to each other's hands, then
moved forward by mutual agreement to flank the bed.

"The doctor should be making his morning rounds soon,"
she said quietly. "He'll be able to tell us more."

About ten minutes later, the doctor showed, going
through what he'd told my mom last night for my benefit. It
helped to talk to him and I was grateful for medical profes-
sionals. To him, Dad was doing really well so the doctor was
positive and optimistic about his recovery. Whereas to us, he
looked awful and gravely ill. Which he still was, but he'd get
better, and that's what the doc wanted us to focus on.

Drawing us out of the room and into the hallway, he continued: "There is plenty of research that says a person in a

coma can be aware of their surroundings and can hear and even understand when people talk to them. So I'd encourage you to talk to him as you would normally. Tell him what you're doing and normal, everyday stuff. Not anything that might cause him concern, you understand."

Mom and I both nodded. I'd heard that before, too.

"It's important that you don't wear yourself out, being here all the time," the doctor said. "It's likely he'll be in this state for a few weeks as he heals, and you getting sick won't help that. So go home, pack a bag, maybe get a hotel close by. Take turns, get other people he interacts with on a daily basis in here to talk to him, too. It's a marathon, not a sprint."

The wheels were already turning in my brain of logistics and things to do and how we could get Dad what he needed, and my mom as well. The last thing I needed was her getting ill on top of everything.

Shultz and Charlie walked up for the tail end of the conversation and caught the doctor's last bit of instructions. Shultz and I glanced at each other in mutual understanding. He'd help me take care of Mom and watch over her so she didn't overdo it.

"I'm going to go check on Parker," I said. "Mom, why don't you go home and pack a bag, like the doctor said. Maybe get a nap before you come back."

She nodded, but hesitated. "I know that's what I should do, but I hate to leave your dad alone."

"I'll stay," Charlie said. "Not a problem at all."

I shot him a grateful look.

"Well...I guess it's all right then." Mom cast one more look through the doorway to Dad, then walked with Shultz down the hallway toward the exit.

To my surprise, Parker was dressed when I got back to him.

"They're actually letting you leave?" I asked, watching dubiously as he put on his shoes.

"I'm fine. Just need something for the infection and some clean bandages." He shot me a quick look before returning his attention to his shoes. "Though they said it might be a little worrisome, my living alone. If I passed out or something, I could hurt myself."

Alarm shot through me. "Then you have to stay! You can't leave now. Just another couple of days—"

But he was already shaking his head. "No," he cut me off. "I need to get back to work and I can't do that from a hospital bed."

"Work can wait," I tried again. He was shrugging on his jacket over his bloodstained shirt. "At least let me call Deirdre. Maybe she can come stay with you." Deirdre was Parker's maid, of sorts. She always was around to tidy the apartment and cook his dinners, which were incredible.

"Didn't I tell you? She and Marco went away for the week. He's taking her to Italy."

I was momentarily diverted. Marco was Parker's butcher and him dating Deirdre was a recent development—and incredibly juicy gossip.

"But they just started dating!" I said. "I can't believe she'd agree to a trip like that so soon."

Parker shrugged, then a tiny wince flashed across his face. "She said something to me about it, that they weren't getting any younger and they got along really well. She seemed to be looking forward to it."

Huh. Well, good for her then, I supposed. I had a slight pang inside that Deirdre—a grandma in her sixties with double-digit grandkids—was more able to take control of her life and go after what she wanted and what made her happy than *I* was.

There didn't seem to be any other answer. I certainly didn't want Parker by himself so soon after getting shot while protecting *me*. "I-I guess I could stay with you," I offered, nearly afraid to utter the words. What if he turned me down? What if he didn't?

Parker finished tying his shoes and stood. "If you wouldn't mind, that would be great," he said. "You don't have to play nursemaid. Just make sure I don't keel over." His lips twisted in a smile that made my pulse triple. I'd forgotten how beautiful he was in the few weeks I'd not seen him on a daily basis. Or else my memory just couldn't do him justice.

"Sure." I headed down the hallway, Parker just a step behind. "I just need to get some things from my apartment and I'll be over."

"I'll come with you."

"No," I argued. "I'll take you home and get you settled, then I'll go."

"I'll be fine and I'm sure it won't take long."

We stood by the door to the hospital, at a standoff, and I frowned as I looked in his eyes. He seemed guileless, his face carefully blank—

And realization dawned. My lips thinned.

"It was a hit, wasn't it," I said.

Parker frowned. "What are you talking about?"

"Last night. It was a hit. Did Charlie come by and talk to you?" My fists were clenched at my sides as I waited for him to answer.

Parker's gaze was steady on mine as he studied me and several beats passed. Finally, he nodded.

"Yeah. It was a hit."

CHAPTER SIX

I thought I'd been prepared for that information, but I wasn't. My veins seemed filled with ice and my knees grew weak.

Someone had deliberately tried to kill my dad.

I turned to head back into the hospital, but Parker caught my elbow, halting me.

"I need to go make sure Charlie has called our security people to guard my dad," I said, trying to tug myself free.

"He's already done that," he said.

I shot Parker a glare. "Why didn't he tell me? Why do *you* know someone tried to kill my dad and *I* don't?"

He hauled me closer to him with laughable ease. "Because your dad was just one of the targets," he said, his voice low and intense. "You were the other."

My mouth went dry and my eyes went wide, staring into the blue depths of Parker's. I didn't want to know that, didn't want to believe it. I'd had too many bad things happen to me lately and it hadn't occurred to me that going to work for my father would be a life-threatening decision.

"Sage, it's okay," he said soothingly. "You're fine and you're going to stay that way."

I wondered why he was talking to me as though reassuring a child, then I noticed my knees had nearly given out entirely and he'd wrapped his other hand around my arm, supporting most of my weight.

"I need a drink." The words put some starch back in my spine and I straightened my clothes and patted my hair (as though anything other than a shower and blow dryer was going to save it at this point).

Parker signaled for a cab and once we'd climbed inside, directed the driver to my apartment.

"So is security covering my place, too?" I asked, staring out the window. That was going to be super fun. Men I didn't know watching my every move. And I wasn't even getting paid for it.

"No. I thought you'd be more comfortable with someone you knew."

I turned to look at him. He raised an eyebrow. My jaw dropped.

"No." *Please tell me I'm wrong.*

"Don't sound so thrilled," Parker said dryly.

"So that whole 'Oh help me, I might keel over' was just a show to get me to stay over so you could keep an eye on me?"

He gave me a shameless smile.

And it would appear I'd been effectively outmaneuvered. "I don't want to insult your masculinity," I said, "but wouldn't the fact that you have a *gunshot wound* somewhat impede your bodyguarding abilities?"

"My gun arm is just fine."

I could tell by his tone that the discussion was over, not

that I was terribly distraught at having to stay with him. I *was* worried about him and wanted to keep an eye on him. If he chose to see it as him protecting me, well then so much the better.

But I knew I needed to keep him at arm's length. I wasn't prepared to trust him again, especially now with Natalie back. I didn't believe that he still harbored feelings for Natalie, but with Ryker acting completely the opposite, I didn't want to muddy the waters between Parker and Ryker now that they'd patched things up.

The cab pulled up to my building and Parker handed him some money as we got out. I felt his eyes on my back as we went inside and was unsurprised when he plucked my keys from my hand and entered my apartment first.

"Stay here," he said, leaving me by the door he closed and locked it behind me.

I pressed my lips together and crossed my arms over my chest. If he wanted to play alpha male bodyguard while still recovering from a gunshot wound, then he could be my guest.

Parker disappeared into the hallway that led to my bedroom, then was back in about five seconds flat.

"Let's go."

There was no compromise in his voice, just a flat order that I instinctively wanted to obey. He pulled open the door and tugged my elbow, but sense prevailed and I planted my feet firmly on the floor.

"I need my clothes!" I'd been wearing the same bloodstained sundress for twenty-four hours and I wanted it *off*.

"I'll come back for them. Let's go." He pulled again and I grabbed on to the door to halt my slow slide into the hallway.

The way he said it, how adamant he was, pricked my spidey sense, and I jerked away.

"Is someone in there?" I asked, suddenly afraid.

"No, no," he said. "Let's just go."

"What is it then? What's in there?" I stepped back out of his reach as he grabbed for me, then spun on my heel and headed for the bedroom. Had someone broken in? Taken anything?

"Sage, wait!"

He reached again for me but I evaded his grasp, stopping short in the doorway to my bedroom, my jaw agape.

I couldn't tell what it was, or what it had been, but there was a mutilated lump of fur in the middle of my blood-soaked bedspread.

For a moment, I couldn't breathe. It felt like someone had punched me in the gut. Then abruptly it changed to my gut deciding to make an appearance. I bolted for the bathroom.

Parker muttered a curse but I was already slamming the door shut and kneeling next to the toilet. Good thing I'd only had coffee today.

Not that it seemed to matter to my stomach, as images of the blood pooling on my quilt ran through my mind. I'd gotten that linen set at Restoration Hardware. And it hadn't been cheap. And now some little furry thing's innards were all over it—

I heaved again and felt my hair pulled back away from my face. My humiliation was complete. My ex-boss was holding back my hair as I puked. I'd averted this particular awkwardness in New York when we'd gone there together and I'd imbibed too much booze one night. So much for my dignity, currently being flushed into the Chicago sewer system.

"I'm fine," I managed, trying to catch my breath.

"Yeah, I can see that." He held a washcloth by my face and I took it, wiping my mouth and lowering the toilet lid. I felt heat creep up my neck into my cheeks and knew I had to be turning bright red. Lovely. I'd match the blood on my bed, I thought somewhat hysterically.

Parker helped me to my feet. I was shaking from shock and from being sick. I didn't throw up delicately, but what with my father would say was "gusto."

"Lean on me," he said, sliding a supporting arm around my waist.

I could've pushed him away, but then I'd just fall on my ass, so I let him help me to the sink. Turning on the tap, I let the water run, splashing some on my face.

I'm okay. I can handle this.

"Of course you can," Parker said, making me realize I'd been muttering aloud.

Looking up in the mirror, I saw him standing behind me. My cheeks were paper white, my hair a bedraggled mess, and my dress wrinkled and stained. Our eyes met and he stared calmly into the reflection, his hands cupping my shoulders.

I'd nearly lost him.

My face crumpled and the nervous breakdown I'd been holding back decided it was done waiting for the appropriate moment. It shoved its way forward and set up camp.

Ugly Crying was right up there next to *Puking* on my list of Things No One Besides My Mother Needs To See. Not that I supposed it mattered when I was bawling so hard I couldn't catch my breath and snot was coming out of my nose.

Parker turned me around and pulled me into his uninjured side, his arms circling me and holding me tight. I'd been strong all night—taking care of my mom, Dad's business, and Parker's job—and it felt so good to lean on someone else. Especially when that someone else was Parker, alive and whole.

"It's all right," he murmured in my ear, his hand sliding

through my hair to cup my scalp. "You're going to be fine. I'm not going to let anything happen to you. I promise."

The promise, spoken in that low raspy whisper of his, calmed me down. I didn't think for that moment, I just felt— his chest rising and falling with his breath, the fuzzy warm feeling inside me at what he'd said, the way his hand was large enough to cover half my head. It all felt so good and so...right.

Which was dangerous territory.

"Thanks," I said, my voice thick from crying. I stepping out of his embrace, turning back to the sink and grabbing a towel to sponge off my face. "We should probably call the cops. Can you take care of that? I want to change and I'll be out."

I could feel his gaze on me in the mirror, but I carefully avoided his eyes. I needed some distance. My feelings for Parker were too near the surface, and I didn't trust his feelings for me.

After a moment, he left the bathroom, softly closing the door behind him.

I let out a breath, my eyes sliding shut as I leaned against the sink, giving up the pretense. But I couldn't stay there, hiding in my bathroom. Parker was out there and there was still the dead furry thing to deal with.

I really hoped it wasn't old Mrs. Judson's cat. She lived a floor above me and that cat looked like it had been around since roughly the Eisenhower administration, just like Mrs. Judson.

When I came out of the bedroom, I'd changed into jeans and a T-shirt. I'd grabbed the first things I'd laid hands on in my closet, deliberately not looking at the bed.

I met Parker in the kitchen. He had my small suitcase sitting by the door.

"I packed some clothes for you and called the cops," he said. "Ryker's on his way."

Shit. "Why Ryker?"

"At this point, who else?"

He had a point, but that didn't mean I had to like it.

A set of uniformed cops led by Ryker in his plainclothes showed up not even ten minutes later.

"What, no Natalie?" I asked when he walked through the door. And yeah, I totally sounded bitchy.

Ryker shot me a look, which softened when he saw my swollen eyes and pale face. He stepped close to me.

"You okay?" he asked in an undertone.

His obvious concern took the bite out of my attitude.

I nodded, adding, "I'm not the one you should be worried about. Parker and my dad were the ones who got hurt. Someone is after my dad."

"And you."

I shot Parker a glare—the last thing I needed was him and Ryker teaming up to go all bodyguard on me.

"We're already running the bullets through ballistics," Ryker said. "Hopefully, we'll pull up a match. In the meantime, someone broke into your apartment. You're not safe here alone."

"She's going to stay at my place," Parker oh-so-helpfully threw in.

Ryker's brows climbed to his hairline, but he didn't protest. He just nodded. "Okay then. I guess I'll know where to find you."

He turned away but I snagged his sleeve. "What are you going to do about Natalie?" I asked.

"I'm going to help her find Jessie," he said.

"Ryker..." I hesitated. "I don't think you should trust her."

His face went blank. "It's really none of your business,"

he said flatly. "I'm here on an investigation about you. You should focus on your own problems and not worry about mine."

Well. That was a big ol' brush off and fuck you wrapped into one. It felt like I'd been slapped and for once in my life, I didn't know what to say. It hurt.

"Natalie already has you being a complete dick," Parker growled. "You're older and supposedly wiser. Try to remember that."

The CSI guy came out of my bedroom and tapped Ryker on the shoulder to show him something. An animal collar with a tag.

It *was* Mrs. Judson's cat—or *had been*—and I insisted on being the one to go tell her, which was even more awful than I'd feared.

She answered the door in her pink housecoat. I'd never seen her wear anything else. She was about a foot shorter than me, and no one had ever been able to ascertain her age, although she looked as if she could be anywhere from about seventy to ninety. I haltingly told her about her cat, trying to find the right words to explain without going into unnecessary gory detail.

"But... why would someone do that?" she asked, blinking her tear-filled eyes behind her thick glasses. "He was *my* cat. Not yours."

"I don't know," I said, which was perfectly true. Guilt crawled up my throat because obviously *I* was to blame. "But I promise, I'll get you another cat."

"I don't want another cat," she said. "I want Morris." The tears she'd been blinking back slid down her cheeks then and she pressed her lips together and closed the door on me without another word. I didn't blame her. If someone had killed my pet, I'd be pretty angry, too.

"Well, that was just the capper on a real shitty twenty-four hours," I said to Parker, who'd insisted on coming with me.

"C'mon," he said, taking my hand. "Let's go."

I didn't resist letting him lead me from the building. The cops were still busy in my apartment and I knew I'd have that lovely yellow police tape over my door yet again. I was becoming That Girl in the building.

"Have you seen that girl lately? You won't believe what's happened to her now." "I heard that girl was in trouble again."

I was the most excitement the building had seen since Prohibition.

Parker held the car door for me and I slid inside. I thought I should offer to drive since he was hurt, but one glance at the hard planes of his face and I knew that wouldn't be happening. I fought to stay awake, but was lulled to sleep before we even hit the freeway.

The slowing of the car woke me and I blinked a few times, trying to figure out where I was. I'd reached that state of exhaustion where I was confused and it took me a good ten seconds to process where I was and get back up to speed.

Clouds had rolled in and a cold rain was falling, making it seem later than it was even though it was only midafternoon. Parker pulled into the parking garage and it didn't take long for him to navigate to his designated spot. He grabbed my small suitcase from the back and took my elbow again as we headed for the elevator.

We didn't speak, but I didn't mind. I was too tired to talk and there was a lot rolling through my head. So much had happened in the past few days. I'd thought I was done with both Parker and Ryker and now they were back in my life, along with Natalie and whatever she was up to. I could vividly picture the way she'd looked at Parker and it made me deeply uneasy. Add to that someone trying to kill both my dad and me... well, a shot of scotch sounded like just the thing.

Parker must've read my mind, because once we'd entered his apartment, that's the first thing he did. After pouring an inch of amber liquid into two cut-crystal glasses, he handed one to me.

"Cheers," he said, clinking his glass against mine, then downed the scotch in one swallow.

I did the same, the liquid burning like fire. I coughed, trying to get air past the inferno inside my throat. Parker's scotch made taking a shot of vodka look like sipping white zinfandel.

"You all right?" He slapped me on the back a few times as I finished choking on air. "Maybe should've gone a little slower on that."

I couldn't yet speak so I shot him a look. *Ya think?* He chuckled, the corner of his mouth twisting upward.

"So I have this theory," he said, grabbing the bottle and refilling his own glass.

"About what?" I sounded three-pack-a-day and cleared my throat again, hoping the liquor hadn't done permanent damage. Glancing behind me, I sank onto Parker's soft leather couch with a sigh. My whole body thanked me.

"About us."

Shit. Not a topic of conversation I wanted to address right now.

"Do you want to hear it?" he asked.

Not really. "Do I have a choice?"

"I think that you wanted me... so long as I didn't want you."

I stared at him, my mouth hanging open. He watched me, calmly sipping his scotch. Finally, I found my voice.

"You've got to be kidding me," I growled. "Do you have any idea how insulting what you just said to me was?"

"I'm not trying to insult you," he said. "I think you're afraid. Wanting something unobtainable is safe, isn't it? Then you don't really have to face the choices and changes and commitments that come with loving someone and them loving you back."

"How about it's the fact that you never looked at me twice until Ryker came along? You tell me you love me, make love to me, all in the heat of thinking Ryker wanted me, too. Then you dumped me, then decided you'd made a mistake, then I thought you were dead. And now Natalie's back." I shook my head. "There's nothing about our relationship that I trust right now."

Parker's face was a blank mask, but his eyes...his eyes burned.

"Do you trust that I'll keep you safe?"

Keeping me alive was a point of honor for Parker and I knew him well enough to know he'd do everything in his power to make sure nothing happened to me. I gave him a slow nod.

"I do, yes."

"What can I do to convince you what we have is real, Sage? That I'm not being fickle and like a child with a toy, only wanting you when Ryker did. I would've died for you last night."

Ouch. The man had a point. He'd taken a bullet for me, after all. Hard to argue with that.

"I know, but I can't snap my fingers and make my doubts disappear, Parker. They're there, and I can't tell you a magic formula to make them go away." I looked away, unable to stare into the blue of his eyes any longer. My own were starting to water. I hadn't been prepared for this kind of conversation, mentally or emotionally.

"Fair enough," he said, and I heard him set down his glass. "Deirdre left things for me to heat up. I'll stick something in the oven to heat while we get some rest. I'm tired and you have to be about dead on your feet."

He reached for my hand and I let him take it. I was such a wuss. I couldn't resist touching him, given any opportunity. His hand was big, strong, and capable, and it swallowed mine.

Parker led me to his bedroom and I kicked off my shoes before crawling under the covers. I heard him leave the room and sighed, trying to figure out if I was disappointed or glad that he'd gone to the couch. But before I could decide, he was back, shedding his shirt and climbing into bed next to me. My eyes shot open.

"I thought you went to sleep on the couch?" I asked, eyeing the rippling muscles of his chest and arms. Hugh Jackman as Wolverine came to mind.

"I told you, I was putting dinner in the oven." He turned on his stomach and stretched his arms underneath the pillow, giving me an absolutely drool-worthy sight of his back. Smooth skin stretched over perfectly sculpted muscle and tendon. His shoulders bulged and my fingers itched to touch.

He was facing me but his eyes were closed, which gave me the luxury of memorizing his face. Perfect cheekbones, straight nose, lush lashes that I would have to use three coats of mascara to duplicate, strong jaw, and his thick chestnut hair, that looked good even tousled as it was. Parker was gorgeous and though I'd seen him nearly every day for almost two years, he could still take my breath away.

And I was in his bed.

Albeit under less than ideal circumstances, but the last time I'd been here, I'd chosen to leave and go to Ryker. I wouldn't be making that same decision again. Ryker was a great guy, but there was no future in the cards for us, not least of which was because my heart was owned by the man doing a really good impression of unconsciousness right next to me.

"Parker?" I whispered.

Nothing.

Wow. I wished I could fall asleep that fast. It took me forever to fall asleep, especially in a bed other than my own...

And that was the last coherent thought I had.

* * *

The gentle clatter of silverware and the smell of something spicy and Italian woke me. I stretched, prying open my eyes when I heard someone step into the room.

Parker, carrying a tray laden with the delicious-smelling food, set it on the end of the bed before sitting next to me.

"I know breakfast is traditional, but I didn't think you'd mind," he quipped, taking a drink from one of two glasses of red wine.

I was ravenous, my eyes glued to the steaming plate of spaghetti and meatballs.

"Where's yours?"

He snorted a laugh and I watched closely. Parker with wine coming out of his nose would be a sight worth remembering.

"I thought we'd share, but there's more if you're still hungry."

Sharing seemed a little too intimate for the discussion

we'd had earlier, but I was too hungry to care. I grabbed one of the two forks and dug in. One bite and I was in heaven. I moaned.

"I love Deirdre," I said around a mouthful of the best meatball I'd ever tasted. "You should give her a raise."

"I already pay her an obscene amount of money as it is," Parker said, taking the other fork and spearing a bite for himself.

"Worth every penny," I said, scooping more noodles onto my fork.

We didn't talk for a few minutes, too busy eating, then we both slowed down at the same time. Pasta was filling and it was only as we were both twining the strands around our forks that it struck me, and I couldn't stop a laugh.

"What?" Parker asked, looking quizzically at me.

"This," I said, motioning to us and the plate. "Isn't this like a live version of *Lady and the Tramp*?"

"Are you calling me a tramp?" He speared a meatball and took a bite. There was a smudge of sauce on his chin that I wanted to lick off, and not just because the sauce was so good I'd put it in a slurpy cup if I could.

"Should I?" I teased. "How many women have known Parker Anderson? And I mean 'known' as in the Biblical sense."

"I had no idea you were so religious."

I took a drink of wine but didn't look away, wondering if he'd answer my question. Parker had always been a bit of a playboy. How many had he been with? I didn't know why I cared...it was one of those questions you always asked, I guessed, out of morbid curiosity.

"More than some. Less than a lot."

I stared. "Seriously? *That's* your answer?" Though I had to admit, it was rather ingenious.

Parker took another bite, still looking innocently at me. "You're the one who asked," he said.

True.

I was full and the wine had relaxed me. I wanted a shower, though a bath would be preferable. Parker either read my mind or saw my glance of longing toward his bathroom. I knew he had a huge soaking tub in there.

"You can go take a bath, if you want," he said. "I promise I won't look."

I gave him the side eye, knowing he was teasing me. As if he hadn't already seen the goods. Not only seen the goods, but touched and licked and kissed—

I cut that off mid-thought. Not going there. My resistance was at an all-time low as it was. But he didn't have to tell me twice. I was in that bathroom and running the water before he could untangle from the bedsheets to help me.

"Stay there," I called. "I can do this. Have you taken your medication yet? You're probably due."

"I'm rolling my eyes at you," he called back.

"I don't care, just so long as you take the meds." The last thing I needed was him getting an infection.

The tub took a while to fill—it was a big tub—but was well worth the wait. I eased back against the side, letting the steaming water wash over me, and let out a long sigh. Yes, this was what I needed. Well, an orgasm and *then* a bath would've been preferable, but beggars couldn't be choosers.

"Another glass of wine?"

My eyes popped open to see Parker sitting on the edge of the tub, holding two glasses. I sat up with a jerk, grabbing the washcloth to hold over my breasts. Which, by the way, wasn't nearly adequate. It was like trying to cover two cantaloupes with a tissue. Not that I was *that* well-endowed, but damn Parker's bath towels seemed way smaller than normal.

"I thought you weren't going to look?" I asked, indignant. And here I'd been relaxing so nicely...

"I'm not looking. I'm bringing you wine," he said. "Totally different."

The look in his eyes told me something else entirely and I had to make myself look away. Parker looking at me with want in his gaze was enough to crumble every defense I had. And sleeping with him would solve nothing, just make things a lot more complicated.

Or so I kept telling myself.

"Thanks for the wine," I said, taking a glass. "You can let yourself out."

"We should talk," he said, making no move toward the door. *Of course he wouldn't leave when I told him to.*

"We've already talked," I said. "I have nothing else to really say about it. Not right now. I just can't do that at the moment." My eyes pleaded with him. I'd had enough emotional turmoil and anxiety over the past few days to last me a while. I needed a break.

"I meant we need to talk about our plan regarding the hit on you and your dad. But it can wait until morning, if you want." He stood to leave.

"No, wait."

He sat back down.

I pulled my knees to my chest, which served to conceal most of my more intimate parts from view. "What do you think we should do?"

"I think we need to call Ryker in the morning, see if they got anything from ballistics or any prints. I'd imagine they pulled security footage from cameras in the building, too."

I nodded. All of that sounded reasonable. Very *Castle* or *Rizzoli and Isles*.

"Then we need to figure out who would have had a motive to kill your dad. And you."

"I'd think after so many years in business, my dad would have a lot of enemies," I said. "But I don't know why anyone would want to kill me. I've just started working for him." I thought for a moment. "Are you sure the hit was for both of us? Maybe I was just a twofer." If you can get more than one, why not? But that didn't necessarily mean I was the target.

Parker hesitated. "I know you were a target... because they sent a message."

I stared at him, waiting. This was the first I'd heard about any kind of message.

He must've read the look on my face, because he spoke again. "They shot Gary. The security guard. Left a note pinned to his chest. Ryker's running it through forensics."

The water was suddenly cold against my skin and goose bumps erupted down my arms. I stared at Parker, wishing I'd misheard but knowing I hadn't. I shook my head and my lips moved, but no sound came out.

Parker cursed, taking the wineglass from my hand. "I'm sorry," he said. "I didn't know how else to tell you."

"I've known Gary for years," I managed. "He used to give me candy when I came to the office with my dad." Going into his sixties, he'd been older but hard as nails. A former Marine drill sergeant, Gary hadn't taken shit from anybody. But he'd had a soft spot for the boss's daughter.

"How?"

Parker flinched, but answered. "Shot to death. They surprised him on his rounds. He drew his weapon and got off a shot, but that's all."

I nodded, swallowing the lump in my throat. "And what did the note say?"

"It said 'The daughter will pay for the sins of the father.'"

Well. They certainly hadn't minced words. "Sounds dramatic," I said, anger forming in my belly. Gary had been a good man.

"So we have to wait to hear from Ryker?"

"No. We could start by going through your dad's files, see if we can make a list. Then we can hopefully start narrowing that list."

My mind was already working. "Okay. A solid plan." I was really glad Parker was including me on this. I'd had a niggle of doubt that he'd leave me locked inside his apartment.

I thought the conversation was over, and yet he still sat on the edge of the tub. I raised an eyebrow.

"The water's getting cold." *Hint, hint.*

But instead of leaving, Parker just grabbed one of his huge, fluffy towels and held it out for me. A flash of memory hit me—Parker doing the exact same thing in New York. It made me sad, which in turn made me angry. I wasn't about to fall for Parker again, not when his idea of "commitment" lasted scarcely twelve hours.

I abruptly stood, water sloshing in the tub, and jerked the towel out of Parker's hands. "I can dry myself, thank you very much."

His lips pressed together but he didn't say anything. Our gazes locked in a staring contest. Then he inclined his head slightly, as if ceding me a victory, and turned and left.

I let out a breath. Though I was glad he'd gone, I could taste the sharp bite of disappointment.

CHAPTER SEVEN

Monday morning dawned bright and early, and I knew that because I was up well before the sun peeked over the horizon.

Parker had slept on the couch in the spare bedroom he used as an office last night, and I was trying hard not to feel guilty about that. He was injured and had let me have his bed. I'd put up a fight, of course, but it had been like talking to a brick wall.

I'd tossed and turned for a while, my mind and logic warring with my heart and emotions. It hadn't helped at all that the sheets and pillows smelled of Parker. My dreams consisted of him and me in various forms of sexual congress, making me awaken horny and frustrated.

Not a good combination.

Coffee cured all ills. Well, most of them. And what coffee couldn't cure, alcohol could, but pouring a shot of bourbon in my coffee seemed like a bad idea, so I went with a heavy pour of half-and-half instead. I'd dug jeans and a long-sleeved cotton shirt out of my suitcase and pulled my hair back into a ponytail. If we were going to be digging through thirty years of my dad's files today, no sense in not being comfortable.

I was watching the first rays of sunrise kiss downtown when Parker emerged from his office. He glanced at me.

"Good morning. Did you sleep well?" he asked as he poured himself a cup of coffee. His voice was as polite and even as if he were greeting me at the office rather than in his apartment. He wasn't wearing a shirt and I scrutinized the gauze over his wound. No bloodstains, so that was good. He didn't seem to be favoring it, either.

"Yes, thanks," I said. "Though I still feel guilty for taking your bed."

He walked toward me, lifting the mug to his lips as he did so. "Well, don't." He took a sip.

I rolled my eyes. "Oh good, well that was easy. So glad you said that."

His lips twitched in an almost-smile. "I'm going to shower and shave. Won't be long. Then we can head out."

I nodded, my mouth suddenly dry at the image of Parker in the shower. He might've read my mind, too, because a gleam came into his eyes and the almost-smile turned into a wicked grin. In another moment, he'd disappeared into his bedroom.

I needed more coffee for this.

An hour later, we were pulling up to my dad's business in Parker's car. He'd gone through a Starbucks drive-thru and the warm smell of a bacon and egg sandwich in the paper bag on my lap was making my mouth water.

Three security guys manned the lobby, all of them looking like they chewed nails for breakfast. Their presence was a reminder of Gary's death and the danger that not only I was in but everyone who worked for my dad and me. The faster we found out who was doing this, the sooner we could neutralize it.

We were a tad early, so only a few other people were in. Carrie smiled a greeting as she passed by us, coffee mug in hand and talking on her Bluetooth headset. I led Parker to my office.

"This is nice," he said as I headed for the windows to open the wood blinds. "No, don't."

The sharp command made me stop in my tracks. "What's wrong?"

"No need to give anyone a target through the window," he said. "Leave them closed."

Oh yeah. Someone was trying to kill me. Wouldn't want to forget *that*.

I dug my half of breakfast out and started chomping as Parker took a tour of my office. It felt odd, him being in *my* office as opposed to the other way around.

"Do you like your new job here?" he asked, taking a sip of coffee.

"Yeah, I do," I said. "It's different when it's something you have a stake in. It's my father's company and I don't want to mess things up."

"You won't."

The certainty in his voice gave me pause. It was a nice vote of confidence that I hadn't expected. He looked at me, his gaze steady, until I had to look away.

"That's nice of you to say," I said for lack of anything better.

"I'm not being nice. I'm being honest. You're smart and a quick learner. You handle people well and are a good problem-solver. I think you'll do very well here." He paused. "Though Rosemary doesn't come close to replacing you."

A tingle of warmth in my belly at that. It was good to be missed. And hearing Parker tell me those things made me happier than it should have. I wondered if he really thought all that or was just trying to build my confidence.

"C'mon," I said, getting to my feet before I did or said something stupid. "The file archive is in the basement."

We took our breakfast and coffee to the elevator and rode it underground. The basement was your typical concrete room. It was large, encompassing the entire footprint of the building, and lit by long, rectangular fluorescent lights. I flipped the switch and they flickered to life with a telltale buzzing noise.

Four aisles of metal storage shelving greeted us, all of it loaded with file boxes.

"Thirty years of paperwork, at your service," I said.

"Good thing we go through paperwork well," Parker replied. Which was true. He and I had a pretty good system when combing through customer files. I hoped it would serve us well today, because hours of reading files until I went blind was not something I was looking forward to.

We dug in.

It was chilly but humid in the basement, an awful combination. A few hours later, I was sticky with sweat and sported a nice layer of dust from head to foot. Parker, of course, looked even more gorgeous with a faint sheen on his skin. I could smell him slightly, his sweat-tinged cologne, and it just made me cranky.

We were quiet as we worked, digging through boxes and reading files. Most were run-of-the-mill orders and invoices. Some were acquisitions of other businesses and for the most part, Parker went through those. A ton of it was legalese and while I had a working knowledge of the terminology, he could get through it quicker and much more thoroughly than I could.

I'd been thinking about Parker's parents and I wondered if they'd called him. Maybe his mother had left a message or told him they would come see him. Parker and I had never discussed his parents, so it was with more than a little hesitation that I asked with deliberate casualness, "So, have you talked to your mom or dad?"

Parker glanced at me, then back down at the file he held. "No."

His tone didn't invite further discussion, so I shut my mouth and went back to work. It was his business, not mine. Though I tried not to let it bother me, it hurt that he wouldn't open up to me about what I knew was a very touchy subject.

"I didn't expect them to call," he said out of the blue a few minutes later.

I paused in flipping pages. "Why not?"

Parker looked as though he were considering his words carefully. "We're not close, my parents and me. I had a younger brother who passed away when he was eight. Leukemia. My parents never got over it, especially my mother. He was everything to her and I think she wished it had been me instead."

Holy shit.

I stared at him as he set aside a file and rummaged in the box for another one. He'd said all of that as though it wasn't a big deal, when it was. It really, really was.

"Why do you say that?" I asked.

"Because she told me so. All the time. 'You should be grateful for the opportunities you're given. Paul never got those.' Or 'Paul would never have thought I was overbearing or had too high expectations.'"

Parker had lost a brother and then paid the price for his own existence by constantly being reminded he wasn't wanted. I couldn't imagine. No wonder he'd latched on to Ryker.

"I'm really sorry," I said. What else was there to say?

He shrugged, flipping through pages rather than looking at me. "It's fine. It is what it is. Everyone has something, right?"

I reached over and set my hand on his arm. He paused and our eyes met.

"You didn't deserve that. Don't deserve that," I said. "It's not fine and I'm really, really sorry. Thank you for telling me."

He didn't move, just let me look into his eyes, and I saw the pain and hurt there. Parker had lost his brother and to an extent, his parents, too.

"I trust you," he said simply.

My heart squeezed and I had to glance away at the sudden tears in my eyes. His hand covered mine on his arm, and for a moment, our fingers touched and held together for a long breath. Then I cleared my throat and sat back and the moment was over. But it had shifted something between us.

Parker had always kept a careful distance when I worked for him, never letting the professional become personal. Then we'd tried to build something in the hurried morass of people trying to kill us and that had fallen into ruin. It made more sense to have this new beginning, spinning strands of trust and intimacy to bind us together with a stronger foundation. I couldn't help the tentative hope I felt.

Carrie sent down a pizza for lunch, along with a couple of pops. We munched on the food, occasionally pointing something out from a file. There was a small stack of Maybes—people who might have a grudge against my dad. Shots in the dark, but all we could do at the moment.

I was up on a stepladder, trying to haul down a box from the top shelf when I felt his hands on my waist.

"Here, let me get that," he said. "I don't want you to fall."

His hands felt as though they burned through the thin cotton T-shirt I wore, and I sucked in a breath.

"I'm fine," I managed, my voice sounding strangled. My thoughts wandered to things like *Could we hear someone coming in time to pull our clothes back on?* And *Exactly how hard is the floor? Like walk-away-with-a-couple-bruises hard or break-my-back hard?*

"Come get down from there," he persisted. "I'll get it." Not leaving me a choice, he circled my waist with his good arm and picked me up. I squealed in surprise, grabbing on to his arm, then my feet touched the ground. He held on to me for a moment, my back touching his chest, and I was glad he couldn't see my face. A shaft of pain went through me.

It'd be so easy to give in, tell Parker I loved him and we could be together. But what if he changed his mind again? What if Natalie decided she wanted him? It was all well and good for him to give lip service to not loving her anymore, but I still couldn't shake the feeling that Parker was the kind of guy who loved the chase and the unobtainable. His entire career was built on fighting impossible odds. Once he'd won...the challenge was gone. As was his interest.

"Thanks," I said, stepping forward out of his hold. His arms dropped to his sides. I didn't look at him—I was afraid my emotions would be too easily read in my eyes.

It was late afternoon and I had too many paper cuts to count when I found something.

"This is weird," I said, flipping through yet another box. "It looks like this is all one file." Most of the boxes had been collections of customers and transactions, but only one name was listed on the file here: SLS Enterprises. "Who's SLS Enterprises?"

"That's Leo Shea's company," Parker replied, setting down the file he was reading and scooting the stool he sat on over next to mine. He read over my shoulder. "The date is twelve years ago."

I could smell him again, but it wasn't like I could tell him to move over. That would just be rude...and telling. I flipped through the pages.

"Handwritten notes," I said, eyeing the scrawl. "I think that's my dad's handwriting." There were a lot of pages and I handed a few to Parker to decrypt. My dad had always had crappy writing. He should've been a doctor.

"Leo's business was a high-profile startup that began eating other businesses like candy," I mused as I read. "Dad listed a bunch of them here, along with the families who ran each." It was a long list.

"Your dad's notes list times and locations," Parker said. "And if I'm not mistaken—victims."

"Victims?"

"And a catalogue of their injuries and deaths."

I swallowed. "So Dad wasn't kidding when he said Shea was bad news."

"No," Parker said, continuing to flip through pages. "And it looks like he targeted your dad, too."

Now it was my turn to lean over to see. My breast brushed his arm and I gritted my teeth, though Parker showed no sign of having noticed. Figured.

"They arranged a meeting," he continued, reading. "But Shea wouldn't agree to any terms. Looks like he wanted a monopoly and your dad was the lone one left standing in his way."

"That's probably why this is all handwritten," I said.

"Dad never learned to type and I doubt he would have dictated it to someone."

Parker shuffled through more pages, then dug in the box. I did as well, but didn't see more handwritten notes. "What happened?" I asked.

"Does your dad keep anything locked up?"

I shrugged. "I have no idea. I just work here, remember?"

Parker gave me a half-smile at the joke. "Let's go see."

Parker carried the box with him as we rode the elevator up. I stopped by Carrie's desk first.

"Carrie, are there any locked files that you know about?" If there was something no one was supposed to know, chances were Carrie knew it.

She glanced around, then leaned over her desk closer to us. "Your dad keeps a locked cabinet in his closet, but I don't know what's in it."

"Do you have a key?"

Carrie just gave me a look.

"It was worth asking," I muttered. I should've known it wouldn't be that easy.

"Charlie might have a key," she said. "He just came in a short while ago."

Good. I wanted to ask him how Dad was doing anyway. I headed for his office, Parker in tow. We dropped the file box off in my office, then rapped on Charlie's door.

"Come in."

Charlie looked tired, but smiled when he saw me, giving a nod to Parker as well. "Your dad is the same," he said, reading my question before I'd asked it. "Stable and doing well. Your mom was there when I left."

"She okay?" I'd need to go relieve her once I got off work.

He nodded. "She's holding up really well."

"Charlie, Parker and I found some files in the basement

about Leo Shea's business about a decade ago, how he was encroaching on Dad, but the files stop after their meeting. Do you know what happened?"

If possible, Charlie looked even older at the question. "It was a rough time," he said. "Your dad ended up handling it. I know he kept notes on all his business dealings so I'm sure he documented the events."

"There's nothing more in the box, but Carrie said he keeps a locked cabinet in his office. Do you have a key?"

Charlie nodded, digging in his desk drawer. "Your dad gave me a set in case something happened to him."

We all grew silent for a moment, since something *had* happened to my dad. It hurt inside my chest to think about it, so I shoved the thought away and cleared my throat, taking the set of keys Charlie handed to me.

I unlocked my dad's office and stepped inside. It smelled so much like him and the cigars he sometimes favored that I stumbled to a halt three feet in.

"You okay?" Parker asked, his hand settling low on my back.

I forced a thin smile. "Yeah. I'm fine. Now let's find out who's behind this." My gut said somehow Shea was involved, even though technically that was impossible since he was dead. I assumed his body had been dropped in Lake Michigan with a set of concrete shoes, but I could be wrong.

The file cabinet wasn't a large one and it didn't take long after I'd unlocked it for Parker and me to find the right files. We began reading.

"He had an informant," I said slowly, my eyes wide. "Somehow, he paid off someone in Leo's organization."

"Your dad isn't a fool," Parker said. "And apparently not someone to be fucked with."

He said it with respect, not disgust, and I agreed.

I flipped through the papers but couldn't find a name. "Can you find a name anywhere?"

Parker shook his head. "No. He just calls him *The Informant*. No details."

"Well, he helped my dad, that's for sure," I said, reading all the notes on what basically boiled down to corporate espionage.

"And was handsomely compensated," Parker added, pointing out the payments made. I gave a low whistle.

"Wow."

"Exactly."

"But it paid off," I said. "Looks like my dad bit back at Shea, nearly sending his business into bankruptcy." Which had been mighty good of him. He didn't have to do that. It looked like he could've crushed Shea and been rid of him for good. Considering what Shea had done to me years later, I would've been okay with that.

"Yeah, but the *way* he did it—" Parker began, flipping through more pages.

Carrie popped her head in. "You have a visitor," she interrupted.

"Who?" Had Ryker come by with information?

"Not you," she said. "Him." She jerked her chin toward Parker, who looked as surprised as I felt.

"Who knows you're here?" I asked him.

"No one." His expression was hard. He'd brought his weapon with him and I saw him reach from where he'd set it on the desk, sliding it into the small of his back.

Okay then.

He followed Carrie and I followed him to the front. When I saw who was waiting, I didn't know who was more surprised—him or me—though I certainly knew who was more pissed.

"What the hell are you doing here?" I asked Natalie, marching toward her, my hands in fists at my sides. "I don't recall issuing you an invitation."

She had the gall to look hurt. "I didn't realize you'd mind so much," she said. "Honestly. I needed to speak to Parker and I thought you'd know where he was. I'm really sorry to bother you." She gave a little shrug, managing to look adorably helpless in that feminine kind of way that men gobbled up like candy.

I ground my teeth together, realizing she'd effectively outmaneuvered me. If I kept at it, I'd just look like a total bitch in front of Parker. But I gave her a hard stare that said she'd entered my territory and that I didn't like it.

"What's going on?" Parker asked.

"I received this today and I don't know what to do." She handed him a note.

"Ten thousand dollars. Gavin's Pub. 10 p.m. tomorrow," he read. He glanced up. "Where did you get this?"

"It was left on the windshield of my car."

"Did you take it to Ryker?"

Natalie hesitated, and I knew why.

"Of course she didn't," I said. "Ryker doesn't have ten thousand dollars." But Parker did.

Parker shot me a look. "I'll handle this."

Oh really?

"Is there somewhere a little more private where we can talk?" Natalie asked, glancing around the lobby.

I gritted my teeth. "My office." I spun on my heel and didn't bother to make sure they followed me.

Sitting in my chair with a heavy desk between Natalie and me seemed like a good idea. I sat in the cool leather chair and watched Parker face off with Natalie.

"We need to call Ryker about this," he said. "A ransom

note is irrefutable, and kidnap cases are automatically under the FBI's purview."

"No, don't!" Natalie said. "We can't get the FBI involved. They'll know and they'll kill Jessie."

"We don't even know who has her or why," I interjected. "If it's just money they're after, why'd they pick your sister?"

Natalie's blue eyes focused on me like a laser. "If I knew that, I wouldn't need to be here," she retorted.

"I don't think we should try to handle this on our own," Parker said.

We?

"I can't take a chance that they'll hurt her," Natalie pleaded. "If they'll give her back for ten thousand dollars, then why can't we just do that?"

"Because it's unlikely they'll stop at just ten thousand," I said, ignoring her body language that said hearing my voice was akin to setting fire to her hair.

"You don't know that."

"She's right, Natalie," Parker said.

There was a rap on the open door and I glanced over to see Ryker had decided to stop by, too. Fabulous.

"Now it's a party," I muttered under my breath. This day was getting worse by the moment.

"I knew I'd find Sage here," Ryker said. "Didn't realize Scooby and the gang were all getting together without me." He fixed Parker and Natalie with a look that would've frozen a criminal at thirty paces.

"Come in," I said, which was completely unnecessary, as he was already plopping down in one of the leather chairs in front of my desk. My fingernails threatened to make permanent crescent-shaped dents in the arms of my chair. "What can I do for you?"

"We went over the security footage for the attack on your security guard last night," he said. "They were in black, but wore a mask. We couldn't get a clear shot and the prints we lifted all belong to employees."

I wasn't surprised. Had I thought it would be so easy as the murderer standing in front of the camera with a sign proclaiming his name, phone number, and current address?

"I just don't understand why," I said. "What were they after?"

"They came up here and tried to break in to your dad's office," he replied, "but tripped the security alarm."

"That doesn't sound like they've had a lot of experience," I said. Yes, we had decent security, but it wasn't state of the art. "And what would they have wanted in here?"

"The files we just unlocked, I'd guess," Parker interjected.

"Why now?"

But no one answered. After a moment, Natalie said, "I hate to interrupt, but I need help with this. Jessie needs me."

"What's going on?" Ryker asked.

Parker showed him the note. "Natalie wants to pay the money."

Ryker's gaze landed on her. "You can't do that. It never ends well."

Tears started leaking from Natalie's eyes. "What am I supposed to do? She's my sister, Dean..."

"Let's get the paper to the lab, see if they can pull any prints. Then we'll decide what to do. We have until tomorrow." He looked at Parker. "Are you fronting this?"

Parker looked grim, but he nodded, and my stomach sank. He was just going to hand over ten thousand dollars, and I still had my doubts as to anything Natalie said. Ryker acted as though he believed everything she said and Parker... well, I couldn't really tell with Parker. Though if he was going to sign over ten grand, he must be feeling there was some truth to this.

Ryker stood. "I'll let you know if we find anything else," he said to me. "Ballistics haven't come back yet on the casings from here or from you and your dad."

Nice to know I was such a priority. But I kept my mouth shut and nodded. "Okay. Thanks."

"Natalie," Ryker said, "we have some photos for you to look at. You said Jessie had a nasty ex, right, but you didn't have a picture of him?"

Natalie nodded. "She broke up with him a while ago," she said.

"If you can recognize him from the photos, maybe we can track him down." He switched his gaze to Parker. "You coming?"

Parker shook his head. "I'm watching out for Sage. I'm not leaving her alone." The emphasis was on *I'm* and the tone of his voice held disapproval. Ryker's gaze swiveled to mine.

"Hey, don't look at me," I said. "I didn't ask Parker to play bodyguard." If he wanted to go support Natalie, I wasn't about to stand in the way, despite the green monster digging its claws into my gut.

A muscle ticked in Parker's jaw.

"We have uniforms watching the place," Ryker said to Parker. "And you're acting like I don't want to keep Sage safe, too. I'm the one trying to chase down every lead we have on the shooting."

"I didn't say you didn't want her safe."

"You implied it."

Their eyes were shooting daggers at each other, but my gaze was drawn to Natalie. Rather than watching the men argue, she was looking at me.

Well, this was interesting.

"Please," Natalie added, her blue eyes turned plaintively up to Parker.

Aaaand my fingernails *just* broke through the leather padding on the arms of my chair.

I was the one with a mutilated cat on my bed, a father in a coma, and a dead security guard. But hey, no worries!

I gritted my teeth. "Go on and go. There are three security guys downstairs. I'll be fine." I wasn't about to try and compete with Natalie and beg Parker to stay. No way.

"Don't leave without me," Parker said, and his tone made me want to stick my tongue out at him like a teenager. At least he hadn't pointed his finger at me.

I settled for, "I'll do my best," which was just this side of snotty bitch, but not by much. If I wasn't trying so hard to hide my disappointment, I'd have been embarrassed.

They left, with Parker taking one last long glance at me. I didn't so much as twitch an eye. They both wanted to go running to Natalie's beck and call? They could be my guest.

Bitterness was a sour taste in my mouth as I headed back to my dad's office. It was after six now and people had cleared out for the most part, but I met Charlie on the way.

"I was looking for you," he said, following me into the room. The blinds were open in here so I moved to the window to start closing them. "I think I know who might be behind this."

"Who?"

"Steven Shea."

I paused, turning to look at Charlie. "Shea? As in a relation to Leo?"

He nodded. "His son. He left Chicago years ago, wanted to become some kind of real estate developer out in California. Apparently when he heard about his father's disappearance, he decided to come back."

His father's disappearance was a nice way of saying my father had Leo killed, then dropped into the black hole of Lake Michigan, mostly because I'd told him to after the man had kidnapped me and tortured Ryker and Parker.

I squirmed uncomfortably. Yes, I'd been upset at the time and Leo had been seconds away from killing me in cold blood, but that didn't mean my conscience was 100 percent clear.

"So Steve decided me and Dad are to blame for his father's disappearance? How could he possibly know that? Is he just guessing? He still has an ax to grind about what happened a decade ago?" I reached for another blind, glancing out the window.

"That's what I was wondering, too," he said. "So I started digging. Who all was there that night?"

But I wasn't listening. Instead, I was watching Ryker, Parker, and Natalie in the parking lot. I was only three stories up so I could see them really well. They stood there talking, and it was easy to see an echo of the photograph Ryker kept hidden in his bottom drawer. Ryker swung his leg over his motorcycle, while Natalie and Parker got in his BMW. Both vehicles left the lot. It felt as though I'd swallowed a lead ball, which was now sitting in the pit of my stomach.

"Sage? Did you hear me?"

I yanked the blinds closed. "Yeah, sorry. Who was there? I don't know. All the men were security guys Dad hired. I'd never seen them before."

"And that was all?"

I forcibly shoved images of Parker and Natalie in his car together out of my mind. Dwelling on them wasn't going to help.

"Um, yeah...I mean, no." I shook my head, frustrated at my lack of ability to concentrate. "There were two other people there, a woman named Branna and this senator guy she worked for." I searched my brain, finally coming up with a name. "Kirk? I think? Parker would know how to reach him. Do you think he would've told Shea what happened?"

I'd find that hard to believe. There hadn't seemed to be any love lost between Leo and the senator, especially if he'd sent in Branna to spy on him.

"I don't know, but I'll find out," Charlie promised. "In the meantime, you need to figure out what to do."

"What do you mean? We've been in touch with our vendors, I've had Carrie reschedule meetings on Dad's calendar, I cancelled his trip to L.A. next week for the conference he was going to attend. What else is there?"

"No. I mean about Steven Shea. If I'm right, he's declared war on you and your dad in a very public and very personal way. This business is full of wolves, Sage. Once there's blood on the ground, they all come circling. And right now that blood is yours."

CHAPTER EIGHT

Charlie's warning was still going through my head when I left two hours later. Parker hadn't returned and he hadn't called. And I was doing a great job not letting that bother me.

Right.

I felt a burning need to find out what was going on with Natalie—why she was *really* here, because I still had my doubts about the missing sister and the dead husband. Plans and ideas to figure out what she was up to churned inside my head as I grabbed a cab and told the driver to take me to the hospital where my dad was staying.

Yes, Parker had told me not to leave. But what did he expect me to do? Wait around all night? I had one of the security guys walk me to the cab and then I was on my way.

My stomach growled—it had been a while since the pizza at lunch—and I tossed around the idea of asking the driver to swing through a drive-thru and whether that would be tacky or not. But before I could decide we'd passed everything and were pulling up to the hospital.

Hospital food it was.

I found Mom where I expected, sitting at Dad's bedside, reading aloud to him from a thick tome. She glanced up when I nodded to the two security guys guarding the door and walked in.

"What are you reading?" I asked, settling into the chair next to hers.

"Tom Clancy."

I gave her a strange look. "Really? That's rather... ambitious."

She shrugged and a tired smile creased her face. "He loves them. I thought it might help."

Taking the book from her, I said, "I'm here now. Go on to the hotel and get some rest. You can come back in the morning."

"You can't stay here all night," she protested. "You need sleep, too."

"I had a long nap today," I lied. "I'll be fine. I promise. Go on." She needed a break, I could tell. There were circles under her eyes and lines of fatigue and worry by her mouth.

"Are you sure?"

"Absolutely. Go on and get some rest, Mom." I got her purse and ushered her to the door. "You're staying close?"

She nodded. "The Marriott across the street."

"Good. Don't worry, okay?" I gave her a hug, squeezing tight. She held on for a long moment before we stepped back.

"All right, sweetheart. I'll see you in the morning."

She walked down the hallway, her back straight and her shoulders back. She was tired and worried, but she always kept her composure and dignity. I wished I could say the same, but I had too much of my father's emotional reckless-ness to always be in control.

I sank back onto the chair, my appetite having fled at some point. Depression about Parker and Ryker and what Natalie was doing to them ate at me. Seeing my father, pale and unresponsive in the bed, only added to the invisible weight on my shoulders.

My cell phone buzzed. I plucked it out of my purse, and my heart sank when I saw "Unknown" on the screen instead of "Parker Anderson." I pressed the button.

"Hello?"

"Sage Muccino?"

That got my attention. I was mostly known as Sage Reese—my mom's maiden name, courtesy of not wanting to capitalize on the family name in college and in my post-college career.

"Who is this?" I asked.

"Senator Kirk. We met a few weeks ago. I believe you met my friend Branna."

The badass Irish redhead with a body like Scarlett Johansson and an attitude like Sarah Connor?

"I vaguely remember her," I lied. She'd scared the bejesus out of me.

"I want you to know that neither of us have or would in the future give any cooperation to the Shea company or its subsidiaries."

Ah. Charlie must've been working the phones since the minute I left. Though why the senator would feel it neces-sary to call me personally was beyond me.

"That's good to hear," I said carefully.

"And if there's anything she or I can do to assist you or your father during this difficult time, please let me know."

And suddenly a gift horse was plopped in my lap.

"Actually," I said, "there is something. I'm looking for information on a woman. She says her husband was in jail about ten years ago, then was killed in a drug deal gone bad. Now she's telling us her sister is missing, possibly kidnapped, and I'm not sure she's telling the truth. Can you help?"

"That's something I can take a look at, yes," he said. "Why don't you send me what you know about her and I'll get back to you." He rattled off an e-mail address, which I scrambled in my purse for paper to jot down, then repeated it back.

"Great, thank you," I said.

"Your father has always been a generous supporter of the party and I'm pleased we can do something to help," the senator said.

Ah. I should've known it came down to money. Since when did politicians do anything just to be nice and helpful?

"I'm sure my father won't forget your kindness once he's fully recovered," I said. "I know I won't." *Hint, hint. Yes, you'll get another donation.*

I'd just hung up from talking to the senator when the door opened and Parker walked in.

I bristled, pulling on an armor of indifference to cover my hurt. What the hell had he been doing all this time with Natalie and Ryker? I wasn't about to ask. I didn't care, right? It wasn't as if I had a claim on Parker's time.

"At least I found you," he said, keeping his voice modulated out of deference to my father and the hour. I could hear the pissed-off tone, though, lurking under the surface.

"I didn't realize you were looking," I said. "For all your claims of indifference, it didn't take you long to go running to Natalie's beck and call." I heard the jealousy in my voice and inwardly cringed.

A nerve ticked in Parker's jaw. "I told you to stay put."

"I'm not a dog, Parker. I needed to come here and let my mom leave."

"Why didn't you call me?"

"Why didn't you come back?"

"I did and you were gone."

"Exactly."

Stalemate.

We stared at each other. Natalie was like a ghost between us. Parker shoved his fingers through his hair and sat down next to me with a sigh. We both stared at my dad, lying impassive in the bed, the machines quietly whirring and doing their thing to keep him monitored and stable.

"I'm sorry," he said. "I was pissed off because I've been trying to leave for over an hour and Natalie was a mess."

"Did she identify anyone?"

He shook his head. "No, but I guess there were trace amounts of DNA on the ransom note that the lab guys think is blood. They're running tests to see if it's Jessie's. Natalie was crying, Ryker was trying to do his job, and I couldn't leave."

Hard to argue with that one, though I wanted to. Jessie could be hurt and Natalie was upset. I'd look like a total bitch to be upset, and yet I was . . . *both* actually—upset *and* a bitch. I bit my tongue to keep from saying anything I'd probably end up regretting.

"Charlie thinks Steve Shea, Leo's son, is behind the attacks and threats," I said, deciding to change the subject. Out of my peripheral vision, I saw Parker glance at me.

"Steve's back in town?"

"Apparently so. Charlie thinks I need to retaliate in some way." It was surreal, thinking in those terms. This wasn't *The Godfather*, and yet he'd tried to kill both me and my dad.

"I don't like the idea of you putting yourself in the middle of a war between Shea and your father," he said.

"Shea's already done that. And I have a feeling he's not going to stop."

Parker was silent, tension radiating from him. He bent, resting his elbows on his spread knees, and looked back at the hospital bed. "I'd feel better if we left town for a while. Let the cops do their job. They'll turn up something to tie Shea to the shooting."

I grimaced. "I wish I could believe that, but somehow I doubt he left a trail of clues leading straight to him. From what Charlie said, he may not have run his dad's business before, but he's not stupid. And who knows what he'll do if I up and leave? What if he targets my mom? I can't leave that to chance."

Parker rubbed the back of his neck and didn't reply.

"How's Ryker?" I asked. "Natalie still have him eating out of her palm?" I couldn't get him out of the back of my mind. Worry ate at me over how easily he'd fallen back into Natalie's orbit. It brought to mind the conversation I'd had with Ryker's friend Amy back on the boat weeks ago. How Ryker just could never see Natalie for what she was, that to him she was this perfect angel who could do no wrong. It was hard to reconcile the badass image I had of Ryker as someone who you couldn't bullshit with a man so smitten by a pretty face that he'd toss aside all common sense and caution.

"You could say that," Parker replied. "Why? Are you jealous?" He said it in a carefully even kind of way, but I stiffened nonetheless.

"I'm worried about him," I said. "I don't like to think of him as being manipulated by anyone. Especially Natalie."

"So you two are over?" he asked.

"I broke up with both of you, remember?"

"Yeah, but you were at his house when Natalie showed up."

"I was returning his things," I said, wondering why I was bothering to explain myself to him. "Now who's jealous?"

The corners of his lips quirked upward and his blue eyes fixed on mine. He was close enough to touch if I stretched my hand out just a little. It would be nice to hold his hand and absorb some of his strength. It felt like my own emotional and mental stability were reaching their limits.

His cell phone buzzed, killing the moment, and he dug it out of his pocket to answer. After speaking for a few minutes (while I pretended not to listen), he covered the speaker with his hand and mouthed at me *be right back* before heading out the door.

I let out a sigh, exhausted. Seeing my dad like this wasn't helping, plus I was starving.

As if to answer my prayers, the doors opened and the warm smell of Italian food hit me, making my stomach grumble. Then I decided God was a cruel joker because who would be holding the bags containing the mouthwatering goodies? Natalie, of course.

Because I hadn't seen enough of her already.

"I hope you don't mind," she said with a tentative smile. "But Ryker told me what happened to your dad, so I thought you might be hungry. Italian is the best comfort food there is, right?"

Okay, this was weird. "Um, yeah. Probably." My dad would definitely agree with that.

She set the bags down on the counter and proceeded to start removing containers, talking as she did. "My parents died when I was six," she said. "Car accident. Jessie and I went to live with our aunt. Didn't have enough money to go to college, so I was working at the local bar and grill when I met Rookie."

"Rookie?"

"Oh yeah, sorry. He was my husband. His nickname. Everyone called him by it because he didn't like his given name. Anyway," she continued, pulling the wrapper off a plastic fork and knife, "we got married when I was desperate to get out of this town. Should've known it was too good to be true."

"Why's that?" I could no longer resist the aroma of marinara and I drifted closer, eyeing the takeout containers. She couldn't have poisoned them, could she? My stomach was growling so loud I didn't know if I cared if she'd poisoned *and* spit in them. I was starving.

"He showed his true colors pretty quick. Broke my arm. Knocked out a tooth." She handed me a paper plate laden with lasagna and Caesar salad. "I was glad when he got caught robbing a liquor store and got put away."

Huh.

I dug in to the lasagna, mulling over what she'd said. She was pretty matter-of-fact about being a victim of domestic violence. A broken arm? And he'd hit her hard enough to knock out a tooth? Regardless of how I felt about her, reluctant sympathy rose in me. If she was telling the truth, she'd led a pretty hard life.

Besides, food was food no matter who'd brought it. Natalie took some as well, though I noticed she only put half as much on her plate as she had on mine. Figured. Just when I was feeling sorry for her, too.

"So why are you here?" I asked. "You don't even know me."

"Dean and Parker know you. You're their friend and a part of their lives. I thought we should be friends, too." Her smile was dazzling.

"You want to be friends?" I asked, my tone laden with skepticism.

"Absolutely. I don't have a lot of girlfriends, and I think we'd get along really well." Still the smile that said we could totally be besties.

Parker walked in, took one look at Natalie and me standing there, and stopped. His eyebrows flew upward as he took in the food and our plates and Natalie, standing right next to me.

"What's this?" he asked.

"I brought Sage some dinner," Natalie said. "I didn't realize you were here, too, but I'm sure there's plenty."

I didn't buy for a second that she hadn't known Parker was there.

"How...thoughtful of you," Parker said as she heaped food onto another plate and handed it to him.

Yeah, *thoughtful* was just the word I'd been thinking.

"Well, I have to admit, I did have a slightly ulterior motive," Natalie said.

Color me surprised.

"And what is that?" Parker asked.

Natalie looked my way. "Well, it's just that I'm kind of low on funds and I've been staying at a hotel while I look for Jessie, but that's not really financially feasible. So..."

Oh my God. I could see where this was going. *Please don't say it. Please don't say it—*

"...I was wondering if I might be able to stay with you for a few days." She finished with another hopeful smile.

"Sage can't stay in her apartment right now," Parker said. "There was a break-in."

Natalie's brow creased in concern. "Oh, wow, that's awful! I'm so sorry. Did they steal anything?"

"It wasn't that kind of break-in," I said. Explaining about

the dead cat wasn't really something I wanted to undertake at the moment.

"So what are you doing then?" she asked.

"She's staying with me for now," Parker replied, taking a bite of the lasagna.

A flash of something crossed her face and was gone, replaced with another smile, though this one held a hint of hurt.

"I see," she said. "I guess I didn't realize...I mean I thought you and Ryker were..." She let the words trail off.

"We were," I said, "but not anymore."

"So you two are...?"

Parker and I spoke at the same time.

"No."

"Yes," he said.

I gritted my teeth. "I used to work for Parker. He's being very gracious to let me stay with him until my apartment is back in order." There was a lot wrong with everything I'd just said, but I didn't feel the need to explain me or my relationships with Parker and Ryker to her any more than I already had.

"Oh." She flashed a relieved smile that made warning signals flare inside my brain. "Well, if that's the case, maybe you might know of someone who wouldn't mind a roommate for a few days? Just until Dean can find Jessie." Tears welled in her eyes and she quickly brushed them away. "Sorry. I keep doing that."

I couldn't help the twinge of sympathy I felt. It was almost impossible not to feel sorry for her.

"Why don't you stay with us?" Parker asked, making me nearly choke on a lettuce leaf.

"Really? You wouldn't mind?" Natalie was looking at him as she asked this, then glanced at me as almost an afterthought.

Yes, I minded. I minded a whole hell of a lot. But Parker did nothing without a reason and I wanted to know what that reason was. Whether it was to rekindle the romance between him and Natalie or some other reason, I'd play along.

I swallowed the lettuce leaf lodged in my throat and forced my lips to curve. "Sure. Why not? It'll be like one big sleepover." Maybe we could ask Ryker, too. I bet Parker's living room would make one hell of a blanket fort.

"Fantastic! Thank you so much. I have my stuff in my car and I'm dying for a shower. Do you mind if I head on over?" She was already grabbing her purse.

"That's fine," Parker said. "I'll call the doorman and let him know you're coming and to let you in." He gave her the address, but she didn't write it down. She must have a really good memory or something. "We'll be in later."

"Perfect. Thanks again, Parker. And you, too, Sage." With a whisper of perfume, she was gone.

"Are you out of your mind?" I asked the minute the door latched closed. "We're really going to let her stay in your apartment? With us?"

"I like the *we* and *us* part of that sentence," Parker said. "It's encouraging."

I shoved another bite of lasagna in my mouth and chewed like it was raw meat rather than noodles. No sense letting good food go to waste. "What exactly is your plan with this?" I asked, trying to keep my cool. "Because I don't see Natalie and me becoming BFFs. I won't be doing her nails and makeup anytime soon while we listen to *Air Supply's Greatest Hits* on the stereo and compare notes on you and Ryker."

"Air Supply? Really? I never got the appeal."

I shrugged. "You're not a chick. Music to slit your wrists to, I know, but I like it. Now back to poor pitiful Natalie."

He grimaced. "You know the saying. Keep your friends close, et cetera et cetera."

"So which is she? A friend or enemy?"

"I'm not sure yet. But I think we'll find out easier and quicker if we go along with her plan than if we fight it. Don't you?"

I couldn't argue with that. He was right. "I don't trust her."

"I know. Neither do I. But the more she's around us, the less she's around Ryker. And I think we both want to protect him from himself. I don't want her screwing with him again." A dangerous glint came into his eyes and his jaw hardened. "He went through enough because of Natalie."

I liked seeing Parker falling back into the role of being Ryker's friend. So even though I dreaded going back to Parker's place like a condemned man on death row, I smiled.

"All right, then. I guess I'm in." And I tried to pretend I wasn't walking right where Natalie wanted us to go.

CHAPTER NINE

I was unprepared to see Natalie wearing one of Parker's shirts when we walked in the door.

"Oh, I hope you don't mind," she said breezily, passing by us to sit on the couch. "I'm washing my clothes and needed something to put on. I'll wash it when I'm through." The man's button-down shirt was big on her and came down to mid-thigh, baring her legs. I was so stunned at her audacity, I could only stare wide-eyed as she flipped on the television.

Parker made a noise that sounded suspiciously like he was smothering a laugh, but when I rounded to glare at him, his expression was one of blithe innocence.

I set my purse down carefully so I wouldn't be tempted to launch it at Natalie's head. For someone whose sister was supposed to be in grave danger, she sure seemed to be taking it well. Except when she wanted to turn on the waterworks, of course.

I cut off the sour thoughts in my head. I didn't need the negativity and continuing down that path would lead to nothing good. I needed to get my game face on and figure out what Natalie wanted and what her strategy was. So far, it seemed she wanted Parker and her strategy was to throw herself in his path as much as possible.

"I see you made yourself at home," I said, walking over to the couch. I tried and failed to keep the bitchy out of my voice. *Sugar not vinegar*, I reminded myself. "Did you need anything else?"

My thinly veiled sarcasm appeared utterly lost on Natalie.

"Yes, actually," she said. "Do you have any underwear I can borrow?" Her smile was sheepish and her cheeks even turned a charming pink as she added in an undertone, "I'm not wearing any right now; they're all in the wash."

If she thought to aim that volume low enough so Parker wouldn't hear, she failed miserably. I saw him almost involuntarily glance over at us. If he so much as tried to get a glimpse…

"Of course," I said. My smile was so stiff, I thought my cheeks would crack. "Come with me and I'll get them for you."

Parker kept his gaze wisely averted as we passed him to go into his bedroom. He was digging in the refrigerator and I hoped he was getting out a bottle of wine because lord knew I needed it tonight.

I dug in the suitcase Parker had packed for me, unsurprised that he'd grabbed the skimpiest and laciest items I possessed. Finding a lone pair of black cotton briefs, I tossed them to Natalie.

"Here you go," I said, striving to sound pleasant. "Will these do?"

"Thanks," she said. "A little big maybe, but I'm sure

they'll be fine for tonight." She smiled sweetly and disappeared into the bathroom.

I unclenched my fists and pried my jaws apart before I permanently ground my teeth to a new level. Natalie was no amateur at this game; that was for sure. *Too big, my ass.* And not in that way.

Parker had said he wasn't interested in her and I believed him... but no sense in letting her have the upper hand. If she was going to be strutting around with nothing but underwear and his shirt, I wouldn't put anything past her.

Digging in my suitcase again, I pulled out the pajamas Parker had packed. A tiny pair of pale pink cotton shorts and a skin-tight matching camisole. I stripped to my skin and pulled on the pajamas, using my fingers to fluff my hair. The pink was ever so slightly see-through.

Perfect.

Natalie was still in the bathroom—no doubt trying to make those tent-size underwear of mine not slip right off her non-existent hips—so I went back out to the kitchen. I'd been right, Parker had opened a bottle of wine, which he promptly choked on when he saw me.

"Holy shit," he rasped.

"You're the one who packed for me," I said with a shrug, my lips curving in a satisfied smile. *Natalie who?*

"I knew that would look good on you. I just didn't realize *how* good." His eyes lingered on my breasts before drifting down my stomach to my thighs. His Adam's apple bobbed as he swallowed.

I felt his gaze as though it was a touch against my skin. His eyes met mine, burning with a hunger that sent a shiver down my spine. I couldn't look away, could barely breathe—

"Oh good! I'd love a glass of wine. That's so thoughtful of you, Parker."

Natalie's voice was a bucket of ice water and was right behind me. Parker kept his cool and poured two more glasses, handing one to each of us.

"To old friendships," Natalie toasted, lifting her glass, her gaze on Parker.

"And new ones," I added meaningfully, clinking my glass against hers. If I was going to get her to talk to me, I had to make her think I trusted her.

There was a knock at the door and we all turned to look before Parker set down his wineglass and picked up his gun.

"Who could that be at this hour?" I asked quietly. It was getting late.

"Guess I'll find out," he said.

The worry on Natalie's face seemed genuine and matched mine as Parker peered through the peephole. A moment later, his body relaxed and he slid the gun into the small of his back before pulling open the door.

"Your timing is impeccable," Parker said as Ryker stepped inside.

Ryker's gaze landed on Natalie first, his eyes widening, then on me. His eyebrows climbed nearly to his hairline as he surveyed our attire, or lack thereof. My face got hot.

"You're having a sleepover? Or did I step into one of your fantasies?"

"If it was a fantasy, you sure as hell wouldn't be here. I don't roll that way."

The words were all said in an easy, lighthearted way, but the look in Ryker's eye was anything but.

"Did you find out something about Jessie?" Natalie interrupted. "Were there any prints on the note or anything?"

Ryker shook his head. "No. It was clean, unfortunately. And our time is running out for the deadline they set tomorrow."

"What are we going to do?" Natalie asked, her voice

strained. "I can't lose my sister. I just…can't." She began to cry, covering her face with her hands, and leaned against Parker's chest. His arms lifted to circle her and he patted her on the back.

Jealousy clawed at my chest like a living thing and I wanted to rip her hair out by the roots. If I could have growled, I would have. Instead, I glanced at Ryker, who was also watching Parker and Natalie, with a look on his face that I knew mirrored mine.

"We'll just give you two a minute," I said, grabbing Ryker's hand and pulling him with me. I dragged him into Parker's bedroom and shut the door. Let those two stew on that.

"They seem to be getting along well," Ryker said. "Why the hell is she here anyway?"

I gave him a quick rundown of her plea for a place to stay and Parker's offer.

"Why are you helping her?" I asked. "Kidnapping isn't your thing. You're homicide, for crying out loud. And I'm not totally convinced all of this isn't one big fat lie. It's awfully convenient, her just showing up out of the blue."

"I'm helping her because of Jessie," he said. "She was a good kid. Whatever happened to her probably leads back to Natalie. She's not telling us everything. And Jessie doesn't deserve to get caught up and possibly hurt due to her sister's scheming."

"Scheming?" I asked, taken aback. "It seemed like you thought Natalie walked on water."

"Natalie goes after what she wants," he said. "That's always been the case."

"And what does she want?"

"I don't know. She wants to find Jessie, I believe that. But how it all fits in with her sudden reappearance to me and Parker…we'll just have to find out."

I hesitated before asking the question I really wanted to ask. "Are you still in love with her?"

Ryker went still, his eyes fixed on mine. "Natalie and I share a history," he said. "A turbulent, painful one, sure, but it's a history. I don't know how I feel about her. I'd like to give her a second chance, but until I find out why she's here and what she wants, I'm not going to commit to anything."

My whole body relaxed. Ryker hadn't been taken in. He'd been playing along. Thank God. "I just don't want to see you hurt again." Which was a helluva thing to say after what he and I had been through, and the irony wasn't lost on me.

A beat passed, then his lips curved in a soft smile. "I'm a grown-up, babe. I don't regret you and me, but I see the writing on the wall." He took a step closer to me and wrapped his hands around my upper arms in a loose grip. "I didn't want to face it, but you've been in love with Parker since long before I came along. I think we had something, could've had more, but you and I both know that Parker's the one you want."

This was awkward. And painful. My chest ached and my eyes burned. I hadn't expected this kind of conversation when I'd brought Ryker in here, and I was unprepared.

"Shh, it's okay," he said, pulling me into his arms. "We had a great time. And we'll still be friends. But I'm not going to stand in the way of you being happy. I saw how much it tore you up to come between Parker and me. I'd like to think I'm not a selfish enough bastard to make you and him miserable just because I'm a sore loser."

Tears wet his shirt as I tried to sniff them back. "I'm sorry," I said, my voice thick. "I never meant for this to happen."

"Don't be sorry," he said, leaning back slightly and brushing tears from my cheeks. "I don't regret a single moment we spent together. And I hope you don't either."

I shook my head, the lump in my throat too big to speak around.

The door flew open and Parker stood there. When he saw me standing in Ryker's arms, the look on his face turned cold and hard. A dangerous fire lit his eyes as he looked at Ryker and I instinctively wanted to take a step back.

"Take it easy, Parker," Ryker said. "I hung a tie on the doorknob. Didn't you see?"

I pinched him, hard, and he winced. No need to antagonize Parker when he already looked like he was ready to murder someone. I maneuvered myself out of Ryker's hold, putting space between us. That's when I noticed Natalie behind Parker, peering curiously at the scene.

"I need to talk to you," Parker said. "Let's go." He turned on his heel and Ryker followed.

"Wait," I said, squeezing by Natalie and hurrying after them. "You're both leaving?" *Me alone with her*, I added silently.

"We'll be back soon," Parker said, grabbing his jacket and swinging it on. It covered the gun still shoved in the small of his back.

"It's okay," Natalie said. "It'll give Sage and me some girl time together."

Kill me now.

Ryker was already out the door and Parker glanced back at me. "Air Supply should be in the left cabinet, upper right. Knock yourself out." The door shut before I could get a retort in.

Asshole.

* * *

"Where are we going?" Ryker asked.

"To see Steven Shea," Parker replied. "Charlie said he's back in town and likely the one behind the attack on Sage and her dad. I thought we'd pay him a visit." He checked the ammunition clip in his Sig as they rode the elevator to the parking garage.

"Steven Shea is a psychopath," Ryker said.

Parker glanced over. "You've met him?"

Ryker nodded. "He didn't run off to college to get away from his dad's business. Leo sent him away. Steven has a sadistic streak. There was an incident that got out of hand."

"What kind of incident?"

"The kind where they needed a garbage bag for body parts."

Nice, Parker thought. "And this sonofabitch has decided he's got a vendetta against Sage. Her dad's protected in the hospital, but God only knows what he'll think of for her. I say we find him and send a message."

"Legally, I can't do that," Ryker said. "He gets one look at my badge and I'm in for a shitload of trouble."

Parker led the way to his car. "I'll do the talking. And you won't have to show your badge."

He drove them out of the building and turned north, heading deeper downtown.

"You know where he is?" Ryker asked.

"I put some feelers out. Got a text while you were talking to Sage in my bedroom."

The words *Sage* and *in my bedroom* hung in the air like little bombs waiting to explode.

"Chill," Ryker said. "I wasn't moving in on you. I was telling her...good-bye."

Parker glanced over at him. "What do you mean?" he asked sharply.

Ryker gave a bitter laugh. "I'm not an idiot," he said. "She's in love with you, not me. I'm through chasing women who'd rather be with someone else."

A tense silence followed as Ryker looked out the window. Parker's hands gripped the wheel.

"I'm sorry," he said at last. "I didn't mean for things to go this way—"

"Just tell me one thing," Ryker interrupted. "If I hadn't come along, would you have ever made a move on Sage? Or would you have just sat on your ass?"

Parker clenched his jaw tight at the accusation and bitterness in Ryker's voice. But he deserved an answer.

"I didn't want a personal relationship with her to affect our working partnership," he said. "But the way I felt about her...that was always there. It just took the thought of losing her—really losing her—to make me realize it was worth the risk. That *she* was worth the risk."

"What risk?"

"Getting my heart broken. Or worse...breaking hers."

They were both quiet for a moment, lost in their thoughts and memories.

"Natalie's up to something," Parker said. "You know that, right?"

"Yeah, I know. But she thinks she's got us both on a string again. No sense disillusioning her. Not yet."

"You really think Jessie's in trouble?"

Ryker nodded. "Yeah. No one's seen her for over a week. I went by her apartment yesterday and there's no trace of her. Her car is in the lot, untouched. And no one broke into her apartment. No sign of a struggle either. It's like she disappeared into thin air."

"You don't think she'd be involved in any of Natalie's shit, do you?" Parker asked. "You knew her better than I did."

"No, she's not like Natalie. When I knew her, she was a sweet and naïve little thing. Wouldn't hurt a fly."

"That was ten years ago," Parker reminded him. "People change."

"Not that much."

That was true. At their core, both he and Ryker were the same, which was probably why they'd been able to fall back into the familiar cadence of what they used to be even after so long a drought.

And they both had Sage to thank for that. Without her, Parker doubted either of them would've reached out to try and repair the damage to their friendship. She'd united them, then tore herself away to keep them together. In other words, the complete opposite of what Natalie had done. Natalie had thrived to see them fighting over her. But not Sage. And that made all the difference.

A few miles passed in silence before Parker pulled over and parked. "It's on the next block," he said.

They both got out, falling into step as they approached the corner. Ahead, the glowing sign of an Italian restaurant blinked lazily. Two men, both in suits with telltale bulges at their sides, stood in too-deliberate casualness by the door.

Parker didn't pay them any attention as he brushed by, but then one of them grabbed his elbow.

"Hey, you can't go—"

His next words were abruptly cut off by Parker's fist in his throat.

Ryker had the other guy down and out with two blows by the time Parker had knocked out the one who'd touched him. Together, they dragged the men to the side of the doorway out of sight, then proceeded into the restaurant.

Parker laid eyes on Steven Shea immediately. In his late twenties, he was tall but shorter than Parker by a good two inches. He was fit in the kind of way that made women look twice, but not fit enough to keep him from getting his ass kicked in a fight.

Glancing away from where Steven was holding court with two other men and a woman, Parker sat at a table toward the back. Ryker sat with him. Both had their backs to the door.

A nervous waiter bobbed over, giving them menus and taking their order for a glass of wine each. They knew ordering anything else would look out of place.

Parker and Ryker pretended to study the menu.

"Do you have a plan?" Ryker asked, perusing the entrees.

"I'm winging it."

"So the usual."

"Pretty much."

"Awesome."

The waiter returned with two glasses of red. "I'll have the lasagna," Parker ordered, his gaze catching on Steven as he got up from his table.

"Make that two," Ryker said, handing the waiter the menu. He glanced at Parker. He'd seen Steven get up, too.

Steven headed for the bathroom, one bodyguard in tow. Parker rose and followed him. Ryker got up as well.

The bodyguard was lax in his vigilance, and his unconscious body was hauled aside embarrassingly quickly. Ryker took up his position as Parker entered the men's restroom.

Steven was standing at a urinal and glanced over.

"What the fuck are you doing in here? This is supposed to be private."

"Maybe you're not familiar with the concept of a public restroom," Parker said, taking a step closer. "Privacy isn't part of the deal."

Steven zipped up and flushed. "Whatever." He headed for the door. Parker stopped him with hard shove in the chest.

"Didn't you forget something?" he asked. "Always wash your hands. Dickwad."

"What the—"

"Let's talk about that," Parker said, shoving him back against the wall. "And some other things."

"Rusty!" Steven called out. "Rusty! Get in here!"

"Oh, you looking for your bodyguard?" Parker asked. "He's been... detained."

Steven's face turned red. "Who the fuck are you?" he snarled. "You hurt me, you're going to regret it. I can promise you that, motherfucker."

"Let me tell you what I'm going to regret," Parker growled, moving his hand to circle Steven's throat. His other hand drew his weapon and he held the barrel to Steven's temple. The man went very still at the touch of the metal against his skin. "I'm going to regret not ending this right here and now, but I'm hoping you're smarter than you look."

"Fuck you," Steven managed to squeeze out.

Parker slammed Steven's head against the tile at his back. The crack of bone against ceramic was loud in the tiled bathroom. "I guess I was wrong. You're a dipshit. If you want to prolong your life expectancy, you'll listen up and listen good. I know about your adolescent vendetta against the Muccino family. Get over it."

"They killed my father. I deserve revenge."

"You deserve nothing. Your father made his choices, and he paid for them. You keep on this path, you'll follow exactly where he went." Parker paused, squeezing the kid's throat harder, cutting off his air supply. "This is your only warning."

He held him for another ten seconds, enough for Steven's

face to start turning blue. Then he abruptly let go. Steven bent forward, coughing and choking. Parker took two steps and was out of the bathroom.

Ryker was waiting. One glance and they were heading for the back door. Sixty seconds later, Parker was unlocking his car.

"Do you think he'll heed the warning?" Ryker asked as they drove away.

"Doubtful. But at least now he knows he's up against someone who can fuck him over. We can hope maybe cooler heads prevail and he'll take advice."

"I'm not betting on it."

"Me neither." Parker sighed. It had been worth a shot.

"Think the girls are okay?" Ryker asked.

A niggle of unease crept through Parker, but he tried to shrug it off. "Yeah. I'm sure they're fine. They're girls. How bad could it get?"

* * *

I ground my teeth as the door shut behind Parker, leaving Natalie and me by ourselves while they went off to do who knew what.

I was so going to kill him for this.

"Didn't I see that Parker has a wine rack over here?" Natalie asked, heading for the kitchen.

Okay, so maybe she and I could agree on one thing: Lubrication was needed to grease these wheels.

I grabbed our glasses while she uncorked another bottle. I didn't ask what kind and she didn't offer to tell me. The silence between us was the kind I imagined Old West gunfighters used to experience right after they'd paced off and before they drew.

She fired first.

"I guess we have a couple of things in common," she said. At my questioning look, she added, "You know. Parker and Dean."

Wow. She wasn't playing around, instead going right for the jugular.

"Oh?" I decided to play dumb. "I thought you were just friends."

She laughed. "We were all much more than friends." Taking a long drink of the white wine, she headed for the living room, leaving me in the unenviable position of trailing after her. She settled on the couch. I sat at the far end, leaving a no-man's-land between us.

"That was a long time ago," I said. "They've moved on."

"To you, apparently."

I took a sip of wine. Decided that didn't need a response. I was feeling very territorial over Ryker and Parker, and Natalie was obviously trying to antagonize me.

"Listen," she said, "I don't want us to be enemies."

"You sure about that?"

She laughed lightly at my dry tone. "I'm sorry. We have a history, the three of us." She shrugged. "I guess I didn't realize how much I've missed them."

"Why didn't you come back before now?" I asked. "Why wait until Jessie went missing?"

"I didn't think they'd want to see me again."

"They thought you were dead."

"Exactly. I'd hurt them enough already. I didn't want to hurt them again."

She looked so remorseful, I almost believed her.

I smiled. "I'm sure they'll let bygones be bygones. What's important now is finding Jessie."

Anxiety crossed her delicate features and I thought it was

real. But then again, I knew she was also a very good actress. I didn't want to minimize the danger to Jessie, but neither did I want Parker or Ryker to put themselves in harm's way for no reason.

What was I saying? *I* was currently the biggest threat to Parker.

Yeah, I really didn't want to think about that.

"You have no idea who could have sent that note? Who would think you had that kind of money?"

"I don't know," she said. "I'm telling the truth. I have no idea."

Hmm. "So . . . what do you do for a living?" I asked. If the kidnapper had asked her for that much money, maybe he was somehow connected to her work, to think she had access to ten thousand dollars.

"I'm a dental hygienist."

Dentists made decent money. Maybe she was sleeping with her boss. *Shocker.*

I cut that judgy thought off right way. Like I was one to talk. Those who live in glass houses . . .

"So in other words, you don't have ten grand lying around and no one who knows you would think you would."

"Right."

"And your sister wasn't involved in anything bad? She hadn't said anything about being in trouble or being afraid?" You'd think there would have been some kind of warning, especially if ransom was involved. But Natalie was shaking her head.

"Not a word."

Reaching over, she refilled our wineglasses. Huh. I hadn't even realized we'd drank it all. It seemed I wasn't the only one who could drink. Which gave me an idea.

"I could use something a little stronger." I got up and

retrieved Parker's bottle of scotch and two shot glasses. I poured some into each and handed her one. "To finding Jessie," I toasted, clinking my glass against hers.

We both tossed back the shot, each one eyeing the other for any sign of weakness. She didn't cough at all. *Dammit. This may be harder than I thought.* People talked when they were drunk, their inhibitions lowered. I just needed to get her drunk, but first I had to outlast her.

I repeated the process and we downed the second shot. Her eyes narrowed, watching me the same way I was watching her.

My throat burned, my lungs wanted desperately to cough. I swallowed the shot down, my eyes watering.

"Good stuff," I managed to squeak out. I cleared my throat as a smile flitted across Natalie's face.

"Parker's always had excellent taste," she said. This time, she poured the shots. "Bottoms up."

Fuck. I was so screwed. A fact that became painfully obvious about an hour later when the room was spinning and I'd decided that listening to Air Supply was the best. Idea. Ever.

"You're every woman in the world...to me..." I warbled. Wine sloshed out of my glass onto the couch. "Oops."

"That's alcohol abuse," Natalie said.

I giggled. "I could lick it up, I guess." I bent over, but was laughing too hard and ended up getting wine on my nose. The couch was slippery and next thing I knew, I was sitting on my ass on the floor.

We both dissolved into gales of laughter. Which was how Ryker and Parker found us when they walked in the door.

"I see you found my scotch," Parker said, picking up the empty decanter and setting it back on the table.

"It was deeelishus." I smacked my lips.

"Yum," Natalie agreed. "The wine, too." Two empty bottles littered the floor.

Mmmm, wine. I went to take a drink from my glass, but it was empty. "It's gone," I said sadly, turning the glass upside down. "No more wine."

"It looks like the remains of a frat party in here," Ryker said, taking the glass from me.

"We're bonding," I explained.

"Is that what it's called?" he asked. "I thought you were just getting stinking drunk."

"You're being awfully judgy." A burp escaped and my eyes went wide as I clapped a hand over my mouth. "'scuse me."

Natalie and I dissolved in a fit of giggles again. I swore I heard identical male sighs of long-suffering.

"Upsy daisy," Parker said, wrapping an arm around me and hauling me up to my feet. My knees weren't cooperating, so I hung on to him. He didn't seem to mind.

"What am I supposed to do with this one?" Ryker asked as Parker started walking me toward the bedroom.

"I don't care. Take her with you."

"You're kidding, right?"

But Parker was already closing the bedroom door behind us.

CHAPTER TEN

I flopped onto the bed and waited for the room to stop turning.

"What possessed you to get drunk with Natalie, of all people?" he asked.

His hands were braced on his hips, which drew my eyes south of the border. I really liked those jeans on him. I wondered if I asked him to turn around whether he'd do it.

"No, I'm not turning around," he said.

Huh. I guess I'd said that out loud.

"Was there a purpose to bonding with your nemesis?" he asked.

"I thought maybe if I got her drunk, she'd let something slip," I said. "But it didn't quite go like I planned."

"No shit."

"Don't get all pissy," I groused. "I'm the one who's going to feel like crap tomorrow."

"Well, did it work?" he asked. "Did she say anything?"

I nodded, then immediately regretted the action. And just

as the room had settled down, too. "It was about three shots and two glasses of wine in."

"And?"

I closed my eyes. Had to get this just right. "She said, and I quote, 'Is it weird that we've both slept with the same two guys?'" I cracked open an eye. "That's when I took another shot."

Parker looked like he'd just bitten into a lemon.

"Yeah, not something I want to dwell on either." I hauled myself up. I wanted a bath.

"What are you doing?"

"I want to take a bath," I said, getting carefully to my feet. So far, so good. The room remained upright. Now to make it into the bathroom.

"Do you always take a bath when you're drunk?" Parker slipped an arm around my waist while I tried to pretend I didn't need the assistance.

"It helps me relax."

"I'd think two bottles of wine and half a bottle of scotch would make you as relaxed as anyone should be."

Smartass. It was on the tip of my tongue, but then we reached the bathroom and sitting down seemed like a really good idea. I didn't protest when Parker leaned me against the counter and began drawing my bath. It was kind of sweet, actually, the way he kept testing the water to make sure it was the right temperature.

"I don't have any bubble bath or salts or whatever women put in their baths," he said. He was frowning, as though this was of vital importance and he'd have to fire someone for the oversight.

"That's fine," I said, unable to stop a smile from spreading across my face.

"What?" he asked, but I just shook my head.

Last night, I'd been feeling uncertain about Parker and me. Tonight... well, tonight he looked pretty darn good in those jeans. My hormones decided they weren't too drunk to stand up and take notice. He was wearing a button-down shirt, too, and I loved undoing buttons...

"Oh no you don't," Parker said, holding up a hand and stopping me. I hadn't even realized I'd moved toward him. "You're drunk. All you're getting tonight is a bath."

"I'm not *that* drunk," I said, sliding my hands up his chest. *Mmmm, hard...* I angled for the buttons.

"You're drunk enough and I'm not about to have you do something tonight that you'll regret tomorrow," he said, grasping my wrists and pulling them away from his body.

"I promise I won't regret a thing." I inched closer until his back was against the wall. "Two consenting adults... and it's not like we haven't done it before." His grip on my wrists was lax and I pulled one hand free, pressing it against the bulge in his jeans.

Parker's Adam's apple bobbed as he swallowed. "You're not making this easy," he said. I was gratified at the roughness in his voice and the way his gaze dropped to my breasts.

"If it's easy, then it's not worth having now, is it?" I murmured, leaning close enough for our bodies to touch. His cock was hard beneath my fingers and an answering heat flashed between my thighs.

Parker's shirt was unbuttoned at the neck, exposing the skin there. It was tan and smooth and begged for me to taste. I stretched up and fastened my lips to his throat, my tongue tasting the salt on his skin. He didn't move away, which I took to be an encouragement.

Hand-eye coordination suffered with alcohol intake, but Parker was the best incentive there was to make the effort to undo a few more buttons on his shirt one-handed while my other hand was busy outlining his erection through his jeans.

Lowering his head, he nuzzled my hair and ear, his lips just brushing against me. The slight touch made me suck in a breath as my skin tingled, so acutely sensitive was I to everything he did to me.

The air was thick with humidity, steam from the bathtub billowing around us. Finally, I felt Parker's palms close over my hips and pull me closer.

Now we were getting somewhere.

My fingers threaded through his hair as my lips inched up his neck to his jaw. I felt a groan vibrate inside his chest. His hands gripped me tighter, his erection pressing against my softness. My body felt like warm butter against his, molding to him. I twined my arms around his neck, moving my mouth closer to his. I could almost taste him on my tongue—

The door flew open and Natalie came bursting in. She ran past us to the toilet and promptly threw up.

Well, that was a mood killer.

The sound of it made my stomach turn over and I bolted out of the bathroom so I didn't end up doing the same damn thing. Parker or Ryker could hold her hair, though neither one looked to be in any great hurry to do so. Instead, Parker followed me.

"Do me a favor," he said to me. "Next time you want to get somebody drunk, drink the cheap stuff, okay?"

Got it.

* * *

I didn't feel as bad the next morning as I'd thought I would. I'd fallen asleep—not passed out (because ladies don't pass out)—on Parker's bed while Natalie was still heaving her guts out in the bathroom. When I woke up, I discovered she'd ended up lying next to me. I grimaced and eased out of bed.

A trip to the bathroom made me feel more human, and I tugged on fresh clothes after my shower. I desperately needed coffee and wandered into the kitchen. Ryker was already awake and sipping on a steaming mug of nirvana.

"I didn't realize you'd stayed," I said, pouring myself a cup. It felt odd—really odd—to be here at Parker's with Ryker. The last time he and I'd had coffee together had been in my kitchen and we'd probably made love before, after, or both. A slight pang of sadness in my chest at the thought made me remember that even being in love with someone else, it would still take some time to get used to our new friend status.

"Parker looked like he might have his hands full with the two of you last night, so I crashed on the couch."

Ah.

"So any news on the shooting or my apartment?" I asked, taking the seat at the table across from him.

"Actually, yeah," Ryker said, pulling out a three-by-four color mug shot. "Forensics found trace DNA on the cat. Like a needle in a haystack, but they narrowed it down to this guy, Rafael Miso."

I was studying the photo when I heard, "Who's he?"

We both turned to see Parker had come out of his office. All he wore was jeans, and I stared. With his hair tousled and a shadow of stubble on his jaw, he looked mouth-watering. He obviously didn't have the same effect on Ryker, because Ryker just answered Parker's question as if nothing were amiss.

"Miso is a common street thug. Hires himself out to the highest bidder for petty crimes, vandalism, theft, B&E... that kind of thing."

Parker poured himself a cup of coffee and sat at the table with us. I tore my gaze away to focus on something else. Anything else. Last night's hormones hadn't gone away with my inebriation and they were acutely reminding me of how very well Parker and I fit together.

"So someone probably hired him to break into my apartment and kill Morris?" I asked, trying to pull my head out of the fantasies I was conjuring of Parker and me.

"It's not like he would have had any cause to go there on his own," Ryker replied, which was just this side of saying *Duh*. I shot him a look. "Sorry," he said. "I just don't particularly like the idea of somebody hiring a guy like him to break into your place."

Yeah, me neither.

"Let's pay Rafael a visit," Parker said.

"We can't just go start cracking skulls and shit," Ryker said. "It's an ongoing investigation. Plus, it's not even technically my case. I've just been calling in favors to stay in the loop."

"You and I both know what's going to happen if the cops pick up Rafael," Parker said. "He'll call for his lawyer and clam up and we won't get anything out of him. If it was Shea who hired him, then we'll know for sure. Let's rule out any third party involvement here."

"Where are you going?"

I turned with a sigh to see Natalie easing into the last remaining chair. She'd brushed her hair and I smelled mint toothpaste, but she still wore Parker's shirt, which was conveniently unbuttoned to show off cleavage. The oh-I-just-rolled-out-of-bed thing might've fooled a man, but I knew better.

"We think we know who killed the neighbor's cat and left it on Sage's bed," Ryker said. "Parker's trying to convince me we should take a field trip to see him."

"Can I come?" Natalie asked.

Both men stared at her. "Why?" Ryker asked.

She shrugged. "I'm going crazy, worrying about Jessie. I need to keep my mind off it. Sitting around here, staring at the walls, isn't helping."

There was no way I was letting her tag along with Parker and Ryker without me. "I'm coming, too," I said.

Parker glanced at Ryker. "It's not a bad idea to have Sage with us, not after last night."

They exchanged a meaningful look I couldn't interpret, but my spidey sense went off. "What happened last night?" They'd been gone for a while together and I'd been too drunk when they returned to quiz them about their whereabouts.

"Nothing," they said in unison.

Right.

"You can either tell me or take us with you," I said. Neither of them hurried to spill their guts—big surprise. "Then it's settled. We're coming." And I could keep an eye on Natalie.

"It could be dangerous," Ryker said, which only made Parker roll his eyes.

"There's two of us and it's not like we'd be walking in on him without a clue," Parker said. "Let's track him down. You can chat with him and maybe I'll do a little breaking and entering."

"Don't *tell* me that," Ryker admonished, glaring.

"Fine. Pretend I didn't say anything."

"And what'll these two do while you're breaking the law and I'm breaking Rafael?"

Two blue gazes landed on me and Natalie.

"We'll wait in the car," I offered. "Won't be any trouble. I swear."

Famous last words, right?

* * *

Everything about Natalie set my teeth on edge. From her laugh, to the way she liked to toss her hair, to how she kept finding excuses to touch Parker.

She'd changed into what I guessed she thought was a "badass" outfit—black skintight jeans and a long-sleeved black T-shirt with a V-neck. The shirt was cut low enough to showcase cleavage that could only be achieved with a state-of-the-art combination of primo elastic and exceptional padding.

I tried to unobtrusively readjust my own assets inside my JC Penney's special as I followed Parker and Natalie through the parking garage. She stuck to him like glue, asking him what he and Ryker were going to do about Jessie and the ransom note.

"Ryker's working on it," Parker said, disengaging her arm from his so he could unlock the car. "We still have time before the deadline."

Natalie chewed her lip and nodded before stepping in front of me to scoot into the front passenger seat. The door slammed shut.

Guess I shoulda called shotgun.

I glanced up and caught Parker's eye above the car. He raised an eyebrow and I swear the corner of his mouth twitched. My eyes narrowed. So he thought this was funny, did he? Maybe he liked the idea of Natalie hanging all over him, hoping I'd get jealous?

Sometimes you should be careful what you wish for.

"So, Sage," Natalie said as Parker drove, following Ryker's motorcycle ahead of us. "What do you do for your dad's company?"

"Um, well, I just started working there," I said. "I'm learning the business right now."

"I just don't think I could do that," Natalie said, more to

Parker than me. "Jump into a business and job I know nothing about just because it's run by family. Seems like a really big responsibility."

My jaw wanted to drop at her audacity, couched in a gosh-I'm-just-being-honest tone. I had to hand it to her; she was really good. I could easily see how Parker and Ryker had been taken in, when they were younger and less worldwise, by the manipulations of this woman.

"Sage is very smart," Parker said. "I'm sure she won't have any trouble at all."

I had a grudging appreciation for his defense of me, but that didn't make me any more inclined to like Natalie.

We drove to a part of the city where my dad would've felt at home, but which made me want to glance over my shoulder constantly. Ryker parked in a side alley where the shadows concealed his bike from the autumn sunshine, while Parker drove another block to park in a half-filled lot.

"You're staying in the car," he said to Natalie and me.

"That's what we promised," I said. Not that I was happy about it, but I'd rather be here than left back at his apartment.

Parker glanced out the rear window to where Ryker stood waiting on the sidewalk. His gaze caught mine and I tried to communicate for him to be careful in the way I looked at him. I didn't want either of them to get hurt, especially tracking down a guy who might have no problem doing to a person what he'd done to Morris.

As though he knew what I was thinking, Parker gave a slight nod, handed me his car keys, and got out.

"We'll be back soon," he said to us, then shut the door.

Natalie and I watched the two of them head down the street and turn into a tenement building that had seen better days. Three men were loitering outside and I saw another guy peeing in the alley.

Eww.

"Nice place," Natalie said.

I didn't bother responding. I had nothing to say to her and wasn't inclined to make small talk. Instead, I just watched out the window.

"You don't like me very much, do you," she asked, and it wasn't a question.

In the interest of diplomacy, I tried to be vague in my answer. "I don't know you well enough to like you or not like you."

"Parker and Ryker like me. I'm sure you will, too. It just takes time."

I thought it was debatable whether Parker and Ryker liked her, but kept my silence. My attention was drawn closer to the building. A man had climbed down the fire escape on the side nearest us and the alley and was running.

"I think that's our guy," I said, shoving open the car door. "And he's getting away."

Natalie popped out of the car, too, and we watched him run toward us, then take a sharp left into a building that could've doubled as a haunted house on Halloween.

"Let's go," Natalie said, and before I could argue the wisdom of that decision—or lack thereof—she'd taken off running.

Shit.

I ran after her, my promise to Parker to stay in the car reverberating inside my head. He was so going to kill me for this. But what was I supposed to do? I kinda felt like her babysitter. If something happened to her on my watch, would Parker and Ryker blame me? I felt like the older sister cleaning up the messes of a younger sibling.

Natalie ran inside the dilapidated building and I followed, first casting a quick glance over to where Ryker and Parker should be. I saw some commotion and prayed they were both all right before I ducked inside.

The inside was different than I'd thought it'd be... it was much worse. A rank smell hit me first in the nearly pitch-black room. The only light was what filtered through the boarded-up windows and open doorway. I couldn't spot Natalie at all, though I'd been just ten seconds behind her.

Belatedly, I realized I was doing a good impression of a perfect target, silhouetted as I was against the light in the open doorway at my back. I scampered farther inside, toward the shadows, which was actually in the opposite direction of where I wanted to be.

Before Parker killed me, I was going to kill Natalie.

In the quiet, I could hear only the sound of my hard breathing loud in my ears—a helluva time to regret not spending more time at the gym. If anyone, such as Freddie or Jason or Chuckie, was waiting to get me in the shadows, I wouldn't be hard to find.

My skin prickled like someone was watching me and the hair stood up on the back of my neck. Where the hell was Natalie?

A muffled sound above me made me look up. Was that Natalie's voice on the floor above? In which case, where were the freaking stairs?

I debated using the flashlight on my phone, but that would make me a target, too, so I waited for my eyes to adjust the best they could do before slowly moving farther into the building.

Empty boxes littered the corners, stretching into a darkened hallway. My fingers itched for something—anything— I could use as a weapon, and I saw a glint of broken glass. Pausing to crouch down, I carefully picked up a shard about as big as my palm. It had a nasty looking point on one end, but I'd have to be real careful using it or I'd cut myself, too. Though I supposed if I did have to use it, cutting my hand would be the least of my worries.

Calling Natalie's name was out of the question, so I kept moving. She had to be in here, probably recklessly running after that guy. If she caught him, I didn't want to think what he would do to her or if that had indeed been her voice I'd heard. I didn't like her and chasing after the guy had been dumb, but I didn't want her to get hurt for being bitchy and stupid.

Dust and grime was thick on the floor, and the air smelled musty and rank. It grew colder as I eased slowly down the hallway, the sunlight not having penetrated this far into the building to warm the previous night's chill.

A soft scuffling ahead made me pause, and my pulse leapt until my heart felt it would burst out of my chest. I listened hard, focusing my eyes in the direction of the sound. Three sets of red eyes blinked back at me.

Well, rats. Like literally . . . rats, complete with beady eyes and nasty-ass long tails.

Eww.

A shiver crawled over my skin, but I shook it off, creeping forward again.

A gaping blackness appeared on my left, taking me by surprise—*hello, horror flicks!*—and I sucked in a breath before I realized it was the stairwell going up that I'd been searching for.

Fabulous.

I consoled myself with images of what I'd do to Natalie when I found her as I gingerly climbed the wooden stairs. It was an older building, to have wooden stairs, and they creaked under my feet, making me wince. *Hey, ax murderer! Here's your next victim!*

The building was only three stories high so when a landing appeared with a barely legible "2" displayed, I took a deep breath and peered into the hallway from the stairwell. When nothing jumped out and said "Boo!" I crept farther, listening for any sign Natalie or Rafael was here. *It's as if they've both disappeared into thin air*, I thought crankily, trying not to let my fear overcome sense.

A noise from above made me jerk my head up to stare at the ceiling. It sounded like a footfall. Someone was above me.

Going back into the pitch-black stairwell required an enormous amount of will. Natalie had been very right. I didn't like her. Not at all.

My hand was sweaty, gripping the shard of glass, and it turned slippery in my hand as I felt for the railing and took the stairs up one step at a time. I hugged the wall, figuring steps would be less creaky there, and I was right. I wiped my palm on my jeans, holding the glass as tightly as I dared.

The doorway to the top floor loomed. I listened, straining to hear as I pressed my back against the wall. My blood was thundering so hard in my ears, it seemed incredible that no one else could hear it. I was breathing too fast, from fear and adrenaline rather than exertion, and I made a conscious effort to breathe more slowly and deeply. *In through the nose, out through the mouth.*

A woman's muffled scream hit my ears. Shit. Natalie.

I rushed through the door and turned right, following the sound, which abruptly cut off. Oh no; what if he'd hurt or killed her?

It was dark and I felt along the wall. My hand hit a door frame, then open space as I passed by a room.

Someone grabbed my arm.

I screamed in reflex, jerking backward, but they didn't let

go. I was pulled into the room and up hard against a man. He smelled like the building.

I was too close to get much leverage, but I had my glass shard. I swung my arm and buried it into his side. There was a grunt and I was suddenly free.

Spinning around, I got two steps before he hurtled into me and we went crashing to the floor. I kicked out, but he was lying on my legs. It was dark and I couldn't see a thing, but neither could he. Squirming, I flipped over. A burning sensation in my leg told me I'd gotten hurt somehow.

He grappled with my flailing legs, and one of my kicks managed to make a solid connection. He grunted again, then growled. I felt his lunge though I couldn't see it, and flung myself to the side just as he buried the point of a knife in the floor by my head. I wouldn't have even been able to see it if the blade hadn't shimmered ever so slightly in a tiny pinpoint of light.

I didn't think; I was just fighting for my life. Grabbing the hilt, I yanked it out of the floor. My hand was slippery. Damn glass must've cut me. The guy grabbed my arm, holding the knife away from him, his breath hot against my neck and his body crushing mine. He was too strong. He squeezed, harder and harder, until I had no choice but to drop the knife.

I twisted, ramming the heel of my palm into his nose and up as hard as I could. He yelped, instinctively cringing away from me. I grabbed the knife just as he saw it and lunged toward me.

The blade sank into his arm, high on his bicep. I think he was as surprised as I was because he stopped, and both of us looked at the knife. I let go; the sickening feel of the blade going through skin and muscle was one I knew I'd never forget. He looked at me, his eyes wide and reflecting light the way a cat's might, or the way the rats' had. I got a good look at him: Rafael.

Someone called my name and we both looked toward the sound. Rafael looked back at me, then suddenly he turned and ran, disappearing into the darkness.

I was shaking and my leg hurt, but the pain was separate somehow, as if it was happening to someone else. Adrenaline and shock, I reasoned. I was alive, Rafael was gone, but I still hadn't found Natalie.

Though I really really didn't want to, I got up to search the floor. My leg hurt and so did my hand as I crept down the hallway, hoping Rafael hadn't stuck around to leap at me like a worker in a haunted house. Then I heard voices.

I stopped in my tracks, straining my ears to listen. I couldn't tell what they said or whether they were male or female. But then they stopped and I heard scuffling, then glass breaking and a man's full-throated yell. It was filled with terror and sent a shiver down my spine. The yell abruptly cut off.

I didn't know what to do. I knew I'd heard more than one voice, which meant there was someone else up here with me. But if I moved, they'd know I was here.

The sound of footsteps coming toward me made my breath freeze in my lungs. They were moving quickly. In seconds, they'd be on me.

My cell rang, the shrill noise nearly making me jump out of my skin.

Muttering curses, I fumbled for the phone, hitting the button to take the call, but I didn't speak. I waited, listening. The footsteps had stopped. They'd heard my phone, of course. They knew I was here.

I began to back up. One step, then two, until I turned and ran for the stairs, throwing caution to the wind—that ship had sailed—and rushing down the flights.

"Hello?" My voice was breathless as I spoke into my cell.

"Where the hell are you?" Parker barked.

"Looking for Natalie. But she's not here." I told him about her running off as I quickly descended the stairs to the exit. I couldn't get out of the building fast enough. Tears threatened and I blinked them back. I would not start bawling like a little girl, though that's exactly how I felt.

Parker was waiting for me outside and the moment he saw me, he grabbed me into his arms, holding me close. "You do realize this is one of the worst places to go wandering off, don't you?" he murmured into my ear.

I nodded, too overcome to speak. My arms were around his neck so tight, it was a wonder he could breathe.

"You're bleeding," he said, pulling back and looking me up and down. His face turned hard. "What happened in there?"

Haltingly, I told him about being jumped from behind. Ryker walked up halfway through my story and I had to start again. Neither man looked pleased when I was finished.

"He sliced your jeans and into your leg," Parker said, "and your hand."

"It was Rafael," Ryker said. Parker stripped off his T-shirt and wrapped it around my bleeding hand. "He took a swan dive from the third floor."

"What? What do you mean?" I asked. Parker tied the T-shirt and I winced.

"He's dead," Ryker said. "The fall killed him. Could've jumped or been pushed."

"Someone was with him," I said. "I heard them talking."

Ryker's gaze sharpened. "So there's someone else in the building?"

"Doubtful now," Parker said. "They're probably long gone."

"Oh my God, there you are!"

We turned to see Natalie sprinting toward us. She was pale and covered in grime. My relief at seeing her alive quickly faded to fury.

"Why the hell did you do that?" I snapped at her when she stopped in front of us. "You nearly got both of us killed."

"I'm so sorry," she said tearfully. "I didn't want him to get away, but he ambushed me and knocked me out. I just woke up inside that awful building, shoved in a corner."

Nice. So she'd been ambushed, but he'd tried to kill me? What'd I ever do to him? Guess the whole gentlemen-prefer-blondes thing worked for non-gentlemen as well.

"I'm calling it in," Ryker said, pulling out his cell and moving a few yards away from us.

"I need to get you to the hospital," Parker said to me. "You may need stitches. And probably a tetanus shot."

"Maybe a rabies shot, too, considering the filth in that place." I gave Natalie another dirty look, but my heart wasn't in it. Now that the adrenaline had worn off and the pain of my injuries was setting in, I just wanted to sit down. Thinking of how close a call that had been made my knees turn to rubber.

Parker's arm tightened around me. "Let's go," he said, mostly supporting my weight as we headed for the car. "Natalie, wait for Ryker."

His order stopped her in her tracks and I wanted to kiss him. The look on her face was inscrutable for a moment, and then she recovered.

"Okay. Call me and let me know how she's doing. Sage, I'm so sorry." She did sound repentant, and I relented. It had been sheer luck and whim that I'd been targeted instead of her. For all I knew, he would've gone back to finish her once he'd finished with me.

"It's fine," I lied. "I'll see you later."

Parker hustled me to his car, pulling open the passenger door, but I hesitated.

"Get in," he urged.

I glanced down at my blood-soaked jeans. "I'll ruin your seat."

He looked at me. "You're fucking kidding me, right? Like I give a shit about the seats. Get in."

"Okay, okay. Don't get cranky." I felt odd; the relief of having survived had melted into an almost jovial feeling. My emotions were giving me whiplash.

"That makes how many times I've not died?" I asked Parker as he slid behind the wheel. "I hate to pat myself on the back, but I'm turning into a total badass."

He glanced at me, grimacing. "You shouldn't have to be a badass," he said.

"C'mon," I urged. "You know you love it. I'm freakin' hot."

Parker shook his head, a smile creeping to his face in spite of himself. "You've always been freaking hot," he said. "Being a badass just means your health insurance premium is about to go up."

I grimaced. Oh yeah. Another ER visit. More stitches. My insurance company was going to put me on the hazard life insurance plan soon. That was enough to take the wind out of my euphoric sails and I settled back in the seat for the drive to Cook County General.

CHAPTER ELEVEN

I figured my mom would be with my dad, so when I got done in the ER, Parker took me back to his place for a change of clothes before going back to check on him and my mom.

"How is he?" I asked, pulling up a chair next to the bed where Mom sat. It was painful, seeing my dad so quiet and still. The machines he was hooked up to were quietly doing their jobs and I had to swallow down the tears that threatened. My mom needed me to be strong, not go on another crying jag.

"The same," she said, setting aside the magazine she'd been thumbing through. "But the doctors say he's healing well and they seem optimistic." She looked more rested today, though I could still see the worry and distress in her eyes. I felt the same. Things just weren't right without Dad.

"Did you need some food?" I asked. "Why don't you come get dinner with us?"

"That's a great idea," Parker said. "I know a quiet spot nearby."

Mom hesitated, but I took her hand. "You need to eat," I said gently. "And we need each other. Come have dinner."

She squeezed my hand and smiled. "You're right, of course. Just let me get my purse and touch up my face."

Mom always looked perfect, her skin criminally good for her age, but I nodded. She went into the bathroom and emerged a few minutes later with her hair freshly brushed and lipstick on. Even just putting on makeup was one of those daily activities that made you feel more "normal" when circumstances were anything but, and she looked more like herself.

Parker took us to a tapas place with Mediterranean cuisine. They'd given me pain medication for the cut on my leg and palm, so I had to reluctantly turn down a cocktail, but Mom didn't.

"Whatever happened to your hand?" she asked, getting a look at the white gauze.

"I broke a glass," I lied. "Klutzy move, then I went and cut myself. I'm fine, though. Just needed a few stitches."

She looked worried, so I smiled. "I'm fine; don't worry. They said I'll just have a little scar but no permanent damage." I didn't mention how very permanent the "damage" would have been if Rafael had gotten his way. Even just thinking about it sent a shudder through me, and I covered it up by taking a hurried sip of water.

"It's good you're here to take care of Sage," she said to Parker. "And myself as well. I know her father will appreciate your concern."

"Sage is very important to me," Parker said, taking my injured hand in his and carefully cradling it in such a way as to hold my hand but not cause me any pain.

My mother watched as she took a sip of the sangria she'd ordered. That crafty look was back in her eye, but I had no desire to dissuade her. If matchmaking Parker and me distracted her from worrying about Dad, then that was fine with me.

"I'm glad to hear that," she said. "You two make a very striking couple. Don't you think so, Sage?"

My face heated and I refrained from saying that anyone standing next to Parker would look good, simply because they were with him. "So what are you having for dinner?" I asked, hopefully deflecting any more pointed compliments.

"I do hope that you've been able to spend some time together, now that Sage is no longer working for you," she continued, ignoring me.

"Not as much time as I'd like," Parker said. "But I'm hoping to change that."

Warmth spread through me from the inside out and I glanced at him. He was looking at me, a softness in his eyes that I hadn't seen before, and it was several moments before I looked away again.

The smile on my mom's face was good to see, and it eased some of the worry lines around her eyes and mouth.

We ordered dinner and chatted about inconsequential things. It felt good—normal—in a way that my life hadn't been for a few weeks. Changing jobs and my evolving relationships with Parker and Ryker had taken a toll on my peace of mind.

After we dropped my mom off, I saw Parker glancing at his watch, and I thought I knew why.

"Did Ryker say what they were going to do about the ransom demand?" I asked. Ten o'clock was just three hours away.

"He was going to try to convince Natalie to get the FBI involved."

"And if she won't? Surely he won't try to handle it by himself, right?"

Parker's lips thinned. "What do you think?"

Shit.

"I need to check in, give him some kind of backup," Parker said. "If he's keeping this off the books, I don't want him to be alone."

I mulled this over as he called Ryker, unsurprised to hear that no, of course Natalie was adamant about not involving the FBI and that yes, Ryker was going to go with her to the location specified in the ransom note.

I wasn't at all happy about any of this. Natalie had somehow gotten both Ryker and Parker involved with dangerous people who she said were holding her sister hostage. The only proof we had that she was telling the truth was her word and the note that had been left.

Natalie's word didn't carry a helluva lot of weight with me.

"What if she's lying?" I blurted.

"What are you talking about?"

"What if Jessie hasn't disappeared and Natalie is playing you both?"

Parker was shaking his head. "She wouldn't do that. She has no reason to."

"Her reason could simply be that she wants you two back in her life," I said.

"So she'd lie about her sister being in danger?" Parker scoffed. "No. That's ridiculous."

Fine. Obviously, I was alone in my suspicions. "Are you absolutely sure you want to risk life and limb for her?" I asked, trying a different tack.

Parker shot me a look. "I'm not doing anything for

her. I'm doing it for Ryker. And because it's the right thing to do."

"It's not the right thing," I argued. "The right thing would be for you and Ryker to turn all this over to the FBI."

"And leave Jessie or Natalie to be killed because we didn't follow instructions and take care of it ourselves?"

"You don't know that's what will happen."

"And if it does, it'll forever be on my conscience."

Parker pulled the car over in front of his building and stopped. "Go inside," he said, "and stay. I'll be back as soon as we're done."

"Just answer me this," I said. "If it wasn't Natalie who was in danger, would you still be so hell-bent on playing the hero and throwing yourself in harm's way?"

"I threw myself in harm's way for you," he countered.

"Considering what you said you feel for me, that doesn't make me feel any better."

"I'm not still in love with Natalie, Sage. Why won't you believe that?"

I wanted to, I really did. But I just couldn't trust his feelings. What if the moment I gave in, the moment I said yes, I loved him, too—what if that was when he decided I wasn't what he wanted after all? That the wanting had been the best part?

"Just go," I said, opening my car door.

"Sage, wait—"

But I was already gone, heading inside. I didn't look back, but heard him drive off. That's when I turned around, staring after his receding taillights.

* * *

I stayed up as late as I could, but the pain meds got to me and when I woke in the morning, it was to the buzzing of my cell phone. Carrie, calling from the office. I glanced over in Parker's bed and saw blond hair.

That made it two days in a row I'd woken up next to Natalie. There wasn't going to be a third.

"You'd better get down here," Carrie said, and the urgency in her voice jerked my attention away from Natalie.

"Why? What's wrong?"

"The cops are here. They have a warrant to search the offices."

* * *

By the time I arrived, the police were tearing the office apart. I watched in horror as men carried box after box of files by me on their way out of the building. Rushing upstairs, I saw Carrie and Charlie standing in the middle of the chaos.

"What's going on?" I asked.

Wordlessly, Charlie handed me a sheaf of papers. I scanned through them.

"Collusion? What the hell?" I looked at Charlie. "They're looking for evidence of collusion between"—I glanced back at the papers—"between us, Johnson & Halloway, M&R Trading, and Sikes? That's absurd." It was every liquor transportation company I'd ever heard of growing up in the area.

"Not absurd, Ms. Muccino." A plainclothes cop spoke from behind me and I turned. "We have reasonable cause to justify this warrant. I suggest you contact your attorney." With that, he gestured to the few remaining officers who followed him to the elevator.

I glanced around at the havoc they'd left in their wake. Employees stood or sat silently, their expressions ranging from confused to scared to resigned. Then I realized...they were all looking at me. Not Charlie. Me. I needed to say something. They were waiting for the boss to reassure them. And since the boss wasn't here, I was next in line.

"Everyone," I began, not even knowing what I was going to say. "First, thank you for maintaining your professionalism during today's events. I appreciate that." I cleared my throat, tightening my sweaty palms into fists. What would I want to hear if I was them? "Second... I can assure you that this company has not broken the law, regardless of what the police say. And last, you can rest assured that your job is safe and that we will fight this. Now please, let's get back to work. Thank you."

People began cleaning and the low hum of conversation picked up. Papers had been scattered and drawers had been pulled out. I overheard someone saying not-very-nice things about cops and their search etiquette, which I rather agreed with.

"Nice job," Charlie said quietly. "Now let's go talk."

I followed him into his office and he shut the door behind us. Collapsing into a chair, I vented my frustration.

"What the hell was this all about?" I asked. "I bet you anything that Shea guy is behind it. Too much crap has happened in the past few days to point to anyone besides him. Did the cops even mention anything about Gary getting attacked the other night and our offices being broken into?"

"No, they didn't, but that's not what I want to talk about," he said, sitting in the chair behind his desk. Something in his tone made me halt my fuming tirade.

"What?" I asked. "Charlie, what is it?"

He didn't answer. He just looked at me. And he looked... tired.

"Oh no," I said, my anger melting into dismay. "Please tell me I didn't just lie to our employees. Tell me this company didn't participate in collusion."

"I wish I could, sweetheart." Charlie heaved a sigh.

I was stunned. "How?" How had my father broken the law? And why?

"It goes back over a decade," he began.

"We've been colluding for that long with these people?" I interrupted.

"No, no. I meant, what happened was over a decade ago," he clarified. "That Leo Shea business. He came on the scene nearly fifteen years ago, over on the north side."

"And he started cutting in on Dad's territory," I said, remembering the files Parker and I had found earlier in the basement. "I read the file."

"Then you know. Shea was intimidating people, threatening them. There were a few who disappeared like Hoffa, never to be heard from again. Your dad was the only one who didn't cave to the pressure. We lost one of our best security men. Gunned down by Shea's people. Your dad, he was devastated. Tony had been a personal friend of your father's since way back in school. Most people"—Charlie shook his head—"most people would've rolled over at that point. But not your dad.

"He went after Shea. The cops wouldn't do anything; too many of them were paid off, so somehow we got somebody on the inside, feeding us intel. I didn't know how your dad did it and I didn't ask. But we got the info and we were able to convince the other suppliers to price match with us to stop Shea in his tracks."

I wasn't surprised that losing a friend would make my father fight back. That's the kind of man he was. He couldn't be intimidated because he'd not only hit back, he'd hit back harder. And while he may have been on the side of the angels, he'd been on the wrong side of the law.

"Okay, so in other words, while it may have been justified

and the only way to put Shea in his place, technically we still broke the law."

"Not you, sweetheart. Me and your dad."

"I realize you two personally may have made those decisions," I said, "but the warrant lists the company, and I'm part owner of the company. So it's not just you two who'll take the fall. Steven Shea is getting back at us over Leo's death. He wants to kill me, kill Dad, and destroy the company. So far, he's making headway on all those objectives."

We both sat in silent contemplation for a moment. I was deep in thought. Dad wasn't available for me to ask for advice. My gut twisted. I had to save the company. I didn't want him to come out of the coma only to see that I'd lost his company. And he *would* come out of the coma.

Finally, Charlie asked, "So what do you want to do, kiddo?"

"Call the lawyers," I said. "Get them in here and start talking strategy. I don't know what files they got or what evidence they may have. Prepare for the worst."

"What about you?"

"I'm going to pay a visit to Steven Shea."

* * *

The offices for SLS Enterprises were north of downtown. With traffic, it took me a while to get there, which was fine with me. I was nervous and had dressed carefully, opting for a black pencil skirt that hit just below my knees and hugged my hips, along with a white silk blouse. I'd left the top two buttons of the blouse undone and tied a scarf around my neck to accessorize. With my hair loosely pulled back and in two-inch heels, I'd hoped to strike the right note of professional yet still feminine. To end this war with Shea, I needed all the weapons in my arsenal.

"I don't like the idea of you walking in to the lion's den like this," Charlie had cautioned me.

"He's not going to kill me in the middle of his office," I'd reasoned. At least, I hoped he wouldn't.

The office building was newer, with five floors and manicured landscaping out front. The company's name and logo were etched in a granite slab artfully placed amidst a bed of marigolds in full bloom.

You'd never guess that the man who ran it had tried to kill me.

I tucked my black clutch bag underneath my arm as I entered the lobby. It was early evening, but I was betting Shea was still there.

A security guard stood behind a counter to my left and a woman sat behind a reception desk straight ahead. I approached the security guard, who asked for my ID, dutifully writing down my name before handing it back, then I headed for the woman.

"Sage Muccino, here to see Steven Shea," I said to her.

"Do you have an appointment?"

"No, I don't."

"Mr. Shea is very busy and doesn't take walk-in visitors—"

"I'm quite sure he'll see me," I interrupted. I tapped her phone with a fingernail. "Just give him a call and tell him I'm here."

She gave me a dirty look, but I just smiled serenely and waited. Finally, she jabbed a button on her phone and spoke into her headset.

"A Sage Muccino is here to see Mr. Shea. She doesn't have an appointment. I told her he won't—" She stopped, glanced up at me, then back down, frowning. "Yes. I'll do that." She ended the call. "Mr. Shea will see you," she said. "Fifth floor."

"Thank you."

I headed for the elevator, taking a deep breath as it took me to the top floor and the doors slid open.

I stepped out into an open floor plan, with huge half-circle windows and tall ceilings. Tasteful décor in modern lines of chrome with bold colors adorned the space, and the floor was a beautiful hardwood in deep mahogany. A man sat behind an imposing desk placed in front of the windows. He stood as I walked toward him, my heels clacking on the floor.

Steven Shea wasn't very tall. With my heels, we were the same height. He was thin and well-built, with dark hair meticulously coiffed and styled. If I'd seen him on the street, I might glance at him twice, as he was striking. He smiled, displaying a perfect set of even, white teeth.

"Miss Muccino," he said. "To what do I owe the unexpected pleasure?"

I sat down in one of the two leather armchairs in front of his desk and crossed my legs. "I think we both know why I'm here, Steven," I said coolly.

He took his seat again, leaning back and steepling his fingers underneath his chin as he surveyed me.

"Giving up already?" he asked. "I didn't expect that, I have to admit. Maybe it's because you're a woman."

His barb stung, but I kept my face expressionless. "No one said I'm giving up. I'm here to make you see sense and stop what you're doing."

Steven's pseudo-smile became a gloating smirk. "And what am I doing, pray tell?" He sat back in his chair, relaxed and smug.

"Should I begin where you tried to have me and my father killed? Or when you broke into our offices? Or with the investigation into allegedly illegal activities from over a decade ago?"

"That is a long list of very serious accusations," he said with a mocking frown. "And I suppose you have evidence of my involvement in all of that?"

"We both know who's responsible," I said. Tension had my body strung as tight as a wire, but I struggled to keep up my façade of indifference. "Your father is dead. Mine, nearly so. Let's let bygones be bygones, Steven. This doesn't have to become a war between us."

He leaned forward suddenly, surprising me, and I jumped.

"Of course it does." His eyes were intense and the curving sneer on his lips looked anything but friendly and logical. "It's much more fun that way."

"This isn't fun," I retorted.

"Of course it is! And I just *love* that you came here today. Aren't you the brave and plucky one?" He laughed.

"This is a business meeting," I gritted out, unwilling to admit how much he was unnerving me.

"Yes, of course it is," he said, waving a hand. "By all means, conduct your business. I'm all ears."

I took a deep breath, trying to steady myself. It was hard to look into his eyes as he stared at me. Something wasn't quite right. His eyes looked…dead inside. A shiver crept down my spine.

"This investigation will cost us both in time and money," I said. "Because if they crawl into my books, I'm pointing them in your direction. Neither of us can afford the business we will lose, especially once word gets out that you're accusing us of collusion. There are enough skeletons in your closet to keep the FBI busy for years."

"On the contrary, my business will do just fine," he said. "Your customers will flee to me as an honest businessman, while the feds drag you through the courts. You may prove your innocence, but by then your customers will be gone."

He grinned. "Bye bye, trust fund. You'll have to actually work for a living, Sage."

"I *have* been working for a living," I fired back. "What about you? Aren't you new to daddy's business? Spending his hard-earned money while he worked to keep up with your booze and drug habits?" Those last two parts were a shot in the dark, but I didn't think I was too far off.

Suddenly, a knife appeared in Steven's hand. It was pointed right at me, clutched in his hand as his elbow rested on the surface of the desk. My breath caught and I shut up.

"Neat trick, right?" he asked. "It took me a while to get the hang of it. There's this sheath on my arm." He casually pushed back the sleeve of his jacket to show me. "And the dagger sits right there. But then when I do this," he did something with his arm, "it springs forward into my hand. Isn't that something?" The knife moved fast and he caught it just as quick. "Of course, it took some time to get it right. If I miss catching it... well, it just flies off at whatever is in front of me. Put a few holes in the Sheetrock, I'm sorry to say."

He laughed and I swallowed, my eyes on the knife as he continued to play with it, the point always directed at me. If he slipped, it would come flying right at me. My palms began to sweat.

"People know I'm here," I said. "If something happens to me, they'll come looking for you."

"Perhaps they would," he replied. "But then... you'd still be dead, wouldn't you." He smiled again.

I don't know if it was his smile or what, but an almost sixth sense had me throwing myself out of the chair just as the knife flew from its sheath. The point buried itself in the soft leather of the chair, right where my chest had just been.

"Oops," he said. "Missed."

"You're insane," I gasped, scrambling to my feet.

"I prefer to call myself a creative thinker."

Rounding the desk, he pulled the knife from the chair. "I'll give you a head start," he said, motioning toward the door to his office. "But fair warning: I don't play by the rules."

There was a breathless moment as we stared at each other. He wasn't smiling any longer. In fact, he looked downright deadly. Adrenaline rushed through my veins and I bolted for the door, slamming my palm against the wood and shoving it open.

"Run, run, little Sage! But wherever will you go?"

His taunt followed me as I raced into the hallway, only to have everything go dark.

The lights were out. He'd turned them off. Now I was as blind as a bat, blinking furiously to try to get my eyes to adjust. I kept going, remembering the length of the hallway from before the light had gone.

Using the elevator seemed a bad idea—like a cage just waiting for me to enter its gaping maw—so I felt for the stairwell door I remembered being at the very end of the hall.

"Little Sage, Little Sage, come out come out wherever you are…" Steven's singsong taunt echoed around me, maybe coming through intercom speakers, I wasn't sure.

He was crazy. Certifiably insane. We were in his *office building*, for crying out loud. There were people around… weren't there?

My fingers found the latch on the door and I pushed it open. The red glow of the Exit sign lit the way and I thanked all the government regulation and bureaucracy that mandated stuff like that as I flung myself down the stairs.

I hit the door at the bottom with speed and it crashed open, spilling me out into the cool evening air. I gulped in breaths, shaking, more rattled by Steven than I wanted to admit. I hurried through the shadowed parking lot, looking back at the innocuous looking building... and ran straight into someone.

A scream clawed its way up my throat and I would have fallen backward on my ass if hands hadn't shot out to grip my arms, holding me steady.

"What the hell are you doing here?" Ryker asked.

My heart was hammering and I was breathing too fast. It took me a second to process what he'd said. "I came to see Steven Shea."

"The man who wants to kill you." The tone of his voice clearly said what he thought of my plan.

"I'd hoped he'd be reasonable," I said with a nervous shrug. "But... uh... he's not so much."

"Shea is a sociopath," Ryker bit out. "And you coming to see him—alone—the height of idiocy."

I stiffened, immediately angry. But then the fear I'd just gone through and everything else that had happened the past few days came crashing down on me, and I burst into tears.

Ryker cursed and dragged me into his arms. "Christ, I'm sorry," he said, holding me close. I buried my face against his shoulder, sobbing. "I was frantic, on my way here, afraid Shea would do something stupid." His hold tightened. "I'm just glad you're okay."

I sniffled, gulping down tears. "H-how'd you know I was h-here?"

He kept an arm around me as we headed toward his motorcycle. "Charlie," he said. "He thought it was a bad idea, too, and got nervous. Thought sending a cop over to get you would be best."

Shrugging out of his leather jacket, he swung it over my shoulders and I pushed my arms into the too-long sleeves.

He held on to the front lapels, pulling me closer until I tipped my head back to look at him.

A grimace creased his brow as he saw my tear-stained face. "What happened in there?"

Haltingly, I told him, a shudder running through me when I got to the part about the knife. Ryker's hands gripped the leather of his jacket, tightening into fists as I finished the story.

"He's a fucking lunatic," he growled. "I should go arrest him now for threatening assault."

"No, don't," I said. "It'll just cause more trouble and he'd be out in hours anyway. I just want to go home." The thought of going back to Parker's—and Natalie being there—was too much for me. "Please take me home." I'd driven myself here in a company car but was more than willing to let Schultz retrieve it in the morning. I was shaking so badly, I doubted my ability to even drive at the moment.

Ryker looked at my face and must have read my desperation because he sighed and gave in without a fight. "All right."

We climbed onto the motorcycle. I wrapped my arms around his torso and held on tight as we roared off into the night.

CHAPTER TWELVE

Carrie had arranged for a new mattress to be delivered for my bed, and a darn good one at that. I thanked the gods above for having a secretary at the company who knew everything about everyone and how to get things done. Ryker helped me put on some new sheets and a blanket. That would do for now.

"How did things go last night?" I asked. "Wasn't Natalie supposed to take the money to them?"

"She did. She followed their instructions and they grabbed the money without us being able to catch them at it."

"You didn't catch them?" I asked, too late hearing the *Really?* in my voice. Ryker's jaw tightened.

"They were armed and took out the drop location," he said. "We split as the emergency personnel were being dispatched."

I shook my head. "What does that mean, 'took out the drop location'? Translation, please."

"It burned to the ground."

Oh. Okay, now I felt kinda bad for pre-judging their competence. "Is everyone okay?" I asked.

"Yeah. But it means we're no closer to finding Jessie."

"I'm sorry," I said. Poor Jessie. "So Natalie lost Parker's ten thousand dollars and has nothing to show for it?"

Ryker flinched. "Pretty much," he said.

"Supposedly, neither one of you trust her," I said, "yet you're both dancing to her tune. Why?"

"I wouldn't characterize it as 'dancing to her tune,'" he replied. "There's Jessie to consider and Natalie is our only link to helping Jessie."

I stood with my arms crossed, staring at him, looking probably for all the world like a pouting child, but I couldn't stop. Neither of them would listen to me about Natalie; both of them seemed hell-bent on following the path she was laying out for them no matter what common sense said to do. And the only reason I could think of as to why...was that neither man was really over Natalie, no matter what they said to the contrary. Actions spoke louder than words, and ten thousand dollars was a helluva statement.

I collapsed onto the bed, dejected and beaten down. I felt foolish. Going tonight to see Shea by myself had been a dumb move, though at least now I knew he wouldn't listen to reason.

"You okay?" Ryker asked, handing me a glass of wine he must've found in the fridge.

I sat up on the bed, taking it from him and swallowing a too-large gulp. "Yeah. I'm fine. Just tired. It's been a hell of a week."

"How are your stitches doing? Need some medicine?"

I nodded and he disappeared into my bathroom, coming back with the prescription bottle. It would help me sleep, which was just what I needed. I was so tired even my bones felt exhausted.

"I ordered some pizza, too," he said. "I don't know about you, but I'm starving."

As if on cue, my stomach growled, prompting a chuff of laughter from him and an embarrassed blush to my cheeks. I couldn't remember when I'd eaten last.

It should've been awkward, eating pizza on my couch with Ryker—now officially an ex—but it wasn't. There was a familiarity between us that was comfortable, but not overtly sexual. I didn't see him *that* way any longer, though I could still appreciate the view.

An hour later, we were stuffed and lethargic, lazing on the couch while watching reruns of *Supernatural*. I could pretend that Shea wasn't trying to kill me and destroy my father's business; Ryker could pretend his ex wasn't back from the dead with inscrutable intentions.

"You should probably go," I said when the latest episode's ending credits rolled, prodding his thigh with my toe. "It's late. McClane's gonna have to pee."

"He's already gone in the house, I'm sure," Ryker said, leaning over to scoop up the last slice of cold pizza. "He throws a temper tantrum if I'm gone a lot, because he knows it ticks me off."

Why did people have dogs again? I couldn't understand it.

"You should still go." Our eyes met. "I'll be fine," I said, knowing why he was sticking around. I wasn't an idiot.

"The lock on your door wouldn't keep out McClane," Ryker said. "Much less someone like Shea."

"I don't want a babysitter," I said. *Especially Ryker.* It was one thing for us to be friendly exes, but another for him to stay the night when both of us were fully aware that Parker was the one who'd decided to pull bodyguard duty. And he was nowhere around.

"Take this then," Ryker said, handing me his handgun. "You do know how to use one of these, right?"

"Duh, yeah, of course," I said. I handled it gingerly. Yeah, in theory I knew how to use one, but they still made me uneasy.

"And keep your cell right by you," he said. "Stick a chair under the door when I leave and don't open it for anyone you don't know. I don't care if they say they're from Publisher's Fucking Clearinghouse."

"Got it." I suppressed a smile at his vehemence, feeling warm inside at the obvious signs that he cared what happened to me. I was glad our breaking up hadn't cost us everything.

I showed him to the door and impulsively gave him a hug. "Thanks," I whispered. "Thanks for caring."

"Of course I care," he said gruffly. "Just because we're not sleeping together doesn't mean I stopped caring."

We were too close and for a moment I was reminded of that strong chemistry between us, but I stepped back before it became something awkward.

"I'll talk to you tomorrow," I called after him, watching as he disappeared down the hallway and through the stairwell door.

I closed and locked my door with a sigh. Oh, what I wouldn't give for a little canine companionship tonight, eat my words though I must. McClane had saved me once before and I had no doubt his ears would hear much more acutely than mine to sound the alarm if someone tried to break into the apartment.

But I didn't have McClane. All I had was me...and Ryker's gun. As for my bodyguard...

Should I call Parker? I hadn't seen him in the apartment

when I'd left this morning and hadn't heard from him. Where was he? Was he with Natalie? Were they even now back at his apartment? Alone?

But no, Parker said he didn't feel like that about Natalie. My head told me to hold on to that while the ache in my gut said that it wasn't so easy to cast aside a woman with whom he had a history.

I went to bed staring at my phone and willing it to ring... but it remained stubbornly silent.

* * *

I blinked blearily and looked at the clock when I woke the next morning. It was after nine, but since it had been well into the wee hours of the morning before I'd fallen asleep, it felt like the crack of dawn.

I had three missed calls on my cell, all from Megan. But before I could listen to her voice mail, the phone rang in my hand. She was calling again.

"Oh my God, you gotta tell me the dirt," she hissed when I answered. "What happened?"

I blinked in confusion, rubbing my eyes. "What are you talking about?"

"You mean you don't know?"

"Know what?"

"Parker quit."

My jaw dropped. I couldn't speak.

"Are you there? Did you hear me? I said Parker—"

"I heard you," I interrupted. "But-but that's impossible. He loves his job. He's good at his job. Why would he suddenly up and quit?"

"I have no idea but it's all anyone's talking about over here. I thought *you* would know."

"I haven't seen him," I said, my mind spinning in shock.

"He left instructions to clean out his office," Megan continued. "And we're supposed to send his things to his new office."

"New office? So he has a new job?"

"Guess so."

"Where?"

"Someplace called SLS Enterprises."

And now my shock turned to full-blown panic. Parker was going to work for Steven Shea? This was bizarre, incomprehensible. I had to find him. Now.

"I gotta go," I blurted, and ended the call. I immediately tried Parker's number, but he didn't pick up and the voice mailbox said it was full. "Shit!" I exploded.

I took a record-breaking fast shower and hit the door running, catching the bus just as it was pulling away. Collapsing breathless into a seat, I checked my phone again.

No missed calls. No texts. No messages. Which made *no* sense.

Parker had been worried for my safety yesterday...and today he was MIA.

The doorman knew me on sight and let me in to Parker's building. Although I'd been remiss in "remembering" to return my key to his apartment, I didn't use it. I knocked politely instead. Okay, maybe not politely. I may have pounded on the door. Several times. Finally, it opened.

And I got another shock. My second of the day.

Natalie stood there, again wearing Parker's shirt and nothing else.

"Oh, it's you," she said with a slight sneer of distaste. "What do you want?"

"I'm looking for Parker," I said stiffly.

"He's at work," she said with a shrug of one delicate

shoulder. "I wouldn't go there, though, if I were you. The boss doesn't like you much, and I don't think Parker's looking for a new secretary."

"Executive Administrative Assistant," I ground out.

"Whatever. And incidentally"—she leaned closer—"he's not looking for a girlfriend anymore either."

My blood ran cold. "What are you talking about?"

"Parker and I...rekindled the flames, so to speak," she said, her lips twisting into a smile. "I must say, it's like not a single day has passed. We connect just as well now as we always did."

"You're lying." The words burst out of me, but I knew in my bones I had to be right. Parker wouldn't do that to me.

"It's sad, how women never want to believe the truth, even when it's staring them in the face. You are, or were, his *secretary*. He deserves better than a cliché romance."

I felt sick to my stomach and clenched my hands into fists so I wouldn't attack her, though I desperately wanted to tear the smile from her face...with my fingernails.

It couldn't be true. The problem was, she didn't *look* like she was lying, not standing there in his shirt, in his apartment, smelling like...his cologne.

Bile rose in my throat and I swallowed it down. Tears threatened but I blinked them back. I absolutely would *not* cry, especially not in front of Natalie.

"Parker will tell me the truth," I managed. My insides felt like I was being torn into a million pieces. "He wouldn't lie to me, whereas everything that comes out of your mouth is a lie."

I had to get out of there. I couldn't stand seeing her like that, looking at me with both pity and triumph in her eyes.

Spinning around, I made a beeline for the elevator, punching a finger blindly at the button because at this point I could no longer hold back the tears. They flowed unchecked down my cheeks and I just wanted to get out of there before anyone saw.

The elevator doors opened and I rushed inside...straight into Parker.

"What the hell?" I burst out, pushing him away with one hand and swiping at my face with the other. Was it too much to ask of the universe that I could've gotten out of here *without* him seeing me like this? And to make matters even better, Natalie still stood at the door, watching.

"Sage, what are you doing here?" Parker asked, reaching out to steady me.

"Tell me the truth," I said, beyond caring that we had an audience. "Are you and Natalie back together?" Pain streaked my voice and I knew my heart was in my eyes, pleading with him to contradict me and tell me no, of course he wouldn't be with her. That he loved *me*.

Parker's face took on that expressionless one I knew so well from too many weeks and months working for him, and my heart squeezed inside my chest.

"We have a history," he said. "You knew that."

"You told me you were over her," I said. "And I *believed* you."

"I'm sorry—" he began.

"You're *sorry*?" I interrupted, anger rising to swallow the hurt burning inside my chest. "I was right not to trust you, not to trust what you said you felt for me. You would've just tossed me aside. *Again*." I was seething now, which was way better than giving in to the heartbreak waiting to split me apart.

"And to add insult to injury, you're working for Shea," I spat. "Are you out of your mind?"

"His company didn't break the law," Parker said, his eyes

narrowing. "I've seen with my own eyes evidence of collusion by your father's company."

"You know why he had to do that. Leo was threatening people's lives! It wasn't like my dad was doing that just to get ahead."

"It was unethical and illegal," Parker said.

"So your solution was to go work for him?"

Parker's eyes were fathomless, his voice even. "He made a very persuasive argument for my employment."

"Enough," I said, pushing past him into the elevator. "I've had enough." I punched the button for the lobby. "You're a fickle bastard, Parker, always wanting what's just out of reach. Stay away from me, and stay away from my company." The door slid shut between us.

I sagged against the wall of the elevator. I felt like I'd been hit by a truck. Everything I'd been telling myself about why I shouldn't give in to Parker was true. Every warning signal inside my head had been proven right. I should feel vindicated. I'd been right to hold out.

So why did I feel like my soul had broken?

The ride home in the taxi was a blur. I tossed a twenty at the cab driver and hurried inside, desperate to get to my apartment and have my private breakdown. Natalie had gotten exactly what she'd wanted: Parker.

A sob escaped and I clapped a hand over my mouth as I unlocked my apartment door and pushed it closed behind me. The ache inside my chest spread like tentacles until it felt like every part of me hurt. I didn't have to stand any longer and pretend, so I sank to the floor, my purse falling unheeded to the side.

I buried my face in my hands as deep, wrenching sobs tore from me. I'd trusted him. I'd trusted Parker that Natalie no longer held the same appeal she once had. Though physically I'd kept him at arm's length, I hadn't on the inside. I'd let myself think there was a future for us, that I might've found the man for me.

I just couldn't understand why he'd make such an about-face. Parker wasn't that much of a flake, not even in his relationships. He was acting more like a jerk with me than with any other woman I'd seen him with, but he'd professed to feeling more for me than for anyone else. So why would he just ditch everything without any kind of explanation?

Now that I'd gotten past the shock of it, my mind was twisting in confusion, trying to make sense of his actions. It was easier to believe he was an asshole, dumping me and taking up again with Natalie, but it just didn't ring true. But try as I might, I couldn't think of another reason other than the one he'd said.

I don't know how long I sat there, feeling sorry for myself, before I finally pulled myself together. You can only cry for so long before the headache becomes unbearable and the nausea in your stomach threatens to overwhelm you.

Even when your dreams fall apart, you still have to go to work.

I was a woman in sole charge of a multimillion dollar company, and my father was counting on me to keep it going. Even if he was in a coma, I wasn't about to disappoint him when he woke up…and he *would* wake up.

It's amazing what a change of clothes can do for your self-esteem. I pulled my hair up into a French twist, and wore a high-neck sleeveless silk blouse tucked into a pair of black slacks. The blouse had a thin gray pinstripe interwoven with a pink floral pattern, so I added a pink belt and pink sparkly earrings. Shrugging into a black blazer, I felt more like the businesswoman I was supposed to be rather than the ex-secretary who'd just gotten dumped. Again.

When I made it to the office, I had a surprise. Megan was waiting for me by the door, holding a grande Starbucks cup and a little brown bag.

"I thought you could use a donut and caffeine," she said.

I gave her a tight hug. I really missed seeing her every day. "You're a lifesaver," I said, heading inside. "I've had neither one yet today." Megan followed me into the elevator.

"Figured as much."

"Aren't you supposed to be at work?" I asked, taking a big bite of the cinnamon sugar cake donut. The elevator dinged and I led her toward my office.

"I'm taking a break," she said with a shrug. She took a seat in one of the chairs in front of my desk.

I glanced up from sucking down way too big a gulp of caramel latte. "Is this a pity coffee?"

"It's a you've-got-a-friend coffee," she said.

I swallowed, the latte swirling uneasily in my stomach. "What kind of offer did they make him? It had to be astronomical. He didn't need money. His job at KLP made him millions."

My phone buzzed, interrupting me, and I hit the button to hear Carrie on the speaker. "Yeah?"

"Something bizarre just happened," she said.

"What?"

"The lawyers just called. The inquiry has been put on hold indefinitely as they found no merit to continue at this time."

Relief unknotted my stomach. "Seriously? This isn't just a bad joke?"

"Seriously. They're sending over e-mail confirmation now. I'll forward it to you." She paused. "Looks like we dodged a bullet somehow."

I shut off the intercom, looking at Megan with what I

knew had to be an openmouthed expression of shock on my face.

"I didn't expect that," I said. "That's...fantastic news. That was a criminal inquiry brought against us, orchestrated by that asshole Parker went to work for. Which is yet another reason I just don't get why he'd do that."

Megan looked at me as if I'd grown two heads. "You're not serious, are you?"

Her reaction took me back. "Serious about what?"

"You really haven't figured it out?"

I just stared at her, the sick feeling in my stomach confirming that a shot of caffeine-loaded milk had been a bad idea.

"He took that job because of *you*, Sage. He had to have. It's obvious now. The inquiry was dropped? The *criminal* one where someone here might've gone to jail or you'd lose your business?"

My mouth was hanging open and I closed it with a snap. Megan just sat there, waiting for me to say something, a grim expression on her face.

"That-that's not possible," I stammered. "Parker wouldn't do that. He wouldn't toss aside his whole career for me. And why would Shea want him, anyway?"

"Oh, gee," Megan said, rolling her eyes. "Why in the world would he want the best investment banker in town, who also happens to be the same guy who handles all *this* company's assets and holdings? It's a real mystery."

"But—" I cut myself off as the pieces fell into place— how *off* Parker's sudden betrayal had seemed, coming out of left field the way it had. Even if Megan was right and Parker's sudden job switch was a martyr's sacrifice on my behalf, that didn't explain why he'd hooked up with Natalie again.

"You take your time," Megan said as she rose, glancing at her watch. "I've got to get back to work."

"Thanks for coming by," I said as she opened the door. Carrie was waiting on the other side, hand poised to knock.

"No problem. Talk soon." Megan flicked a finger wave and was gone as Carrie stepped inside.

"Are we sure this has really gone away?" I asked, shoving thoughts of Parker to the back of my mind. I had to deal with the business first. Personal matters could come later.

"I set up a two o'clock with our attorneys," Carrie replied. "You can all go over it then. I'm sure they'll have paperwork for you to sign and go over in your father's stead."

"Has Mom called?"

She nodded. "Condition still the same, but the doctors say he's healing really well. They might be able to try and bring him out of the coma by next week."

My heart leapt. Finally. Some good news.

"Thanks," I said.

Carrie motioned to a stack of files on my desk. "Those reports need to be looked over and you have a four o'clock with Jane regarding seasonal inventory and a five o'clock weekly managers' meeting."

"Got it."

But Carrie was right and the lawyers confirmed it. The lawsuit had miraculously gone away. I didn't know who Shea had paid off to do what he'd done, but I knew in some way Parker had to be a part of it, just like Megan had said. The timing was too coincidental and there was no way he'd just up and quit his job without a very good reason.

I had to talk to him.

The thought kept reverberating in the back of my mind as I sat through the meetings. I had to do double-duty as both my dad and Charlie, as the latter was keeping the former company at the hospital. For someone who'd just started officially working there—even as the boss's daughter—it was a formidable challenge.

Finally, I was free. I had a pounding headache and lunch had been a long time ago, but I still asked Schultz to drive me over to SLS Enterprises. My stomach churned at the thought of seeing Steven the psycho again, but I had a feeling Parker would still be there. At least, I hoped he would be. I didn't think I could face showing up at his apartment again and seeing him with Natalie. Not like that.

Jealousy twisted inside, along with the sick sensation in my gut that hadn't gone away all day. My anger had faded as I tried to make sense of what he'd done and what had happened today. What didn't I know?

I had Shultz drive through the darkened parking lot as I searched the shadows for Parker's car. No way did I want Steven to see me and would definitely avoid that at all costs, but I could wait by Parker's car until he showed.

"Please still be here, please still be here," I muttered over and over under my breath. Wait...there. I checked the plates. Yep, that was his all right. "I see it," I said to Schultz. He dropped me off by Parker's car to wait and he parked several rows over, out of sight. I wanted privacy and the element of surprise.

I leaned against the spotless driver's side door and waited. It was getting late. Surely he'd leave soon. I wasn't sure what I'd say, but I hoped something would come to me.

Unfortunately, the butterflies in my stomach short-circuited my brain, because when he finally emerged about fifteen minutes later I still hadn't come up with a good opening line.

I watched him walk toward his car, his attention on the

phone in one hand. In his other he carried his briefcase. God, he looked good.

Pushing myself away from the car, I lifted my chin and squared my shoulders. I didn't want to get emotional.

Parker spotted me when he was about ten feet away. Surprise flashed across his face, quickly replaced by an expression I knew well. He was pissed.

"What are you doing here?" he asked when he was close.

"I needed to talk to you," I replied. I hated that he was angry, but so was I.

"So you came here? You could've met me at my apartment."

"And see Natalie wearing your shirt again?" I shot back before I thought about it. "No thanks."

His lips pressed together, his blue eyes hard to read in the dim light. A breeze ruffled his hair and I caught a hint of his cologne. The smell hit me like a fist in my gut, taking my breath away.

"The investigation went away," I blurted, wanting to get this over with and get away as soon as possible. "I find that and your sudden change of employment highly coincidental. Not to mention that you don't seem concerned that Shea's about to off me anymore."

Parker said nothing.

"So what was the deal you made?" I asked, pressing on. "Because that's what it was, right? Shea never wanted to put my dad's company out of business. He wanted you."

"Let it go, Sage."

His non-confirmation only infuriated me more. "No, I'm not going to *let it go*," I retorted. "Your job was your life. I know how hard you worked to get there. Nothing is worth you giving that up—"

"You are."

I stopped speaking, the words cut off in my throat. For a moment, I wasn't sure I'd heard him correctly.

"You and I both know your dad is guilty," he said. "If they investigate, all that will come out. He'll go to jail and the fine they levy on him will probably put you out of business. This alleviates all of that . . . with some addendums I insisted on."

Addendums? I was confused for a moment, then realized. He'd bargained for my safety as well. I swallowed.

"You think it's acceptable, on any level, for you to trade your life for mine?"

Parker didn't reply to my question, not that I expected a response.

"It's not okay," I said. "And I'm not going to let you do it."

"You don't have a choice." His voice was flat, that same tone he used when arguing was a very bad idea.

"So you're just taking my decision away from me? Just like that?"

His hand closed around my upper arm, hauling me toward him. "Do you think I'd do this if there was any other way?" he hissed. "I may have lost you, but at least you're still alive. And so is your business."

Abruptly, he let me go. "Now go on and get out of here," he ordered. "I don't want you anywhere near Shea." He unlocked his door and tossed his briefcase inside.

"Wait," I said, grabbing on to the door as he slid into the seat. "Are we over, Parker? Is this it for us?" I couldn't help asking. Part of me still hoped, no matter how much I'd been hurt.

Parker's gaze drank me in, lingering on my face before he met my eyes. It took him a moment to answer. "Part of the deal," he said, his voice a harsh rasp of sound. "A part

I couldn't renegotiate. Too much of a 'conflict of interest.' "
The Adam's apple in his throat moved as he swallowed.
"Now go. Take care of yourself."

I was too numb to protest, pain held in check by sheer force
of will. Mutely, I took a few steps back so he could close his
door. I watched his car back out of the space and drive away,
his taillights blurring as tears swam in my vision.

I didn't know what to do or how to feel. Parker had
done the unthinkable. I couldn't even process it as I walked
numbly back to Schultz and climbed into the back of my
family's car. Schultz must have known by the look on my
face that things hadn't gone well.

He drove me home and I thanked him as I got out of the
car and went in to my apartment. I sat on my couch, staring
into space and thinking. I don't know how much time passed
before I was startled from my thoughts by the ringing of my
cell phone. I didn't recognize the number, but I answered it
anyway.

"Um, is this Sage Muccino?" an unfamiliar female voice
asked.

"Yes. Who is this?"

"You don't know me, but I think you know my sister,
Natalie. My name's Jessie."

CHAPTER THIRTEEN

I sat nervously in the diner, waiting to meet the woman who said she was Natalie's little sister. She'd been adamant that I not tell anyone about her. Had said she couldn't trust anyone. Never having met her before, I didn't know if she should be taken seriously, or if she was merely being overly dramatic. But I kept my word regardless and sat waiting in the all-night diner per her instructions.

I'd finished a first cup of the diner's coffee and had started on my second, a brew so dark and strong I needed twice as much cream and sugar as usual. I stirred as I listened to Dolly Parton sing about Jolene and stared at the booth opposite me, where the torn vinyl seating was held together by duct tape. The glass door swung open and I glanced over to see a woman enter.

She looked young, younger than me, and I could tell immediately she was related to Natalie. They looked very similar, though Jessie was a brunette as opposed to Natalie's blond locks. Her face was heart-shaped with delicately arched brows and a nose that turned up slightly at the end. About Natalie's height and build, she wore jeans and a long-sleeved zip-up hoodie.

Spotting me, she hurried over. It wasn't hard to figure out who I was—I was the lone female customer. A group of three guys sat two booths down, laughing and putting away a frightening amount of greasy cheeseburgers and fries. Another two men sat by themselves at the Formica counter, one sipping coffee, the other working his way through a piece of chocolate cream pie that I'd been eyeing earlier.

Chocolate sounded like nirvana after the week I'd had, and I was all out of peanut M&Ms at home.

"Sage?"

I nodded. "You must be Jessie."

Relief flashed across her face and she slid into the booth opposite me. "Thanks so much for meeting me."

"I don't even know how you got my name," I said. "Or my number."

"That's kind of a long story," she replied, ordering a cup of coffee for herself as the waitress stopped by to refill my cup.

"I've got all night."

"Natalie's always been up to some scheme or another, all her life," she began. "And I've always been the one to pick up the pieces. This time is no different."

"No offense," I interrupted, "but she said you'd been kidnapped. And she gave someone ten thousand dollars to get you back."

Jessie winced. "I'm so sorry. I didn't know she'd gone through with it."

"Gone through with what?"

"The plan that I was 'kidnapped.'" She used quote-y fingers for *kidnapped*.

I knew it. I'd been suspicious of Natalie the whole time she'd been back. The story of Jessie having disappeared had been so convenient and far-fetched.

"So you obviously weren't kidnapped," I said. "Why the story then? Why would she lie? Especially about something so serious." Though it did explain why she hadn't wanted to get the police or FBI involved. I wasn't a cop, but I thought it was probably against the law to make up a story about someone being kidnapped.

"She needed a reason to find Dean again."

I stiffened, instinctive protectiveness filling me at the thought of her hurting him again. "You know she lied to him," I said. "She faked her own suicide and made him think it was all his fault. For years she let him think that."

Jessie looked sad. "I know. Natalie is a compulsive liar, and she's a manipulator. I should know. She's been lying to and manipulating me for years."

"How do I know you're not the same?" I asked. "Why should I trust you?"

"Because I'm here, telling you. She may have wanted to be back in Dean's life, but you're the one she's been obsessing about."

"Me?" I was startled. "Why me? She just met me a few days ago."

"You're Dean's girlfriend, right?"

"I was. Not anymore. We're just friends now." There was a pang inside at that, but not as bad as it had been a couple of days ago. It was hard, moving on from someone, even when you knew it was the right thing to do.

"So you're with Parker?"

I pressed my lips together. For just meeting me, Jessie sure was nosey. Not to mention that I didn't want to answer the question. "You know a lot," I said instead. "And I still don't know if I should trust you. Why come to me? Why not go straight to Ryker yourself?"

"Because I wanted to warn you," she said, taking a sip of her coffee. "I think Natalie may do something really crazy this time."

"You mean crazier than faking her own suicide or lying about her sister being kidnapped?" My sarcasm was as thick as the diner's coffee.

"If she found out I was here, telling you this, I don't know what she'd do."

Okay, that gave me pause. I studied Jessie, looking hard into her eyes, and I saw fear there. My gut told me she wasn't lying, that she really was afraid of Natalie.

Shit.

"I think we need help." Luckily for us, I'd already foreseen this possibility. I wasn't about to trust some unknown quantity—i.e., Jessie—when I had no idea who she was or what she wanted. I'd called Ryker before I came here. I knew he'd not only know what to do, he deserved to hear for himself what Jessie had to say. I knew he was still giving Natalie the benefit of the doubt, but he needed to protect himself from any more of her machinations.

Jessie didn't argue, just grimly sipped from her cup as I took out my cell and dialed, telling Ryker it was time to come in.

Ryker walked in wearing his usual beat-up jeans, T-shirt, and leather jacket. I could see the outline of his dog tags through the cotton as his heavy boots ate up the linoleum between us and him. He stopped at our booth, his gaze on Jessie.

She swallowed hard, a tentative smile on her face. "Hey, Dean. It's been a while."

"Come here," he said roughly, pulling her to her feet and into his arms for a tight hug. "I've been worried sick about you."

Her whole body relaxed in his arms as she melted against him. Obviously, she'd been apprehensive at the kind of reception she'd receive.

"I'm sorry," she said. "I couldn't let her lie to you like that. Not again."

"What do you mean?" he asked, pulling back.

She sighed. "Sit down. I have a lot to tell you."

Ryker slid into the booth next to me and Jessie started over again with all she'd told me.

"Why didn't you tell me before that she wasn't dead?" he asked once she'd finished. His face was a grim mask and I couldn't imagine how he must be feeling, hearing the truth about Natalie after idolizing her all this time.

Tears shined in Jessie's eyes, but she didn't cry. "I'm so sorry, Dean. I was fifteen. I didn't know what to do. She's my sister. I didn't even know the extent of her lie to you and Parker until recently."

I believed her; the earnestness on her face couldn't be faked, as though she was desperate for him to know she was telling the truth. And after a moment, Ryker nodded.

"It's okay," he said, reaching across the table to squeeze her hand. "It's not up to you to apologize for or try to fix Natalie's mistakes."

I felt like an intruder between them, and the idol worship I saw in her eyes made me realize she saw Ryker as quite a bit more than just a big-brother/little-sister thing that he'd portrayed their relationship to be.

I cleared my throat. "So," I said, feeling a vague twitch of regret for interrupting their Moment. "What do we do now? Go confront Natalie?" But Ryker shook his head.

"I don't think so. I have a gut feeling she did all this for something more than just coming back into our lives. Otherwise, she would've done it before. The question is, why now? Why concoct this elaborate plan now?"

"She got Parker's ten thousand dollars," I said. "Maybe she just wanted the money."

"Ten grand isn't a lot," he replied. "If it was for money, I think she'd have asked for more."

"She's been researching Sage," Jessie offered. "I thought it was because of her involvement with you and Parker. But maybe it's more than that."

"For now, Natalie is staying with Parker," Ryker said. "I think we should keep you hidden and wait and see what she does next."

"Hidden? Where am I going to hide?" Jessie asked.

"You can stay with me," he replied.

Surprise flickered across Jessie's face, then her cheeks turned pink, making me wonder what she was thinking about staying with Ryker.

"I couldn't put you out like that," she said, shaking her head.

"I think it's a good idea," I interjected. "She has to finish this somehow, your supposed kidnapping. And I'd like to know what she wants with me." Surely she wasn't just all *Fatal Attraction* on Ryker and Parker? There seemed like there should be more to the story, but I wasn't a manipulator or compulsive liar, so what did I know? Maybe getting Parker back was all she'd wanted. Either way, I wanted to know... and I wanted to finish her.

I wondered what Parker would have to say about Jessie's information on Natalie... or if he'd even care.

"Then it's settled," Ryker said, pulling out his wallet and tossing some money on the table to cover our coffee. "You'll stay with me and we'll see what Natalie's next move is. I take it you're communicating with her?"

Jessie nodded. "She's supposed to call me today."

"Then we'll wait and see."

Ryker had come on his motorcycle and after making sure I didn't mind grabbing a cab, he and Jessie roared off into the night. Seeing another woman clinging to him on the back of his bike sent a spark of jealousy through me, which I immediately quashed. I wasn't going to be one of *those* women—begrudging Ryker finding someone else.

Parker was on my mind even more than everything else as I locked my apartment door and got ready for bed. The stitches in my hand itched, reminding me of how adept he'd been at taking my mind off what the doctor was doing when needles were involved.

I'd failed him. Well, maybe not me personally, but my father had done something illegal. Perhaps justifiable, considering the circumstances and Leo's ruthlessness, but still illegal. And now Parker, of all people, was having to pay the price.

An ache inside made me curl into a ball underneath the covers. I stared at the light seeping through the slats of the blinds on my bedroom window, wondering what he was doing... and if it was with Natalie. We'd been so close to being together, so close to being happy, that it was a physical pain to realize that chance was lost.

I couldn't sleep, my thoughts churning as the minutes and hours ticked slowly by. My cell phone buzzed and I glanced at it, wondering who could be texting me at two in the morning.

It was Parker.

I snatched up my phone and opened the text.

Are you there?

I quickly texted back. Yes, I'm here. I waited, the little el-
lipses telling me he was typing.

I'm sorry, Sage. This wasn't how it was supposed to be.

Tears stung my eyes and the screen blurred as I typed
back. I'm the one who's sorry. You shouldn't have done what you
did.

Don't be ridiculous. I'm glad I could help.

It figured. Parker had to pick now to be all chivalrous and
self-sacrificing. I sighed. I don't want to argue. Why are you up
so late?

Having a drink.

A drink? At this hour and by the tone of his texting, he'd
had more than one.

Are you drunk?
Maybe. Possibly.
Why don't you just call me?

There was a long wait before he texted back.

Natalie. Sleeping.

That sick feeling was back in my stomach. I didn't understand. He'd willingly tie himself to a woman he didn't want,
just to spare me and my dad?

Please don't do this, I typed. Go back to KLP. I'm a big girl.
I can handle the fallout from my dad's mistakes.

No.

Shit. I huffed at my phone, staring at the one-word response. Chivalrous and stubborn plus drunk. A dreaded combination and one nearly impossible to reason with. Before I could think of how to reply, he'd sent more.

Did Steven follow through? Investigation dropped and no more attacks?

I grudgingly texted back. Yes. Everything appears to be back to normal. Except us, I wanted to add.

Good.

I sighed, pulling my knees to my chest as I stared at my phone. I wanted him so badly, it was eating me up inside. Not just physically, but I missed *him*—talking to him, looking at him, seeing his lips quirk in a smile, and the way his eyes softened when he looked at me.

I miss you, I typed.

I miss you, too, lover.

My heart thudded a bit harder at the endearment, and I wondered just how drunk Parker was.

I'm not your lover anymore. Natalie is.

I waited for a response, hoping I wasn't going too far.

If you think I could possibly be with her after being with you, then you don't know me at all.

A wave of relief swept through me. He hadn't slept with Natalie. She'd been lying about that part at least.

Then what are you doing with her?
Biding my time.
Until . . . ?
Until she goes away.

Considering how badly I thought Natalie wanted Parker, I had sincere doubts that she would just "go away" anytime soon.

I couldn't help myself, though I knew it would make me look needy. Come see me.

I held my breath, hoping beyond hope he'd do it, he'd come to me.

I wish I could. I'm being watched. If I come there, they'll know, and it'll have all been for nothing.

Tears rolled down my cheeks and I swiped them away, staring helplessly at his text. Steven and Natalie held us both hostage, and there wasn't a damn thing I could do about it.

Shh, don't cry.

I didn't question how he knew. Of course he would. He knew me, knew how I felt about him, though I'd been remiss in saying it.

I love you. My hand shook as I typed out the letters.

I know. I love you, too. That won't ever change, no matter what.

I rested my wet cheek on my bent knees, trying to ease the ache inside. The phone buzzed again.

We're being too maudlin. What are you wearing?

I snorted a laugh. Ever the unexpected, that was Parker; just another of the many things I loved about him. He could make me smile in even the most dire and bleak of circumstances.

A navy blue satin chemise with pink lace trim, I lied, tugging down the hem of my faded Mickey Mouse T-shirt.

Send me a pic.

I laughed again as I typed, No way. Do I look like I have Stupid stamped on my forehead?

Don't you trust me?
Nope.
I'm devastated...

I giggled again as I texted back, I'm sure you'll get over it.

So just the chemise, that's all? Nothing else?

Nope. Unless you counted very unsexy white cotton panties, but he didn't need to know that.

Touch your knee.

My breath hitched as I stared at the screen. Okay...this was getting interesting. Tentatively, I rested a hand on my bare knee.

Okay, I typed one-handed.

Your skin is so soft, like velvet. I miss touching you. Pretend I'm there. Trail your fingers down the inside of your thigh, slow and gentle.

I swallowed, my mouth suddenly dry. I might need a glass of wine for this, I thought, yet found my fingers doing exactly what Parker was telling me to do.

Can you picture me?

Yes, I texted back.

I'm hard, thinking about you. You have the most amazing eyes.

Okay, I hadn't ever put much stock in "sexting" before, but this was starting to work. My pulse was racing and there was definite slither of heat through my veins at the thought of an aroused Parker.

I could come from just looking in your eyes.

Okay, yeah, definitely working. I tried to think what to text back. It went both ways, right? I should say something, but it wasn't like I'd done this before.

I miss touching you. Your chest, your arms. It wasn't much, but it was true. Parker had a rock hard chest and his arms looked carved from marble. My fingers itched just thinking about him.

I miss you touching me, too, he sent back. But I miss your kiss more.

Oh, wow. That melted me and I was still staring at the
words when the next text came.

Touch yourself.

I could feel heat flood my face. I'm touching my leg.

That's not what I meant and you know it. Touch between
your legs.

I hesitated and he texted again.

I'm touching myself, thinking about you.

That mental image flashed inside my head and I slipped
my hand inside my panties.

Are you wet?

Okay, so we're Going There. I could do that, even without
the wine.

Yes. I'm imagining it's you, touching me.
If I were there, I'd put my head between your legs and
lick you. I love how you taste.

I swallowed. Parker was really, really good at this. I
should step up my game.

If you were here, I'd want you inside me. That was good, right?
Not too vulgar, but definitely edging into R-rated territory.

Slide a finger inside and rub your clit. Say my name.

It was getting very warm in my apartment.

My cock is hard for you. I'm stroking myself, pretending
I'm inside your tight pussy.

I threw my inhibitions out the window.
Your cock feels so good. I want you to come inside me. I
sent it before I could rethink it and get embarrassed.

I want to feel you come, feel you gripping my cock.
Come for me.

I wouldn't have thought something like this would work,
but the mind is a powerful thing, especially when stimulated.
And Parker knew how to flick my Bic.

I'm coming. Tell me you are too.
God yes.

There was a brief silence from both of us as I caught my
breath. Good lord, that was a first, not that I was complain-
ing. A giggle escaped. My phone buzzed.

Was it good for you?

I replied with the most shit-eating grinning emoji I could
find.
You're so beautiful, he typed. I've always thought so.
I hesitated, then decided to go out on a dicey limb. You don't
know how many times I imagined slipping under your desk. A
true statement, when I'd let my imagination run away with me
and he'd looked particularly mouthwatering. I'd be under his
desk and reach up to undo the zipper of his slacks…

I imagined that, too, **he texted back.** And you on my desk, skirt around your waist, staring into your gorgeous eyes as I took you.

How long have you imagined that? **I couldn't help asking. The answer came back immediately.**

Since the day we met.

That was a revelation. I hadn't realized Parker had felt the chemistry between us as acutely as I had. It was gratifying to know he hadn't been as immune as I'd assumed he'd been—just exercising enormous self-control as he'd never so much as hinted he felt anything but a professional interest in me.

You wore peach toenail polish.

Yes, I had. And he remembered. My throat closed up again.

And you wore your purple tie with the thin silver stripes.
It's not purple. It's eggplant.

I laughed, dashing a hand across my cheek to wipe away the tear tracks.

It's scary you know that. I may have to take your man card.
I think I lost that when I bought Air Supply's Greatest Hits.

I chuckled as I texted. You did take a bullet for me. So I'll let it slide this time.

There was a pause and I was staring at my phone, a stupid smile on my face. It felt so good to be talking to him.

I miss you.

I didn't hesitate. I miss you too.
It'll work out, **he texted.** I promise.
How?? **I saw no way out of the box Steven and Natalie had stuck us in.**

I'll think of something. Don't worry, baby.

The endearment curled around my heart like a hug.
It's late, go to sleep, **he sent.** Dream of me.

Be careful.
I will be.
Goodnight.
Goodnight.

I set the phone down and cuddled back underneath my covers, staring at the window again. It was absurd, being held hostage at the whim of two thugs with enough crazy between the two of them to keep a slew of psychiatrists busy for years.

I had to think outside the box, that was all. There had to be a way out for us; I just had to find it.

CHAPTER FOURTEEN

Flowers were waiting for me at work the next day, a full dozen peach roses. I was smiling before I'd even read the card.

Peaches and cream are my favorite.

~P.

"Who are they from?" Carrie asked, taking my jacket and hanging it up. "I've been dying to know since they arrived."

Blushing, I hurriedly shoved the card in my purse. "Parker Anderson."

Her brows rose. "Our investment manager at KLP?"

"No longer our investment manager," I said, smoothing my skirt as I sat behind my desk. "He's gone to work for Steven Shea at SLS."

Her jaw dropped. "You've got to be joking," she said.

"He's a good guy. Why would he go work for a slimeball like Shea?"

"To keep Shea from going after us," I said. "He made a deal."

"But that makes no sense," she said, dropping into the leather armchair across from me. "You wouldn't need someone like Parker Anderson on staff, not unless..." Her voice trailed away and she got a vague look in her eye.

"Unless what?" I asked. Then repeated myself when she didn't immediately answer. "Carrie, not unless what?"

Her eyes refocused. "Not unless you were getting ready to do a buyout and needed to keep all your ducks in a row to stay off the radar as a monopolistic entity."

That got my attention. "What other companies besides us and SLS move liquor through the tristate area? Are all the companies listed in the inquiry still in business?"

"Well, not all of them. Johnson & Halloway sold to Fulton Foods about six years ago," she said. "They got out of the business. Then M&R Trading went belly up about a year ago. That leaves only Shelton Sikes's company, us, and Shea. Shelton covers a lot of Wisconsin, but he still has a few territories in Illinois."

"Has he been having trouble lately?" I asked. "Financial trouble?"

"Funny you should ask that," Charlie said. I glanced up to see him striding through the doorway, newspaper in hand. "Look what's front page of the business section." He tossed it down on my desk as he sat next to Carrie in her chair's twin.

Thirty-Two-Year-Old Company Prepares to Go Public

The story was relatively short. Shares for Sikes would go on sale tomorrow. The big news of the story wasn't that it was going public, but that a majority of the shares would be for sale. The owner wasn't keeping a controlling interest.

"They must be in trouble," I said.

"Old Man Sikes made the announcement a few months ago," Charlie said. "Your dad had approached them, wanting to buy, but Sikes turned him down."

"Thought he'd make more money going public?"

"I think so."

And no one was better equipped to handle buying controlling stock in another company than Parker Anderson.

"So you think he wanted Parker to ensure his control of Sikes?" I asked.

"Once Shea controls Sikes, we'll be the only other distributor in the region," Charlie said. "And he's got our head on a chopping block already."

"So we'll go down along with everyone else." Regardless of the deal Parker had made, I knew Shea wouldn't stop until we were out of business. We were already on the government's radar, and even if he'd paid someone off to file and then withdraw the allegation, someone was bound to follow up at some point.

All of us were silent, considering the implications.

"We need dirt on Steven Shea," I said. "That's the only way we're going to get out of this, by finding something we can hold against him."

"Blackmail?" Carrie asked.

I hesitated, wondering if she'd have qualms.

"Not that I have a problem with that," she hurriedly added. "Steven Shea is nuts. The things I've heard about him..." She glanced at Charlie, who nodded grimly. It appeared I was the only one in the dark about Steven Shea.

"I don't want to blackmail him," I said, "but he's the one who went for the jugular first. He nearly killed us. As far as

I'm concerned, the gloves are off. We fight back with everything we've got.

"So what do we know about Steven Shea?" I looked expectantly at them.

"Leo kept a lid on that kid," Charlie said, settling back in the chair. "He was wild, with a mean streak. There was some business a few years back, but just rumors. That's when Leo sent him away."

"I've heard through the grapevine that he's violent with women," Carrie added. "My daughter has a friend who went on a few dates with him. His temper is on a hair trigger and she got out quick."

I digested all of this. Rumors and hearsay. Not a lot to go on, but where there was smoke...

"Where did Leo send him off to?" I asked.

"There's a place about an hour and a half from here," Charlie answered. "It's not really a juvenile delinquent place, but it's where rich people send their kids when they need to be dried out or rehabbed."

"It sounds like we should pay a visit," I said. "Carrie, want to get out of the office for a while?"

She grinned. "I'm all about job security."

"Charlie, will you hold down the fort for me?"

"I always do. But you girls be careful. I don't want to have to call our lawyers to bail you outta jail."

"Understood," I said, grabbing my purse. "Let's go."

Carrie had a car, so she drove. She was a few years younger than my mom and I'd known her my whole life, but we hadn't ever spent a lot of one-on-one time together. I thought it might be awkward at first, but I shouldn't have worried. She chatted away as she drove, telling me about her son Paul, who had just landed his first job out of college as a junior architect at a firm in San Francisco.

"What about you?" she asked, taking me aback.

"What about me?"

"Well, you've never shown much of an interest before in the business," she said. "I thought you wanted a career in art, but then you seemed to really like your job at KLP."

"KLP was a good transition from college to real life," I said. "I think I needed that time. And while I love art, I don't think I want to make it my career."

"So your job at KLP was all about you finding yourself?" A smile played about her lips as she glanced at me. "And didn't have anything to do with Parker Anderson?"

Carrie wasn't stupid. She'd known my family forever and she was a mom. I'd found moms had a built-in bullshit detector, and Carrie was no exception, so I didn't even try lying.

"It was about ninety percent Parker and ten percent finding myself."

She laughed and so did I. "Well, at least you're honest," she said. "The worst lie you can tell is to yourself."

"I like the business," I said. "I like being a part of something my dad built. It's different, I think, when it's a family legacy. It's not really just a job."

"You're right. It's different when it's your own."

A couple of miles passed in silence, each of us in our own thoughts, then she asked, "So what will you do about Parker? Are you in love with him?"

I slowly nodded. "Yeah. I am. I can't be without him. It's just not in me. I have to find a way to get us both out of this, even if it means stooping to Shea's level."

"You're not stooping to his level," she said. "You're doing what needs to be done to save your livelihood and the man you love. There's nothing wrong with that. Once upon a time, your father had to make the same choice."

"I guess that old saying is true," I said ruefully. "Don't judge another man until you've walked in his shoes."

"Or her shoes, as the case may be," Carrie added.

We pulled into a long, black asphalt driveway lined with huge oak trees. After about a quarter of a mile, it opened up to a large expanse of lawn with a huge stone mansion situated squarely center. Beautifully tended flowerbeds and manicured bushes flanked the home. I started counting the windows in the three-story structure and gave up after reaching twenty-nine.

"What is this place?" I asked as Carrie navigated to the discreet parking area west of the main house. Numerous out-buildings dotted the acreage.

"I'm guessing they turned an old family mansion into a hospital for the wealthy," Carrie said, turning off the car. "Looks less like an institution and more palatable if you have to stay here."

Considering that those who couldn't afford a place like this were relegated to state-run hospitals with more concrete than grass, I could understand wanting to pay to send your kid to a nicer place. But those with addictions battled the same demons, regardless of the size of the bank account.

Carrie and I walked toward the entrance. We saw a few people on the way, some sitting under the trees in the shade, and a man pushing a young woman in a wheelchair. She was so thin, she had to be anorexic. It hurt me to look at her, with her pinched face and deep shadows under her eyes. I said a quick prayer for her as we passed by.

"So what's the plan?" Carrie muttered as we climbed the flight of stone steps to the grand double doors. They had to be at least twelve feet tall.

"I think we're taking a look at this place for your son,

my brother," I said, thinking on the fly. "You can talk and I'll...wander. See what I can find."

"You got it."

The interior was every bit as impressive as the exterior, though I noticed the little security details they couldn't really hide—the card swipes on the walls next to doors, the cameras in the ceilings, the infrared motion detectors. The shining wooden floors and curved staircase didn't conceal that this was still part prison.

"May I help you?"

A woman intercepted us. Dressed conservatively in sweater and pearls, she looked like a maiden aunt, her smile warm and kind.

"We're visitors," Carrie said. "I'm looking for a place that might be able to help my son."

"Of course," she said. "I'm May. Come with me, please, and we'll be able to answer your questions and show you around."

She led us down the hall and we passed an open doorway. I peered inside and saw a handful of people seated in a circle by the windows, talking. Looked like a group therapy session to me, and I hurried on.

The sitting room was just outside an office and I wandered to the windows as Carrie sat down.

"I'll get Dr. McIntosh to speak with you," May said. "He's just finishing up his rounds. Can I get you something to drink?"

We both requested coffee and May left the room. I settled next to Carrie on the sofa.

"Not at all *One Flew Over the Cuckoo's Nest*," I murmured.

She grimaced. "Just let me know if you spot Nurse Ratched."

I snorted just as May returned with a coffee tray. After

leaving it on the table in front of us, she pulled the door shut, closing out the ambient sound of echoing footsteps and voices from the hallway.

By mutual agreement, neither Carrie nor I broke character. I didn't know if we were being monitored, but I'd rather operate under the assumption that we were. I poured coffee for us both while we waited. A few minutes later, the door opened and a man wearing a white lab coat hurried inside.

"I'm so sorry to keep you waiting," he said as we stood. "I'm Dr. McIntosh."

"I'm Carrie and this is my daughter, Sage." We all shook hands before taking our seats again. The doctor sat in a chair opposite us.

"So I understand you're looking for a place for your son?" he asked.

"Yes. He's been...having trouble," Carrie said, and I could only admire her acting skills. Her face was creased in lines of worry and she was twisting her hands in her lap. "He's always had anger management issues, but I think lately he's started using drugs, and that's only exacerbated the problem."

"What kind of anger management issues?"

"He gets violent, verbally abusive. We believe he's mutilated animals before, though he won't admit to it."

Dr. McIntosh looked very serious. "We do take those kinds of cases," he said, "though the fee is higher, due to the staffing required to make sure they don't present a danger to themselves or others."

"I understand," Carrie said. "Do you have a lot of experience with those kinds of cases?"

"We do." He launched into an explanation of their treatment and schedule. After a couple of minutes, I interrupted to excuse myself to use the restroom.

"Down the hall and to the right," he said. "And please don't wander."

"Of course," I lied.

I bypassed the restroom and headed for the stairs. I wasn't sure what I was looking for, maybe a file room or office, something that would have a record of Steven's stay. It'd be real handy to just ask the staff, but I knew HIPAA rules would prevent them from disclosing anything about him to me.

On the second floor was a long corridor stretching out to either side, lined by what I assumed were patients' rooms. The key to breaking in anywhere is to look like you belong there. Any kind of sneaking or looking furtively around would be like a flashing neon sign to anyone who spotted me.

With that in mind, I walked down the corridor at a good clip, hoping one of the rooms wouldn't just be a patient room, and it wasn't until the very last doorway that I was rewarded.

OFFICE was printed in block letters across the frosted glass window and I turned the brass knob, knowing it was probably locked... and it was.

"Shit," I muttered.

"Who are you?"

I jumped and spun around, knowing as I did so that I looked guilty as sin. So much for my great plan to blend in and look like I belonged.

A guy stood there: maybe twenty years old, a few inches taller than me. He was thin, too thin for his frame, and his eyes were shadowed. But he didn't look angry at spotting me, just curious.

"I-I'm Sage," I said. "Who are you?"

"Jerrod, but my friends call me TJ," he said.

"What's the T stand for?"

"Trouble."

Okay then.

"Are you new here?" he asked. "I don't think I've seen you before, and I'm damn sure I would've noticed." He smiled crookedly, showing a dimple in his cheek. He was cute and the smile made his eyes less sad.

"I'm...visiting," I said. "What about you? How long have you been here?"

"I've been in and out of here since I was twelve," he said with a shrug, his smile fading. "I suppose one of these days they'll just give up and throw away the key."

The way he said it was so resigned, the look in his eyes so full of hopelessness that it made my chest hurt. Instinctively, I reached out to touch his arm.

"Don't say that," I said. "Things can get better. They *will* get better. You have to believe that. Your family wouldn't send you here if they didn't have that hope for you."

He glanced down at my fingers on his bare arm and I hurriedly pulled my hand back, heat creeping into my cheeks. "Sorry about that," I said. I knew it wasn't a good idea to touch without asking.

"No, don't apologize," he said. "It's been a long time since a beautiful girl touched me." The sheepish grin was back. "So tell me why you're trying to get into the office."

I swallowed, debating. Something instinctively told me I could trust TJ. And he'd been around this place for a while, if I were to believe his story.

"I'm looking for information on a former patient," I said. "A Steven Shea. Do you know him?"

TJ's smile was gone again. "Yeah, I knew him," he said. "If I'm fucked up, he's a psycho lunatic. Crazy, sick bastard. He was here for a couple of years, then he left. That was maybe three years ago? Haven't seen him since."

"What can you tell me about him?" I asked. "Why was he sent here? Did his family come visit?"

"We were roommates for a while," TJ said. "Until they moved him into a room by himself. He was really pissed when they first brought him here. Tried to escape, hurt a couple of workers. They threatened to turn him over to the State."

"What happened?"

"He was smart. Knew it'd be even worse there, so he settled down. He quit doing the drugs, which took the edge off, but he never stopped being a dangerous fucker." TJ suddenly looked abashed. "Sorry for the language."

I couldn't help a smile. "It's okay." I refocused. "Why do you say he never stopped being dangerous?"

"He had a way of making sure no one messed with him," TJ said. "There was a guy who took a real dislike to him, gave him a lot of shit in front of people. One day he was missing a finger. It'd been totally sliced off. He never said what happened, but he never so much as looked at Steven again.

"Some of the nurses would refuse to deal with him," he continued. "Though they'd never say why. After a while, everyone just tried to pretend Steven didn't exist."

Considering how Steven had scared the crap out of me in his office, I could understand the desire to stay far away from him. "Did he ever have any visitors?"

"Just his dad," TJ said. "Though there was some girl he obsessed over. Said she was his wife, but I always thought he was full of shit because no girl ever came to see him."

"And they just let him go?" I asked.

"Said he was cured, I guess." TJ shrugged. "Up and checked himself out one day. I never heard from him again."

"He could just leave?"

"Some people are here voluntarily," he said. "Some aren't."

"Okay, well, thank you, TJ. You've been very helpful."

His smile was sweet. "I don't suppose you'll be coming back anytime?"

"I'm sorry, but no, probably not."

TJ looked somewhat crestfallen and I impulsively leaned forward and kissed his cheek. "Take care of yourself," I said. "I really appreciate you talking to me."

"Talk to a beautiful girl for a few minutes? Not really a hardship."

That coaxed a smile from me, which quickly faded when I heard footsteps and voices on the stairs.

"I've gotta go," I said, glancing around, but there was only the one staircase. I didn't know what they'd say about me exploring on my own, much less talking to a patient without permission, and I didn't want to find out.

"This way," he said, reaching out and grasping my hand. He pulled me with him into an open room that looked like a lounge. A couple of guys were at a table playing cards and they looked up as we hurried past.

"There's a back staircase through here," he said, stopping in front of a door.

"But there's a keypad," I said. "Isn't it locked?"

He winked at me. "Of course it's locked." He punched in six numbers and the door clicked open. "Lucky for you, I've been around here a while."

I hurried through the door. "Thanks, TJ. I'll see you."

"Bye, Sage."

I hurried down the stairs as the door closed behind me. Voices floated in the air.

"Has anyone seen a woman come through here? Tall, long brown hair?"

I stopped in my tracks, listening.

"Nope. Why? You guys lose another patient?"

I didn't recognize the voice as TJ's, so it must have been one of the two guys playing cards.

"TJ, why are you by the door? Going somewhere?" The question had an edge to it.

"At some point, but probably not today," TJ retorted.

I let out the breath I'd been holding and kept going, keeping my steps as light as I could. So my disappearance had been noticed. Well, at least I'd gotten information worth our trip.

The door at the bottom opened into the courtyard behind the house and I stepped out onto a cobblestone path. Slowing my pace and my breathing, I strolled through the manicured flowerbeds, stopping at a pond filled with koi and lily pads.

"There you are."

I turned and saw May heading toward me, her steps purposeful. The warm, friendly smile was gone and now I saw more than a hint of Nurse Ratched.

"We've been looking for you," she said when she was closer. "I believe Dr. McIntosh warned you not to wander off. Not all of our patients respond well to strangers."

"If my brother is going to be staying here, surely a tour of the grounds isn't off limits," I fired back. "But it doesn't matter. We need to be going anyway. We have other appointments today."

I caught sight of Dr. McIntosh and Carrie walking down the steps from the back. She saw me at the same time and waved. I watched as they shook hands and Carrie headed my way.

"Thank you for your time, May," I said. "We'll be leaving now." I turned toward Carrie, effectively dismissing May. We didn't speak until we were in the car.

"Did you find out anything?" Carrie asked.

I nodded. "Steven was here for a couple of years dealing

with drug addiction and anger management. He was violent and cunning." I paused. "And married."

Carrie's brows flew up. "Married? Really? I never heard anything about Steven Shea being married."

"Neither have I. But supposedly she never came to visit him while he was here."

"I wonder if she's still around," Carrie said.

"I'm thinking the same thing. If we can find her, maybe she'd be key to calling off Steven. If she was married to him, surely she'd know all the dirt.

"Marriage records are available to the public," I said. "The Cook County Clerk's Office would probably be the best place to start."

"Then that's where we'll go."

Two hours later, we were fighting downtown traffic as we jockeyed for a parking spot outside the Clerk's Office.

"I'll just hop out and go in," I said. "Go on back to the office and I'll grab a cab."

"You sure?"

The person in the car behind us laid on their horn. I hopped out of the car and leaned back in so Carrie could hear me over the blaring noise. "I'm sure. I'll be back soon." I shut the door and she drove off. I made sure to signal my irritation to the horn-blower as he went by and he responded in kind. Jerk.

It took longer than I expected to search the records, because I had no idea of the time frame when Steven would've been married. All I had was his name, so I wasn't surprised when I turned up nothing, despite digging through archive records for the past decade.

"Need some help on that Steven Shea?" The woman who'd shown me the computer database had come to check on me.

"I'm not finding anything," I explained. "Though I'm pretty sure there's a marriage record."

"These are the computer records and much more easily searched," she said. "But everything is still on paper. It's possible, though unlikely, that something was missed. If you want to take a look, I can show you where those are kept."

"That'd be great, thanks."

She took me down a staircase to the basement. I followed her down a hallway, her low heels clacking on the concrete floor, and she unlocked a door. Stepping inside, she turned on the lights. The fluorescent bulbs flickered to life, showing row after row of filing cabinets.

"They're by year," she said, "so maybe searching won't be easier, but if it's not here, it didn't happen."

"Okay, thank you."

"We close at four," she said. "I'll lock the door behind me so you can just leave when you're through without hunting me down."

After she left, I stared at the aisles of dull gray filing cabinets and sighed. "Good thing I sent Carrie on back," I muttered. I'd had no idea I'd take this long.

I started at three years ago and quickly found out that a) a lot of people got married in Cook County and b) a lot of their last names began with S. After my third paper cut, I was gritting out curse words and wondering if I wasn't on a wild goose chase.

A decade ago, Steven Shea would've been nineteen. Old enough to marry. Or maybe it had all been a figment of his imagination. Maybe TJ was right and he hadn't married at all, which meant I was looking for a ghost.

It wasn't until I reached that ten-year mark and was digging through musty records in the far reaches of the cavernous room that I actually found a lead.

"It's about time," I muttered, pulling out a thin folder for *Shea, S.*

The sound of the door closing up front made me look up. Had that lady come back? I glanced at my watch. It was nearly five o'clock. Crap. Not good.

"Hey, I'm almost done," I called out, flipping open the file.

It took me a moment to realize no one had answered me.

"Hello?" I called again, frowning as I listened hard.

Nothing. Then I heard the slight scuff of a shoe.

The hair on the back of my neck rose. Someone was in here with me, and they didn't want me to know it.

As quietly as I could, I stuffed the file inside my purse and got to my feet from where I'd been crouching on the floor. Reaching down, I slipped off my heels, carrying them in one hand as I crept down the aisle.

The lights went off.

CHAPTER FIFTEEN

I froze, blinking rapidly to try and get my eyes to adjust. If I'd had any doubts as to whether I was imagining things, they were now gone. Someone had turned off the lights and was sneaking around the room...hunting me.

Every noise I made seemed amplified, from the rustle of my skirt to my rapid breathing. I reached the end of the aisle and waited, straining my ears. I took a step just as I heard the gunshot. Papers exploded inches from my shoulder and I cried out, instinctively ducking. Then I ran.

Running down the aisle toward the door, I heard the footsteps behind me. Just as I reached the end of the row, I turned, grabbed the metal stand housing the file cabinets, and heaved. For a terrifying second it didn't budge, then it began to topple as though in slow motion.

Drawers flew open as the stand fell and I heard a man grunt in pain. Metal slammed against metal, but I didn't wait to see how or if he got himself out. I got to the door and turned the knob.

It was locked. Someone had thrown a dead bolt on the outside.

I looked around frantically for anything I could use to get out. I could hear the man digging out from the stacks. Lacking any other option, I gripped my shoe tightly and, using the heel, I smashed it into the glass window. Luckily, it wasn't shatterproof glass and it broke easily. Thrusting my hand through, I twisted the dead bolt and flung open the door.

The hallway was deserted—government employees gone at the stroke of quitting time—and the corridor stretched endlessly in front of me.

I didn't hesitate. I ran. An EXIT sign glowed over a door at the far end. But there was nowhere in between and I was a sitting duck.

The door banged open and I chanced a quick glance behind me...just enough to see the gun pointed in my direction.

I dodged to the left as a shot rang out. Twenty more feet and I'd be at the door. My pocket buzzed. Someone was calling me. I dodged back to the right as I yanked the phone out. I didn't even look at the screen, just hit the button and talked.

"Please help me!"

Another gunshot barely missed. Panic was taking over, adrenaline flooding my body in a chilling rush through my veins. Ten feet.

"Sage? Are you—"

Parker. But he cut out.

"Help..." I gasped, putting forth one last burst of speed to shove through the exit door. My hand hit the crossbar and it flew open, crashing into the wall with a loud metal bang.

"—wrong? What's happen—"

He cut out again. My signal was crap in here. "Someone's shooting at me."

"Carrie sent me to get you," Parker said, and this time his voice was clear. "I'm out front of the Clerk's Office, but the building is locked."

"I'm coming out the side exit," I said, my bare feet flying up the flight of stairs leading to the outside. "Please, Parker..." I was near tears, terrified that whoever was shooting was following me and that I'd feel the bite of a bullet in my back at any second.

"I'm here."

I shoved open the door and burst outside. An arm snagged me around the waist, lifting me off my feet. I yelped in surprise, twisting until I could see his face.

Parker had me.

"Thank God," I breathed, relief flooding me. I gripped the lapels of his jacket, resting my forehead against his shoulder.

"What's going on?" he asked. "Who's shooting at you?"

"I don't know," I said, stepping away now and pulling on him. "Let's just go. Please." I couldn't bear the thought of Parker intervening and something possibly happening to him. Fear still had a grip on my mind.

"It's okay. Just tell me where you saw him last. Was it a man?"

"Please, let's go," I said, starting to cry. I felt hysterics coming on and tried not to let it show. "Please don't go in there. Just take me home." I pulled again on his arm, tugging him away from the door and the building.

His hand closed over mine. "Okay, okay," he said soothingly. "We'll go. I'll get you out of here right now."

"Yes, thank you." This time when I tugged on his hand, he came along. His other hand held his gun.

I couldn't get away fast enough and was glad Parker's car was parked right there on the street. He bundled me inside, rounded the car, and slid behind the wheel. It wasn't until we were roaring down the street that I felt I could breathe normally again.

"Start at the beginning," he ordered.

I told him about Carrie and me going to the institution to look for information on Steven, then about how he'd been married and our reasoning that his wife would know more about him than we would.

"First of all," he said when I was through, "you shouldn't have been trying to investigate Steven. He's dangerous. Everything I just did was to keep you safe. Then you go throw all of it away in a hope you'll find some kind of smoking gun?"

"Smoking gun? Not funny, given the fact someone was just shooting at me. Besides, I was trying to rid us of him," I protested. "You can't be mad at me for that."

"I can and am," he shot back. "Someone was *shooting* at you back there. What would've happened if they hadn't missed? You think I want to have to identify your body on a slab in the morgue?"

I flinched. That was certainly an image I didn't need, thank you very much.

"Freeing you would be worth it," I said.

"Bullshit. I can take care of myself. What is patently obvious is that you are ruled by your emotions, not logic."

Okay, now I was starting to get pissed off. "What's that supposed to mean? That I'm some kind of emotional basket case female who leaps headfirst without looking?"

"Pretty much."

"Dammit, Parker! I'm doing this for us!"

"So am I."

We fumed in silence. Or at least, *I* fumed. I couldn't tell what Parker was thinking. Other than the tight grip he had on the steering wheel, his face was starkly blank.

He pulled into my parking lot and turned off the car, then faced me. "Promise me you'll stop. Steven Shea is dangerous. I don't want you having anything to do with him. Let me handle it."

"You're not handling it!" I burst out. "You're letting him run our lives. He has me over a barrel and is using you. Or don't you know why he wants you?"

"I know about Sikes going public, if that's what you're getting at."

"If you do that deal, you'll be positioning Shea as a monopolistic interest," I said. "All he'll have to do is shut us down and he'll own the liquor trade in three states."

"Of course he will. Did you really think this was about his dad? He doesn't give a shit about his dad."

I was surprised by the bitterness in Parker's voice. "I thought he wanted revenge—"

"He doesn't. It's all about the money. It always has been."

Parker got out of the car before I could reply. He opened my door and I had no choice but to step out. He stood too close, our bodies only inches apart, and for a moment I couldn't breathe. A sharp pang of longing went through me.

"Thanks for coming to get me," I said, my voice much too breathless.

"Carrie was worried when you didn't show up," he replied, shutting the door behind me. His arm brushed mine and it felt as though I'd been burned. "She said she tried calling your cell but it went straight to voice mail."

"Um, yeah," I said, struggling to think past the heartbroken yearning I felt. "I had a crappy signal in the basement."

"C'mon. I'll walk you up."

No argument there. Any time I could prolong with Parker was well spent. I missed him and I missed us. I missed what might have been... what should be.

We were walking down my hallway when I made the words come out of my mouth.

"Do you miss me?"

We stopped in front of my door. Parker's fingers brushed my chin, lifting my downcast face up.

"You know I do."

His words were a balm to the burning wound inside that ached for him. I drank in the clear blue of his eyes, the curve of his jaw, the wave of his dark hair over his forehead. He was so beautiful, it hurt to look at him.

Tears stung my eyes. "Is it always going to be like this?"

"I hope not. I can't be without you."

"I feel the same."

He was so close, I could feel the heat from his skin. He was watching me with a look in his hooded eyes that sent a shiver of anticipation down my spine.

"Come inside with me," I said, my voice a husky whisper.

"We shouldn't."

I didn't want to beg... but "Please, Parker," I whispered. My hand crept up to the back of his neck, my fingers threaded through his hair. His whole body stiffened and his eyes slipped shut. "I want you."

For a breathless moment, I didn't think he'd give in and I'd be left feeling like a needy idiot.

Suddenly I was against the wall, with Parker's body pressed against me and his mouth hungrily devouring mine.

I clung to him, holding on tight. My lips opened and his tongue delved inside. The taste of him was as intoxicating as I remembered and I moaned.

He opened the door and swept me inside. I barely heard the door close, too busy kissing his neck and jaw and any other part of him that I could reach.

He lifted me and my legs circled him. My skirt pushed up my thighs and my back went up against the wall. His kiss was as desperate as mine. Parker's hips were cradled between my thighs and I tightened my legs.

"God, Sage," he rasped against my lips. His erection pressed against me, sending a rush of heat through me. I whimpered, wanting him so badly I thought I'd die if he didn't take me right there, right then.

"Fuck me, Parker," I whispered. Part of me was embarrassed that I had the guts to say that, but the other part of me really didn't give a crap, other than hoping Parker liked taking that particular order.

I squirmed a hand between us and managed to undo his pants. Another deft tug and his hard cock was in my hand. Parker was sucking on my neck and I gently squeezed him.

"You're sure?" His voice in my ear sent a shiver across my skin.

"I'd be the worst kind of tease if I wasn't," I replied dryly.

He snorted. "Just making sure."

I was glad Parker worked out because somehow he managed to tug aside my panties and bury himself inside me all while still keeping me against the wall.

"Where there's a will, there's a way," I breathed, smiling. He felt incredible and I clung to him.

"God, I've missed you."

I didn't have a chance to respond before he was kissing me again, not that I had much coherent thought at that point. Just vague thoughts of *yes please* and *oh yeah, just like that*.

He gripped my hips, thrusting inside me, his tongue tangling with mine. Our breath mingled and the sound of my pulse racing throbbed in my ears. His taste, his touch, the feel of his body covering mine—all of it was overwhelming in the very best kind of way.

Parker tore his mouth from mine. "My memory didn't do you justice," he said, carrying me from the wall toward the couch.

I thought we would lay down, but he bent me over the side and shoved my skirt up to my waist. I felt air on the backs of my thighs as Parker yanked my panties down and off my legs. His leg nudged my knees apart and I gladly obliged, emitting a wholly unfeminine groan when he thrust inside me.

It was hard and fast and oh so thorough, Parker taking me like this. I felt his wanting me, needing me, and it was an incredible turn-on. When he reached around to slide his fingers against my clit, I was already almost there.

"Oh God, Parker," I moaned, knowing I sounded like a bad porno flick but not caring. "Oh God..."

"Come for me, Sage. I want to feel you."

He thrust harder, filling me, and I shattered, crying out his name. I heard him cursing as his body jerked into mine, his cock pulsing inside me.

Parker was draped over me, both of us struggling to get our breath. He swept aside my hair and pressed his lips to my skin. I closed my eyes at the feel of his gentle, slow kisses on my neck.

"I love how you smell right here," he said in a voice just above a whisper. "It's a warm smell. It combines your perfume, your hair, and your skin."

If I wasn't already boneless from my mind-blowing orgasm, I would have melted on the spot.

He pulled out of me and swept me up in his arms. I

hooked an arm around his shoulder and nuzzled his neck as he carried me to the bedroom.

We didn't speak. He gazed into my eyes as he laid me down and sat down next to me. Reaching over, he flipped on the bedside lamp. His fingers tangled in my hair, combing slowly through the strands. The touch made me feel like a cat being stroked and I watched him, the air heavy between us.

"Come lie down with me," I said.

"You know I can't."

My stomach sank. "Why not?"

"I have to leave. Natalie will be waiting for me."

"You've got to be kidding me," I said, sitting up. "You're going back to her?"

"I have no choice. Not right now. And I'm not going *back to her*. I'm going to my apartment, where she happens to be."

"This is ridiculous," I said, channeling my hurt into anger. "I refuse to let those…those assholes dictate our lives."

"I'm working on it," he said. "But in the meantime, we're going to play by their rules. I'm not going to allow him to hurt you or your business."

Okay, so he was *working on it*. "What does that mean?" I asked.

His eyes searched mine. "Trust me," he said. "I need you to just trust me. Can you do that?"

I hesitated. I wanted to, I really did, but he was going home to Natalie, who was beautiful and wanted him…

"You can't, can you," he said, disappointment evident on his face.

"No," I denied. "I do trust you, it's just…"

"Just what?"

"I don't trust *her*," I blurted. "She practically throws herself at you." And that had been with me around. I couldn't imagine what she was doing now that I wasn't there.

"It takes two," he said. "Now kiss me and try not to worry." His hand slid underneath my hair to cup the nape of my neck.

One of those requests was easily done. The other...not so much.

I kissed him as though it might be our last kiss ever, because well, you just never know. It was several moments before we came up for air.

"You certainly don't make it easy to leave," Parker said, his voice roughened in a way that made me smile with satisfaction.

"I don't know what you're talking about," I said, pretending innocence, though the look I gave him was pure take-me-now.

He groaned, kissing me again, a hard press of his lips against mine. His hand moved between my legs to touch me. I was still sensitive and gasped. He deepened the kiss as he slid a finger inside and I clutched at his shoulders. I was wet and it felt divine, sweeping away thoughts of Natalie and Steven.

Parker didn't stop kissing me until I was crying out, my body shuddering with the force of another orgasm. Even the light stroke of his finger was too much and I grabbed his wrist, stilling him.

"Now who's using sex as a distraction," I managed to say.

His lips twisted in a half-smile. "Couldn't resist making you come again," he said. "I love watching you."

Heat flooded my face and I knew I was blushing something awful.

"Go to sleep and don't worry," he said, pressing a kiss to my forehead. "I'll be in touch." He rose to leave.

"Wait," I said, grabbing on to the hem of his jacket. "I love you. You know that, right?"

His smile was sweet and made his eyes soften as he looked at me. "I do. And I love you, too." Another quick kiss, one last smoldering look at me lying half-naked on my bed, and he was gone.

CHAPTER SIXTEEN

I was smiling like a lovesick fool the next morning, pleasantly sore in all the right places, and it took until my second cup of coffee before I remembered the all-important fact that I'd stolen government property last night—namely, Steven Shea's marriage document file.

No sense letting a good felony go to waste...

Digging in my purse, I pulled out the folder and flipped it open. Several papers were inside and I scrutinized them. A marriage license application all right, dated over a decade ago... with the name of the prospective bride utterly blacked out.

I stared in disbelief. It looked like a Top Secret file I'd seen in the movies, where information had been blacked out with a marker.

"You've got to be kidding me," I muttered, flipping through the entire file. It was all like that. Someone had gone to some trouble to make sure no one knew the name of Steven's wife. Why? If he'd regretted getting married, he could've just had an annulment or gotten a divorce.

TJ had said Steven was always talking about his wife, so it didn't sound like he'd regretted getting married.

But maybe his father had, especially if there hadn't been a prenup. Given Leo's history of bribing officials and politicians, it didn't seem like much of a stretch to think he could've paid someone off to do this.

I tossed aside the file, thinking. Now what? I'd hit a dead end in looking for something on Steven. Parker had said to trust him, Jessie and Ryker were waiting for Natalie's next move, and I was cooling my heels doing nothing.

That didn't sit well with me.

My cell phone rang and I glanced at the caller ID. My mom was calling.

"Hey, Mom, everything okay?" Fear for my dad was always in the back of my mind, that on one of these calls she was going to say that no, everything *wasn't* okay.

"Yes, things are fine," she said. "I called to tell you that they're going to start easing your father off the drugs today. If all goes well, he might wake up as soon as tomorrow."

"That's great!" It would be a huge relief to have my dad awake, even though I knew he'd still be in the hospital for a while recovering. "I can come by later and see you."

"Okay. I'll see you soon then. Love you, dear."

"Love you, too, Mom."

I was in a good mood when I got dressed. Things were looking up. Yes, my father had broken the law and yes that put me in a very bad situation now, but Parker had something up his sleeve he wasn't telling me about. All I had to do was trust him, which was a hell of a lot easier after last night.

Memories made my smile wistful as I brushed my hair, not seeing my reflection, but reliving the moment he'd pressed me against the wall. He'd wanted to stay, I'd bet my life on it. And we'd said we loved each other. It was the first time in a while that we'd done that and a lot had happened since then.

I hoped that though our relationship had been through a lot of fires, it had strengthened and reinforced what we felt for each other. It wasn't a crush and it wasn't fleeting. It was that soul-deep, abiding, can't-breathe-without-the-other kind of love that poets wrote about and artists tried to portray on canvas. I knew I didn't want to live my life without him...I just hoped he felt the same way.

I was on my way to work when I noticed the car following us. Schulz had been kind enough to drop by to take me in and I'd seen a rather nice white Mercedes idling on the corner. I probably wouldn't have even looked twice if it hadn't been just on this side of flashy, but it was hard to miss as we navigated through downtown Chicago traffic and it stayed exactly two cars behind us the entire time.

Was this Steven again? Sending a flunky to try and hurt me? The thought enraged me. Parker had made a deal that had sacrificed his job and possibly his career. That Steven, the shit, would renege wasn't a surprise to me.

When we reached the office, I jumped out of the car before Schultz could get out. "I'll see you later, thanks!" I called to him. No need for him to get involved and possibly hurt.

I headed for the office, keeping an eye on the car that had pulled to the curb three cars down. There was a crowd of people waiting to cross the street and I blended into them, sidling up to the car from the back, and trying to pretend my heart wasn't pumping triple-time.

Hoping it was unlocked (or I'd look really stupid), I pulled on the driver's side door handle. It swung open.

"Why the hell are you—" I stopped, staring in surprise at Natalie. "You!" I recovered. "What are you doing following me?" Reaching inside the car, I grabbed on to her arm and yanked her out.

Her face turned red. "I'm not…following you."

"Oh, really. You just *happened* to be outside my office right now?"

"Okay, fine, I was following you," she said. "But it's just that—" She stopped.

"Just that what?"

She hesitated, then blurted, "I just have to know. Do you love Parker? Like really love him?"

Okay, this was out of left field. "Why do you care?"

Her eyes filled, but she didn't cry. "Parker is a good man, and he deserves someone who loves him for who he is, not a stepping stone in their career."

I stiffened, but before I could retort, she blundered on.

"Not that I'm accusing you of doing that and I'm probably the last person in the world who should be holding anyone accountable for how Parker is treated, it's just that…I care about him. And I want to see him happy."

"If you want to see him happy, then why are you forcing a relationship on him?" I countered.

"I-I…I can't answer that right now," she said. "But I know he needs you to trust him, and in a small way, I do, too."

"How can I possibly trust you and why should I?"

"Because Parker does."

Her frank response silenced me. I took a moment, looking into her eyes, trying to read the truth there.

"I don't know if I believe any part of your story," I said at last. "But I love Parker, and I trust him. He took a bullet for me." It was hard not to look at that and realize I *could* trust Parker, no matter what. Even if it involved Natalie.

"So...truce?" she asked, holding out her hand.

"Truce." I shook her hand. I'd officially crossed over into the Twilight Zone. I wanted to ask her why the lies about Jessie's kidnapping, but held my tongue.

I headed inside the building, glancing once behind me to see Natalie getting into her car and driving off.

Hmm.

Carrie greeted me with coffee and breakfast. "Monthlies from Rick are on your desk for review and I'm off to the first floor to grab the mail. I'll be back in a flash." And she was out the door.

Carrie was back shortly with another stack of papers for me to go through and quizzed me as I read. I told her about the records office, someone shooting at me, and finding Steven's electronic file missing and the paper original censored.

"I can't believe someone *shot* at you! Thank God I called Parker."

"Yeah, no kidding," I said grimly.

"Do you think they knew you were looking for information on Steven?" she asked.

I thought about it. "Maybe. It doesn't make sense, though, why they'd go to the trouble to censor the file and still leave it to be found, right? And the only person who would've known what I was looking for was—" I stopped, struck by a thought.

"Was who?"

"It had to be that girl in the office," I said. "I told her what I was looking for and she was the only one who knew I was in that room. She was probably the one who locked me inside."

"Do you remember her name?"

"Yes." I'd seen her name tag and closed my eyes to remember. "It was Ashley...something. Started with a W. Waters...no. Woods...no. It was something from someone famous..." My eyes popped open. "Wilkes. Ashley Wilkes." That's right. The totally wussy guy Scarlett had been in love with in *Gone With the Wind*, something I'd never understood. Why would anyone pick Ashley over Rhett?

"I can Google her."

"Okay, do that. I'll call Ryker, see if I can find her address." I reached for my cell.

"You're going to her house?"

"I think it's time we played hardball," I said. "Sikes goes public tomorrow. We're running out of time."

Ryker answered on the third ring.

"So what's the plan now?" I asked.

He sighed heavily. "Natalie still says Jessie is missing. Said she was going to track down her ex-boyfriend or something and took off. I don't know where she went."

"She came to see me," I said, explaining what had transpired between us. "Do you know what's going on between Parker and Natalie?"

"No, but he's my next phone call."

Maybe Parker would tell Ryker what he wouldn't tell me.

I hesitated, then asked, "Is it bothering you, Natalie and Parker?"

"Parker is in love with you," he said. "I have no doubt about that. Whatever he's doing, it's for you, not her."

That made me feel better. Other than myself, Ryker probably was the only other person who knew Parker as well.

"And Natalie?"

There was a long pause before he answered this time, leaving me wondering if I'd overstepped. "Seeing her again, talking to her...it's like not a day's gone by." His voice grew rougher as he spoke. "I don't know what's going to happen or why she's doing what she is, but I want things to work out…somehow. I'm not going to lie to you or myself."

That was hard to hear, but then again, you can't choose who you love, right? And I could sympathize with falling in love with someone utterly inconvenient. I decided to change the subject.

"I called because I needed the home address of a government employee," I said. "Can you help me?"

"Why do you need that—wait, do I want to know?"

"I'm not going to hurt her or anything," I said, hoping I wasn't telling a little white lie. "I just need to talk to her away from the office."

"What's her name?"

"Ashley Wilkes. She works in the Cook County Clerk's Office."

"Okay. I'll call you back."

I hung up just as Carrie came back in carrying a few papers.

"What'd you find?" I asked as she handed me half of them.

"That she's twenty-two, newly divorced but currently *In a relationship*, according to her Facebook status. She has an unhealthy appreciation for cat videos, Theo James, and wine."

"Sounds like we could be friends," I said. Theo James was pretty hot.

"She also has massive credit card debt." I looked at Carrie and she shrugged. "I ran a credit report on her."

"So if she needed money, she would've made an excellent target for Steven to bribe."

"My thoughts exactly."

My phone buzzed. Ryker.

"I'm not going to regret telling you this, am I?" he asked.

"Of course not. I'm a very trustworthy person."

He snorted, then reeled off an address that I jotted down.

"Thank you," I said. "I promise I'll be good." I ended the call.

There was a tap on my door and I glanced up to see Charlie standing there.

"Shelton Sikes is here to see you," he said.

I glanced at Carrie, then back to Charlie in confusion. "Really?"

"Really."

"Show him in." What Sikes would want with me, I had no idea. His company was basically being auctioned to the highest bidder tomorrow, which should allow him to retire in relative comfort.

Charlie ushered in a man who looked to be in his early seventies. He was tall and reminded me a bit of Clint Eastwood, with deep-set eyes and crow's feet. His skin was weathered for a man in his profession, but the suit he wore was tailored and fit him well.

I stood to greet him. "Good afternoon, Mr. Sikes. I'm Sage Muccino."

"Nice to finally meet you," he said, his voice the deep rasp of a career smoker. He grasped my hand and his skin was as rough as his voice. The hands of a hardworking man.

"Please, sit down." I gestured to the chairs as I took my seat again. He sat in one and Charlie in the other. Carrie left, closing the door softly behind her.

"I'm sorry to hear about your father," he said. "How's he doing?"

"He's getting better," I replied. "They think they'll be able to bring him out of the coma tomorrow."

"That's good news. Your father and I . . . well, we go way back."

"Really?"

He chuckled. "Oh yes. Granted, we're also competitors, but your dad's always been an honest man, someone I could trust. In this business, that's hard to come by."

"I guess I didn't realize you and he were friends."

"Oh, maybe not friends, per se, but we had a healthy respect for one another. And we worked together, when the times necessitated it."

I read between the lines. "You mean when Leo Shea was trying to shut you both down."

He nodded. "Desperate times called for desperate measures. We did what needed to be done to save our businesses."

"What you did was against the law," I said.

"And Leo's intimidation wasn't?" he retorted. "Judging is so much easier in hindsight."

"I'm not judging," I said. "But those actions are having repercussions now."

"That's why I'm here."

"I'm listening."

"As I'm sure you know, tomorrow Sikes, Ltd. goes public. Forty-nine percent of the company will be held for employees only. Fifty-one percent will be available for purchase." He paused. "I'm here to offer you my five percent share of that fifty-one."

"Five percent?"

"As owner, I have the right to purchase up to five percent prior to the IPO. In turn, I will sell it to you."

"And what's five percent going to do?" I asked. "Unless there's a majority percentage, Shea will still buy the remainder and control your company."

"The employees' forty-nine plus our five will be the controlling interest," Charlie interrupted. "With that, we'll be able to incorporate the company as a Muccino holding."

"A merger," I said.

"Exactly," Shelton said. "And since he'll then be a share-holder, Shea won't be able to bring charges of collusion up against his own parent company. You'll be in the clear."

It sounded like an excellent plan to me, almost too good to be true, but the part of me that no longer relied on the kindness of human nature was suspicious. "Why are you doing this?" I asked.

"I want to retire, go take my wife and sit on the beach somewhere," he said. "But I built this and don't want it to fall into Shea's hands. Plus, I owe your dad one. This is my way of paying him back."

"Okay, so what do we need to do?"

He reached into his briefcase and withdrew a sheaf of papers. "The paperwork's already been drawn up," he said. "You just need to sign it." He handed it to me.

"Who prepared all this?" I asked, flipping through the pages.

"Parker Anderson."

I paused in my signing, glancing over at Charlie, who maintained a poker face. I hurriedly finished signing and handed the papers back.

"I'll have these filed and the agreement faxed over by tonight," Shelton said, sliding them back in his briefcase. He stood and I followed suit. "It was good doing business with you."

"Likewise," I said, shaking his hand again.

"I'll see you out," Charlie said, holding open the door.

I sat back down with a thump. Obviously, this was what Parker hadn't told me about. I wondered what else he had up his sleeve because once Shea found out his plan to mo-nopolize the business was gone, he was going to be pissed. And considering he was a psycho, I wasn't sure what form his temper would take; I just knew it wouldn't be pleasant.

Would he find out about Parker's involvement?

Apprehension still filled my gut. Yes, Parker may have saved my company and my father, but who was going to save him?

I needed to find something on Steven. If I did, then I could maybe turn the tables and get him to leave my company—my father's company—alone. Which meant I was still going to see Ashley. But in the meantime...

I picked up my cell and dialed.

"Parker Anderson," he answered.

"Shouldn't it be 'knight in shining armor'?"

There was a low chuckle on the line. "I take it Sikes came by."

"Yes, he just left. So why didn't you tell me this last night?"

"We were kind of busy last night." The way he said it sent a shiver down my spine.

"Yes, we certainly were," I replied, my voice dropping into what I hoped was a sexier register. Phone-sex operator, I was not.

"Been thinking about you all day," he said. "I kept smelling you on my fingers when I drove home last night. Gave me another hard-on."

Hooboy. That sent my blood in a southerly direction. Okay, maybe I could channel my inner phone-sex operator. "Then it's too bad you left or I could've taken care of that for you." Hmm. Surely I could do better...

Another low laugh. "I'd ask you to tell me, in detail, how you would've done that, but I'm afraid I need to go."

"Yeah, about that," I hesitated. "While I appreciate what you did, Steven's not going to be happy about it."

"I'm not worried."

I rolled my eyes. Alpha males. "I didn't think you would

be, but *I* am. He's certifiable. What if he does something crazy? He could hurt you."

"I can take care of myself, Sage," Parker said.

"That's what you keep telling me," I said. "Pardon me if I'm not convinced of that."

He sighed. "This isn't my ideal, no. But you're safe and so is the company. If Steven gets out of hand, I'll take care of it."

I let my silence speak for me.

"I've gotta go, sweetheart. I'll call you later, okay?"

"Yeah, okay. Bye."

"Bye." He ended the call.

I know he meant to be reassuring, but I still didn't feel any better.

* * *

I caved and asked Schultz to leave one of the family cars at my apartment—it was just so much easier than calling a cab—then I drove myself to Ashley's house.

I decided to go for badass and wore black jeans, a fitted black long-sleeved shirt, and slicked my hair back in a ponytail. I didn't trust myself with a gun, so I brought a knife. I intended to leave with information, and Ashley was going to give it to me, even if I had to scare ten years off her life.

It was dark and I parked half a block away but near enough to where I could see her house. There were no lights on and there was no car in the driveway. She wasn't home yet.

Hmm.

Breaking and entering wasn't high on my list of Things I Excelled At, but her house was old and so were the locks. I used my knife to jimmy the dead bolt at the back door and eased inside. I stood still for a moment, waiting to see if a dog might be waiting for me or if I'd triggered an alarm. Neither happened.

I released my breath and let my eyes adjust to the darkness. I'd entered the kitchen, so I walked through to the hallway. Waiting in the bedroom would probably be the best location and give me the most bang for my buck.

Sure enough, her bedroom was the master at the end of the hallway. It was girly enough not to be anyone else's. She had a slipper chair in the corner opposite the door and I sat there.

I'd been sitting in the dark for several minutes when something touched my leg. I squeaked in alarm—some threat I was—and looked down to see a white Persian cat rubbing against my leg. He glanced up at me, then hopped onto my lap. After kneading my legs for a moment with clawless paws, he settled down.

After I started hesitantly petting his head, he began to purr. Oh, this was too good. I felt like Dr. Evil, sitting here with a cat on my lap while I waited for my victim. I nearly snorted.

Time passed slowly and I was bored. Glancing at my watch for the umpteenth time, I wondered why they never showed *this* in the movies. Bond wouldn't be so glamorous if people saw him nodding off as he awaited the bad guy, who was late getting home.

Bookshelves on the wall drew my eye. I stood, the cat leaping down to floor and giving me a kitty glare of disdain. I used the flashlight on my phone to peruse the titles of the books. Typical fiction and a few photo albums lined the shelves. I was about to sit down again when a line of yearbooks caught my attention. They were for a high school not far from mine. It appeared Ashley and I had practically been neighbors.

Curious, I slid one off the shelf and opened it. Typical class photos lined the pages. I searched out her name under the Ws. *Hmm.* A cheerleader. Why was I not surprised?

Idly, I scanned the rest of the page, then stopped short.

No. It couldn't be. But it was. Jessie was pictured in the same class. Ashley knew Jessie?

I heard the front door open and hurriedly replaced the book on the shelf before going back to my chair. It was showtime.

I took a deep breath, my nerves strung tight and my heart racing. I had to look the part if I wanted answers.

Steps advanced down the hall and a light was flicked on. My eyes adjusted just as Ashley appeared in the doorway. To my surprise, she didn't notice me but walked right in and slipped off her shoes. She released a heavy sigh.

"Hard day?"

She spun around and yelped at the sound of my voice, her eyes widening when she spotted me.

"Remember me?" I smiled as maliciously as I was able, and she went pale.

She took off running, but I'd been expecting this and wasted no time chasing after her. I remembered some of my short lesson with Parker in moves and I grabbed a handful of her hair as well as the waistband of her slacks. Planting my foot, I leveraged her suddenly off-balance body and she was flat on her back, the wind knocked out of her.

"Nice try," I puffed, more out of breath than I should've been for that short of a sprint. "I take it you were expecting me to be dead. That's what was supposed to happen last night, right? When you locked me in that room?"

I thought about the knife in my pocket, but I just couldn't pull it out. I'd heard somewhere that you shouldn't show a weapon unless you were prepared to use it. And I knew there was no way I'd be using a knife on Ashley, not unless I was suddenly fighting for my life.

"I swear, I didn't know that was going to happen," she said. "I was just supposed to let him know if anyone came snooping."

"Let who know?" I asked, wanting confirmation.

"Steven Shea."

"And he paid you off?"

She nodded.

"Did he also pay you to scrub the files?"

She hesitated, her eyes glancing past me toward the door, but I resisted the instant urge to turn and look.

"He almost killed me last night," I said. "That makes you an accessory. You should tell me now or I'm going to the cops."

"Please don't," she said. "Yes, he paid me to delete the electronic file and destroy the paper one. Then I just had to call if anyone came looking."

"But you didn't destroy the paper," I said. "Why?"

"Because I didn't ask to get involved in this mess!" She was near tears. "It was bad enough deleting the electronic file. I couldn't bring myself to destroy the paper one. Someone should know he's trying to hide it, and if I destroyed everything, no one would have."

"But you still went through with calling him?"

"I thought you were a test," she said. "And he'd already threatened me. If I hadn't called..." She swallowed hard. "So I did and a man showed up. He told me to lock the door when I left. That's what I did. I swear, I didn't know he was going to try and kill you."

"What exactly did you think was going to happen?" I retorted. It didn't take a rocket scientist to figure out she'd put me in imminent danger. I felt kind of bad for threatening her like this, but her pretending she hadn't taken an active role in nearly getting me—a total stranger—killed, wasn't helping her either.

"I'm so sorry," she said.

I sighed. She sounded sincere, and I could relate to being threatened and scared. I reached down and took her hand, helping her to her feet. "Steven Shea is bad news," I said. "Tell me the name you marked out of the file. Who'd he get married to?"

The sound of a gunshot and crashing glass exploded in my ears. Ashley's body jerked, then red began leaking from her chest. She crumpled to the floor.

I stood for a second, stunned, then dropped to my knees. Ashley was limp. I pulled at her arm.

"Ashley! Ashley!"

She didn't respond. Her head lolled to the side and I saw her eyes, glassy and empty. She was dead. Shot by someone outside.

Fear was a bitter taste in the back of my throat as I crawled toward the door. There was no further gunfire, but I didn't know if it was because the shooter had left or was waiting for me to present a good target.

The thought that someone was watching you, had a gun pointed at you, was enough to turn anyone's knees to jelly. I got to the hallway and stood, my breath a sharp intake that caught in my chest. Should I run outside? What if he was waiting? Was it the same guy who'd been after me before?

Sirens screamed in the distance as I stood in indecision. Oh, thank God. The cops were coming.

Please be coming here, I prayed.

Apparently someone was listening tonight because sure enough, the sirens pulled up outside and I heard a pounding on the front door.

"CPD! Open up!"

I went into the living room just as the front door burst open. I threw up my hands in the universal gesture of surrender as men in uniform streamed inside, weapons at the ready.

"Please don't shoot me!" That would really suck.

The swarm of police moved around me and before I even knew what was happening, I was facedown on the floor, my hands behind my back.

"I'm so glad you're here," I babbled. "He killed Ashley. He's still outside—"

"Woman down in the back! Paramedics!"

I knew it was too late to help Ashley, even as two men rushed by carrying equipment. Tears leaked from my eyes and it felt like I couldn't breathe. I was numb as I was handcuffed, watching as they rolled a gurney with Ashley's body on it out the door. They put me in the back of a police car and we drove away.

CHAPTER SEVENTEEN

It wasn't until they were fingerprinting me and taking my mug shot that I realized I'd been arrested. I'd broken into Ashley's house and had a knife on me, not to mention that my outfit, which I'd thought was so "badass," was also a red flag proclaiming *I'm Up To No Good*.

I'd never been arrested in my life and while I was trying to keep calm, on the inside I was quaking. The cop processing me took me into a tiny room with a table and two chairs. He handcuffed me to the chair, then left me alone. The heavy metal door swung shut behind him.

Time inched by, my own panic not helping matters any. I was supposed to get a phone call, right? But so far, no one had offered. They'd fired questions at me about my name and address, but that was all.

Oh yeah, and that Miranda Rights question about whether I'd understood.

I shuddered. Hearing that had made this all turn more surreal. Ashley had died right there in front of me. Why? She'd done what he'd told her to do. Had Steven just been tying up loose ends? She'd been about to tell me the name of his bride.

The door opened, cutting off my thoughts. Ryker walked in.

"Oh, thank you, God," I breathed. "I'm so glad you're here." My throat thickened with relieved tears.

"What the hell happened?" he asked, unlocking my handcuffs. I rubbed my sore wrists. "I told you not to do anything stupid."

"I didn't! I was just talking to her, and she told me Steven paid her off to scrub his files. Then someone shot her."

"Jesus, Sage! What were you thinking? You could've been killed!"

My face crumpled. "P-please don't yell at m-me," I blubbered through my tears.

Ryker cursed, then pulled me into his arms, hugging me tightly as I sobbed against his shoulder. His T-shirt grew wet as I cried. Every time I closed my eyes, I saw Ashley's slack face and the livid red wound in her chest. I'd been strong for a while now, and I couldn't take any more. The hits just kept coming, no matter which way I turned.

He let me get it out for a while, until my sobs had degenerated into the kind of hiccupping you do after a bad crying jag. My nose was clogged, my eyes were swollen, and my head pounded.

"Come on," he said. "You could use a drink, I think."

"Are they g-gonna let me go?" I stammered, using my sleeve to wipe my face.

"The shot came from outside," he said. "They know you didn't kill her. And Flanagan owes me one anyway."

I kept my gaze lowered as Ryker took my hand and led

me outside. Although I hadn't killed Ashley, I'd been arrested, and that humiliation was still fresh.

Ryker had his bike there and he climbed on first, then helped me. I wrapped my arms around his torso, glad to be able to lean on someone else for a while, even if it was just for a motorcycle ride.

Ten minutes later, we were pulling up outside the cop bar where we'd had our first dinner together. Ryker ushered me inside and we slid onto two stools at the bar.

"Hey, Ryker," the bartender said. "Your usual?"

"Better make it the hard stuff this time, Sammy. One for my friend, too."

Sammy nodded. Adding ice to two glasses, he poured an inch of Irish whiskey on top of each, then slid them in front of us.

Ryker lifted one. "To Ashley," he said in a somber toast. I lifted my glass and we both drank to a girl we didn't know, but who had gotten caught up with the wrong kind of people.

The whiskey went down smooth, its cool fire spreading warmth in my belly.

"So what did she tell you before she was killed?" he asked.

I recounted what she'd said, right up until she'd been about to tell me the name of Steven's wife.

"...and that's when she—" My throat closed up and I hurriedly took another sip of the whiskey.

"And you thought if you found out who Steven was married to, you'd be able to find her and she'd give you dirt you could use to blackmail him?" Ryker asked. I nodded, and he looked pissed. "You do realize that blackmail is illegal, no matter how justified you might think your motives, not to mention that Steven is batshit crazy enough to just kill you rather than cave meekly to your demands."

I nodded, disconsolate.

Ryker sighed heavily. "I'm sorry, babe. I'm just trying to look out for you. Parker's got this handled. Let him take care of it."

"He doesn't have this *handled*," I retorted. "Going to work for that scumbag is not *handling* it. And I have this nasty suspicion that this wife Steven doesn't want us to find is none other than Natalie." I waited, wondering what Ryker would say to that particular bombshell.

His brows rose. "You think Steven Shea is Natalie's husband?"

I nodded. "It makes sense, doesn't it? Why else come back so suddenly just at the same time Steven returns to take over his dad's business? He wants Parker and guess who has a relationship with Parker already? Natalie. Think about it."

Ryker frowned. "I understand it looks plausible, but why would she say Jessie was kidnapped? And why make up the whole story about the dead abusive husband?"

"To get your attention, gain your sympathy, and have a way in," I said. "Plus gets her ten thousand dollars. Don't forget the supposed ransom money Parker gave her."

Ryker downed the rest of his drink. Sammy looked his way and Ryker tapped the edge of the glass for a refill.

"Okay," he said. "Now, don't take this the wrong way..."

That never, ever boded well.

"...but are you sure that maybe you're not grasping a little bit at straws here? Maybe because you don't like Natalie?"

I gritted my teeth. Men. Always thinking it had to be personal. "You're absolutely right," I said calmly. "I don't like Natalie. However, perhaps you're so blinded by your feelings for her that you refuse to see that there's just a few too many coincidences here."

"Natalie has her faults," he said, "but I'm not ready to say she's gone that far down the rabbit hole."

I took another drink, thinking. "At least think about it," I said. "Don't write off the possibility."

"I'm a cop," he said. "I don't rule out anything."

"Fair enough."

We lapsed into silence, drinking the whiskey and lost in our own thoughts. I could hear the strains of John Cougar Mellencamp singing about Jack and Diane on the jukebox in the corner. My stomach growled loud enough for Ryker to hear it.

"Shit, Sage," he said. "When was the last time you ate?"

I scrunched up my face, thinking. "Breakfast, maybe?" Hadn't Carrie made sure I ate this morning? It seemed so long ago...

"You know you gotta be a special kind of stupid to forget to eat," Ryker said, signaling Sammy for a menu.

"Shut up," I groused.

"Order something. And it better only have vegetables as a topping."

Got it.

I ordered a bacon cheeseburger with cheese fries. Ryker ordered the same.

"You didn't eat dinner either?" I asked.

"Of course I did. No reason to turn down a cheeseburger." Ryker glanced at me. "There's that smile. Knew it was there somewhere."

He was right. I hadn't had much reason to smile lately. "Sorry," I said. "It's been a little rough. My dad, the company, nearly getting killed a few too many times, plus—" I stopped. I'd been about to say *Parker*, but realized Ryker probably wouldn't want to discuss my love life troubles.

"Plus Parker, you mean," he said.

I needed another drink for this.

"He's with Natalie…kind of," I said with a shrug. "I miss him and I want this whole thing over and done with."

"Give it time. Things have a way of working themselves out."

I just looked at him.

He snorted a laugh at my expression. "I know, it sounds like a fucking bumper sticker, but I'm serious. It'll be okay."

"Whatever." I shrugged, taking another swig of my refilled whiskey. I was starting to feel the effects, which were wholly welcome.

Our burgers came and it was the best burger I'd had in a really long time. I ate every bite, washing it down with more whiskey. Although the grease soaked up some of the booze, I was feeling full and pretty carefree by the time I'd chomped the last of my fries.

"Do you have a dollar?" I asked, eyeing the jukebox. Ryker handed over a bill and I eased off the stool. The room tilted for just a moment, but then I steadied myself.

"You got it?" he asked.

"*Pfffft*, yeah." *Duh*. I could walk to the jukebox, no problem.

A dollar bought four songs. Turned out, Ryker'd given me a five. "That's…" I did the math in my head. "…twenty songs. Cool."

I scrolled through the list and picked as many favorites as I could find. Happily I headed back to Ryker, now nursing a beer, as No Doubt began to play.

"Gwen Stefani? Really?"

I stuck my tongue out at Ryker as I hopped back on my stool. "So this is weird, right?" I blurted.

He took another swig of his beer. "What's weird?"

"Me. You. So we're like friends now."

"Yeah," he said. "Why's that weird?"

"Because." I shrugged. "We used to...you know..." *Have sex*, I thought but didn't say. Here's hoping he could fill in the blanks.

"Doesn't mean we have to never see each other again," he said. "I care about you. I think you care about me, too, right?"

"You know I do."

"Then don't think so much."

Excellent advice. Really, really excellent.

"Let's dance." Ryker grabbed my hand and pulled me onto the tiny parquet floor that could be called a dance floor if you were really loose in your requirements. He spun me around until I was laughing and nearly falling on my ass. Then we did two shots of tequila and decided we were experts at doing the Thriller dance, even if Thriller wasn't playing.

I wanted to play pool, but couldn't remember if I was stripes or solids. Ryker kept making fun of me for hitting his balls in, then the conversation degenerated into bad sexual puns about balls.

At some point, Sammy called us a cab and we tumbled into the backseat. I had no idea what time it was and for once, I didn't care.

"I'm so tired," I mumbled, leaning on Ryker's shoulder. My eyes slipped closed.

"You should be. It's been a long fucking week."

"Thanks for taking care of me tonight."

"No problem." He put his arm around me and squeezed.

I had vague impressions of my building, the elevator, and Ryker taking the keys from me to unlock my door.

"I need a bath," I said, stumbling toward my bathroom.

"You're not serious?" Ryker called after me.

"I need to relax."

"Relax any more and you'll be comatose."

Hardy har har.

A steaming tub of water later, and I felt much better. A knock on the bathroom door made my eyes pop open.

"You alive in there?" Ryker said through the door.

"Yep."

"All right. Don't drown. I'm going to bed. I'll go home in the morning."

"'kay."

I stayed in the water a little while longer, until my fingers began to prune. Finally, I pulled the plug and got out. I knew there were a lot of things I should be upset about, but I just couldn't remember what. And it was a blessed relief not to be upset.

Dragging a T-shirt over my head and pulling on some underwear, I smothered a yawn as I headed for my bed. There was already a lump there proclaiming Ryker wasn't going to sleep on the couch, but I didn't care. He was snoring and all I wanted was to do the same (except ladies don't snore, of course).

Slipping under the covers, I sighed, snuggling into my pillow. The room spun when I closed my eyes, making me think I might lose that bacon cheeseburger after all, but I was out before my stomach had the chance to revolt.

* * *

The pounding in my head made me groan. Damn. Should've taken ibuprofen before I'd gone to bed. Or better yet, not had that second shot of tequila. Or had it been the third whiskey on rocks that had done me in?

I realized a second longer than it should have taken that

the pounding was on my front door, not just inside my head.

"Shit," I muttered, rolling out of bed. Ryker still snored on his side. It figured. So much for those fabled *cop instincts* they made movies about. Real life was so much more mundane.

"I'm coming, I'm coming," I called out as I navigated my hallway and kitchen. Then I winced as my voice echoed with malicious intent through my head. The pounding stopped, thank God. I peered through the peephole.

Parker.

That was enough to put a smile on my face and I fumbled with the lock in my haste to open the door.

"Hey!" I said, once I had it open. He looked good. Really good. A deep charcoal suit so dark it was nearly black, with a stark white shirt and silk tie in swirling jeweled shades of emerald, topaz, and amethyst. He was in a *fantastic* mood this morning. "You look incredible."

Parker smiled, that sweet slow spread of his lips that made his eyes soften and my insides turn to melted caramel.

"Good morning," he said, his voice a teasing lilt. "Rough night?"

Oh yeah. I probably looked like a disaster. Had I remembered to take my makeup off? Raccoon eyes only looked sexy on models.

"A little bit," I said, rubbing my face and combing my fingers through my tangled hair.

"Sage, who are you talking to?"

I turned to see Ryker stepping out of the hallway. He was pulling on his shirt, but his jeans were still unfastened. I opened my mouth to tell him Parker was there when Parker suddenly flew past me. Faster than I could take a breath, he'd landed a solid fist into Ryker's jaw.

"Oh my God! Parker!" I ran toward them as Ryker shoved him away.

"What the fuck are you doing?" Ryker spat.

"You piece of shit," Parker growled, furious. "You've been waiting, haven't you, just waiting to get me back." He hit Ryker again and I flinched at the sound.

"Are you of your mind?" I yelled. "Stop it!"

Now they were both enraged and hitting each other. I shoved my fingers into my hair, gripping my head in helpless frustration. I couldn't stand to see them doing this and when I saw blood, I couldn't just watch any longer.

Rushing forward, I grabbed Parker. "Stop!"

He sidestepped, off-balance, and suddenly there was a blinding, smashing pain in my head. I stumbled and fell, unable to see anything. My head felt like it was going to explode.

"Shit! Oh my God, Sage, I'm so sorry—"

I heard Ryker, but couldn't respond. The pain was so bad, nausea clawed at my throat.

"Leave," Parker snarled. "Haven't you done enough?"

I couldn't concentrate on them, though I felt someone's hands on me as I lay on the floor, my knees drawn up to my chest in the fetal position.

"You're the fucking asshole who did it," Ryker retorted. "You of all people should know not to believe everything you see."

The nausea wouldn't abate and to my mortification, I turned over and began dry heaving. Someone—Parker, I think—gently brushed my hair back from my face as I retched. If I stained my six-hundred-dollar rug from Pier One, I was going to be so pissed...

When I could finally catch my breath, I said the only thing that I could think of.

"Both of you, get out."

Neither of them spoke for a moment. Maybe they hadn't heard me.

"I mean it," I managed, pushing myself to a sitting position. "You're both acting like idiots. I'm not some kind of bone to be fought over. Get out."

Ryker looked ashamed of himself, especially when I caught him looking at my cheek and temple where he'd accidentally hit me. Parker looked...emotionless. As though whatever he was feeling and thinking had been sucked into a vacuum and locked away tight. I hated when he did that. Especially when it was obviously not true. He'd gone apeshit when he'd shown up and thought he was seeing the proverbial Morning After between Ryker and me.

Too bad he should've known me better by now.

"I'm not Natalie," I gritted out through the pain in my head. "And I'm *not* playing a game. Both of you. Out."

Ryker left first, still looking embarrassed and upset. I felt kind of bad considering he'd just been helping me out last night. But he also had retaliated against Parker rather than stopping everything. Men. The first chance they had to unleash some frustration, and they take it out on each other.

Parker's gaze burned a hole in me as I got off the floor, trying to ignore him. His tie was askew and a button torn off his jacket, but I didn't think he noticed.

"I'm not leaving you when you're hurt," he said.

"You're the reason I'm hurt," I snapped back. "Did you think you could just come in here and pick a fight for no reason?"

"I thought—it looked like—"

"It's obvious what you thought it looked like," I said. "And it's insulting. To me and to Ryker. You owe him an apology and you know it."

He said nothing.

"I'm fine," I said. "You can go." I was dangerously close to tears and I didn't want him to see me cry.

"Sage, I'm sorry—" he began.

I cut him off. "I don't want to hear it right now," I said. "I need some space."

Parker shoved his fingers through his hair in frustration, his lips pressed tightly together. I saw a bruise darkening his jaw and steeled myself against the urge to get some ice for him. If anyone needed ice, it was me.

Parker gave me a curt nod, his gaze penetrating. "Fine. I'll go." He headed to the door but stopped halfway out and turned. "Natalie has nothing to do with you and me. I just want you to know that. She and I are over. I swear to you."

I studied him. "What aren't you telling me?" There was something there, I could tell by the flicker in his eyes.

"Trust me. Please."

A beat passed. I gave him a slow nod. "Okay."

Something like relief flashed across his face, then he was gone.

But just because I trusted Parker, didn't mean I trusted Natalie.

* * *

I called Carrie and told her I wouldn't be in today. She wasn't surprised, given everything I'd been going through, and I didn't disillusion her assumption that I was going to chill at home. What I was going to do was a shot in the dark and she'd likely try to talk me out of it.

I'd come up with a plan, something that would get Natalie to tell the truth for once. I felt as though I was in a holding pattern with Parker. We wouldn't be able to move forward until this mess with Natalie was resolved. Since he'd elected to keep me in the dark about whatever I was supposed to "just trust" him about, I decided to take matters into my own hands. Maybe some women would have meekly sat at home, but I wasn't that kind of girl.

Sitting down at my kitchen table, I wrote a very carefully worded note. I folded it and stuffed it in an envelope, then sealed it. Then I wrote two more notes and did the same thing.

Time to put things into motion.

CHAPTER EIGHTEEN

It took me the better part of the afternoon to arrange for delivery of my missives. One to Natalie and one each to Parker and Ryker.

Then it was time to prepare... and wait.

The location I'd specified in my notes was a warehouse our company no longer used. That area of town had become too riddled with crime; we'd elected to pull out and put the building on the market. So far, no takers, but it stood empty and that suited my purposes. Although at ten o'clock at night, it wasn't the most welcoming of locations.

I could hear dogs barking a street over. Up the block I saw a small group of teens walking down the side of the street in a clump.

"Yeah, this isn't creepy or anything," I muttered to myself, my breath coming out as a puff of cold air. I shivered, and it wasn't just from the autumn chill.

I unlocked the main door and went inside. There was an office so coated in dirt and dust from the gravel lot that I immediately began sneezing. It was dark and musty and I refrained from turning on more than just one light. A weak fluorescent lamp flickered overhead, the buzzing of it sounding overly loud in the empty room.

The door on the other side of the office led to the interior of the warehouse. I stepped through, moving to my right, to the bank of switches. Although I threw them all, only a scattering of lights came on, high overhead, leaving much of the warehouse in shadows.

I was armed. The small revolver fit in my back pocket. I'd had to go by my parents' house to get it from Dad's gun case. Luckily, my mom was still at the hospital.

Anxiety itched underneath my skin. My dad should be coming out of the coma anytime, but so far I'd heard nothing from my mother. I couldn't give up faith, though. He'd come out of it. My dad was a fighter. He had to wake up. He would.

Pushing those thoughts aside—I didn't need any distractions—I found an empty nook between stacks of moldy wooden pallets. It afforded me a good view of the space, kept me hidden, and I'd have my back to the wall. All necessary if this was to work.

I went over my plan in my head while I waited.

On the note to Parker and Ryker, I'd written *I have proof she's lying*. Then to Natalie I'd sent *I escaped. Come get me.* I'd signed it: *Jessie*.

On all three I'd put this address. If all went as planned, Natalie would show up, expecting to find Jessie. I'd confront her, let Parker and Ryker overhear how she'd been using them on his behalf, and hopefully that'd be the end of it.

Natalie would arrive first. I waited, my palms sweating

even though the interior of the warehouse was cold. I just hoped Parker and Ryker would forgive me for yanking the wool from their eyes about her.

Thirty minutes later, the scrape and squeak of the door told me someone was there. Right on time.

But it wasn't Natalie who stepped out of the office and into the dim light of the warehouse. It was Jessie.

Shit.

"Jessie, what are you doing here?" I asked, hurrying toward her. I had to hide her before Natalie got there.

She started, her head jerking toward me. "Sage?"

"Yeah, who else?" I grabbed her arm as I glanced at my watch. "Come on. We need to hide. Natalie will be here any second."

"Why is Natalie coming?" she asked, keeping up with me as I nudged her inside my hiding spot and scooted in next to her.

"I sent her a note," I said grimly. "She'll want to come, believe me."

"You're the one who sent Ryker the note?"

I shot her a look. "You got it? It was for Ryker."

"He's been at work all day, so I opened it," she said. "I thought it was better for me to come than Ryker. He's been put through enough already."

Dammit. I cursed under my breath. The last thing I wanted was Jessie getting caught in the middle of this and possibly being hurt. The situation was dicey enough as it was.

"Okay, well, it's too late for you to leave, so you'll just have to stay," I said. "Just keep quiet, okay?" Even if Ryker didn't show, Parker would still be there.

"Why is Natalie coming?" she asked quietly.

"Because I sent her a note," I said, glancing at her. "I think she's married to Steven Shea. I know she's been working with him to get Parker and use him to gain control of another company and force us out of business."

Jessie's eyes widened. "Married? She's his wife?"

I nodded. "She made up some story about him being in jail ten years ago and then getting out and that's why she faked her death, but really they're working together." I glanced sideways at her. "Don't tell me you didn't know." I was suspicious of everyone now.

"She told me her husband died," Jessie said. "He was killed."

"She lied to you." It didn't surprise me at all that Natalie would lie to her sister. "She used you in her schemes, saying you'd been kidnapped. Then she pulled in Parker and Ryker."

The door squeaked again and I shut up, watching to see who appeared.

Natalie stepped tentatively through the door.

"Stay here," I said to Jessie in a bare whisper.

I waited until she'd taken a few more steps before emerging from my hiding place.

"Glad you could make it," I said.

Natalie's eyes narrowed. "You. I should've known."

"The game's up, Natalie. I know the truth, and I'm through watching you lie and manipulate Parker and Ryker."

"What 'truth'? What do you think you know?" she sneered. "You're supposedly so smart. Go on and tell me."

"I know you were lying about your dead husband," I shot back. "He's not dead at all, is he, Natalie?"

Her face paled. "What do you mean?"

"We both know he's alive. You've been doing his dirty work all this time."

Confusion etched her face. "You have it wrong. I don't know what you—"

"Stop lying!"

My furious yell echoed and she jumped. Her eyes went to my hand. Without even realizing it, I'd pulled my gun and was pointing it at her. Natalie's throat moved as she swallowed.

"I'm sick of your lies," I said, my voice normal again. I wouldn't lose control. I was just pissed and I'd had enough. Enough of her, enough of being hurt, enough of watching the man I loved sacrifice himself time and again for me, enough of life kicking me in the teeth.

Natalie didn't say a word or move an inch. We were locked in position and every muscle in my body was tense, ready to strike.

I got the eye of the tiger...

The sound of my cell phone's ringtone echoed through the building. Shit. I'd forgotten to silence it. I didn't move, didn't take my eyes off Natalie.

...and you're gonna hear me roar...

"You going to answer that or what?"

"Fuck!" I grabbed for the phone and jabbed the button. "Yeah?"

A pause. "Ms. Muccino?"

"Yes. Who's this?"

"Senator Kirk."

Oh. Oh, wow. Talk about bad timing. "Um, yeah, Senator. How are you?"

"I'm well, thank you. I apologize for taking a while to get back to you. I did some digging on the information you sent me. A Natalie Wilson?"

Yeah, way too late. I'd already found out what I needed to know. It'd be good for confirmation, though. "Yes. What did you find out?"

"Ms. Wilson was married—"

Duh.

"—and her husband, a Chad Reynolds aka Rookie, was killed nine months ago. Shot to death in what was later characterized by the local PD as a drug deal gone wrong. Currently unemployed, her whereabouts are unknown."

My stomach sank to my toes.

"Her younger sister, Jessica, was reported as missing to the Chicago police approximately three weeks ago. Local law enforcement have no leads currently in her disappearance."

I stared at Natalie, unable to believe what I was hearing. I'd been wrong. But...how?

"Ms. Muccino? Are you there?"

My mouth was utterly dry. "Yes," I managed, barely audible.

"I did a little more digging, just to be thorough," he continued. "And I found something else that might interest you. SLS Enterprises was run by Leo Shea, as I'm sure you know. His son, Steven Shea, is his heir and I believe has taken up the reins of the company."

There was a pause and the nausea in my stomach increased tenfold, as though I knew what he was going to say before he even said it.

"Ms. Muccino, Steven Shea is married. And his wife is Jessica Wilson. Your friend Natalie's sister."

"Hang up the phone."

I felt the hard metal of a gun barrel to my temple even as I heard Jessie's voice. I swallowed.

"Hang. Up."

I pressed the button to end the call without looking.

"Drop it."

I let go and the phone clattered to the concrete floor. A second later, Jessie had smashed her foot on top of it. That was going to be expensive. I'd already had the screen replaced twice.

"Now toss your gun over to the side. *Not* toward Natalie."

I hated doing it, but what choice did I have? I tossed the gun. Natalie's eyes and mine met. I waited for her to join Jessie.

"What are you doing?" Natalie hissed. "Are you out of your mind?"

"I got sick of waiting for you," Jessie retorted. "You always think you know what to do. Steven's idea was better."

"He's no good, Jessie. I keep telling you that. We're going to get away from him. I almost have enough money so he won't find us."

"Newsflash, big sister: I don't want to get away from him."

Natalie said nothing, her mouth falling open slightly as she stared at Jessie.

"You think you're the only one in the family who knows how to lie. Steven and I have been together for years. You left me, too, when you ran away. Steve took care of me. When he found out his dad was dead and the business was his, he knew he could make it bigger and better. We just had to get rid of the competition first."

"I'm guessing I'm the competition," I said grimly.

Jessie laughed. "You were incredibly easy," she said to me. "So handy, you being with both Parker and Ryker. Just like Natalie. Steven cooked up the whole kidnapping thing to control Natalie. All she had to do was infiltrate and find a weakness he could exploit."

"You're my sister," Natalie said. "I trusted you. You let me believe Steven was holding you against your will so you could just use me? What was the ten grand for, Jessie?"

"Steven needed capital," Jessie said. "And it helped make things look more...authentic, don't you agree?"

"It wasn't my money. It was Parker's," Natalie said stiffly. "I can't believe you'd do this to me, Jessie."

"Don't play the victim card," I ground out. "You killed my security guard when you broke in to our offices. You mutilated my neighbor's cat. And don't forget Rafael, *falling* to his death. You pushed him out that window."

"Please," Jessie snorted in disdain. "Natalie doesn't have the guts to do that. I did. Rafael had to die before he talked, and he would've talked."

"*You* knocked me out in that building?" Natalie asked. "You could've killed me."

Out of the corner of my eye I saw Jessie shrug. "But I didn't, did I?"

"Jessica, please tell me you're not telling them the details of our evil plan, like the villain in some Bond film."

All of us turned to see Steven Shea striding toward us.

I lunged, knocking Jessie's hand away from my head. My hand fastened around her wrist and I hammered a vicious blow to her solar plexus.

She doubled over, the gun falling from her grip to the ground. I grabbed for it—

A gunshot sounded, then another, as pain exploded in my leg. I fell, my leg refusing to hold my weight, just as Steven's foot kicked Jessie's gun well beyond my reach.

"Gotta watch this one," he said to a coughing and gasping Jessie. "She's scrappy." He grinned at me.

I grimaced, clutching my calf as blood seeped through my jeans and onto my hands. "So glad you could make it," I ground out.

"Can we just get this over with and get out of here already?" Jessie asked. She'd recovered, but still clutched her gut where I'd hit her. *Hope I left a mark, bitch.*

"Get what over with?" Natalie asked. "You shot her.

You think she's just going to forget that? Or what you've said?"

"Of course not," Steven replied. "And I have to say, I'm kind of glad Jessie opened her big mouth. It makes this so much easier."

Before I could process what he'd said, he'd turned the gun on Jessie and shot her point blank in the chest. She was dead before her body hit the ground. Natalie screamed and ran forward.

"Ah ah ah..." Steven warned, turning the gun on Natalie, who skidded to a halt. Tears were streaming down her face, which was contorted with rage.

"You killed my sister, you sonofabitch!" Her yell echoed around us.

"Jessica was a loose end," Steven said. "And I don't like leaving loose ends. Besides, *I* didn't kill her. *You* did. You killed Sage, and your sister, then in a fit of despair, turned the gun on yourself. It's tragic, really."

A cold shiver of dread crept down my spine. Steven was a psyho, and a smart one at that. He was going to kill us all and walk away.

"And what will that get you?" I asked, desperately trying to think of a way to outsmart him. "You still won't have a monopoly in this town. Even if I die, my dad is still alive and we own a controlling share in Sikes now. You can't come against us."

"I'm so glad you mentioned that." Reaching inside his jacket, he pulled out a sheaf of folded papers. "I just need you to sign these papers, releasing those shares to SLS Enterprises."

"You can rot in hell before I do that."

"I thought you might say that." He tossed the papers at me and reached for his cell phone. I watched, but his gun hand remained steady, pointing at me. "So I have a backup plan." He turned the screen of his phone so I could see it.

It was my mom. She wasn't looking at the camera, but focused on my dad, still unconscious in his hospital bed. I thought it was a photo, but then she moved, and I realized I was watching live video. Someone was right there in the room with my mom and dad. They were both in danger and didn't even know it.

Panic and rage shot through me. "No! Don't you dare do anything to them! I will kill you!"

"There is really nothing like the love between a child and her parents, is there," Steven said, ignoring my threat. "All you have to do is sign, and your parents will remain alive. Refuse and... well, do I really need to say any more?"

"You won't get away with this," I said, desperate to buy some time. I winced at how movie-cliché that sounded.

He pocketed the phone, then tossed a pen at me. "Of course I will. Now sign."

"Parker will find a way to stop you," I said. "You won't get my company, no matter what these papers say."

"I'm not worried about Parker. I imagine he's next in line to show up here? Too bad for him. He'll be walking into an ambush."

"So you're just going to leave a trail of dead bodies in your wake? You really think no one's going to question that?"

"Nothing links any of you to me," he said. "But you and Parker and Natalie... well, that's a different story. Lovers' quarrels so often turn deadly."

I hated him in that moment. I hated his self-assurance and his deadly arrogance.

"You think you have it all figured out, don't you," I sneered. "Did you ever stop to wonder why I picked this spot? This building in particular?"

For the first time, doubt flickered in Steven's eyes.

"I mean, do you *really* think I'd lure you out to a deserted warehouse, knowing what a fucking lunatic you are?"

In two steps he was in front of me, the barrel of his gun pressed against the center of my forehead.

"I'd be very careful if I were you. This *fucking lunatic* is holding a gun to your head."

My breath was lodged in my chest as I stared into his empty, soulless eyes. I swallowed, careful not to move a muscle.

"Explain," he demanded.

"This is a bad neighborhood," I said. "The warehouse got broken into a lot. So much so, that we suspected an employee was behind it. So we had security cameras installed."

"Bullshit. There are none. I looked."

"They're not meant to be seen. That would've defeated the purpose," I said. "But the point is, they're watching and recording. Everything you've said and done. You won't get away with anything."

Steven's jaw went tight and I could feel cold sweat break out all over my body. It would take just a twitch of his finger, and I'd be dead. This was a very dangerous gamble I was taking.

"Well," he said at last. "Aren't you just full of surprises." His smile was thin.

I swallowed. "We can make a deal. I can give you the recording."

"What do you want?" he asked.

"My parents. You call off your guy."

"Fine." Reaching for his cell phone, he held it to his ear. "Abort," he said. "Repeat, I said abort." He ended the call. "Satisfied?"

"And Natalie. She gets to leave."

He laughed outright. "That is rich," he said. "You're bargaining for *her* life? She wouldn't do the same for you, trust me."

He might be right on that one, but it didn't matter. "Natalie gets to leave," I repeated.

Steven took a step back and glanced at Natalie. She wasn't looking at us. Her gaze was on Jessie and her face was wet with tears.

"Out," Steven said to her. She didn't move.

"Natalie," I said sharply. She jerked, as though awakened from a trance, and looked at me. "Go."

She took two hesitant steps backward, watching Steven as one would a snake preparing to strike, then she turned and ran toward the office. I watched her disappear into it, then heard a door slamming shut.

Now I just had to hope she had enough sense to send help and I could delay long enough for them to get here.

Steven motioned with the gun. "Your turn."

Turning, I headed for the far corner of the warehouse. There was a panel there, hidden behind a plain metal cupboard. I opened the cupboard to reveal a number key touchpad. I tapped in ten numbers and a click sounded as the panel unlocked.

Behind it was a black box that held a rotation of tapes. Pressing a button, I had it eject the current tape and handed it to Steven, who pocketed it.

"Now what?" I asked.

The gun went off.

I stared in shock at the smoke rising from the barrel of Steven's gun, then I looked down.

Blood was spreading on my chest, on the right side. I touched it, certain it couldn't be real. Red stained my shaking fingers. My knees gave and I collapsed onto the ground.

Steven crouched down. "That's what," he said. "You're an idiot. Giving up your only leverage to save Natalie? Dumb. She would've let you rot."

"No, I didn't, asshole."

Natalie stood in the doorway, Jessie's gun in her hand. Steven whirled to face her and she pulled the trigger.

The impact made him stumble back, and she shot again. And again. And again. His body hit the wall and he slid down, leaving streaks of red in his wake. He hit the ground and didn't move, his eyes staring sightlessly ahead.

"Help," I managed to whisper. It was hard to breathe and the pain that I hadn't felt earlier now burned.

Natalie knelt next to me and pulled out her phone. She was talking on it. "My friend's been shot...please send help." She rattled off the address, then listened. "Yes, in the chest. There's some blood." She listened again and looked at my mouth. "Yes, there's like a pink foam." More listening. "Okay."

Tucking the phone between her cheek and shoulder, she leaned over and placed her hand over the wound. I groaned at the pain of her touching it, but I could breathe slightly easier.

"Just hurry!" The panic in her voice made my eyes open. They'd been drifting shut. I didn't want to pass out from shock. I wanted to stay awake. I was terrified if I blacked out, I wouldn't wake up.

"Please," I managed. "Please tell—"

"Shh, don't try to talk," she urged me. Pity and fear were in her eyes, and I didn't know which scared me more.

"Gotta...listen," I whispered. "P-Parker. Tell him...I l-love him..."

It took forever and every ounce of will I had to get that sentence out. It exhausted me.

"Of course I will, but you'll tell him yourself," she said, tears wetting her lashes. "The paramedics will be here any second."

"Y-you even l-look pretty when you c-cry," I stammered. I could still be disgruntled, even as I lay drowning in my own blood.

She huffed a laugh. "Don't be stupid. Stop bleeding and you'd look prettier, too."

There was something else I needed to say. "I'm sorry," I said, unable to do more than whisper. My lips felt wet. "About Jessie."

Tears tracked down Natalie's cheeks. "Me too."

I couldn't understand why Parker hadn't come. "P-Parker..."

"I'll get him for you. I promise."

My eyes closed and I lost some time. When I opened them again, I saw two men I didn't know kneeling next to me. They wore latex gloves and uniforms. Where was Natalie? And Parker? I needed Parker...

I lost some more time.

Vague impressions hit me then and I couldn't tell when I was awake or if I was dreaming. People talking, their voices urgent. Being lifted and moved. Sirens. Then the white of ceiling tiles and fluorescent lights going by fast overhead. More voices, saying things I couldn't understand. I closed my eyes.

* * *

The next time I opened my eyes, I felt no pain, but neither could I move. Everything was blurry and it took a moment to focus.

Movement in my peripheral vision startled me, then I saw it was Parker. He was there.

"You're awake," he said, moving closer to me. He'd been sitting, but now stood. I felt his hand cover mine.

I tried to speak, but couldn't. My eyes widened in panic.

"Shh, don't try to move," he said. "You were shot."

Shot. There was something vague in my memory... Steven. Steven had shot me. I was so tired, it was hard to concentrate. Parker's hand tightened on mine.

"You're going to be okay," he said, his voice thick. "You have to be. I won't lose you."

I wanted to reassure him, but I was too tired, and the darkness pulled me back under.

* * *

The next time I woke, I could move. There seemed to be fewer machines around me. I didn't know if it was morning or evening, based on the weak sunlight coming through the blinds on the window. It did seem like I was in a different place. I didn't remember a window last time I woke.

I moved my legs, relieved when they obeyed my command. As before, Parker appeared a split second later.

"Hey, baby," he said with a smile.

I stared at him. He looked... haggard. There was no other word for it. At least two days' growth of beard shadowed his jaw, his eyes were bloodshot with dark circles underneath them, and his clothes were so wrinkled they looked like he'd slept in them.

"Why do you look like that?" I asked, my voice hoarse and raw. I winced. Ouch.

"Your throat is going to be sore," he said. "You had to have a breathing tube for a while."

"How long?" I didn't want to say much; it hurt. Hopefully, Parker would figure out what I meant.

"It's been two days," he said. "They brought you in and operated. They took the chest tube out yesterday, the breathing tube this morning. You're very lucky. If Steven had used a larger caliber bullet or if it had hit your heart instead..." His voice trailed off and he stopped to clear his throat. "But you're going to be okay. You should be able to go home in a few days."

"Natalie?"

"She's fine. She called me right after the ambulance got there."

"Where were you?" I didn't mean to sound accusatory, but it came out that way.

"I'm so sorry, baby. I'm so damn sorry. It was Jessie. She called me, told me you were in trouble. Sent me on a wild goose chase. I tried calling you, but couldn't reach you."

That's right. Jessie had destroyed my phone. She must have realized I'd sent Parker the same message as the one she'd intercepted to Ryker and made sure he wouldn't show up.

"Mom and Dad?"

"Your dad is awake," he said. "He woke up the night they brought you in. You two will probably be going home at the same time."

I couldn't believe it. Everyone I loved was okay? Despite Jessie and Steven? It didn't seem possible.

"SLS Enterprises has declared bankruptcy," Parked continued. "They were teetering on the brink, the effort to get Sikes and shut you down would've saved them, but those options are both gone now. The board of directors voted unanimously, especially considering their recently deceased CEO was guilty of murder and attempted murder."

Money. It was hard for me to imagine doing what Steven had done just because of money. Then again, most crimes were committed in a moment of passion or because of money.

"Psychotic," I said.

"Yes. And if I'd known you were going to do something so stupid as to provoke him, I'd have locked you in my apartment."

There was anger there, and I understood. It was the kind of anger that comes from fear. But I'd nearly lost Parker once because Steven had come after me. I wouldn't have risked him again by telling him ahead of time.

"Sorry," I said. "Wrong about Natalie." It had stared me in the face, the truth about Jessie. She'd been the tie between Ashley and Steven, had known Ashley in high school so knew where she worked at the records department. But I'd been so set on making Natalie the villain, I hadn't put the pieces together. If I had, maybe she might still be alive. I swallowed down the lump of guilt in my throat.

"I told you to trust me," he said, but his anger was gone. He took my hand, cradling it in both of his. "Natalie finally came clean about Jessie and what Steven was doing. She didn't know her sister would double-cross her like that. I was working with her, trying to feed him enough information to keep you and her safe, until I had enough to press charges and have him arrested." He looked grim. "Unfortunately, I wasn't fast enough."

Ah. So that's what he hadn't been able to tell me. Trying to protect everyone. As usual.

"Why didn't you tell me the truth?" I asked.

"Steven was watching me too closely. He didn't trust me not to double-cross him, which was smart of him because that's exactly what I was doing. If he had an idea that you knew what was going on, I was afraid he'd use you against me."

Steven would absolutely have done that, and I shuddered to think of what methods he would have used on me to control Parker. "So it's over?" I asked.

"It's over, baby."

It was a relief. My eyes slipped closed. "Tired," I murmured.

"Go to sleep. You need the rest."

My eyes popped open when I felt him place my hand back on the bed.

"Don't go," I said, panicked at the thought of Parker leaving me.

"Shh, I'm not going anywhere," he soothed. He brushed my hair back from my forehead and smiled. "I promise you. I'm not leaving until you do."

I believed him, belatedly realizing that's probably why he looked the way he did. He'd been with me since I came in. I hated that he hadn't been taking care of himself, but couldn't bring myself to tell him to leave.

Parker softly stroked my hair and face until I fell asleep.

CHAPTER NINETEEN

Mom, I'm fine. I don't need a wheelchair."

"Hospital policy," the nurse said.

I rolled my eyes. "I'm fine—"

"Get in the damn chair, Sage." When my father spoke, people listened, and I was no exception.

I plunked down in the chair, feeling ridiculous.

"If I have to be wheeled out, so do you," Dad said, which was how it came to be that both of us were wheeled side by side down the hallway.

Ryker and Natalie were waiting outside. To my surprise, she came over and hugged me.

"I'm glad you're okay," she said as I got out of the wheelchair. The nurses left and went back inside.

"Thanks to you," I replied. "But I'm sorry. I'm sorry for not believing you."

She shrugged. "I didn't exactly work hard to gain your trust."

"Natalie," my dad said, coming up next to me. He was moving slowly and had a cane, but was determined to walk. "My goodness, it's been years. How are you?"

"I'm fine, Mr. Muccino. Good to see you out of the woods."

I looked at them in surprise. "You know each other?"

"Since you're the new CEO, I should probably tell you," Dad said. "Natalie here helped us out a while back. What, was that ten years ago now?"

"I think so," Natalie replied.

"What do you mean *helped us out*?"

"The business with SLS," Dad said. "We needed someone on the inside, and Natalie here was friendly with Steven for a while. She knew what a crackpot he was, but couldn't get rid of him. She got me the information I needed. I paid her and helped her disappear." His gaze switched to Natalie. "Faked your suicide, I believe?"

My jaw was hanging open and Natalie said nothing, just nodded.

"Obviously, that didn't work out since you're back here," my dad continued, oblivious.

"Steven ended up going after my sister," she said. "She... wasn't as fortunate as I was."

"I'm sorry to hear that," Dad said, contrite. I could see he was tiring and Schultz had pulled up in the car.

"You need to get home, Dad," I said, taking his arm so he could lean on me because I knew he wouldn't ask.

"You catch that part about the CEO?" he asked as we headed for the car.

"Hmm?" I was concentrating on both of us not falling.

Dad stopped, making me look at him.

"What?" I asked.

"I'm retiring. The company is yours now."

I stared. "You're serious?"

He nodded, the hint of a grin appearing. "As a heart attack. I'm done. Time for me and your mother to settle into our dotage."

I laughed. "Like you could ever do that."

"The paperwork's being done even as we speak," Dad said. "Hope you're ready to go on Monday."

"But what about Charlie?" I asked. "He's been your right-hand man for twenty years."

"Charlie's great," Dad said. "But you're my blood."

And I could tell by the way he said it that it was final. Family was everything to him. Charlie may have been a devoted employee and friend, but he wasn't family.

I loaded my mom and dad into the car and watched it drive off. Parker's hands settled on my waist as he stood behind me.

"Well, that was a nice little bomb to drop," I said.

"Yep. Do I say congratulations or I'm sorry?"

I turned to him, narrowing my eyes. "Did you know about Natalie?"

He held his hands up in a gesture of surrender. "I didn't. I swear. I don't really care why she left. It's as much of a surprise to me as to you that she was working for your dad."

"Let's go have a chat with her," I said.

Natalie was eyeing us as we headed back to where she stood next to Ryker. I glanced at him. He looked as shocked as I felt.

"...the truth?" he was asking her. "Which is it? Abusive husband or paid-off informant?"

"Both," she said with a sigh. "I was married to Chad when he went to jail. His best friend was Steven. Steven decided he'd help me through it. He was just as much of an asshole. I met you two during that time." She indicated

Ryker and Parker. "At first, I thought maybe you could help me get away from Steven, but then I was offered the job from Mr. Muccino. I needed the money. Jessie needed the money. So I took the job. And when I needed to get out of town because Chad was released, he helped me get out.

"I'm sorry I couldn't tell any of this to you," her gaze had gravitated to Ryker. "I wanted to. I really did. I believed you did care about me. Maybe even love me. But Chad and Steven weren't going away, and I was afraid for me and for you. I didn't want to hurt you by just leaving, so I tried to make you hate me."

"By sleeping with my best friend," Ryker said.

Natalie nodded, her eyes filling with tears. "But even then, you still loved me. I wanted you to despise me, think the very worst of me. Everyone else did."

Guilt washed over me as I listened. I could understand a little too well, and she was right. Everyone—their friends, Parker himself, and even me—had spoken of Natalie with contempt. The only one who had forgiven her was the man who loved her.

"I knew I had to make the break with you permanent or I'd always be tempted to come back. Pretending to be dead was best solution I could think of. I was forced to leave and start over again somewhere else."

"But Chad found you," Ryker said.

She nodded. "Unfortunately. And although I didn't know it, I guess Steven moved on to Jessie while I was gone."

"It's okay," Ryker said, pulling her into his arms. "I understand. I wish you would've trusted me—trusted us—to help you. But I understand why you made the choice you did."

Her body relaxed into his. I felt bad for her, I really did. She'd had a tough life, had lied to people she cared about to try and protect herself and her sister. That same sister she'd seen murdered right in front of her just a few days ago. We might not ever be besties, but I could understand why she'd done what she had.

"I'm tired," I said to Parker. "Take me home?"

"You got it."

I half expected him to take me to his place, but he drove me to my apartment instead. It felt good to be in my home, though, so I was glad for it. But I didn't want him to go and wasn't sure how to approach the topic.

Parker settled me on my couch. He grabbed a blanket and tucked it around me. Then he started fussing over the blinds and television, getting my trio of remotes and setting them next to me. I grabbed his wrist.

"Stop."

"Stop what?"

"You're coddling me."

"Maybe I like coddling you," he said.

"Sit with me." I tugged him down onto the couch, then rearranged myself up next to him. "Can you stay a while?"

"I'll stay as long as you want."

I really hoped he meant that literally.

We hadn't talked about "us" since everything had blown up in my face. I realized now that Natalie and he hadn't been "together" while she was staying with him, though I'd been glad to see her move out.

I flipped the television to a rerun of *Castle* and we watched for a few minutes. It felt really good to be in Parker's arms. I felt safe for the first time in too long.

"So what do you think about Ryker and Natalie?" I asked.

"If it's what he wants, good for him," he said. "I told you, he's never gotten over her. And I think she's finally in a place where maybe they can work things out."

"Guess we'll see."

"Yeah." There was a pause. "What about you and me?"

I twisted so I could look up at him. "What about us?"

His fingers trailed through my hair. "You forgive me for not telling you?"

I nodded. "Lives were at stake."

Something close to relief flickered in his eyes. "So we're good?"

I smiled. "We're good." Stretching up, I went for a kiss and he leaned down until our lips met.

His mouth was warm and soft as it moved over mine. My eyes drifted closed and I wrapped an arm around his neck, pulling him closer. He deepened the kiss, his tongue sliding between my lips, and a mewling sound escaped my throat.

"No," he murmured against my lips. "You *just* got out of the hospital. I'd be the biggest dick alive to make you have sex right now."

"You're not *making* me do anything," I said, trailing kisses along his jaw. He smelled good. Mmmm. "And I'll be the judge of the size of your—"

"No," he said again, pulling my questing fingers away from his belt. "You're not well yet."

"I'm well enough." I squirmed in his lap, gratified to feel that he was as primed for me as I was for him. "It'd be a shame to let a good erection go to waste."

He laughed. "I'll tell you what," he said. "I can make you feel good, and I'd really like to do that." He talked as he stood, lifting me in his arms.

"You always make me feel good." I nestled against his chest. There was nothing quite like having a man carry you. Maybe it touched something primal from the caveman days, of claiming and being claimed. I could analyze it, I suppose, but whatever the reason behind it . . . I liked it. I liked it a lot.

"Not true," he said, heading down the hall. "Remember that time I got mad because I thought you'd forgotten to amend the Houston file? I got all pissy with you."

Now it was my turn to laugh. "That's right. I still remember the look on your face when you realized you'd deleted it. I had to call IT and have them restore the backup."

"I was a dick. Did I even apologize?" He laid me on the bed.

"You may have grunted something at me," I said. "I do recall you being very generous on my birthday, which was about two weeks after that little incident."

He lay down on top of me, bracing himself on his arms so his weight was supported. "I don't know how I got along before you," he said. His fingers pushed into my hair as his hands cradled my head. I felt his thumbs brush my cheeks, but I was captivated by his eyes.

"I love it when you look at me like that," I murmured.

"Like what?"

"Your eyes are like windows into your soul," I said. "Everything else about you is hard to read, but your eyes... your eyes are so expressive. When you look at me, they change. Sometimes they burn right through me and I can feel how much you want me. Other times, like now, they're soft and warm, like you're thinking of how much you love me."

"What an odd coincidence. That's exactly what I'm thinking." He kissed the tip of my nose.

"Great minds think alike," I quipped.

"And fools seldom differ," he finished.

"Well, that puts a whole different spin on it," I huffed.

He smiled, then said, "Enough talking." His lips moved to my neck and my eyes closed again. His breath was warm against my neck, and the weight of his body covering me was bliss.

Parker moved down, unbuttoning my shirt and sliding it off my shoulders. He kissed my collarbone and the dip at the base of my neck. I wasn't wearing a bra and my breasts practically tingled in anticipation of his touch.

Parker pushed upward so he could look at me. My nipples hardened under his gaze. His blue eyes lifted to meet mine.

"There's that look," I murmured. The searing look sent a jolt through me and told me more than any words how much he wanted me, desired me, had to have me.

"You're beautiful," he said, his lips closing over a nipple.

The heat of his mouth felt like heaven, and the brush of his tongue like liquid fire. He spent a lavish amount of attention to my breasts, until my clothes were too constricting and my body burned for him.

"Please," I begged, tugging at his shirt. He let me pull it off, and the touch of his skin against mine was a relief and further incentive. Time for the belt...

"No," he said, pushing my hand away. His tongue dipped into my navel and I forgot to breathe.

Parker's fingers hooked into the waistband of the leggings I wore, pulling them over my hips and down my legs. He dragged my panties with it and tossed the whole bundle aside.

"I've missed your taste," he said, pushing my thighs apart.

Okay, that was totally hot was my last coherent thought before Parker went about setting a new personal record for how many orgasms I was capable of.

I was sweating and panting, my fingers clutching his hair, when I knew I couldn't take any more. I tugged on his hair. Lazily, he lifted his head from between my legs, brushing his lips against my inner thigh, then my hip.

"That was..." I didn't know what to say. Amazing? Incredible?

"Words don't do me justice, I know."

That got a laugh out of me. Parker lay next to me, pulling me close in his arms. I rested my head on his chest.

"Arrogant, too," I teased.

"I prefer confident."

I could see that not only was he confident, he was also very aroused. Although I wouldn't have thought I could do anything more, my body had other ideas. I reached for his belt.

"I said no; you're not up to it," Parker said.

I pushed his hands away. "If you don't let me have my way with you *right now*, you're going to be on the business end of a hissy fit." This time I got his belt undone. Jackpot.

"Are you threatening me?" I could hear the smile in his voice.

"Absolutely. Now be still." Button? Check. Zipper? Easy there... got it.

"For how long?"

I didn't answer because I'd managed to bare the part of him I was most interested in at the moment. I closed my mouth over the head of his cock and smiled when I heard his sharply indrawn breath. *That should shut him up.*

I planned on paying a great deal of attention to Mr. Happy, so I settled between his legs and got comfortable. Parker was well endowed and it took some practice to handle all of him without embarrassing myself by gagging. I circled the base of his shaft with my hand, squeezing lightly as I moved up and down. He was making encouraging noises as he watched me, which turned me on even more.

"You know you hold your pinky up when you do that, like you're having a spot of tea."

I burst out laughing, which is really hard to do with a mouth full of Mr. Happy. I turned aside, resting my cheek on his thigh as I giggled.

"It's like getting a *Downton Abbey* blowjob," he said, adding a British accent for effect.

I giggled harder. "Now how am I supposed to go back to doing that now that you've made me laugh!" I complained.

"If you can't laugh during sex, when can you?" he asked with a shrug. Grasping me under the arms, he pulled me up until I was straddling him.

The feel of his erection between my legs stilled my laughter, though I was still smiling.

"You make me very happy," I said.

"I try," he replied. "And I think I can try a little harder." Reaching between our bodies, he adjusted himself and lifted his hips, pushing his cock inside me.

"Mmmm, yeah, that'll do it."

"Swear you'll say something if it hurts," he said.

"I swear." The pleasure far outweighed the twinge of discomfort from the stitches pulling a little.

And this was the reason I spent so much time doing squats and burpees, I thought, moving on top of him. It wouldn't do to be the first to wear out or succumb to a leg cramp.

It turned out, I didn't have to worry about any of those things. Parker could go all night, literally, but took it easy on me today. He waited until I came, yet again, before allowing himself to come, too.

Our lips were locked, tongues entwined, when he finally had to pull his mouth away to gulp more air, his orgasm wracking his body. I watched him, his beautiful face contorted in pleasure as he gasped my name.

I rested against him, our bodies slick with sweat, a satisfied smile on my face. This was bliss. This was happiness. Being with the man I loved beyond all reason, and knowing without a doubt that he loved me just as much.

Parker kissed the top of my head, then turned us, scooting down until we were lying back-to-front spoon style.

"Get some sleep," he whispered in my ear.

"Stay with me?"

"Always."

CHAPTER TWENTY

It was another week before I could go back to work, but I felt 100 percent better and was in a great mood. Parker and I had stayed over together either at his place or mine each night. He'd gone back to work for KLP and I'd even managed to get him to go easy on yet another new assistant. I was hoping this one would actually last longer than a week.

"Welcome back!" Carrie greeted me when I walked in. Jumping up from her chair, she rounded the counter to hug me tight. "I'm so glad you're all right."

"I know, right? More excitement than *Cagney & Lacey*."

"Isn't that show before your time?" she teased.

I shrugged. "I grew up with Mom watching that and *Magnum, P.I.*" I headed for my office and she followed me.

"Nothing wrong with Tom Selleck," she said. "A girl's gotta have standards."

I grinned, shrugging out of the light coat I'd worn today. Fall was hitting hard, which was fine with me. Curling up in front of the fire with Parker and a bottle of wine tonight sounded like heaven.

"Breakfast is on your desk and I'll grab you some coffee from the Starbucks across the street," she said.

"Ooh, is it that pumpkin spice latte time of year yet?"

"You bet." She winked. "Extra whip?"

"You know me well."

I sat down at my desk as Carrie disappeared. There was a huge stack of paperwork, and I saw over a hundred e-mails in my inbox, but it felt good to be back at work.

I was in the middle of digging my way out from under the pile when there was a knock on my open door. I glanced up and saw Charlie standing there.

"Can I come in?" he asked.

"Absolutely," I said with a smile. I was acutely aware that I'd been promoted—someone with much less experience than he—and needed Charlie's expertise. "I'm glad you came by."

He closed the door and took a seat opposite me. "How are you feeling?" The lines on his face were creased in concern.

"I'm okay," I said. "It wasn't an experience I care to repeat but from what I've been told, it could've been a lot worse."

"True," he said. "You and your dad are very lucky."

Something about the way he said that made me frown, but I let it pass. "Charlie, I wanted to talk to you about Dad's resignation." I took a deep breath. "I'm sure you expected to be the next CEO—"

"Don't worry about it," he said. "You're his daughter. It doesn't surprise me."

I smiled, relieved. "Good. I'm glad you're not upset. I really am going to need you while we transition."

"Of course. I'll be glad to help." His smile faded. "I got

an e-mail this morning from our lawyers, and we need to discuss the collusion investigation."

Alarm shot through me. "I thought that had gone away," I said. "I spoke with them—"

"Steven may be dead, but once he woke that sleeping giant, it wasn't just going to go away," Charlie said. "I'd expect a formal indictment to show up pretty soon."

Fuck. Just when I thought fate was smiling on me and life decided to give me a break, it knocked me down and stole my lunch money.

"I don't even know how he found out about it," I mused. That point had bothered me, but I hadn't spent much time analyzing it. I'd been busy healing from a gunshot wound. "I guess Jessie was the one that broke in here, but she didn't find the documents. Those were locked in Dad's office at the time."

Charlie didn't say anything and I glanced at him. "Charlie?"

Our gazes met and something clicked. I gasped, stricken. "Was it...was it you, Charlie?"

His lips twisted just a fraction. "You always were smart, Sage."

I gaped at him. "You betrayed my father? But...why?"

He snorted. "I knew the day you showed up that any chance I had of getting this company was down the toilet. It didn't matter that I've worked for him for decades, given my entire adult life to making this company a success and him a millionaire. I'm not *blood*."

"You were his friend," I said. "You gave confidential information to Steven Shea about this company?"

"Please," he said contemptuously. "If that idiot would have been as smart as he was nuts, that would've been all he needed."

I puzzled over this for a moment, my thoughts spinning.

"You," I breathed. "You were the one in the hospital room with Mom and Dad, on the phone." At the time, I'd thought it was just another of Steven's lackeys. But it would have had to be someone who could get that close without arousing suspicion. And Mom wouldn't have thought twice about Charlie being in there. Charlie had been alone with my dad a number of times.

"Was it you?" I asked. "Was it Shea or you that arranged that hit on me and Dad?"

"Thought I could get rid of you both in one fell swoop," he said. "Should've known it wouldn't be that easy."

I couldn't believe what I was hearing. It was like I was inside a living, breathing nightmare.

"I've known you my whole life," I said. "And you tried to kill me?"

"Did your dad ever tell you how we met?" he asked. I shook my head. "But I bet he's told you about how he was threatened when he first went into the business."

"He said that my mom had car trouble one day and that a man had stopped to supposedly help her, but ended up threatening her instead." When I'd asked Dad what had happened to the man, he'd said *I made him understand that messing with me was a bad idea.*

"I was that guy," Charlie said.

I stared.

"Your dad showed up at my house three days later," he continued, "and he knew everything about me, including the fact that I'd killed a union boss up in Detroit. Your dad's family, they know people everywhere, and he dug up enough information and witnesses to put me away for life. But he didn't give it to the cops. Instead, he offered me a deal."

"Work for him instead," I guessed.

"Yep. I've been at his mercy for decades, knowing that at

any time he could turn me in. Not only for that, but for the shit I've done since."

"It wasn't like that," I said. "Dad wouldn't have done that to you."

"It doesn't matter anymore. I'm done. And so's your dad."

"You sonofa—!"

"Ah ah ah," he interrupted, and it wasn't so much what he said but the gun in his hand that shut me up. "Let's keep it down, shall we?"

I clenched my fists. "What do you want?" I asked, my voice tight but even.

"Well, I hadn't intended for this particular cat to get out of the bag, but I should've known you'd figure it out. You always did have your mother's smarts."

"What do you want?" I repeated. I was trying very hard not to look at the gun. My entire body had broken out in a cold sweat and I was shaking. The pain from when I'd been shot by Steven was still fresh in my mind, as was the fear and helplessness I'd experienced that night.

"Grab the checkbook, Sage. Let's go make a withdrawal. I've decided on an early retirement."

I opened my desk drawer—

"Easy now," Charlie said. "I'm old and I'm afraid my hands aren't as steady as they used to be."

I let not an ounce of reaction appear on my face, though on the inside, I was freaking out. I was enraged, terrified, and on the verge of panic. Somehow, I had to pull myself together. Charlie had tried to have me killed. That wasn't quite the same as pulling the trigger himself, but desperate men do desperate things.

The company ledger was inside my drawer and I removed a check. Picking up my purse, I slid it inside and stood. "Let's go."

"Ladies first." Charlie put his hand holding the gun inside his jacket pocket, then motioned for me to go ahead of him. "Act natural," he said as I opened my door.

"Of course," I said bitterly.

We passed by Carrie's empty desk. The line at Starbucks must have been really long. I was both disappointed and glad she wasn't there. I didn't want anyone to get hurt, but I also didn't want to be shot again.

"And how much are you expecting me to withdraw?" I asked in an undertone as we approached the elevator.

"I think two million should be sufficient," he said. "Besides, I couldn't carry any more than that."

Always so practical, that was Charlie.

We stood in front of the elevator and when the door slid open, I sucked in a breath.

Parker stood inside, holding a bouquet of flowers.

He saw me and a smile broke across his face as he stepped out. "Hey, babe. You read my mind. Was just coming to see you, wish you a good first day back."

I forced myself to smile. "That's so sweet. And thoughtful." I wracked my brain for any kind of code word or phrase I could use to tell him what was going on…and came up empty. I couldn't risk Charlie suspecting something. Employees were around, as well as Parker.

Parker glanced to my right. "Charlie," he said. "Good to see you, too."

"Good morn—"

Parker moved so fast, he was a blur. One second Charlie was standing there beside me, the next he was flat on his back on the floor. I'd seen his head snap back when Parker's fist shot out.

Openmouthed, I stared at Charlie. His eyes had rolled back in his head, his mouth slack.

"Is he dead?" I asked.

"No, unfortunately," Parker replied grimly.

I looked at him in astonishment. "How did you know?"

"I was talking to your dad this morning," he said, "finishing up the final touches on the paperwork for the Sikes merger. He mentioned how he was glad he'd gotten to see Natalie again. How she'd really helped ten years ago when they—your dad and Sikes—blackmailed Leo Shea."

"Excuse me?"

"They blackmailed him," Parker repeated. "Natalie found out that Steven had killed a guy. Beat him to death. Leo was covering it up and Steven went to jail for a couple of years on a misdemeanor charge. Natalie told your dad about the murder and he was able to dig up enough circumstantial evidence to blackmail Leo. That's what made Leo back down. Not collusion."

"But Charlie said—"

"Charlie didn't know," Parker interrupted. "He manufactured evidence on collusion and planted it, figuring he could get away with it since your dad was in a coma and was the only one who knew the truth, that it was blackmail."

"So when Dad told you that . . ."

"I put the pieces together and came straight here."

I held up the flowers he'd given me, raising an eyebrow.

"Yeah, those came out of the vase on the pedestal in the foyer downstairs."

"I thought they looked familiar."

The elevator dinged again and this time, Ryker stepped out along with two uniformed policemen.

"I got your message," he said to Parker. He glanced at Charlie, still out cold. "Must've been your right hook. It's a real bitch."

Charlie would probably agree . . . when he came to.

They searched and disarmed him, splashing some cold water on his face to wake him up before promptly cuffing him and leading him away. I watched the elevator door close on my dad's oldest employee, my stomach bottoming out.

"You okay?" Parker asked, putting his arm around my shoulders and pulling me close.

"Yeah," I sighed. "It just sucks. I can't imagine what Dad's going to say. He and Charlie were close, friends as well as boss and employee."

"Your dad's been around a while," he said. "I doubt anything surprises him anymore."

We had just turned to head back to my office when the elevator opened and Carrie popped out, breathless and holding two large Starbucks cups.

"You will not *believe* the line today!" she said, handing me one. "I think it was the barista's first day because she took absolutely forever. But I did get you a free scone." She proudly brandished a little paper bag.

A free scone and a grande pumpkin spice latte, with extra whip. The day was looking up.

EPILOGUE

Have a glass of champagne," Mom said, handing me a flute of bubbly golden liquid.

"I don't want to get married drunk, Mom!"

"Please," she said with a wave of her hand. "If one glass of champagne gets you drunk, then you're not your father's daughter."

Okay, she had a point. I took a long swallow.

"Sip it, don't gulp it," she chastised me. "Now hold still and let Jeffrey finish your hair."

Jeffrey was cursing under his breath at my thick mass of hair, which he'd spent the past two hours painstakingly curling and arranging into an artful up-do with a mountain of bobby pins. Ten minutes later and he was finally through.

"Voilà!" he pronounced with a flourish. "You look amazing!"

I surveyed the stranger in the mirror, a way better-looking version of the usual me, in an Oscar de la Renta wedding gown. My eyes caught on the diamond necklace at my throat.

"They were your grandmother's," Mom had said when she'd put them on me. She and Parker had colluded ahead of time and he'd had matching earrings made. Something old and something new. He'd given them to me last night after the rehearsal dinner, before he'd gone back to his apartment (alone—Mom had been quite adamant about our being apart from then until the ceremony).

"Oh, Sage," Megan breathed, clasping her hands in delight. "You look like a princess!"

She was my Maid of Honor. I had six other attendants who were all various cousins and second cousins on my dad's side, but they were all getting ready in another room. Only Megan, Jeffrey, and my mom were in here. Thank goodness Catholic churches like this one were huge.

I hadn't wanted a big wedding, but Dad had cajoled and begged and even at one point broke down and cried (which I'd been sure were crocodile tears since once I'd caved they'd magically disappeared). So now Parker and I had fourteen attendants, a flower girl and ring bearer, plus a miniature bride and groom.

Okay, the miniature bride and groom were super cute.

"You're going to be just as beautiful on your wedding day," I said. Brian had proposed at Christmas.

She grinned. "Maybe. But my wedding won't include half of Chicago."

She was referring to the over five hundred guests currently waiting in the nave. I started to sweat.

"No no no!" Jeffrey cried, grabbing a tissue and carefully blotting my forehead. "The makeup is perfect!" He gestured to my mother and Megan. "Quick, fan her."

"Shit! I'm sorry, Sage!" Megan said, hurrying to obey him.

The sight of three people grabbing the nearest hymnal or Bible and using it to fan a nervous bride-to-be had me bursting out laughing.

"Well, laughing is better than sweating," Mom said, setting aside her hymnal and tossing back the rest of her champagne.

"I thought you said to sip it!" I said.

She covered a delicate burp. "The bride should sip it. The mother of the bride should drink a gallon before seeing her only daughter walk down the aisle." Her eyes shone with tears as she looked at me, but Jeffrey began *tut-tut*ting and muttering things about mascara, so she blinked them back with a smile. Which was a good thing because I was pretty sure if my mom started crying, I would, too.

There was a knock on the door. "Ten minutes!" Ah. The wedding planner.

"We'd better go," Mom said. "I'll send your dad in." I nodded and she left along with Megan and Jeffrey.

I took deep breaths. I wasn't nervous about marrying Parker. I was nervous about *getting married*. All those people out there watching me walk down the aisle...I could feel the sweat coming on again.

"Dammit," I muttered, grabbing for more tissues as the door opened. I turned around, expecting my father, but it was Ryker.

I smiled. "Hey! You know you're not supposed to be in here." He looked great in the tuxedos I'd picked out.

"Shh. Don't tell the dragon lady," he said.

"The wedding planner is the best in the city," I said. "I can't help it if you don't take orders well."

He shrugged, not looking a bit repentant at the teasing he'd given our planner last night. It was lucky for him he was good-looking and a cop, otherwise I think she would've boxed his ears.

"I just wanted to say how happy I am for you and Parker," he said. "He's like a brother to me and now, well, now I get a new sister." He smiled.

It was sweet of him and felt genuine. It had been almost nine months since we'd been together, but it felt like a lifetime ago. His heart and mine had moved on, but there would always be a special tenderness between us.

"Thanks, Ryker." I reached to give him a hug, but he jumped back, evading my arms.

"No way am I messing up the bride," he said. Leaning forward, he gave me the merest brush of his lips on my cheek. "Good luck, sweetheart."

He turned back at the door. "Wait. Do you have all your 'something old, something new' stuff?"

"Megan let me borrow her Jimmy Choos," I said. "But I didn't find anything blue."

Ryker stepped back toward me. "Please, allow me." Reaching in his pocket, he pulled out a tiny bottle of Bombay Sapphire gin.

I laughed in surprise and delight. "Where the heck am I supposed to put that?" I asked. "Down my cleavage?"

Ryker glanced around and spied my bouquet, still in the florist box and waiting for me. He picked it up, nestled the gin deep among the peach roses, eucalyptus, and greenery, so only a bit of it peeked out. He handed it to me.

"It's perfect," I said with a smile. "Thank you."

He smiled, then went out the door.

My dad was a blubbering mess when he saw me, his eyes red as he manfully tried to hold back the tears. I hugged him and patted him on the back, so glad I had parents who loved me so much.

Butterflies filled my stomach as we headed for the nave, with me on my dad's arm. The music was beckoning—my dad had somehow gotten ten members of the Chicago Symphony to play for our wedding—which made my stomach turn somersaults. Then we turned the corner and I looked down the aisle...and saw Parker. Ryker stood at his side.

Our eyes met and I smiled. The butterflies settled down as I walked down the aisle to my groom.

* * *

"You are the most beautiful bride I've ever seen," Parker said, slowly turning me around the dance floor.

"And how many brides have you come across?" I teased.

He laughed, his eyes shining as he looked at me, the look on his face one I wanted to memorize. As though I indeed was the most beautiful, perfect thing he'd ever seen.

The wedding had been perfect. The dinner and reception had gone off without a hitch. Now we were dancing and enjoying the celebration.

"What a lovely wedding!"

I looked over my shoulder and saw Natalie in Ryker's arms as they danced next to us. I smiled.

"Thank you," I said. "I'm glad you came."

Natalie and I had buried the hatchet. I'd saved her life. She'd saved mine. She and Ryker had been dating steadily ever since Thanksgiving. They both looked happy and I hoped things worked out for them. I had a feeling it would.

Ryker had held a torch for Natalie for a decade. He wouldn't let her go now. And she'd been amazed that he still loved her, crying to me one night over too many bottles of wine that she didn't deserve him. I'd told her not to be stupid, of course she deserved him, and to have another piece of chocolate cake. Then I'd eaten half her piece of cake.

"So where's the honeymoon?" I asked Parker as Natalie and Ryker spun away. He'd refused to tell me, saying it was a surprise. He'd even had Megan do the packing for me so I didn't know if it was somewhere warm or cold.

"You'll see," he said. "You don't want to ruin my surprise now, do you?"

"Well, when do we get to leave?"

"As soon as you want."

I raised my eyebrows. "Really? Are we driving?" Hmm... what was within driving distance...

"Nope."

"So we're flying."

"Yep."

"But we can leave anytime?"

His eyes twinkled at me. "Yep."

That could only mean... "Someone loaned you their private plane," I guessed.

He winked at me.

I squealed. That was so cool. "Let's go now," I said. "Is that okay?"

"Now would be perfect," he said. "Because I really don't want to wait any longer to start the rest of my life... with you." And he kissed me.

THE END

Sage Reese lives for her debonair boss,
Parker Anderson. But when she runs into
tough Detective Dean Ryker, Sage
becomes caught between the man she's
always wanted—and the one who makes
her feel wanted like never before...

Please see the next page
for an excerpt from

Power Play

Book 1 of the Risky Business series

CHAPTER ONE

Y ou're dumping me?"

I couldn't believe it—not that it was completely out of the blue—but I hadn't even had a chance to order dessert.

"Listen, Sage, I just don't think it's working out," Brandon said. "I mean I like you, I really do, but it just doesn't seem as though you have time for a relationship—"

The buzzing of my cell phone cut him off. I didn't have to look to know who it was. Fighting my instinct to pick it up, I said, "I have plenty of time for a relationship!"

"Sage, we've been dating for three months and we've yet to have a dinner that wasn't interrupted by your cell."

"That is not true," I protested, frantically trying to remember a time when I'd had *any* meal without my phone ringing. My phone buzzed again, and I swear my eye twitched with the need to answer it.

But Brandon was shaking his head, a resigned look on his

face. "I'm sorry. I really am." He took some money out of his wallet and placed it on the table.

More insistent buzzing, as if the person on the other end knew I was there and not picking up. I clenched my hands into fists in my lap.

"Brandon," I tried again as he stood. He nodded toward my phone.

"Sage, you may not want to admit it, but you're already in a committed relationship. And he doesn't share."

I stared in dismay at Brandon's retreating back as he left the restaurant. The phone buzzed. Glaring at it, I reached out and snatched it up, knowing it could only be one person.

"What?" I snapped, allowing the hovering waiter to remove my plate. I grabbed the wine bottle and emptied the rest into my glass.

There was a long pause on the other end of the line. "Excuse me?"

I held in a sigh and rubbed my forehead. I felt a headache coming on. "I'm sorry, I thought it was someone else," I lied, modulating my voice into the usual pleasant tone I used for work. "What can I do for you, sir?"

Sir was Parker Anderson, and Parker Anderson was my boss.

"I need the margin projections on the Layne acquisition. Where are they?"

"Lyle brought them by this afternoon," I said. "I put them on your desk."

"I'm looking and I don't see them."

"They're underneath the stack of quarterlies that I printed off this morning," I guessed.

There was a shuffling of paper. "Okay. Found it. Thanks." He ended the call.

"You're welcome," I muttered, tossing down my phone.

Parker never apologized for calling me after official work hours. I thought it was because he worked so much. He never considered any hour as being free from work, for either himself or those who worked for him. Usually, I didn't mind because... well, it was complicated.

The wind had picked up and I pulled my wrap tighter around my bare arms as I gazed out at Lake Michigan. Brandon had picked one of the nicest restaurants in Chicago to break up with me, a place with outdoor seating and a great view. I guessed that was something.

I watched as the last bit of twilight faded into evening and sipped my wine. Brandon had already paid for it so no sense letting it go to waste. We'd met on Valentine's Day of all things and over the next three months I'd become more and more convinced that maybe he could be Mr. Right.

Apparently, I was Ms. Wrong.

On that depressing thought, I got drunk. Well at least I *think* I got drunk. I was vaguely aware of the valet calling me a cab and me stumbling into my apartment. I may or may not have taken a bubble bath—a weird predilection that came out when I was very drunk, no matter the time of night—since I had little memory of anything up to my head hitting the pillow. Some might say I passed out, but I'm a lady and ladies don't *pass out*. I just... slept very deeply.

The alarm woke me at the usual time and I groaned, slamming my hand on the button to silence it. My head ached from too much wine and I stood too long in the shower. By the time I was rummaging through my closet trying to find the match to the shoes I wanted to wear, I was already going to be late.

"Damn it!" I yelled in frustration, then heard my mom in my head.

Ladies don't use vulgar language.

"Ladies probably never have to take the bus to work either," I groused to no one.

The bus was just closing its doors when I ran up, out of breath and carrying my shoes. I rapped on the door and the driver opened it for me.

"Running late today?" he asked with a grin.

I was too out of breath to reply so I just smiled. He was a nice guy and knew all the regulars on this route.

Work was just under five miles away and I was one of the first off the bus, shoes now on my feet. It was a cool spring morning and probably too early in the season for the peep-toe sunny yellow heels, but I'd worn them anyway. I'd added a matching yellow scarf around my neck to go with the navy skirt and white blouse I wore. The yellow added a touch of whimsy to the otherwise staid clothes. I didn't mind. It was expected attire for the assistant to the Director of Investment Analytics at KLP Capital, which was *the* investment bank in Chicago.

Robin worked the morning shift at Starbucks and had my standing order ready when I walked in.

"Thank you!" I said, blowing an air-kiss in her direction as I grabbed the two cups and paper bag. A second later I was out the door and scurrying across the street. The wind whipped at my hair, but I always kept it pulled back tight. My hair was dark, thick, and long, and I never wore it down to work. A French braid tucked up into a bun kept it from getting in my way.

Used to juggling coffee, Parker's breakfast, and my purse, I showed my pass to Security, who let me by to the elevators. Thirty-five floors later, I stepped out.

It was still early enough for me to get things set the way Parker liked. I hurried to drop off my purse and coffee before getting a plate and silverware from the kitchen. After placing the scone on the plate and setting the coffee in precisely the right spot, I hurried back to my desk to listen to his voice mails, taking notes as I scrolled through them. Finally setting down the telephone, I let out a sigh. All set for Parker's arrival in—I looked at my watch—three minutes.

At eight o'clock on the dot, Parker Anderson stepped off the elevators and headed my way.

It was secretly my favorite part of the day.

Parker Anderson wore five-thousand-dollar suits and walked like he owned half the city. There was no one he couldn't intimidate, and he knew it. Some called him arrogant; he said it was confidence.

This morning he'd worn his usual kind of power suit, this one a dark gray pinstripe with a light gray shirt and what I recognized as a Burberry tie. His dark hair was long on top, parted on the side, and lay in a smooth wave back off his high forehead. It made a nice contrast to the clear blue of his eyes. His face was perfect symmetry, an oval with a straight nose that conjured adjectives like *aristocratic*. A strong jaw and chin were the perfect complement, while his lips—his lips were in the sweet spot between too-thin and too-feminine, not that I spent much time staring at his lips. At least, I tried not to stare. He was thirty-five, incredibly handsome, successful, wealthy—and as unobtainable as the moon.

But that didn't mean I couldn't enjoy the view.

"Good morning, Sage," he said, the deep baritone of his voice as smooth as a shot of twenty-year-old scotch. He took the stack of messages I handed him and glanced through them. This was our morning routine, too.

"Good morning," I replied with a smile. I caught a whiff of his cologne mixed with his aftershave. I'd become so accustomed to the slightly spicy scent that I didn't think I'd ever be able to smell it and not think of Parker.

Usually he'd give me a polite smile, then disappear into his office, but today he hesitated.

"I, um, I didn't get you at a bad time last night, did I?" he asked, still looking through his messages.

My eyes widened. He had never asked me that before and there had been plenty of times that had been "bad." I was gonna have to mark this one down on my calendar.

I was so surprised, I blurted out the truth. "I'd just gotten dumped."

Parker looked up at that. If my candor had shocked him, I couldn't tell. His blue eyes were steady on mine for a long moment in which I may have stopped breathing. He rarely ever focused that intently on me and I found myself wishing for the umpteenth time that Parker were a less attractive man. It would make concentrating at work a helluva lot easier.

"I'm sorry to hear that," he said at last.

My smile was as fake as the name-brand purse I'd bought off a street vendor on Michigan Avenue.

"It's fine," I said quickly with a nervous wave of my hand as I tried to figure out what to say. It wasn't like Parker and I often chatted about our personal lives. "He was bad in bed anyway."

Oh. My. God. Had I just said that? To *my boss*?

I gasped in dismay, both my hands flying to cover my mouth. Talk about too much information.

His lips twitched slightly and I swear his eyes crinkled at the corners, as though he were holding back a full-blown grin. He cleared his throat.

"Yes, well, um, that's . . . too bad. Guess you're better off then." With another fleeting smile, he headed into his office, the glass door swinging closed behind him.

If he couldn't see me through the glass wall, I would have

put my head down on my desk and moaned in sheer mortification. I'd mentioned sex to my boss. And that I'd been having *bad* sex. Maybe he thought it was me? What if he thought I was bad in bed?

"It doesn't matter!" I hissed to myself, grabbing my coffee and taking a steadying swig as though it were bourbon rather than a nonfat-grande-caramel-no-foam-latte (add whip). Who cared if Parker thought I was bad in bed? It wasn't like I'd ever get the opportunity to—

Nope. Not going there. I was not a secretary-with-the-hots-for-her-boss cliché. Any woman with eyes could appreciate the many wonderful attributes of Parker Anderson. I was just... normal.

Right.

It was business as usual after that and I made myself put aside my embarrassment and stop thinking inappropriate thoughts. Parker was as normal as ever as I transcribed from his voice memo recorder, edited a Power Point presentation he was giving in New York next week, coordinated the quarterly performance reviews, and all the usual things that made the day fly by. Mondays were busy so Parker always ate lunch at his desk. At noon, I ran out to get his usual from the restaurant four blocks down. He had their Monday special of Tuscan-style salmon with rosemary orzo.

I had a hot dog from a street vendor that I scarfed down while hurrying back from the restaurant. I always ate it plain because one time I'd dropped mustard on my blouse, which had sent me into a panicked tizzy and resulted in thirty minutes in the bathroom trying to unsuccessfully scrub it out. I'd tried to hide the stain, but Parker had seen when I'd had to take him some files.

"Problems at lunch?" he'd inquired with a pointed look at my stained blouse.

I hadn't eaten mustard, or anything else, on my hot dog since.

Parker was still in a meeting when I set the tray on his desk, arranging the plate and cutlery just so. The mouth-watering aroma of the salmon filled the air, making my stomach growl even after my hot dog.

I was just finishing folding the napkin into a bird of paradise when the door to Parker's office swung open. Surprised, I glanced up...and promptly forgot all about the napkin fold.

Holy shit.

Bradley Cooper all buff and badass in *The A-Team* immediately sprang to mind.

He was over six feet tall, his broad shoulders encased in a white T-shirt and leather jacket, with the outline of dog tags underneath the thin fabric stretched across his chest. Chestnut hair that had a hint of curl in it was slicked back from his face and begged for a woman's fingers to run through it. His jaw was grizzled with two days of whiskers while his eyes were obscured behind mirrored sunglasses.

The man slipped the sunglasses off and I swear my knees went weak. His eyes were a bright blue, the corners showing fine lines from either smiling or squinting. I chose to think it was from smiling because with looks like his, why would he *not* smile?

"Where's your boss, sweetheart?" he asked, hooking his sunglasses on the front of his shirt. He glanced curiously around the office.

I realized I was gaping and closed my mouth with a snap. The "sweetheart" set my teeth on edge. I wasn't his sweetheart—at least, not without dinner first.

My smile was like saccharine. "Who's asking, *sugar pie*?"

His eyebrows shot up and his gaze whipped around to mine. Then he gave a low chuckle and took a few steps toward me until he stood right in front of the desk. He held up a badge.

"Detective Ryker, CPD."

Now it was my turn to be taken aback. The police? Here to see Parker?

"Oh, um, are you sure you're looking for Parker Anderson?" I asked.

The detective snorted in derision as he pocketed his ID. I glimpsed a gun and holster. "Oh yeah. I'm sure. Where is he?"

"He's in a meeting," I said, hurrying to finish folding the napkin. "He'll be back any minute for his lunch."

Detective Ryker glanced at the tray as I carefully set the bird of paradise napkin to the side. I frowned, nervously chewing my lip. If Parker didn't hurry, the salmon would be cold and I'd have to nuke it in the microwave. And if this cop was here to talk to him, chances were that might take a while so he wouldn't get the chance to eat until later. Maybe I should take the tray to the kitchen for now?

My thoughts were interrupted by the detective. "You've got to be fucking kidding me."

Shocked, I glanced around to see what he was talking about; then I realized he was referring to the lunch, or me, or maybe both.

"What?" I asked. "What's wrong?"

But the detective just shook his head. I was starting to get a bad feeling about this.

"Listen," I said, rounding the desk to approach him. "Why don't you come with me for a few minutes? I can get you a cup of coffee or some tea perhaps, while you wait." Yeah, because this guy looked like he'd cool his heels in the lobby sipping hot tea, but whatever. I used the tone I always adopted when placating an irate or obstinate—usually at the same time—Parker, adding a soft smile. It nearly always worked on him.

However, it seemed the cop was a tougher nut to crack.

"Nice try, but I think I'll wait." Turning, he settled himself onto the black leather sofa in the corner.

I stared in dismay. He seemed wholly at ease, one ankle resting on the opposite knee while his arms were spread wide on the back of the couch. It was obvious he wasn't going anywhere until he was darn good and ready.

Parker was going to kill me.

"Please wait in the lobby," I urged, starting to panic. "It's really nice. There's a television, and magazines..."

He just looked at me.

I went for blunt honesty. "He'll get mad at me," I blurted. "Please wait in the lobby."

Honestly, I didn't know if Parker would be upset or not, though I did know he'd prefer some warning before finding a police officer waiting in his office. I'd rather err on the side of caution because nothing was as devastating as when Parker was angry with me.

"He'll get mad at you?" Detective Ryker asked in disbelief, his eyebrows climbing. "What a fucking prick," he added under his breath.

I winced at the name-calling and wondered what in the world the police thought Parker had done for this guy to say such things about a man he'd never met.

I didn't know if the detective would've done what I asked or not because that's when Parker walked through the door. If he was surprised to see a strange man sitting in his office, he didn't show it.

"Ryker," he said, barely glancing at the man as he passed

me and rounded his desk. "Isn't there a murder to investigate or somebody you should be arresting?" His voice was cold. To anyone who didn't know him as well as I did, he appeared unfazed, but I could see the tension in his body.

"Aw, you've kept tabs. I'm touched," Ryker sneered.

Parker didn't even glance up from his plate. He spoke around a bite of salmon. "Don't flatter yourself. Only a cop could get in this building armed, and only homicide gets away with dressing like shit."

I'd never heard Parker speak to someone like that. Ruthless and cutting? Yes. But deliberately insulting cops usually wasn't high on his To Do list.

"I'd rather dress like shit than treat people like shit. You make your secretary serve you lunch without even a thank you? Color me surprised to see you're still a narcissistic dick."

My face grew so hot my ears burned as Parker's eyes flicked my way, as though he were just now noticing me in the room.

"Was there something else, Sage?" he asked stiffly.

"O-of course not, sir," I stammered, hurriedly retreating. "Excuse me." I couldn't get out of there quick enough.

My desk was a haven after the tension in Parker's office and I eyed them covertly, pretending to work, though likely neither would have noticed even if I'd pressed my nose to the glass.

Parker seemed to be barely paying attention to Ryker, though I'd seen him do that before and it was always a fake out. Nothing slipped by him.

For his part, Ryker had abandoned his earlier relaxed pose and was now bent forward, his elbows braced on his knees as he talked.

Neither of them smiled.

They knew each other, and apparently hated each other—or at least Ryker hated Parker. "Narcissistic dick" and "fucking prick" usually weren't terms reserved for a good buddy. It was an engrossing mystery and I did nothing but speculate, my imagination running rampant for the ten minutes Ryker was there.

Finally, he stood and walked to the door. He didn't appear to say good-bye and Parker was seemingly already absorbed in a file before Ryker even left his office.

I expected him to head straight for the elevators, but he caught sight of me watching him. A look I couldn't read flashed across his face and he changed direction, stopping in front of the raised counter that served as two walls of my "cubicle."

"So…Sage, was it?" he asked.

I eyed him suspiciously, tapping the nameplate that sat on the counter rather than answering him.

"Sage Reese," he read. "Executive Administrative Assistant."

"You can read," I said, raising an eyebrow. "I was worried you'd have trouble with the big words." If Parker didn't like Ryker, and it seemed pretty clear he didn't, chances were I wasn't going to like him either.

He grinned at me despite my sass and he had an honest-to-God dimple in his cheek. His teeth were perfectly straight and white, and his smile drastically altered the hard expression on his face to one of sexy mischief. I momentarily lost my train of thought.

Ryker leaned down like he was going to tell me a secret. The aroma of leather and something musky drifted in the air and I caught myself taking a deep whiff of it.

"I know what you're doing after work," he said. I looked at him in confusion. "What?"

"You're having dinner with me."

That was the absolute last thing I expected him to say. I gaped at him.

Ryker reached toward me and my breath caught. His fingers brushed the fabric of the scarf tied around my throat. I was frozen in place, my eyes wide as I looked up at him and my pulse racing. I felt the softest touch of the back of his knuckles against my jaw; then he was reaching past me to snag a couple of peanut M&Ms from the little candy dish on my desk for when I absolutely had to have a bite of chocolate. Tossing them in his mouth, he grinned again, the knowing look in his eyes telling me he knew exactly how he was affecting me.

"Pick you up at six," he said with a wink, and then he was gone, striding toward the elevators, his jeans and leather jacket utterly out of place in the sea of suits and business attire. But you would have thought he was a model wearing the latest from Armani by the way he walked.

When he got to the elevator, it dinged as though it already knew he was coming. He'd slid his sunglasses back on and he turned before he stepped inside. I was still staring at him and he caught me at it, another knowing grin spreading across his face before he disappeared from my view.

"Wow. Who was that?"

I turned around to see Megan, my friend and fellow secretary. She worked for a group of analysts who reported to Parker.

Sliding her glasses up her nose, she turned to me. "Seriously. Please tell me he was interviewing and starts work tomorrow."

I laughed. Megan was an incongruous package. She was tiny, barely five feet tall, with curly blond hair and a heart-shaped face—a stereotypical sweet, shy type. She was sweet, that much was true, but she had a biting wit and an irreverent humor that made her a favorite with nearly everyone at KLP.

"Sorry," I said with an exaggerated sigh. "He already has a job."

"As a movie star, right?"

"He's a detective," I said with a grin. "And I think I have a date with him tonight."

"Get out!"

I shrugged. "He asked me out." I thought for a second. "Actually, he didn't ask. He just told me I was going to dinner with him." Which should have ticked me off, but instead I found it to be kind of . . . sexy.

"If I didn't like you so much, I'd hate you right now," Megan sighed. "As if it's not bad enough you work for the hottest guy in the building. Now you have a date with a sexy detective."

"There are some days I'd gladly trade you bosses," I said dryly. "You know that."

"I know Parker can be a total pain in the ass," she said. "But don't give me that. We both know you'd come to work even if you were miserable sick—and have—if Parker said he needed you. So don't play that 'I hate my job' card with me. I know you're full of crap."

"He's not that bad," I said.

Megan snorted. "You're the only one here who'd put up with him. Even I could only let that pretty face go so far before I'd have to slip something in his coffee."

I couldn't argue with her. There were some days I wanted to slip something in Parker's coffee.

"So I take it Brandon's no longer in the picture if you're going to dinner with a smokin' hot detective dude?" she asked.

"His name is Ryker and no. I got dumped last night."

"No shit," she said, looking completely unsurprised.

I held up a finger. "Don't say it."

"Say what?" she replied, all innocence. "You know what."

"You mean that I've been telling you for months now how you're never going to have a decent relationship so long as you let Parker rule your every waking moment? That I keep reminding you that this is a job and not your life? That Parker doesn't appreciate you and that I can't for the life of me understand why you allow yourself to be at his beck and call to the point where you can't even date? Is that what you *don't* want me to say?"

I sighed. I couldn't be mad at Megan. Nothing she said was wrong. I knew she only said those things because she loved me and worried about me, but it was what it was. I needed this job. I liked this job, despite the demands it made on me. The pay was awesome, the benefits were great, and I liked living in Chicago. Though Megan would call me a masochist—and probably had at some point—because most of my waking hours were consumed by Parker and my job, I liked it that way.

At my silence, Megan looked contrite. "I'm sorry," she apologized. "I should just keep my mouth shut sometimes."

I shook my head. "No, it's okay." It was kind of depressing when I thought about Brandon dumping me—yet another short-lived relationship to add to my tally—so I pushed the thought aside.

"So I texted Brian this weekend," she said, and I was glad for the change of subject. Brian was a guy who worked in IT. He was really nice and very good-looking, but I thought he wasn't terribly bright when it came to women.

"And?" I asked. Megan had had a thing for Brian since the day she first met him a year ago. They'd had to work together on a project and had become good friends. "Did he text you back?"

"Yeah, a little," she said with a sigh. "I think I'm permanently friend-zoned, though. He doesn't seem to get it no matter how much I flirt."

"Of course he doesn't," I said. "He's in IT. You'd have to parade in front of him topless for him to get it."

She laughed. "I don't know what it is with him. Any other guy, I'd just ask them out. But him...I don't know." She sighed.

"It's because he's different from all the other guys you've dated," I said. "You're actually friends, which is awesome. They're supposed to make the best husbands."

Now it was Megan's turn to look slightly uncomfortable. "What was a detective doing here anyway?" she asked, changing the subject.

"No clue," I replied. "But I think they know each other, him and Parker. Their conversation was a bit...hostile." A massive understatement.

"Huh. Weird. Maybe he'll tell you?"

I shrugged. "No way to know. But I'll definitely give you the gossip if he does." I shot her a grin. Megan loved gossip.

"You'd better."

After I swore to tell her all the juicy details of my date with Ryker, Megan headed back to her desk and I went to retrieve the lunch tray from Parker's office.

He was deeply involved in something, judging by his frown and fierce look of concentration, so I didn't speak. His jacket had been discarded and flung onto the sofa. I picked it up and hung it on the valet in the corner closet so it wouldn't wrinkle. Parker always kept an extra suit and a couple of extra shirts at the office. Once I'd done that, I picked up the tray he'd pushed to the side of his desk.

"Thank you," he said.

I glanced at him, for a moment wondering if he was speaking to me, but he was still engrossed in the computer screen. Since there was no one else there and he wasn't on the phone, he must have been speaking to me. It was a little odd. He didn't usually say anything when I took away his tray or hung his jacket.

"You're welcome," I murmured, since it would have been weird to just ignore him. I couldn't help but wonder if Ryker's biting comment earlier was why I was getting a thank-you now, which kind of took the pleasure from it. Not that I did my job for thank-yous; I did it for a paycheck. But still.

"Could you get me the file on that new Russian firm we've been buying from?" Parker said. "Rogers has it, I believe."

I frowned, thinking. "You mean Bank ZNT?"

"That's the one."

"Of course." I headed for the door, then hesitated, glancing at Parker. He looked up.

"Yes?" he asked.

"I was just wondering, and it's probably none of my business, but about the detective who was here earlier. Um, is . . . everything okay? Do you need anything? Something I could do . . ." I was rambling now so I shut up.

Parker was looking at me in that intense way of his, which had me rethinking sticking my nose in something that was obviously private. I looked down at the tray I held, unable to meet his gaze, and uneasily shifted my weight from one foot to the other.

"Never mind. I shouldn't have pried," I blurted, balancing the tray on one arm so I could pull open the door.

"Sage," Parker called out, stopping me. I looked back at

him. "There's nothing you can do, but I...appreciate the offer."

That eased my embarrassment somewhat and I gave him a fleeting smile and short nod before hurrying out of the office.

I watched the clock much too closely that afternoon, the butterflies in my stomach getting more fluttery with each passing hour. By five forty-five, I gave up working at all and just started cleaning off my desk. I didn't know if the butterflies were from nerves, anticipation, or both.

What if he'd just been messing with me? The men I'd dated tended to be safe types, men who had solid white-collar jobs and worked in office buildings. I'd never in my life dated a man who knew how to shoot a gun, much less carried one on him. All my dates wore suits and ties, drove sensible cars, and didn't own leather jackets. And none of them embodied the guy-my-mom-warned-me-about cliché quite like Ryker did.

I must be out of my mind.

I went to the ladies' room to check my hair and touch up my makeup, looking myself over critically. I looked very...businesslike, I guessed. My pretty yellow heels and scarf at least dressed up the dreary white blouse and navy skirt. I had a decent body that should probably get to the gym more often, but my waist was narrow, my hips curved, and I filled out a C cup bra reasonably well.

Digging in my purse, I added some more blush to my cheeks and reapplied my pale rose lipstick. My skin was a warm peach and in the summer I tanned to a golden brown. My dark hair went well with my deep brown eyes, though I often wished I had light eyes, which was probably why I was always attracted to men with blue eyes.

After tucking some wayward strands of hair back into

my braid, I took a deep breath. I eyed my blouse. Should I maybe undo a button? It was done all the way up with only about an inch of skin showing between the bottom edge of my scarf and the top of my blouse. I hesitated, then undid a button, then one more. I had decent cleavage, might as well show it off. And now I looked a bit more like a woman who'd get asked on a date by a cop named Ryker.

Glancing at my watch had me scurrying out the door. It was six o'clock and I was going to be late, not that it was necessarily a bad thing. I'd rather he show up and wait than me stand downstairs waiting for a man who never arrived.

Parker seemed to be packing up, too, when I rapped lightly on his door and stepped inside his office.

"Anything else for today?" I asked, as was my custom to do before I left.

"No, I don't think—" Parker glanced up from where he'd been adding files to his briefcase. When he caught sight of me, he stopped talking. I waited, but he didn't continue, his gaze dropping to my chest.

Okay, maybe cleavage wasn't businesslike, but it wasn't like it was eight in the morning. Technically, business hours were over. I glanced at my watch again. Crap. Six oh-five. "Um, okay, well I'll see you tomorrow then," I blurted. I tossed a "Have a good night" behind me as I rushed out the door.

Grabbing my purse from my desk, I hurried to the elevator and punched the button, waiting impatiently for the car to arrive. What would I do if Ryker wasn't there? What would I do if he was?

I didn't race across the lobby. Instead, I took my time and walked at my normal speed, joining the dozen or so other people exiting the building. When I hit the sidewalk,

I glanced around, trying not to be too obvious that I was searching. But within seconds, my eyes found him and I froze.

Ryker was waiting all right, his sunglasses on and arms crossed over his broad chest as he leaned against a massive black and chrome motorcycle parked at the curb. He saw me and his lips curved in a slow grin that made a warm tingle spread underneath my skin.

I got my feet moving again and Ryker pushed himself upright as I approached, waiting until I was near to speak.

"About time," he teased. "I almost thought you were blowing me off."

"Does any woman blow you off?" I asked.

His grin widened. "Nope."

I rolled my eyes, but I could admit it. Arrogance and cockiness turned me on, and Ryker had them both in spades.

Gesturing toward the motorcycle, I said, "I hope the restaurant is within walking distance because there's no way I'm getting on *that*."

"Ever ride a bike before?"

"A bike, yes," I said. "A death machine that can do ninety miles an hour with only a helmet for protection when my head hits the asphalt? No. I'm allergic to danger."

Ryker stepped closer, right into my personal space, and I tipped my head back to look him in the eyes. All I saw was my own reflection staring back at me. His proximity was electric, though, making my body hum as though a current ran from him into me.

"Sweetheart, I'm as dangerous as it gets."

The low thrum of his voice sent my heart into triple time. My gaze drifted down from Ryker's sunglasses to his lips, still curved in that shit-eating grin. What would it be like to be kissed by a man like him? To be swept off my feet?

"Whaddya say, Miss Prim and Proper? Wanna take a walk on the wild side?"

My eyes flew back up to his. "Did you just call me—" I began, indignant.

"Yep. Now let's get out of here. I'm starving." Grabbing a helmet from the back of his *bike*, he plopped it on my head. I would have protested, but was immediately flustered when he began fastening the strap beneath my chin. His fingers brushed my skin and suddenly it was harder to breathe.

"Well, don't you look as cute as can be," Ryker said once he'd finished.

I bet. Helmets were just oh so sexy.

He swung a leg over the bike and moved the kickstand back with his booted heel. A moment later, the engine fired up. At the noise, people nearby turned to look.

I stood, staring dubiously from the sidewalk. As if going to dinner with Ryker hadn't made me nervous before, the prospect of riding a motorcycle with him made me lightheaded. My mother was so going to kill me.

"C'mon," Ryker said over the noise. "You know you want to. Don't be a scaredy-cat." He held out his hand to me.

My eyes narrowed. Schoolyard taunts were for children. And that's what I told myself as I reached out to take his hand. He tugged me forward, his mischievous smile changing to one of triumph.

I wouldn't have worn a skirt had I known I'd be climbing on the back of a motorcycle. For a girl whose mom had drilled into me the appropriate way a lady exits a car in a skirt, hiking my skirt up my thighs made me cringe.

Shoving aside thoughts of what my mother would say, I quickly got on behind Ryker, letting out a squeak when he reached back and pulled me tighter against him. At least the strap of my purse was long enough to hook over my chest so it rested against my back.

Grabbing his leather-clad shoulders, I steadied myself. I would've been showing the entire street the fabulous black satin and lace panties I wore if they weren't currently pressed against Ryker as I straddled the bike. His hand drifted down my thigh to hook around the back of my knee, his calloused palm warm against my skin. I gasped at the sensation, a flash of heat and want racing through me.

"You have to hold on like this," Ryker explained, turning his head to talk to me. He let go of my leg to reach up, moving my hands from his shoulders to circle his chest beneath his arms. "And hold on tight."

I was shaking now, fear—and, yes, a tinge of excitement—making adrenaline rush fast through my veins. "Scared?" Ryker asked.

"Do I have reason to be?" I asked rather than admit to my fear.

I could feel him laugh, though I couldn't hear it over the noise.

"Trust me, sweetheart. I've got you." The motor revved and I tightened my grip around him.

Glancing at the sidewalk and people passing by, I suddenly saw Parker standing just outside the building entrance. He had an unreadable expression on his face, which wasn't unusual, but he was staring right at Ryker and me. There was something about the set of his jaw and tension in his body that made me uneasy.

Then the bike was moving and I lost sight of Parker as we shot down the street.